My room was touched by moonlight. I sat up with a start. Something had awakened me.

I was in danger. An extra sense seemed to be telling me this. I stared in dismay, for someone was in my room. I saw the outline of a figure seated in an armchair, watching me.

I gave a stifled cry, for the figure had moved. I thought, I have always thought the Abbas was haunted. Now I know. . . .

Fawcett Crest Books
by Victoria Holt:

BRIDE OF PENDORRIC
THE CURSE OF THE KINGS
THE DEVIL ON HORSEBACK
THE KING OF THE CASTLE
KIRKLAND REVELS
THE LEGEND OF THE
  SEVENTH VIRGIN
LORD OF THE FAR ISLAND
MENFREYA IN THE MORNING
MISTRESS OF MELLYN
MY ENEMY THE QUEEN
ON THE NIGHT OF THE
  SEVENTH MOON
THE PRIDE OF THE PEACOCK
THE QUEEN'S CONFESSION
THE SECRET WOMAN
THE SHADOW OF THE LYNX
THE SHIVERING SANDS
THE SPRING OF THE TIGER

THE LEGEND

OF THE

SEVENTH
VIRGIN

Victoria Holt

FAWCETT CREST • NEW YORK

1

Two days after the bones of the walled-up nun were found in St. Larnston Abbas, the five of us were together. There were Justin and Johnny St. Larnston, Mellyora Martin, Dick Kimber and myself, Kerensa Carlee—with as grand a name as any of them, for all that I lived in a cob-walled cottage and they were the gentry.

The Abbas had belonged to the St. Larnstons for centuries; and before they had owned it, it had been a convent. Impressive, built naturally of Cornish stone, its battlemented towers were pure Norman; it had been restored here and there and one wing was obviously Tudor. I had never been inside the house at that time but I knew the surrounding district very well; and it was not the house which was unique, for, interesting as it was, there were many more in England—and even Cornwall—as interesting and as antiquated. It was the Six Virgins who made St. Larnston Abbas different from all the others.

The Six Virgins was the name by which the stones were known. If the legend could be believed they were misnamed because, according to that, they were six women who precisely because they had ceased to be virgins had been turned into stones. Mellyora's father, the Reverend Charles Martin, whose hobby was delving into the past, called them the menhirs—"men" being the Cornish word for stone and "hir" for long.

The story about there having been seven virgins came from the Reverend Charles, too. His great-grandfather had had the same hobby, and one day the Reverend Charles found some notes which had been tucked away in an old trunk and among these was the story of the Seventh Virgin. He had had it printed in the local paper. It made quite a stir in St. Larnston, and people who before had never bothered to glance at the stones, then went to stare at them.

The story was that six novices and a nun had ceased to be virgins and the novices were driven from the convent. As they left they danced in the nearby meadow to show their defiance and because of this were turned into stones. In those days it was believed that good luck was brought to a place if a living person was what they called "walled-up," which meant putting that person into a space in the wall and building round her, leaving her to die. The nun, having sinned more deeply than the others, was condemned to be walled-up.

The Reverend Charles said the story was nonsense; the stones must have been in the meadow years before the convent was built for, according to him, they were older than Christianity. He pointed out that there were similar ones all over Cornwall and at Stonehenge; but the people of St. Larnston liked the story of the Virgins best, so that was the one they made up their minds to believe.

They had been believing it for some time when one of the oldest of the Abbas walls collapsed and Sir Justin St. Larnston ordered that it should be immediately repaired.

Reuben Pengaster was working on the spot at the moment when the hollowed wall was exposed and he swore he saw a woman standing there.

"She were there one second," he insisted. "Like a nightmare she were. Then she were gone and there was nothing but dust and they old bones."

Some said that was the start of Reuben's being what was called in Cornwall piskey-mazed. He wasn't mad but he wasn't quite like other people. He was slightly different from the rest of us, as though, it were said, he'd been caught by the piskies one dark night, and having become piskey-mazed had stayed like that.

"He looked on what weren't intended for human eyes," they said. "It's made him piskey-mazed."

But there *were* bones in that wall, and it was said by experts that they had belonged to a young woman. There was fresh interest in the Abbas, just as there had been when the Reverend Charles had had his piece printed in the paper

6

about his menhirs. People wanted to see the spot where the bones had been found. I was one who wanted to see.

The day was hot and I left the cottage soon after midday. We had had a bowl of quillet each—Joe, Granny Bee, and myself—and for anyone not Cornish who doesn't know what quillet is, it's peas made into a sort of porridge. It was used a great deal in Cornwall during the hungry times because it was cheap and sustaining.

Of course they wouldn't have quillet at the Abbas, I was thinking as I went along. They would be eating roast pheasant off gold plates; they would be drinking wine out of silver tankards.

I knew very little of how the quality ate, but my imagination was vivid; and I could clearly see the picture of the St. Larnstons at their table. In those days I was continually comparing my life with theirs; and the comparison angered me.

I was twelve years old, black-haired and black-eyed; and although I was very thin, there was something about me which was already causing men to look twice at me. I did not know very much about myself, not at that time being given to self-analysis, but there was one characteristic of which I was aware even then: I was proud—with that sort of pride which is one of the seven deadly sins. I walked in a bold and haughty way as though I wasn't one of the cottage people but belonged to a family like the St. Larnstons.

Our cottage stood apart from the others in a small copse, and I felt that made *us* apart, although ours was exactly the same as the others; it was merely a rectangle with walls of whitewashed cob and a thatched roof—about as primitive as a dwelling could be. Still, I was constantly assuring myself, ours *was* different, just as we were different. Everyone would admit that Granny Bee was different; and so was I with my pride; as for Joe, whether he liked it or not he was going to be different, too. I was determined to see to that.

I ran out of our cottage, past the church, and the doctor's house, through the kissing gate and across the field which was a short cut to the Abbas drive. This drive was three quarters of a mile long and there were lodge gates at the end; but coming this way and scrambling through a hedge I struck the drive close to where it opened onto the lawns which stood in front of the house.

I paused, looking about me, listening to the rustle of

7

insects in the long grass of the meadow. Some distance away I could see the roof of the Dower House where Dick Kimber lived and briefly I envied him for living in such a fine house. I felt my heartbeats quicken because very soon I should be on forbidden ground—a trespasser—and Sir Justin was hard on trespassers, particularly in his woods. I'm only twelve, I said to myself. They couldn't do much to a child!

Couldn't they? Jack Toms had been caught with a pheasant in his pocket and it had been transportation for him. Seven long years in Botany Bay—and he was still serving them. He had been eleven when he was caught.

But I was not interested in pheasants. I was doing no harm; and they said Sir Justin was more lenient with girls than boys.

Now I could see the house through the trees and I stood still, disturbed by my unaccountable emotion. It was a grand sight, with its Norman towers and mullioned windows; the stone carvings were more impressive, it seemed to me, because after hundreds of years the noses of griffins and dragons had become blunted.

The lawn sloped gently down to the gravel path round the house. This was the exciting view because on one side was the lawn divided only by a box hedge from the meadow in which were the Six Virgins. Seen from a distance they did look like young women. I could imagine how they would appear at night—in starlight, say, or by the light of a crescent moon. I made up my mind to come and look at them one night. Close by the Virgins, incongruously, was the old tin mine. Perhaps it was the mine which made this such a startling sight, for the old balance box and beam winding engine were still there and one could go right up to the shaft and look down into the darkness below.

Why, it had been asked, did the St. Larnstons not have all evidence that there had once been a mine there, removed? What purpose did it serve? It was unsightly, and something like sacrilege to leave it there beside the legendary stones. But there was a reason. One of the St. Larnstons had gambled so heavily that he had become almost bankrupt and would have been forced to sell the Abbas if tin had not been discovered on his estate. So the mine was worked, although the St. Larnstons had hated the fact that it had to be within sight of their mansion; and down into the earth the tinners had burrowed, working with their crooks and pokers, picking out the tin which was to save the Abbas for the family.

But once the house was saved, the St. Larnstons, hating

the mine, had closed it. There had been hardship in the district, so Granny told me, when the mine was closed; but Sir Justin didn't mind that. He didn't care about other people; he was all for himself. Granny Bee said that the St. Larnstons had left the mine as it was to remind the family of the rich tin underground to which they could turn in times of need.

The Cornish are a superstitious race—the rich no less than the poor—and I believe that the St. Larnstons looked on the mine as a symbol of prosperity; while there was tin in their land they were safe from financial disaster. There was a rumor in existence that the mine was nothing but an old scat bal—a disused mine—and some of the old men said they remembered their fathers saying that the lode was running out when it closed. The rumor persisted that the St. Larnstons had known this and had closed down the mine because it had nothing more to offer; but they liked to be thought richer than they were, for in Cornwall tin meant money.

Whatever the reason, Sir Justin did not wish the mine to be worked and that was the end of it.

He was a man both hated and feared in the country; on the occasions when I had seen him riding on his great white horse or striding along with a gun on his shoulder, I had thought of him as a kind of ogre. I had heard tales about him from Granny Bee and I knew he considered that everything in St. Larnston belonged to him, which might have some truth in it; but he also believed that the people of St. Larnston belonged to him, too—and that was a different matter; and although he dared not practice the old seignioral rights, he had seduced a number of the girls. Granny Bee was always warning me to keep out of his way.

I turned into the meadow so that I could go close to the Six Virgins. I paused beside them and leaned against one of them. They were arranged in a circle looking exactly as though they had been caught swaying in a dance. They were of various heights—just as six women would be; two were very tall and the others were the sizes of fully grown women. Standing there in the stillness of a hot afternoon, I could believe that I was one of those poor virgins. I could well imagine that I should have been as sinful and having sinned and been found out I should have danced my defiance on the grass.

I touched the cold stone gently and I could have deceived myself quite easily that one of them bent towards me as

9

though she recognized my sympathy and the bond between us.

Crazy thoughts I had; it was because I was Granny Bee's granddaughter.

Now was the dangerous part. I had to run across the lawns where I might be seen from one of the windows. I seemed to fly through the air until I was so close to the gray walls of the house I knew where to find the wall. I knew too that the workmen would be sitting in a field some distance from the house eating their hunks of bread, all brown and crusty, baked that morning on the open hearth; we called them manshuns in these parts. Perhaps they would have a little cheese and some pilchards or, if they were lucky, a pasty which they would have brought from home wrapped in their red handkerchiefs.

Making my way cautiously round the house I came to a small gate leading into a walled garden; on these walls peaches grew; there were roses, too, and the smell was wonderful. This was trespassing proper, but I was determined to see where those bones had been found.

On the far side propped against a wall was a wheelbarrow; there were bricks on the ground with the workmen's tools, so I knew I was in the right place.

I ran over and peered through the hole in the wall. Inside it was hollow, like a little chamber, about seven feet high and six feet wide. It was clear that the thick old wall had been deliberately left hollow; and studying it I was certain then that the story of the seventh virgin was a true one.

I longed to stand in the spot where that girl had stood, and to know what it felt like to be shut in, so I scrambled through the hole, grazing my knee as I did so for it was some three feet from the ground. Once inside the wall, I moved away from the hole, turning my back to the light, and tried to imagine what she must have felt when they forced her to stand where I was standing now, knowing that they were going to wall her up and leave her for the remainder of her short life in utter darkness. I could understand her horror and despair.

There was a smell of decay about me. A smell of death, I told myself, and so strong was my imagination that in those seconds I really believed I *was* the seventh virgin, that I had extravagantly cast away my chastity and was doomed to frightful death; I was saying to myself: "I would do it again."

I should have been too proud to show my terror, and I

10

hoped she, too, had been for although pride was a sin, it was a solace. It prevented your demeaning yourself.

I was brought back into my own century by the sound of voices.

"I *do* want to see it." I knew that voice. It belonged to Mellyora Martin, the parson's daughter. I despised her, for her neat gingham dresses which were never dirty, her long white stockings and black shiny shoes with straps and buckles. I should have liked to possess shoes like that but, because I couldn't, I deluded myself into the belief that I despised them. She was twelve years old, the same age as I was. I had seen her at one of the parsonage windows, bent over a book or sitting in the garden under the lime tree with her governess reading aloud or sewing. Poor prisoner! I said then, and I was angry because at that time I wanted more than anything in the world to be able to read and write; I had a notion that it was the ability to read and write, more than fine clothes and manners that made people equal with one another. Her hair was what some would call gold but which I called yellow; her eyes were blue and big; her skin white and delicately tinted. I called her Melly to myself, just to rob her of a little dignity. Mellyora! It sounded so pretty when people said it. But my name was as interesting. Kerensa the Cornish for Peace and Love, Granny Bee told me. I have never heard that Mellyora meant anything.

"You'll make yourself dirty." That was Johnny St. Larnston speaking.

Now I shall be found out, I thought, and by a St. Larnston. But it was only Johnny who, it was said, would be like his father in one respect and one only—that was as far as women were concerned. Johnny was fourteen. I had seen him sometimes with his father, a gun on his shoulder, because all the St. Larnstons were brought up to hunt and shoot. Johnny was not much taller than I, for I was tall for my age; he was fair although not as fair as Mellyora and he didn't look like a St. Larnston. I was glad it was only Johnny and Mellyora.

"I shan't mind. Johnny, do you really believe the story?"

"Of course."

"The poor woman! To be shut up . . . *alive!*"

"Hello!" A different voice this. "You children, come away from the wall."

"We're looking to see where they found the nun," said Johnny.

"Nonsense. There's absolutely no evidence that it was a nun. It's just a legend."

I crouched as far from the hole as I could while I wondered whether I ought to dash out and run. I remembered that it would not be easy to scramble out of the hole and they would almost certainly catch me—particularly now that the others had come.

Mellyora was looking in through the hole and it took a second or so for her eyes to become adjusted to the dimness; then she gasped. I was certain that in those few seconds she thought I was the ghost of the seventh virgin.

"Why . . ." she began. "She . . ."

Johnny's head came through. There was a brief silence; then he murmured: "It's only one of the cottage children."

"Be careful there! It might not be safe." I knew the voice now. It belonged to Justin St. Larnston—heir to the estate—no longer a boy, but a man, home from the University on vacation.

"But I tell you there's someone in there," Johnny replied.

"Don't tell me the lady's still there?" Yet another voice, and one I knew as that of Dick Kimber who lived in the Dower House and was at Oxford with young Justin.

"Come and see for yourself," called Johnny.

I was crouching closer to the wall. I didn't know what I hated most—the fact that I was caught or the way they looked on me—"one of the cottage children!" How dared he!

Another face was looking in on me; it was brown, crowned by untidy dark hair; the brown eyes were laughing.

"Not the virgin," commented Dick Kimber.

"Does she look like it, Kim?" said Johnny.

Now Justin pushed them aside to look in. He was very tall and thin; his eyes were serene, his voice calm.

"Who is it?" he said.

"It's not an 'it,'" I replied. "It's a Miss Kerensa Carlee."

"You are a child from the cottages," he said. "You've no right to be here, but come out now."

I hesitated, not knowing what he intended to do. I pictured him taking me to the house and accusing me of trespassing. Also I did not want to stand before them in my scanty Holland smock which was becoming too small for me; my feet were well shaped though brown, but I had no shoes and they would be grimy. I washed them in the stream every night because I was very anxious to keep myself as clean as

12

the gentry but, having no shoes to protect them, they were always dirty by the end of the day.

"What's the matter?" demanded Dick Kimber, whom they called Kim. I should always think of him as Kim in future. "Why don't you come out?"

"Go away," I retorted, "and I will."

He was about to step into the hollow when Justin warned: "Careful, Kim. You might bring the entire wall down."

Kim remained where he was. "What did you say your name was?" he asked.

"Kerensa Carlee."

"Very grand. But you'd better come out."

"Go away."

"Ding dong bell," sang Johnny, "Kerensa's in the well."

"Who put her in?" continued Kim. "Was it due to sin?"

They were laughing at me, and as I stepped out of the hole preparing to run, they made a circle round me. In half a second I thought of the circle of stones and it was as uncanny a feeling as that which I had experienced in the wall.

They must have been noticing the difference between us. My hair was so black that it had a blue sheen in it; my eyes were big and they looked enormous in my small face; my skin was smooth and olive. They were so neat and civilized, all of them; even Kim with his untidy hair and laughing eyes.

Mellyora's blue ones were troubled and in that moment I knew I had underrated her. She was soft but she wasn't silly; she knew far better than the others did, how I felt.

"There's nothing to be afraid of, Kerensa," she said.

"Oh, isn't there!" contradicted Johnny. "Miss Kerensa Carlee is guilty of trespassing. She's been caught in the act. We must think up a punishment for her."

He was teasing, of course. He wasn't going to hurt me; he had noticed my long black hair and I saw his eyes on the bare skin of my shoulder where it showed through my torn smock.

Kim said: "It isn't only cats who die of curiosity."

"Do be careful," ordered Justin. He turned to me. "You've been very silly. Don't you know that scrambling about a wall that has just collapsed could be dangerous? Moreover, what are you doing here?" He didn't wait for an answer. "Now get out . . . the faster the better."

I hated them all—Justin for his coldness, and talking to me as though I was no different from the people who lived in the cottages on his father's estates, Johnny and Kim for their

13

teasing, and Mellyora because she knew how I felt and was sorry for me.

I ran, but when I came to the door of the walled garden and was at a safe distance from them, I stopped and looked back at them.

They were still standing in a semicircle watching me. Mellyora was the one I had to stare at; she looked so concerned—and her concern was for me.

I put out my tongue; I heard Johnny and Kim laughing. Then I turned my back on them and sped away.

Granny Bee was sitting outside the cottage when I reached home; she often sat in the sun, her stool propped up against the wall, her pipe in her mouth; her eyes half closed as she smiled to herself.

I threw myself down beside her and told her what had happened. She rested her hand on my head as I talked; she liked to stroke my hair which was like her own, for although she was an old woman her hair was thick and black. She took great care of it, sometimes wearing it in two thick plaits, at others piling it high in coils. People said that it wasn't natural for a woman of her age to have hair like that; and Granny Bee liked them to say it. She was proud of her hair, yes, but it was more than that; it was a symbol. Like Samson's, I used to tell her, and she would laugh. I knew that she brewed a special preparation which she brushed in every night and she would sit for five minutes massaging her head. No one knew what she did except Joe and me, and Joe didn't notice; he was always too busy with some bird or animal; but I would sit and watch her do her hair and she used to say to me, "I'll tell you how to keep your hair, Kerensa; then you'll have a head of hair like mine till the day you die." But she hadn't told me as yet. "All in good time," she added. "And if I was to be took sudden, you'd find the receipt in the corner cupboard."

Granny Bee loved Joe and me and it was a wonderful thing to be loved by her; but what was more wonderful still was to know that I was the first with her always. Joe was like a little pet; we loved him in a protective sort of way; but between Granny and me there was a closeness which we both knew about and were glad of.

She was a wise woman; I don't mean merely that she had good sense; but she was known for miles round for her special powers and people of all sorts came to see her. She

14

could cure them of their ailments and they trusted her more than they did the doctor. The cottage was filled with smells which changed from day to day, according to the remedies which were being brewed. I was learning what herbs to gather in the woods and fields and what they would cure. She was also believed to have special powers which enabled her to see into the future; I asked her to teach me, too, but she said it was something you taught yourself by keeping your eyes and ears open, and learning about people—for human nature was the same all the world over; there was so much bad in the good and so much good in the bad, that it was all a matter of weighing up how much good or bad had been allotted to each one. If you knew your people you could make a good guess as to how they would act and that was seeing into the future. And when you became clever at it, people believed in you, and they'd often act the way you had told them to, just to help you along.

We lived on Granny's wisdom; and we didn't do too badly. When someone killed a pig, there would be a good joint for us. Often some grateful client would put a sack of potatoes or peas on our doorstep; there would often be hot baked bread. I was good at managing, too. I could cook well. I could bake our bread and pasties, and turn out a fine pie of taddage or squab.

I had been happier since Joe and I had come to Granny than I was before.

But the best thing of all was this bond between us; and I felt it now as I sat beside her at the cottage door.

"They mocked me," I said. "The St. Larnstons and Kim. Mellyora didn't though. She was sorry for me."

Granny said, "If you could make a wish now, what would it be?"

I pulled at the grass and didn't speak, for my yearnings were something I hadn't put into words, not even to her.

She answered for me. "You'd be a lady, Kerensa. Riding in your carriage. You'd be dressed in silks and satins and you'd have a gown of bright, rich green and there would be silver buckles on your shoes."

"I'd read and write," I added. I turned to her eagerly: "Granny, will it come true?"

She didn't answer me and I was sad, asking myself why, if she could tell others the future she couldn't tell me. I gazed up at her pleadingly, but she didn't seem to see me. The sun glinted on her smooth blue-black hair which was braided about her head. That hair should have been on Lady St.

Larnston. It gave Granny a proud look. Her dark eyes were alert although she hadn't kept those as young as her hair, there were lines about them.

"What are you thinking?" I asked.

"Of the day you came. Remember?"

I laid my head against her thigh. I was remembering.

Our first years—Joe's and mine—were spent by the sea. Our father had a little cottage on the quay which was rather like this one where we lived with Granny, except that ours had the big cellar underneath where we stored and salted the pilchards after a heavy catch. When I think of that cottage I think first of the smell of fish—the good smell which meant that the cellar was well stocked and we could be sure of enough to eat for a few weeks.

I had always looked after Joe because our mother had died when he was four and I was six and she told me always to look after my little brother. Sometimes when our father was out in the boat and the gales blew, we used to think our cottage would be swept into the sea; then I would cuddle Joe and sing to him to stop him being frightened. I used to pretend I wasn't frightened and found that was a good way not to be. Continually pretending helped me a good deal, so there wasn't much I was afraid of.

The best times were when the sea was calm and at harvest time when the shoals of pilchards came to our coast. The huers who were on watch all along the coast would sight the fish and give the warning. I remember how excited everyone was when the cry of "Hevva" went up, for "hevva" means in Cornish "a school of fish." Then the boats would go out and the catch would come in; and our cellars would be full. In the church there would be pilchards among the sheaves of wheat and the fruit and vegetables, to show God that the fishermen were as grateful as the farmers.

Joe and I would work together in the cellar putting one layer of salt between each layer of fish until I thought my hands would never be warm again or free from the smell of pilchards.

But those were the good times, and there came that winter when there was no more fish in our cellars and the gales were worse than they had been for eighty years. Joe and I with the other children used to go down to the beaches at night to twitch the sand eels out of the sand with our small iron crooks; we would bring them home and cook them. We brought back limpets too, and caught snails with which we made a sort of stew. We picked nettles and boiled them. I can remember what hunger was like in those times.

We used to dream we heard the welcome cry of "Hevva Hevva," which was a wonderful dream but made us more despairing than ever when we woke up.

I saw desperation in my father's eyes. I saw him looking at Joe and me; it was as though he came to a decision.

He said to me: "Your mother used to talk to you a lot about your Granny."

I nodded. I had always loved—and never forgotten—the stories of Granny Bee who lived in a place called St. Larnston.

"I reckon she'd like to have a look at 'ee—you and little Joe."

I did not realize the significance of those words until he took out the boat. He, having lived his life on the sea, was well aware of what was threatening. I remember his coming into the cottage and shouting to me. "They'm back!" he said. "It'll be pilchards for breakfast. Take care of Joe till I come back." I watched him go. I saw the others on the beach; they were talking to him and I knew what they were saying, but he didn't listen.

I hate the southwest wind. Whenever it blows I hear it as it blew that night. I put Joe to bed but I didn't go myself. I just sat up, saying "Pilchards for breakfast," and listening to the wind.

He never came back, and we were alone. I didn't know what to do but I still had to pretend for Joe's sake. Whenever I tried to think of what I could do, I kept hearing my mother's voice telling me to look after my brother; and then my father's saying: "Take care of Joe till I come back."

Neighbors helped us for a while, but those were bad times, and there was talk of putting us into the workhouse. Then I remembered what my father had said about our Granny and I told Joe we were going to find her. So Joe and I set out for St. Larnston, and, in time and after some hardship, we came to Granny Bee.

Another thing I shall never forget was the first night in Granny Bee's cottage. Joe was wrapped in a blanket and given hot milk to drink; and Granny Bee made me lie down while she bathed my feet and put ointment on the sore places. Afterwards I believed that my wounds were miraculously healed by the morning, but that couldn't have been true. The feeling of deep satisfaction and content comes back to me now. I felt I had come home and that Granny Bee was dearer to me than anyone I had ever known. I loved Joe, of course, but never in my life had I known anyone so wonderful as Granny Bee. I remember lying on the bed while she took down her marvelous black hair and combed it and rubbed it—for even the unexpected arrival of two grandchildren could not interfere with that ritual.

Granny Bee healed me, fed me, clothed me—and she gave me my dignity and my pride. The girl I was at the time when I stood in the hollow wall was not the same one who had come exhausted to her door.

She knew this, because she knew everything.

We adjusted ourselves to the new life quickly, as children do. Our home was now in a mining community instead of a fishing one; for although the St. Larnston mine was closed, the Fedder mine provided work for many of the St. Larnston people who walked the two miles or so each day to and from their work. I discovered that miners were as superstitious as the fishermen had been, for each calling was dangerous enough for those who followed it to wish to please the gods of chance. Granny Bee would sit for hours telling me stories of the mines. My grandfather had been a miner. She told me how a didjan had to be left to placate the evil spirits, and that meant a good part of a hungry man's lunch; she spoke angrily of the system of paying tribute instead of wages which meant that if a man had a bad day and his output was small, his pay was correspondingly so; she was equally indignant about those mines which had their own tommy shops at which a miner must buy all his goods, sometimes at high prices. When I listened to Granny I could imagine myself descending the mine shaft; I could see the men in their red-stained ragged clothes and their tin helmets to which a candle was stuck with sticky clay; I was conscious of dropping down to darkness in the cage; I could feel the hot air and the tremor of the rock as the men worked; I could feel the terror of suddenly coming face to face with a spirit, who had had no didjan, or a black dog and white hare whose appearance meant imminent danger in the mine.

I said to her now: "I'm remembering."

"What brought you to me?" she asked.

"Chance?"

She shook her head. "It was a long way for little ones to come, but you didn't doubt you'd find your Granny, did you? You knew if you went on walking far enough you'd come to her, didn't 'ee now?"

I nodded.

She was smiling as though she had answered my question. "I'm thirsty, lovey," she said. "Go get me a thimbleful of my sloe gin."

I went into the cottage. There was only one room in Granny Bee's cottage, although a storehouse had been built on and it was in this that she brewed her concoctions and often received her clients. The room was our bedroom, and living room. There was a story about it; it had been built by Pedro Balencio, Granny Bee's husband, who was called Pedro Bee because the Cornish people couldn't pronounce his name and weren't going to try. Granny told me how it had been put up in a night to fit the custom which was that if anyone could build a cottage in a night they could claim the ground on which it was built. So Pedro Bee had found his ground—a clearing in the copse—had hidden in the trees the thatch and poles, together with the clay which would make the cob walls; and one moonlit night, with his friends to help him, had built the cottage. All he had to do that first night was make the four walls and the roof; gradually he would put in the window, the door, and the chimney; but Pedro Bee had built what he could call a cottage in a night and satisfied the old custom.

Pedro had come from Spain. Perhaps he had heard that according to legend the Cornish had a streak of the Spaniard in them because so many Spanish sailors had raided the coast and ravished the women, or having been wrecked on the rocks had been befriended and settled down. It's true that although so many have hair the color of Mellyora Martin's, there are as many again with the coal-black hair and flashing dark eyes—and the quick temper to go with them, which is different from the easy-going nature that seems to suit our sleepy climate.

Pedro loved Granny who was named Kerensa—as I was; he loved her black hair and eyes which reminded him of Spain; and they married and lived in the cottage which he had made in a night and they had one daughter who was my mother.

Into that cottage I went to get the sloe gin. I had to pass through it to reach the storehouse where her brews were kept.

Although we had only one room we also had the talfat which was a wide shelf about halfway up the wall and which protruded over the room. It served as a bedroom—mine and Joe's; and we reached it by means of the ladder which was kept in the corner of the room.

Joe was up there now.

"What are you doing?" I called.

He didn't answer me the first time and when I repeated the question he held up a pigeon.

"He broke his leg," he told me. "But twill mend in a day or so."

The pigeon remained still in his hands and I saw that he had constructed a sort of splint to which he had bound the leg. What surprised me so much about Joe was not that he could do these things for birds and animals, but that they remained passive while he did them. I had seen a wild cat come to him and rub her body against his leg, even before she knew he was going to feed her. He never ate all his meals but kept some back to carry about him, for he was certain to find some creature who needed it more than he did. He spent all his time in the woods. I had come upon him lying on his stomach watching insects in the grass. Besides his long, slender fingers that were amazingly clever at mending the broken limbs of birds and animals, he had an extra sense where animals were concerned. He would cure their sickness with Granny's herbs and if any of his charges needed something he would help himself from her store as though the needs of animals were more important than anything else.

His gift for curing was a part of my dream. I saw him in a fine house like Dr. Hilliard's, for doctors in St. Larnston were respected; and if people thought more highly of Granny Bee's remedies, they wouldn't bob a curtsy or pull a forelock for her; in spite of her wisdom she lived in a one-roomed cottage, whereas Dr. Hilliard was gentry. I was determined to raise Joe up with me; and I wanted the rank of doctor for him almost as passionately as I wanted that of a lady for myself.

"And when it's mended?" I asked.

"Well then he'll fly away and feed himself."

"And what'll you get for your pains?"

He didn't take any notice. He was murmuring to his pigeon. If he had heard me he would have wrinkled his brow, wondering what he should get beyond the joy of having made a maimed creature whole.

The storehouse had always excited me, because I had never seen anything like it before. There were benches on each side and these were laden with pots and bottles; there was a beam across the ceiling and attached to this were different kind of herbs which had been hung up to dry. I stood still for a second or so sniffing that odor which I had never smelt anywhere else. There was a fireplace and a huge blackened cauldron; and beneath the benches were jars of Granny's brews. I knew the one containing sloe gin and I poured some into a glass and carried it back through the cottage and out to her.

I sat down beside her while she sipped.

"Granny," I said, "tell me if I'll ever get what I want."

She turned to me, smiling. "Why, lovey," she said, "you talk like one of these girls who come to me to ask me if their lovers will be true. I don't expect it of 'ee, Kerensa."

"But I want to know."

"Then listen to me. The answer's simple. Clever ones don't want the future told. They *make* it."

We could hear the shots all through the day. It meant that there was a house party at the Abbas; we had seen the carriages arriving and we knew what it was, because it happened at this time every year. They were shooting pheasants in the woods.

Joe was up on the talfat with a dog which he had found a week before when it was starving. It was just beginning to be strong enough to run about; but it never left Joe's side. He shared his food with it and it had kept him happy since he had found it. But he was restless now. I remembered how he had been the year before and I knew that he was thinking of the poor frightened birds fluttering up before falling dead on the ground.

He had banged his fist on the table when he had talked of it and said: "It's the wounded ones I be thinking of. If they'm dead, there's nothing 'ee can do, but it's the wounded ones. They don't always find 'em and . . ."

I said: "Joe, you've got to be sensible. Don't do no good worrying about what can't be helped."

He agreed; but he didn't go out; he just stayed on the talfat with his dog whom he called Squab because he found it the day the pigeon whose leg he had mended, flew away and it took the place of the bird.

He worried me because he looked so angry and I was beginning to recognize in Joe something of myself. Therefore I was never sure what he would do. I'd told him often that he was lucky to be able to roam around looking for sick animals; most boys of his age were working in the Fedder mine. People couldn't think why he wasn't sent to work there; but I knew Granny shared my ambitions for him—for us both—and while there was enough for us to eat we had our freedom. It was her way of showing them that there was something special about us.

Granny knew I was worried, so she said I was to go into the woods with her and gather herbs.

I was glad to get away from the cottage.

Granny said: "You mustn't fret yourself, girl. It's his way and he'll always grieve when animals suffer."

"Granny, I wish . . . I wish he could be a doctor and look after people. Would it cost a lot of money to make him a doctor?"

"Do you think it's what he'd want, m'dear?"

"He wants to cure everything. Why not people? He'd get money for it and people would respect him."

"Perhaps he don't care what people think like you do, Kerensa."

"He's *got* to care!" I said.

"He will, if it's meant."

"You said nothing was meant. You said people make their own future."

"Each makes his own, lovey. Tis for him to make what he will, same as tis for you to."

"He lies there on the talfat most of the day . . . with his animals."

"Leave him be, lovey," said Granny. "He'll make his own life the way he wants."

But I wasn't going to leave him be! I was going to make him understand how he had to break out of this life into which he had been born. We were too good for it—all of us. Granny, Joe, and me. I wondered why Granny hadn't seen it, how she could be content to live her life as she had.

Gathering herbs always soothed me. Granny would explain where we had to go to find what we wanted; then she would tell me about the healing properties of each one. But on that day, as we picked, every now and then I would hear the distant sounds of the guns.

When we were tired, she said we should sit down under the trees and I persuaded her to talk of the past.

When Granny talked she seemed to put a spell on me, so that I felt I was there where it was all happening; I even felt that I was Granny herself, being wooed by Pedro Bee, the young miner who was different from all the others. He used to sing lovely songs to her which she didn't understand because they were in Spanish.

"But tain't always necessary to hear words to know," she told me. "Oh, he were not much liked in these parts, being a

22

foreigner and all. There wasn't enough work for Cornishmen some of them did say—let alone foreigners coming to take the manshuns out of their mouths. But my Pedro, he laughed at 'un. He did say that once he'd seen me that was enough. He was going to stay, for where I be that was where he belonged to be."

"Granny, you loved him, truly loved him."

"He was the man for me and I wanted no other—nor ever have."

"So you never had another lover?"

Granny's face was set in an expression I had never seen there before. She had turned her head slightly in the direction of the Abbas and seemed as though she were actually listening for the guns.

"Your grandfather was not a mild man," she said. "He'd have killed the one who wronged him as lief as look at 'un. That were the man 'e were."

"Did he ever kill anyone, Granny?"

"No, but he might have . . . he would have . . . if he'd known."

"Known what, Granny?"

She didn't answer, but her face was like a mask that she'd put on so that no one should see what was beneath.

I lay against her, looking up at the trees. The firs would stay green all through the winter but the leaves on the others were already russet brown. The cold weather would soon be with us.

Granny said after a long pause: "But it was so long ago."

"That you had another lover?"

"He weren't no lover, I'll tell 'ee. Perhaps I should tell 'ee—for a warning. Tis well to know the way the world wags for others, for maybe it'll wag that way for you. This other one were Justin St. Larnston . . . not this Sir Justin. His father."

I sat bolt upright, my eyes wide.

"You, Granny, and Sir Justin St. Larnston!"

"This one's father. There wasn't much difference in them. He was a wicked one."

"Then why . . ."

"For Pedro's sake."

"But . . ."

"Tis like you to come to a judgment afore you've heard the facts, child. Now I'm started, I must go and tell you all. He saw me; he fancied me; I was a St. Larnston girl, and I was bespoke. He must have made inquiries and found I was

23

to marry Pedro. I remember how he cornered me. There's a little walled garden close to the house."

I nodded.

"I were silly. Went to see one of the maids that was in the kitchens. He caught me in that garden, and that was when he fancied me. Promised a job for Pedro that'd be safer and better paid than working in the mine—if I'd be sensible. Pedro never knew. And I stood out against him. I loved Pedro; I was going to marry Pedro; and there weren't going to be nobody for me but Pedro."

"And then . . . ?"

"Things started going wrong for Pedro. The St. Larnston mine was being worked then, and we was in his power. I thought he'd forget me. But he didn't. The more I stood out, the more he wanted me. Pedro never knew. That was the miracle. So one night . . . before we was married I went along to him, for I said that if it could be secret and he'd let Pedro alone . . . it would be better than the way it were."

"Granny!"

"It shocks you, lovey. I'm glad. But I'm going to make you see I had to do it. I've thought of it since and I know I was right. It was like what I told you . . . making your own future. Mine was with Pedro. I wanted us to be together always in the cottage and our children round us . . . boys looking like Pedro, girls like me. And I thought what's once if it'll buy that future for us? And I was right, for it would have been the end of Pedro. You don't know what we were like, that long-ago Sir Justin. He didn't have no feelings for the likes of we. We were like the pheasants they be shooting now . . . bred up for his sport. He'd have killed Pedro in time; he'd have put him on the dangerous work. I had to make him leave us alone because I could see that this were like a sport to him. So I went to him first."

"I hate the St. Larnstons," I said.

"Times change, Kerensa, and people change with them. Times is cruel hard but not quite so cruel hard as they were when I was your age. And when your children come, then times'll be a little easier for them. It's the way of things."

"Granny, what happened then?"

"It weren't the end. Once weren't enough. He liked me too well. This black hair of mine that Pedro loved so much . . . he liked it, too. There was a blight on my first year of marriage, Kerensa. It should have been so fine and grand, but I had to go to him, you see . . . and if Pedro had known, he would have killed him—for passion ran high in his dear heart."

24

"You were frightened, Granny."

She frowned as though trying to remember. "It were a sort of wild gamble. And it went on for nigh on a year, when I found I was to have a child . . . and I didn't know whose. Kerensa, I wouldn't have his child, I wouldn't. I saw it all through the years . . . looking like him . . . and deceiving Pedro. It would be like a stain that would never be washed out. I couldn't do it. So . . . I didn't have the child, Kerensa. I was very ill. I came near to dying, but I didn't have the child; and that were the end as far as he were concerned. He forgot me then. I tried to make up to Pedro. He said I was the gentlest woman in the world with him, though I could be fierce enough with every one else. It pleased him, Kerensa. It made him happy. And sometimes I think the reason I was so gentle with him and did all I could to please him, was because I'd wronged him; and that seemed strange to me. Like good out of evil. That made me understand a lot about life; that was the beginning of my being able to help others. So, Kerensa, you should never regret any experience, good or evil; for there's some good in what's bad just as there be bad in good . . . sure as I sit here in the woods beside you. Two years later, your mother was born—our daughter, Pedro's and mine; and her birth nearly killed me and I couldn't have no more. It was all along of what had happened before, I'm thinking. Oh, but it were a good life. The years pass and the evil is forgotten and many a time I've looked into the past and I've said to myself you couldn't have done different. It was the only way."

"But why should they be able to spoil *our* lives!" I demanded passionately.

"There's strong and weak in the world; and if you're born weak you must find strength. It'll come to you if you look."

"*I* shall find strength, Granny."

"Yes, girl, you will, if you want. It's for you to say."

"Oh, Granny, how I hate the St. Larnstons!" I repeated.

"Nay, he is dead and gone long since. Don't hate the children for the parents' sins. As lief blame yourself for what I did. Ah, but it was a happy life. And there came the day of sorrow. Pedro had gone off for his first shift of the day. I knew they'd be blasting down in the mine and he were one of the trammers who'd go in when the fuses had been blown and load the ore into trucks. I don't know what happened down there—no one can ever truly know, but all that day I waited at the top of the shaft for them to bring him out. Twelve long hours I waited, and when they brought him—he

25

weren't my gay and loving Pedro no more. He were alive though . . . for a few minutes—just time to say goodbye afore he went. 'Bless you,' he did say to me. 'Thank you for my life.' And what could he have said better than that? I tell myself even if there hadn't been a Sir Justin, even if I'd given him healthy sons, he couldn't have said better than that."

She stood up abruptly, and we went into the cottage.

Joe had gone out with Squab, and she took me into the storehouse. There was an old wooden box there which was always kept locked and she opened this and showed me what was inside. There were two Spanish combs and mantillas. She put one of the combs in her hair and covered her hair with the mantilla.

"There," she said, "that was how he liked me to look. He said when he made his fortune he would take me to Spain, and I'd sit on a balcony and fan myself while the world went by."

"You look lovely, Granny."

"One of these is for you when you're older," she said. "And when I die, they are both for you."

Then she put the second comb and mantilla on my head and as we stood side by side it was surprising how much alike we were.

I was glad that she had confided in me something which I knew she had told to no other living person.

I shall never forget that moment when we stood side by side in our combs and mantillas, incongruous among the pans and the herbs. And outside the sound of the guns.

I awoke to moonlight, although not much of it came into our cottage. There was a silence about me which was unusual. I sat up on the talfat and wondered what was wrong. No sound of anything. Not Joe's breathing nor Granny's. I remembered that Granny had gone out to help at a childbirth. She often did and then we never knew when she would be coming home, so it was not surprising that she was absent. But where was Joe?

"Joe!" I said. "Joe, where are you?"

I peered to his end of the talfat. He wasn't there.

"Squab!" I called. There was no answer.

I descended the ladder; it did not take more than a second or two to explore the cottage. I went through to the storehouse but Joe wasn't there either and I suddenly thought of the last time I had been in here when Granny had dressed

26

my hair and decked me out in Spanish comb and mantilla; I remembered the sound of the guns.

Was it possible that Joe had been such a fool as to go into the woods to look for wounded birds? Was he mad? If he went into the woods he would be trespassing, and if he were caught. . . . This was the time of year when trespassing was considered doubly criminal.

I wondered how long he had been gone. I opened the cottage door and looked out, sensing it to be just after midnight.

I went back to the cottage and sat down, not knowing what to do. I wished Granny would come in. We would have to speak to Joe, make him understand the danger he ran in doing such a reckless thing.

I waited and waited and still Granny did not come—nor did Joe. I reckoned that I had sat there for an hour when I could endure it no longer, so I dressed and, leaving the cottage, made my way towards the Abbas woods.

It was a still and beautiful night. Everything seemed slightly weird but enchanting, touched by moonlight. I thought of the Six Virgins and wished that I were making that trip to see the stones, which I had promised myself, instead of coming out to look for Joe.

There was a chill in the air but I was glad of it and I ran all the way to the woods. I stood on the edge of them wondering what to do next. I daren't call Joe, for if any of the gamekeepers should be about, that would attract their attention. Yet if Joe had gone into the woods, it would not be easy for me to find him.

Joe, I thought, you fool! Why do you have to have this obsession, when it makes you do things like this which could bring trouble . . . great trouble?

I stood by the board which I knew said PRIVATE, and told people that if they trespassed they would be prosecuted. These boards were all over the woods as a warning.

"Joe!" I whispered, then wondered if I had spoken too loudly. I went a little way into the woods and thought how silly I was. It was better to go home. He might be there by now.

Horrible pictures kept flashing in and out of my mind. Suppose he found a wounded bird? Suppose he were *caught* with the bird. But if he were foolish, there was no need for me to be. I should go back to the cottage, climb to the talfat, and go to sleep. There was nothing I could do.

But I found it difficult to leave the woods because Joe was

27

my charge, and I must look after him. I should never forgive myself if I failed him.

I prayed, there in the woods that night, that nothing bad should happen to my brother. The only time I thought of praying was when I wanted something. Then I prayed with all my being, desperately and earnestly, and waited for God to answer.

Nothing happened, but I still stood, hoping. I was delaying returning, because something told me that Joe wouldn't be back at the cottage, if I did go back, when I heard a sound. I was alert, listening; it was the whine of a dog.

"Squab!" I whispered, and I seemed to have spoken louder than I thought, for my voice echoed through the woods. A rustling of undergrowth and then, there he was, thrusting against me, making low whining noises, looking up at me as though he wanted to tell me something.

I knelt down. "Squab, where is he, Squab? Where's Joe?"

When he ran a little distance from me, stopped and looked back at me, I knew he was trying to tell me that Joe was somewhere in the woods and he could take me to him. I followed Squab.

When I saw Joe, I was numb with horror. I could only stand still, staring at him and that hideous contraption in which he was held. I could think of nothing, so great was my despair. Joe, caught in the prohibited woods—caught in a mantrap.

I tried to pull at the cruel steel but it would not yield to my puny strength.

"Joe!" I whispered. Squab whined and rubbed against me, looking up at me, imploring me to help, but Joe did not answer me.

Frantically I pulled at those hideous teeth but I could not pry them apart. Panic took hold of me; I had to release my brother before he was found in that trap. If he were alive, they would take him before the magistrates. Sir Justin would have no mercy. *If* he were alive! He *must* be alive. One thing I could not bear was that Joe should be dead. Anything but that, for while he lived I could always do something to save him. I would do something.

You could always do what you wanted to . . . provided you tried enough, was one of Granny's maxims and I believed everything she told me. And now when I was confronted by something different . . . the most important task that I had ever had to perform . . . I couldn't do it.

My hands were bleeding. I did not know how to prize

open this frightful thing. I was putting all my strength into it and I couldn't do it. There must be another way. One person alone could not open a mantrap. I must get help. Granny must come back with me. But Granny for all her wisdom was an old woman. Would she be able to open the trap? She could do anything, I assured myself. Yes, I mustn't waste any more time. I must go back to Granny.

Squab was looking up at me with expectant eyes. I touched him and said: "Stay by him." Then I sped away.

I ran more quickly than I ever had before and yet how long it seemed to take me to reach the road! All the time I was listening for the sound of voices. If Sir Justin's gate-keepers found Joe before I could save him it would be disastrous. I imagined my brother cruelly treated, whipped, enslaved.

My breathing sounded as though I were sobbing as I flung myself across the road; perhaps that was why I was not aware of the ring of footsteps until they were almost upon me.

"Hi," said a voice. "What's wrong?"

I knew the voice; it was that of an enemy, the one they had called Kim.

He mustn't catch me; he mustn't know, I told myself; but he had started to run and he had longer legs than I.

He caught my arm and pulled me round to look at him.

He whistled. "Kerensa of the well!"

"Let me go."

"Why do you fly through the countryside at midnight? Are you a witch? Yes, you are. You threw away your broomstick when you heard me coming."

I tried to twist my arm free, but he wouldn't let me go. He brought his face close to mine.

"You're frightened," he said. "Of me?"

I tried to kick him. "I'm not frightened of you."

Then I thought of Joe lying in that trap and I was so miserable and felt so helpless that the tears came into my eyes.

His manner changed suddenly. He said: "Look, I'm not going to hurt you." And I felt there must be something kind about someone who could speak in a voice like that.

He was young, strong, and towered above me; and in that moment a thought came to me: he might know how to open the trap.

I hesitated. I knew we had to act quickly. I wanted Joe to

live more than anything; if he was going to live he had to be rescued quickly.

I took a chance and the moment I had taken it, regretted it; but it was done and there was no turning back.

"It's my little brother," I said.

"Where?"

I looked towards the woods. "In . . . a trap."

"Good God!" he cried. Then: "Show me."

When I led him there, Squab came running to meet us. Kim was very serious now. But he knew how to set about opening the trap.

"Though I don't know if we can manage it," he warned me.

"We must." I spoke fiercely and his mouth turned up slightly at the corners.

"We will," he assured me; and I knew then that we could. He told me what to do and we worked together but the cruel spring was reluctant to release its prisoner. I was glad—so glad—that I had asked his help because I knew that Granny and I could never have done it.

"Press with all your might," he commanded. I put all my weight on the wicked steel, as, slowly, Kim released the spring. He gave a deep sigh of triumph. We had freed Joe.

"Joey," I whispered, just as I used to when he was a baby. "Don't be dead. You mustn't be."

A dead pheasant had fallen to the ground as we had pulled my brother out of the trap. I saw Kim's quick glance at it but he did not comment on it.

"I think his leg's broken," he said. "We'll have to be careful. It'll be easier if I carry him." He lifted Joe gently in his arms and I loved Kim at that moment, because he was quiet and gentle and he seemed to care what became of us.

Squab and I walked beside him while he carried Joe, and I felt triumphant. But when we reached the road I remembered that, as well as being gentry, Kim was also a friend of the St. Larnstons'. He might well have been a member of this afternoon's shooting party; and to these people the preservation of the birds was more important than the lives of people like us.

I said anxiously: "Where are you going?"

"To Dr. Hilliard. He needs immediate attention."

"No," I said in panic.

"What do you mean?"

"Don't you see? He'll ask where we found him. They'll

know someone's been in the trap. They'll *know*. Don't you see?"

"Stealing pheasants," said Kim.

"No . . . no. He never stole. He wanted to help the birds. He cares about birds and animals. You can't take him to the doctor. Please . . . *please*. . . ."

I caught at his coat and looked up at him.

"Where then?" he said.

"To our cottage. My Granny's as good as a doctor. Then no one will know. . . ."

He paused and I thought he would ignore my plea. Then he said, "All right. But I think he needs a doctor."

"He needs to be home with me and his Granny."

"You're determined to have your way. It's wrong, though!"

"He's my brother. You know what they would do to him."

"Show me the way," he said; and I led him to the cottage.

Granny was at the door, frightened, wondering what had become of us. While I told her in breathless jerks what had happened, Kim didn't say anything; he carried Joe into our cottage and laid him on the floor where Granny had spread out a blanket. Joe looked very small.

"I think he's broken his leg," said Kim.

Granny nodded.

Together they bound his leg to a stick; it seemed like a dream to see Kim there in our cottage taking orders from Granny. He stood by while she bathed Joe's wounds and rubbed ointment into them.

When she had finished, Kim said: "I still think he ought to see a doctor."

"It's better this way," Granny answered firmly, because I had told her where we had found him.

So Kim shrugged his shoulders and went away.

We watched over Joe all that night, Granny and I, and we knew in the morning that he would live.

We were frightened. Joe lay there on his blankets too sick to care; but we cared. Every time we heard a step, we started up in terror, afraid that it was someone come to take Joe.

We talked about it in whispers.

"Granny," I pleaded, "did I do wrong? He was there and he was big and strong, and I thought he would know how to open the trap. I was afraid, Granny, afraid you and I wouldn't get Joe out."

31

"You did right," Granny Bee soothed me. "A night in the trap would have killed our Joe."

Then we fell into silence, watching Joe, listening for footsteps.

"Granny," I said, "do you think he'll . . . ?"

"I couldn't say."

"He seemed kind, Granny. Different from some."

"He did seem kind," agreed Granny.

"But he's a friend of the St. Larnstons', Granny. That day I was in the wall he were there. He mocked like the rest."

Granny nodded.

Footsteps near the cottage. A rap on the door.

Granny and I were there simultaneously.

Mellyora Martin stood smiling at us. She looked very pretty in a mauve and white gingham dress, white stockings and her black, buckled shoes. On her arm she carried a wicker basket which was covered by a white cloth.

"Good afternoon," said Mellyora in her sweet high voice.

Neither Granny nor I answered; we were both too relieved to show anything but our relief.

"I heard," went on Mellyora, "so I brought this along for the invalid."

She held out the wicker basket.

Granny took it and said, "For Joe . . . ?"

Mellyora nodded. "I saw Mr. Kimber this morning. He told me how the boy had had an accident climbing a tree. I thought he might like these. . . ."

Granny said in a voice meeker than I'd ever heard her use before: "Thank 'ee, Miss."

Mellyora smiled. "I hope he will soon be well," she said. "Good afternoon."

We stood at the door watching her as she walked away; then without speaking we carried the basket inside. Under the cloth were eggs, butter, half a roast chicken, and a loaf of homemade bread.

Granny and I looked at each other. Kim wasn't going to tell. We had nothing to fear from the law.

I was silent thinking about my prayer in the woods and how, providentially, it seemed, I had received help. I had snatched the opportunity given; I had taken a great risk; but I had won.

I had rarely felt as happy as I did in that moment; and later when I thought what I owed to Kim, I told myself that I would always remember.

Joe took a long time to recover. He used to lie on his blanket with Squab beside him for hours, doing nothing, saying nothing. He couldn't walk for a long time, and when he began to, we realized that this had made a cripple of him.

He didn't remember very much about the trap; only that terrifying moment when he had walked into it and he had heard it snap, as it crunched his bones. Fortunately, pain had sent him into speedy oblivion. It was no use scolding him, no use telling him it was his fault; he would have done it again if he could.

But he was listless for many weeks and it was only when I brought him a rabbit with an injured foot that he began to cheer up; in looking after the rabbit he regained some of his spirits and during that time it was like having the old Joe back. I could see that I would have to make sure he always had some maimed creature to care for.

The winter came and it was a hard one. Winters were harder inland than they had been on the coast, but, even so, the Cornish winters were usually mild; this year, however, the wind turned from the usual southwest and came from the north and east bringing blizzards with it. The Fedder mine where many of the villagers now worked, was not yielding the tin that it had up till now and there were rumors that it might in a few years become an old scat bal.

Christmas came and there were hampers of food from the Abbas—a custom which they had kept through the centuries—and we were allowed to gather kindling from some parts of the woods. It wasn't like the last Christmas because Joe wasn't able to run about and we had to face the fact that his leg would never be right. Still, the events of that night were too recent for us to complain; we all knew what Joe had narrowly escaped and we weren't likely to forget.

Troubles don't come singly. It must have been in February that Granny took a chill; she was hardly ever ill, so we didn't take much notice during the first few days; and then one night her coughing awakened me and I scrambled down from the talfat to get her some of her own syrup. It soothed her temporarily but it didn't cure the cough and a few nights later I heard her talking and, to my horror, I discovered that she didn't know who I was when I went to her. She kept calling me Pedro.

I was terrified that she was going to die, for she was very ill. I sat beside her all that night and in the morning she stopped being delirious. When she was able to tell me what

33

herbs to brew for her, I felt better. I nursed her for three weeks, on her instructions, and gradually she began to recover. She was able to walk about the cottage but when she went out her cough started again, so I made her stay in. I gathered some herbs for her and made a few of the brews; but there were many which needed her special skill. In any case, not so many people came to ask her advice now. They were getting poorer and so were we. Moreover I heard some of them questioning the power of Granny Bee. She couldn't cure herself, could she? That boy of hers was a cripple, wasn't he, and all he'd done was fall off a tree! It didn't seem as though Granny Bee was so wonderful after all.

Those tasty joints of pork did not come our way. There were no grateful clients now to leave a sack of peas or potatoes on our doorstep. We had to eat sparingly if we wanted to eat twice a day.

We had flour, so I made a kind of manshun in the old cloam oven, and it tasted good. We kept a goat who gave us milk, but we couldn't feed her properly and we got less milk.

One day at breakfast I spoke to Granny of an idea which had come to me during the night.

The three of us were sitting at the table, our bowls before us containing what we called sky blue and sinkers—a dish which was being eaten a great deal that winter. It was made of water with a dash of skim milk which we got cheaply from the farmer, who sold what he didn't need for his pigs; we boiled this and dropped pieces of bread into it. There was a tinge of blue in the liquid and the bread always sank to the bottom of the bowl—hence its name.

"Granny," I said, "I reckon I ought to be bringing something in."

She shook her head, but I saw the look in her eyes. I was nearly thirteen. Whoever heard of a girl in my station, who wasn't Granny Bee's granddaughter, living at lady's leisure? Granny knew that something would have to be done. Joe couldn't help, but I was strong and healthy.

"We'll think about it," she said.

"I have thought."

"What?" she asked.

"What is there?"

That was the question. I could go to Farmer Pengaster and ask if he wanted someone to help in the dairy, with the animals, or in the kitchens. There would be plenty yearning to give their services if he did! Where else? One of the houses of the gentry? I hated the thought. All my pride rose in revolt; but I knew it had to be.

"It might only be for a time," said Granny. "In the summer I'll get on my feet again."

I couldn't bear to look at Granny or I should have told her that I would rather starve than work as I was suggesting. But I wasn't the only one to be considered. There was Joe who had had this terrible misfortune; and there was Granny herself. If I were away working, they could have my share of the sky blue and sinkers; my share of the potatoes and bacon.

"I'll put myself up at Trelinket Fair next week," I said firmly.

Trelinket Fair was held twice a year in the village of Trelinket—a good two miles from St. Larnston. We had always gone to it—Granny, Joe, and I—in the old days; and those were red-letter days for us. Granny Bee would dress her hair with special care and we would walk proudly through the crowds; she used to take some of her cures and sell them to a stallholder, who bought as many as she could provide. Then she would buy us gingerbread or a fairing. But this year we had nothing to sell; and as Joe couldn't walk the two miles to the fair everything was changed.

I set out alone, with my heart like a piece of lead; my pride debased. How many times, walking through the fair with Granny and an uncrippled Joe, had I glanced at those men and women who stood on the hiring platform and been so happy because I was not like them. It seemed to me the depth of degradation that men and women should have to hire themselves out. It was like being in a slave market. But it was what had to be done if one needed work, for employers came to the fair for the purpose of hiring likely-looking servants. Now, today, I was to be one of them.

It was a bright spring day and somehow the sunshine made it worse; I envied the birds who seemed mad with joy after the unusually hard winter; in fact I was ready to envy everyone that morning. Once the fair had offered a feast of enjoyment. I had loved the bustle of it, the smell, the noise— everything that made up Trelinket Fair. On the refreshment stalls there was hot beef and boiled goose; you watched them cooking on fires beside the stalls. There were stalls of pies, golden pasty enclosing the delicious contents baked the day before in some farmhouse kitchen or cottage oven. The stall-holders called out the tantalizing descriptions as the people strolled past. "Try a piece of this old muggety, m'dear.

Reckon you ain't never tasted the like." And one of them cut open a pie to display the entrail of sheep or calves, which was muggety, or those of pig which were nattlins. A special treat was the taddage pies made with sucking pig; and the more common squab or pigeon pie was there, too.

People would stand by the stalls sampling and buying the pies to take away with them. There was that part of the fair where the cattle were on show; there were the cheap-Jacks selling almost everything you could think of—old boots and clothing, saddlery, pots, pans, and even cloam ovens. There were the fortunetellers and the healers—those who shouted the merits of their medicines and who had been customers of Granny Bee's.

And close by the spot where a goose was being roasted over an open fire was the hiring platform. I viewed it with shame. Several people were already standing there; they looked a wretched and dejected lot; and no wonder. Who could enjoy displaying themselves for hire! And to think that I, Kerensa Carlee, must join them. I thought I should hate the smell of roasting goose forever after. Everyone around me seemed to be laughing; the sun had turned hot and I felt angry with the whole world.

But I had given my word to Granny that I would stand for hire. I could not go back and tell her that my heart had failed me right at the last moment. I couldn't go back and be a burden to them; I, who was well and strong.

Resolutely I approached the platform and mounted the rickety wooden steps at the side; then I was standing there among them.

Prospective employers regarded us with interest, weighing up our possibilities. I saw Farmer Pengaster among them. If he took me, it wouldn't be too bad. He was reckoned to be good to his workpeople and I should be able to take little titbits home to the cottage. It would ease my bitterness considerably if I could go home now and then and play the lady bountiful.

Then I saw two people who made me start back in dismay. I recognized them as the butler and housekeeper at the Abbas. Only one purpose could have brought them to the fair and they were making straight for the hiring platform. Now I was beginning to be frightened. It had been a dream of mine that one day I should live at St. Larnston Abbas; I had lived with that dream, because Granny Bee had told me that if you created a dream and did all you could to make it come true, it was almost certain that in time it would. Now I

36

saw this dream of mine could easily come true—I could live at the Abbas—as a servant!

Hundreds of images flitted through my mind. I thought of young Justin St. Larnston haughtily giving me my orders; of Johnny jeering at me, reminding me I was a servant; of Mellyora coming to drink tea with the family, and myself standing by in cap and apron to serve them. I thought of Kim there. There was another thought too. Ever since Granny had confided in me that day in the woods, I had thought a good deal about that Sir Justin who was the father of the present one. They were very much alike and I was like Granny. There was a possibility that what had happened to Granny might happen to me. I burned with rage and shame at the thought.

They were coming nearer, talking earnestly, then scrutinizing one of the hiring girls who was about my age. What if they should pass along the line? What if they should choose me?

I was wrestling with myself. Should I leap from the platform and run home? I pictured myself explaining to Granny. She would understand. Hadn't it been my suggestion—not hers—that I should come at all?

Then I saw Mellyora—dainty and fresh in mauve gingham, with a flounced skirt and a neat close-fitting bodice, neck and sleeves edged with lace; with white stockings and black walking shoes with straps; and her fair hair showing from under her straw bonnet.

The moment I saw her she saw me, and in that second I was unable to hide my apprehension. She came over swiftly, her eyes troubled, and she stood right before me.

"Kerensa?" She said my name softly.

I was angry because she had seen me in my humiliation, and how could I help hating her, standing there neat, clean, fresh, so dainty—and free.

"You're hiring yourself?"

"Twould seem so," I answered truculently.

"But . . . you haven't before."

"Times are hard," I muttered.

The pair from the Abbas were coming nearer. The butler already had his eyes on me and they were shining in a warm and speculative manner.

A look of excitement came into Mellyora's face; she caught her breath and started to speak in a hurry as though the words wouldn't come out quickly enough.

"Kerensa, we're looking for someone. Would you come to the parsonage?"

It was like a reprieve. The dream was not turning sour on me. I was not going to St. Larnston Abbas by way of the back door. If I did that, I felt the real dream would never come true.

"To the parsonage!" I stammered. "So you are here for the hiring?"

She nodded eagerly. "Yes, we need . . . someone. When will you be ready to start?"

Haggety the butler was close to us now; he said: "Morning, Miss Martin."

"Good morning."

"Nice to see you, Miss, at the fair. Mrs. Rolt and myself's here to find us a pair of girls for the kitchens." He was looking at me now, his little eyes shining.

"This looks a likely 'un," he said. "What's your name?"

I lifted my head haughtily. "You're too late," I said. "I'm hired."

There was a feeling of unreality in the air that day. I had the impression that this really wasn't happening to me, that soon I would wake up and find myself on the talfat, dreaming as always or laughing with Granny Bee.

I was actually walking along beside Mellyora Martin; and she had engaged me to work at the parsonage—she, a girl of my own age.

Mr. Haggety and Mrs. Rolt had looked so astounded that they had only gaped when Mellyora said a gracious good-bye. They stared at us as we walked away and I heard Mrs. Rolt murmur: "Well, did 'ee ever see the like!" I glanced at Mellyora and I felt a vague alarm; I sensed that she was beginning to regret a rash action. I was certain then that she had not come to the fair to hire anyone, that she had acted on an impulse to save me from going to work at the Abbas, just as she had tried to save me from the mockery of the boys when she had found me in the wall.

I asked: "Is it all right?"

"What?"

"For you to hire me?"

"It'll be all right."

"But . . ."

"We'll manage," she said; she was very pretty when she

38

smiled and the sparkle and defiance in her eyes made her prettier.

People turned to look at us as we went through the crowds, past the cheap-Jack who was shouting the merits of his wares, how a bottle of this or that would cure all the ills in the world; past the roasting goose and the stall of fairings. We were such a contrast—she so fair, myself so dark; she so neat, and myself, though clean, for I had washed my smock and my hair the day before, so poorly dressed; she in her black shining shoes, myself barefoot. And it wouldn't occur to anyone that she had hired me.

She led me to the edge of the field in which the fair was set up and there was the pony and trap which I knew belonged to the parsonage: in the driving seat was the middle-aged governess whom I had seen often in Mellyora's company.

She turned as we approached and said: "Good gracious, Mellyora! What does this mean?"

I presumed the "this" referred to me, so my head shot up and I gave the governess my haughtiest stare.

"Oh, Miss Kellow, I must explain . . ." began Mellyora in an embarrassed flutter.

"Indeed you must," was the answer. "Pray do."

"This is Kerensa Carlee. I've hired her."

"You've . . . what?"

I turned to Mellyora, reproach in my eyes. If she had been wasting my time . . . if she had been playing some game of pretense . . . if this was supposed to be some amusing sort of game. . . .

She shook her head. Again that disturbing habit of reading my thoughts.

"It's all right, Kerensa," she said. "Leave this to me."

She talked to me as though I were a friend, not a hired girl; I could have liked Mellyora if I could only rid myself of this bitter envy. I had imagined her foolish, meek, quite dull. It wasn't true though. There was a great deal of spirit in Mellyora, as I was to discover.

Now it was her turn to be haughty, and she managed this very well. "Get in, Kerensa. Miss Kellow, pray drive us home."

"Now, Mellyora . . ." She was a dragon, this Miss Kellow; I judged her to be in her early forties, her lips were tight, her eyes alert. I felt an extraordinary sympathy for her because she, in her superior way, was after all only a servant.

"This," retorted Mellyora, still the haughty young lady, "is a matter between myself and my father."

We clop-clopped along the road back to St. Larnston, and none of us spoke as we passed the cottages and the blacksmiths' shops and came to the gray church with its tall tower and the graveyard with its toppling tombstones. Beyond was the parsonage.

Miss Kellow drew up at the door and Mellyora said: "Come along, Kerensa."

I alighted with her and Miss Kellow drove the trap to the stables.

I said: "You hadn't any right to hire me, had you?"

"Of course I had a right," she retorted. "If I hadn't you would have gone to the Abbas, and you would have hated that."

"How did you know?"

She smiled. "I guessed."

"How do you know I won't hate it here?"

"Of course, you won't. My father is the best man in the world. Anyone would be happy in this house. I have to explain to him, though." She hesitated, uncertain what to do with me. Then she said: "Come with me."

She pushed open the door and we went into a large hall in which was a bowl of daffodils and anemones standing on an oak chest. A grandfather clock ticked in a corner and facing the door was a wide staircase.

Mellyora signed to me to follow her and we mounted the staircase. On the landing she threw open a door.

"Wait in my bedroom," she said, "until I call you."

The door shut on me and I was alone. I had never been in such a room before. There were soft blue curtains at the big window and a blue coverlet on the bed. There were pictures on the wall and pale-blue lover's knots on the pink wallpaper. What struck me most, though, was the little bookcase near the bed. The books Mellyora read! They brought home to me the gulf between us, so I turned my back on them and looked out of the window. Below me was the parsonage garden; about half an acre, with lawns and flowerbeds. And working in the garden was the Reverend Charles Martin, Mellyora's father. As I watched, I saw Mellyora appear; she ran straight to him and began talking earnestly. I watched intently, knowing that my fate was being discussed.

The Reverend Charles was looking startled. Mellyora was being emphatic. They were arguing; she took his hand and went on talking vehemently. She was pleading for me. I wondered why she cared so much.

I could see she was winning; he couldn't refuse anything to his lovely daughter.

He nodded resignedly and they started to walk towards the house. In a few minutes the door opened, and there stood Mellyora, smiling the smile of triumph.

The Reverend Charles came towards me; he said in the voice he used for the pulpit, "So you are coming to work with us, Kerensa. I hope you will be happy here."

2

I soon began to realize what a great opportunity Mellyora had given me, and although later strange things were to happen about me and to me, that first year at the parsonage seemed to me, while I lived it, the most exciting time of my life. I suppose it was because that was when the realization came to me that I could begin to climb into another world.

Mellyora *was* my opportunity. I understood that she was attracted by me in the same way that I was by her. She had discovered in me this tremendous urge to escape from an environment which I hated, and she was fascinated.

I had my enemies in the house, naturally. The most formidable of these was Miss Kellow. Prim, a parson's daughter herself, she was constantly on her dignity, eager to prove that only misfortune had forced her to earn her living. She had an affection for Mellyora, but she was an ambitious woman and I, who possessed that quality in excess, was quick to observe it in others. Like myself, she was dissatisfied with her lot and planned to improve it. There was Mrs. Yeo, the cook-housekeeper who looked upon herself as head of the staff, including Miss Kellow. There was a feud between those two which worked to my advantage, for although Mrs. Yeo couldn't, as she said, for the life of her see why I had been brought into the house, she didn't resent me quite as much as Miss Kellow did, and was inclined, at times, to take my part, simply because to do so was to be in opposition to Miss

Kellow. There was the groom, Tom Belter, and the stable-boy, Billy Toms; they were inclined to view me more favorably, but I would have none of the familiarities they gave to Kit and Bess, the two maids, and I quickly made this clear; even so, they bore me no grudge and they were inclined to respect me for it. Kit and Bess regarded me with awe; this was because I was Granny Bee's granddaughter; they would sometimes ask me questions about Granny, they wanted her advice in their love affairs, or some herb that would improve their complexions. I was able to help them, and this made life more comfortable for me, because in exchange they would do some of the tasks which had been allotted to me.

For the first few days in the parsonage I saw little of Mellyora; I thought then that she had done her good deed and left it at that. I was handed over to Mrs. Yeo, who, when she had done complaining about my unnecessary presence, found jobs for me to do. I did them uncomplainingly for those first days.

When Mellyora had brought the parson to her bedroom on that first day, I had asked if I might run and tell my Granny where I was going to be and permission was readily granted. Mellyora had come with me to the kitchen and herself packed a basket of dainty food which I was to take for my poor brother who had fallen off the tree. So I was in a rather exalted state when I arrived at the cottage to tell the result of my standing for hire at Trelinket Fair.

Granny held me in her arms, nearer to tears than I had ever seen her. "The parson's a good man," she declared. "There's no better in the whole of St. Larnston. And his girl's a good girl. You'll do well there, my love."

I told her about Haggety and Mrs. Rolt and how they had nearly hired me, and she laughed with me when I told her how flabbergasted they were to see me walk off with Mellyora.

We unpacked the basket but I wouldn't eat a thing. It was for them, I said. I should eat very well at the parsonage.

This in itself was like a dream coming true because hadn't I imagined myself playing the lady bountiful?

The elation faded during those first few days when I didn't see Mellyora and was set to scouring pots and pans or turning the spit or preparing vegetables and swabbing floors. But there was the compensation of eating well. No sky blue and sinkers here. But I remember during those first days hearing a remark that astonished me. I was cleaning the slate floor of

43

the cooling house where the butter, cheeses, and milk were kept, when Belter came into the kitchen to talk to Mrs. Yeo. I heard him give her a noisy kiss and that made me more alert. "You give over, young man," said Mrs. Yeo, giggling. He didn't give over and there were sounds of scuffling and heavy breathing. Then she said: "Sit down then, and stop it. Them maidens'll be seeing you. Twouldn't do for they to get to know what sort of man you be, Master Belter." "Nay, that be our secret, eh, Mrs. Yeo?" "Give over. Give over." Then: "We've got that Granny Bee's girl here, did you know?" "Ay, I've seen 'un. Sharp enough. What beats me . . . why do we have her here then? Parson finds it hard enough, lord to you know, to feed us all. Then they brings this one in—and she can give a pretty good account on herself when it comes to the table. Better she be at that than doing her work, I can tell 'ee." "So things be bad then?" "Oh, you do know, if parson has a halfpenny, he'll give away a penny."

They quickly found something of more interest to them than the parson's affairs or my arrival; but I went on thinking as I swabbed the floor. Everything had seemed luxurious in the parsonage; it was astonishing to consider that in this house they found it difficult to make ends meet.

I didn't really believe it. It was just the servants' gossip.

I hadn't been a week at the parsonage when I realized my great good fortune. I had been sent to clean Mellyora's room while she was having her lesson in the library with Miss Kellow, and as soon as I was alone in the room I went to the bookcase and opened one of the books. It had pictures in it with captions underneath. I stared at these, trying to understand what they were. I felt angry and frustrated, like someone shut up in a prison while the most exciting things in the world are happening just outside.

I wondered if I could teach myself to read if I took one of the books and looked at it, learned the shape of the letters, copied them, remembered them. I forgot all about cleaning the room. I sat on the floor, took one book after another, tried to make comparisons of letters to give me a clue as to what they meant. I was still sitting there when Mellyora came into the room.

"What are you doing?" she demanded.

I shut the book hastily and said: "I'm cleaning your room."

She laughed. "Nonsense. You were sitting on the floor

reading. What were you reading, Kerensa? I didn't know you could read."

"You're laughing at me," I cried. "Stop it. Don't think because you hired me at a fair you bought me!"

"Kerensa!" she said haughtily as she had spoken to Miss Kellow.

Then I felt my lips tremble and her face changed at once. "Why were you looking at the books?" she asked gently. "Tell me, please. I want to know."

It was the "please" which made me blurt out the truth. "It's not fair," I said. "I could read if someone would show me."

"So you want to read?"

"Of course I want to read and write. More than anything in the world I want to."

She sat on the bed, crossed her pretty feet, and looked at her shiny shoes. "Well, that's easy enough," she said. "You must be taught."

"Who'll teach me?"

"I will, of course."

That was the beginning. She did teach me, although she admitted afterwards that she thought I would soon tire of learning. Tire! I was indefatigable. In the attic which I shared with Bess and Kit, I would wake with the dawn and write the letters, copying those Mellyora had set for me; I would steal candles from Mrs. Yeo's store cupboard and burn them half the night. I threatened Bess and Kit with horrible misfortunes if they should tell on me, and because I was Granny Bee's granddaughter, they meekly agreed to keep my secret.

Mellyora was astounded by my progress and on the day I wrote my name unaided, she was quite overcome by emotion.

"It's a shame," she said, "that you have to do this other work. You ought to be in the schoolroom."

A few days later the Reverend Charles summoned me to his study. He was very thin, with kind eyes and a skin that seemed to grow more and more yellow every day. His clothes were too big for him and his light-brown hair was always ruffled and untidy. He didn't care much about himself; he cared a great deal about the poor and people's souls; and more than anything in the world he cared for Mellyora. You could see that he thought of her as one of the angels he was always preaching about. She could do exactly what she liked with him, so it was lucky for me that one thing she had inherited from him was this caring about other people. He always looked rather worried. I had thought that this was because he was thinking of all the people who would go to hell, but after I overheard the conversation between Mrs. Yeo and Belter, it occurred to me that he might be worried about all the food being eaten in this house and how he was going to pay for it.

"My daughter tells me that she has taught you to write. That's very good. That's excellent. You want to read and write, do you, Kerensa?"

"Yes, very much."

"Why?"

I knew I mustn't tell him the real reason, so I said craftily: "Because I want to read books, sir. Books like the Bible."

That pleased him. "Then, my child," he said, "since you have the ability, we must do all we can to help you. My daughter suggests that you join her with Miss Kellow tomorrow. I shall tell Mrs. Yeo to excuse you from the duties you would be doing at that time."

I didn't try to hide my joy because there was no need to, and he patted my shoulder.

"Now if you find that you would rather be at your tasks with Mrs. Yeo than those set you by Miss Kellow, you must say so."

"I never shall!" I answered vehemently.

"Go along," he said, "and pray earnestly that God will guide you in all you do."

The decision which would never have been made in any other household caused consternation in this one.

"I never heard the like!" grumbled Mrs. Yeo. "Taking that sort and making a scholar of her. Mark my words, it'll be Bodmin Asylum for some people afore long—and them not far distant from this room where I do stand. I tell 'ee, parson's going out of his mind."

Bess and Kit just whispered together that this was the result of a spell Granny Bee had put on parson. She wanted her granddaughter to be able to read and write like a lady. Just showed, didn't it, what Granny Bee could do if she wanted to. I thought: this is going to be good for Granny, too!

Miss Kellow received me stonily; I could see that she was going to tell me that she, an impoverished gentlewoman, was

46

not going to sink so low as teaching such as I was, without a struggle.

"This is madness," she said when I presented myself.

"Why?" demanded Mellyora.

"How do you think we can continue with our studies when I have to teach the ABC."

"She already knows it. She can already read and write."

"I protest . . . strongly."

"What are you going to do?" asked Mellyora. "Give a month's notice?"

"I might do that. I would like you to know that I have taught in the house of a baronet."

"You have mentioned it more than once," retorted Mellyora acidly. "And since you so regret leaving that house, perhaps you should try to find another like it."

She could be sharp when she had something to campaign for. What a champion she was!

"Sit down, child," said Miss Kellow. I obeyed meekly enough because I was anxious to learn all she could teach me.

She tried to spoil everything, of course; but my desire to learn and to prove her wrong was so great that I astonished not only Mellyora and Miss Kellow but myself. Having mastered the art of reading and writing, I could easily improve without anybody's help. Mellyora gave me book after book which I read avidly. I learned exciting facts about other countries and what happened in the past. Soon I should equal Mellyora; my secret plan was to surpass her.

But all the time I had to fight Miss Kellow; she hated me and was continually trying to prove how foolish it was to waste time on me, until I found a way to silence her.

I had watched her closely because I had already learned that if you have an enemy it is as well to know as much about him as you can discover. If you have to attack you must go for the vulnerable part. Miss Kellow had a secret. She was frightened of insecurity; she hated being unmarried, seeing in it some slur to her womanhood. I had seen her flinch at the reference to "old maids," and I began to understand that she hoped to marry the Reverend Charles.

Whenever I was alone with her in the schoolroom, her manner to me would be disdainful; she never praised what I did; if she had to explain anything she would sigh with impatience. I disliked her. I should have hated her if I hadn't known so much about her and recognized that she was as insecure as I was.

47

One day when Mellyora had left the schoolroom and I was putting our books away, I dropped a pile of them. She gave her unpleasant laugh.

"That's not the way to treat books."

"I couldn't help dropping them, could I?"

"Pray be more respectful when you speak to me."

"Why should I?"

"Because I have a position here, because I'm a lady—something you will never be."

Deliberately I set the books down on the table. I faced her and I gave her a look as scornful as the one she had given me.

"Leastways," I said, lapsing into the dialect and accent which I was learning to drop, "reckon I wouldn't be chasing an old parson, hoping as how he'll marry me."

She turned pale. "How . . . dare you!" she cried; but my words had struck as I had intended they should.

"Oh, I dare all right," I retaliated. "I dare taunt you as you taunt me. Now listen, Miss Kellow, you treat me right and I'll treat you right. I won't say a word about you . . . and you'll give me lessons just like I be Mellyora's sister, see?"

She didn't answer; she couldn't; her lips were trembling too much. So I went out, knowing it was my victory. And so it proved to be. In future she did her best to help me learn, and stopped taunting me and when I did well she said so.

I felt as powerful as Julius Caesar whose exploits were fascinating me.

No one could have been more delighted than Mellyora at my progress. When I beat her at lessons she was genuinely delighted. She looked on me as a plant she was cultivating; when I didn't do so well she was reproachful. I was discovering her to be a strange girl—not the simple creature I imagined. She could be as determined as I—or almost—and her life seemed to be governed by what she considered right and wrong, probably instilled by her father. She would do anything—however daring or bold—if she believed it to be right. She ruled the household because she had no mother and her father doted on her. So when she said that she needed a companion, a personal maid, I became that. It was, as Mrs. Yeo continually complained, something she had never heard the like of, but the parsonage was like a madhouse, she reckoned, so she couldn't be expected to know what would happen next.

I was given a room next to Mellyora's and was spending a great deal of time with her. I mended her clothes, washed them, shared her lessons and went for walks with her. She was very fond of teaching me and she taught me to ride, taking me round and round the meadow on her pony.

It didn't occur to me how unusual this was. I simply believed that I had made a dream which was coming true, as Granny had told me that it would.

Mellyora and I were about the same height, but I was much more slender than she and when she gave me dresses which she no longer wanted, I only had to take them in to make them fit. I remember the first time I went home to the cottage wearing a blue and white gingham dress, white stockings, and black shiny shoes—all gifts from Mellyora. I carried a basket on my arm, because whenever I visited the cottage I took something.

Mrs. Yeo's remarks had been the only disconcerting note to a perfect day. As I packed the basket, she said: "Miss Mellyora be like parson—very fond of giving away what she can't afford to."

I tried to forget that remark. I told myself that it was just another of Mrs. Yeo's grumbles; but it was like a tiny dark cloud in a summer sky.

As I walked through the village I saw Hetty Pengaster, the farmer's daughter. Before that day I had set myself up for hire at Trelinket Fair I had thought of Hetty with envy. She was the farmer's only daughter, although he had two sons—Thomas, who farmed with him, and Reuben, who worked at Pengrants the builders, and was that young man who had thought he had seen the seventh virgin when the Abbas wall collapsed and consequently had become piskey-mazed. Hetty was the darling of the household, plumply pretty in an over-ripe way which made the old women shake their heads pro-phetically and say that Pengasters ought to watch out that Hetty didn't have a baby in a cradle before she had a wed-ding ring on her finger. I saw what they meant; it was in the way she walked, in the sidelong glances she gave the men, in the thick, sensuous lips. She always had a ribbon in her auburn hair and her dresses were always showy and low cut.

She was all but affianced to Saul Cundy who worked in the Fedder mine. A strange alliance this would be—for Saul was a serious man who must have been some ten years older than

Hetty. It would be a marriage approved of by her family, for Saul was no ordinary miner. He was known as Cap'en Saul and had the power to employ men; he was clearly a leader and one would have thought him scarcely the sort to come courting Hetty. Perhaps Hetty herself thought this and wanted to have some fun before settling down to sober marriage.

She mocked me now. "Well, if it bain't Kerensa Carlee—all dressed up and fit to kill."

I retorted in a tone I had learned from Mellyora: "I am visiting my Grandmother."

"Ooo! Are you then, me lady. Mind 'ee don't soil your hands with the likes of we."

I heard her laughing as I went on and I didn't mind in the least. In fact I was pleased. Why had I ever envied Hetty Pengaster? What was a ribbon in the hair, shoes on the feet, beside the ability to write and read and talk like a lady?

I had rarely felt as happy as I did when I continued on my way to the cottage.

I found Granny alone and her eyes shone with pride when she kissed me. No matter how much I learned I would never cease to love Granny and yearn for her approval.

"Where's Joe?" I asked.

Granny was exultant.

I knew Mr. Pollent, the vet, who had a good business out Molenter way? Well, he had called at the cottage. He had heard tell that Joe was good with animals and he could do with someone like that . . . someone who would work for him. He would train him and make a vet of him, maybe.

"So Joe has gone to Mr. Pollent?"

"Well, what do 'ee think? Twas a chance in a lifetime."

"A vet. I was planning for him to be a doctor."

"A vet has a very good profession, lovey."

"It's not the same," I replied wistfully.

"Well, tis a start like. Get his keep for a year, then he'll be paid. And Joe be happy as a king. Don't think of nothing but they animals."

I repeated Granny's words. "Tis a start."

"Tis a load off my mind, too," Granny admitted. "Now I see you two settled like, I be at peace."

"Granny," I said, "I reckon anything you want can be yours. Who'd have thought I'd be sitting here in buckled shoes and a gingham dress with lace at the collar."

"Who'd have thought it," she agreed.

"I dreamed it; and I wanted it so much that it came. . . .

Granny, it's there, isn't it? The whole world . . . it's there if you know how to take it?"

Granny put her hand over mine. "Don't 'ee forget, lovey, life bain't all that easy. What if someone else has the same dream? What if they do want the same piece of the world as you. You've had luck. It's all along of parson's daughter. But don't 'ee forget that was chance; and there be good chance and bad chance."

I wasn't really listening. I was too content. I was faintly chagrined, it was true, that it was only the vet to whom Joe had gone. If it had been Dr. Hilliard I should have felt like some magician who had found the keys to the kingdom on earth.

Still, it was a start for Joe; and there was more to eat in the cottage now. People were coming to see Granny. They believed in her again. Look at that granddaughter of hers worming her way into the parsonage! Look at that grandson! Mr. Pollent himself riding to the cottage to ask "Could I train him please?" What was that but witchcraft. Magic! Call it what you will. Any old woman who could do that could charm the warts off you, could give you the right powder to cure this and that, could look into the future and tell you what you belonged to do.

So Granny was prospering, too.

We were all prospering. There had never been such times.

I was singing to myself as I made my way back to the parsonage.

Mellyora and I were together a great deal now that I was a fit companion for her. I imitated her in lots of ways—walking, speaking, remaining still when I spoke, keeping my voice low, holding in my temper, being cold instead of hot. It was a fascinating study. Mrs. Yeo had ceased to grumble; Bess and Kit had ceased to marvel; Belter and Billy Toms no longer called out when I passed; they even called me Miss. And even Miss Kellow was polite to me. I had no duties in the kitchen at all; my task was to look after Mellyora's clothes, do her hair, walk with her, read with her and to her, talk to her. The life of a lady! I assured myself. And it was now two years since I had put myself up for hire at Trelinket Fair.

But I had much to achieve. I was always a little downcast when Mellyora received invitations and went off on visits. Sometimes Miss Kellow accompanied her, sometimes her father; I never did. None of those invitations, naturally, was extended to Mellyora's maid, companion, whatever one liked to call her.

She often went to call at the doctor's house with her father; on very rare occasions she went to the Abbas; she never went to the Dower House because, as she explained to me, Kim's father was a sea captain and he was rarely at home, and during the vacation Kim wasn't expected to entertain; but when she went to the Abbas she often found him there, because he was a friend of Justin's.

After Mellyora returned from a visit to the Abbas she was always subdued and I guessed that the place meant something to her, too—either that or the people. I could see reason in this. It must be wonderful to go boldly into the Abbas as a guest. One day that would happen to me. I was sure of it.

One Easter Sunday I learned more about Mellyora than I had ever known before. Sundays were naturally busy days at the parsonage because of all the church services. The sound of bells went on for most of the day and since we were so near they appeared to be right in the house.

I always went to morning service which I enjoyed, chiefly I have to admit because I would be wearing one of Mellyora's straw hats and one of her gowns; and sitting in the parsonage's pew I felt grand and important. I loved the music, too, which always put me in a state of exultation and I liked to praise and give thanks to God who made dreams come true. The sermons I found dull for the Reverend Charles was not an inspired speaker and when, during them, I studied the congregation, my eyes invariably came to rest on the Abbas pews.

These were at the side of the church—set apart from the rest. There were usually quite a number of servants from the house in church. The front row where the family sat was almost always empty.

Immediately behind the Abbas pew were the lovely glass windows said to be some of the best in Cornwall—blue, red, green and mauve glinting in sunshine; they were exquisite and had been given to the church by a St. Larnston a hundred or more years before; on the two walls on either side of the pews were memorials dedicated to past St. Larnstons. Even in church one had the impression that the St. Larnstons owned it like everything else.

The whole family was in the pew this day. I suppose because it was Easter. There was Sir Justin, whose face seemed more purple—just as the parson's seemed more yellow—every time I saw him; there was his wife, Lady St. Larnston, tall with a long, somewhat hooked nose, very imperious and arrogant-looking; and the two sons, Justin and Johnny, who hadn't changed a great deal since that day I had encountered them in the walled garden. Justin looked cold and calm; he was more like his mother than Johnny was. Johnny was short compared with his brother, and lacked Justin's dignity; his eyes kept roaming round the church as though he were looking for someone.

I loved the Easter service and the flowers which decorated the altar; I loved the joyous singing of "Hosanna." I felt I knew what it must be like to be risen from the dead; while, during the sermon I studied the occupants of the Abbas pews, I was thinking of Sir Justin's father fancying Granny and how she went to him in secret for Pedro's sake. I wondered what I should have done in Granny's place.

Then I was aware that beside me, Mellyora was also studying the Abbas pew; her expression was rapt and completely absorbed—and she was looking straight at Justin St. Larnston. There was a sheen of pleasure on her face and she looked prettier than I had ever seen her look before. She is fifteen, I said to myself, old enough to be in love, and she's in love with young Justin St. Larnston.

There seemed to be no end to what I was discovering about Mellyora. I must find out more. I must make her talk about Justin.

I kept my eyes on the St. Larnston family and before the service was over I knew who Johnny was looking for. Hetty Pengaster! Mellyora and Justin—that was understandable. But Johnny and Hetty Pengaster!

That afternoon the sun shone warmly for the time of the year and Mellyora had a fancy to go out of doors. We put on big shady hats because Mellyora said we mustn't let the sun spoil our complexions. Her fair one was very susceptible to sunshine and she freckled easily; my olive skin seemed indifferent; all the same I liked to put on a shady hat because it was what ladies did.

Mellyora stood in a solemn mood and I wondered whether it had anything to do with seeing Justin in church that morning. He must be twenty-two, I thought, which would be about seven years older than she is. To him she would seem only a child. I was becoming worldly wise and I wondered whether it would be considered fitting for a future Sir Justin St. Larnston to marry a parson's daughter.

I thought she was going to confide in me when she said, "I want to tell you something this afternoon, Kerensa."

She led the way on our walk as she often did; she had a way of reminding one now and then that she was the mistress, and I didn't forget that I owed my present contentment to her.

I was surprised when she led the way across the parsonage lawn to a hedge which divided the garden from the churchyard. There was a gap in this hedge and we passed through it.

She turned to smile at me. "Oh, Kerensa," she said, "it is good to be able to go out with you instead of Miss Kellow. She is rather prim, don't you think?"

"She has her job to do." Strange, how I stood up for the woman when she wasn't there.

"Oh, I know. Poor old Kelly! But, Kerensa, you serve as a chaperone. Don't you think that's amusing?"

I agreed.

"Now if you had been my sister I suppose we should have been plagued by a chaperone."

We picked our way over the gravestones towards the church.

"What were you going to tell me?" I asked.

"I want to show you something first. How long have you been in St. Larnston, Kerensa?"

"I came when I was about eight years old."

"You're fifteen now, so it must have been seven years ago. You wouldn't have heard. It's ten years since it happened."

She led me round to the side of the church where one or two more recent headstones rose from the ground, and standing before one as though reading the inscription she beckoned me over. "Read it," she said.

"Mary Anna Martin," I read, "thirty-eight years. In the midst of life we are in death."

"That was my mother. She was buried here ten years ago. Now read the name below."

"Kerensa Martin. Kerensa!"

She nodded, smiling at me with a satisfied expression.

"Kerensa! I love your name. I loved it the moment I heard it. Do you remember? You were in the wall. You said 'It's not an "it." It's Miss Kerensa Carlee.' It's strange how you can recall days and days in one little minute. I remembered when you said that. This Kerensa Martin was my sister. You see, it says 'aged three weeks and two days'; and the date. It's the same as the one above. Some of those gravestones have

54

little stories to tell, don't they, if you go round reading them."

"So your mother died when Kerensa was born?"

Mellyora nodded. "I wanted a sister. I was five years old and it seemed as if I waited for her for years. When she was born I was so excited. I thought we could play together right away. Then they told me I had to wait until she was grown up. I remember how I kept running to my father and saying: 'I've waited. Is she big enough to play yet?' I made plans for Kerensa. I knew she was going to be Kerensa even before she was born. My father wanted a Cornish name for her and he said that was a beautiful name because it meant peace and love which, he said, were the best things in the world. My mother used to talk about her and she was certain she would have a girl. So we talked about Kerensa. It went wrong, you see. She died and my mother died, too; and everything was different then. Nurses, governesses, housekeepers . . . and what I had longed for was a sister. I wanted a sister more than anything in the world. . . ."

"I see."

"Well, that was why when I saw you standing there . . . and because your name was Kerensa. You see what I mean?"

"I thought it was because you were sorry for me."

"I'm sorry for all the people on the hiring platform, but I couldn't bring them home, could I? Papa is always worried about bills as it is." She laughed. "I'm glad you came."

I looked at the gravestone and thought of the chance which had given me all I wanted. It might have happened so differently. If that young Kerensa had lived . . . if her name hadn't been Kerensa . . . where should I be now? I thought of Haggety's little pig's eyes, Mrs. Rolt's thin mouth, Sir Justin's purple complexion, and was overawed by this sequence of events called Chance.

We were closer than ever after our talk in the graveyard. Mellyora wanted to make believe that I was her sister. I was nothing loath. When I brushed her hair that night I started to talk about Justin St. Larnston.

"What do you think of him?" I said, and I saw the quick color in her cheeks.

"He's handsome, I think."

"More so than Johnny."

"Oh . . . Johnny!" The tone was contemptuous.

"Does he talk to you much?"

"Who . . . Justin? He's always kind when I go there, but he's busy. He's working. He'll graduate this year and then he'll be home all the time."

She was smiling secretly, thinking of the future when Justin would be home all the time. Riding through the country one would encounter him; when she called with her father he would be there.

"You like him?" I said.

She nodded and smiled.

"Better than . . . Kim?" I ventured.

"Kim? Oh, he's wild!" She wrinkled her nose. "I like Kim. But Justin, he's like a . . . knight. Sir Galahad or Sir Launcelot. Kim is not like that."

I thought of Kim's carrying Joe through the woods and to our cottage that night. I did not believe Justin would have done that for me. I thought of Kim's lying to Mellyora about the boy who had fallen off the tree.

Mellyora and I were like sisters; we were going to share secrets, adventures, our whole lives. She might prefer Justin St. Larnston. But Kim would be my knight.

Miss Kellow had one of her bouts of neuralgia, and Mellyora, who was always sympathetic towards the sick, insisted on her lying down. She herself drew the curtains and gave Mrs. Yeo orders that she was not to be disturbed until four o'clock when tea was to be taken to her.

Having looked after Miss Kellow, Mellyora sent for me and said that she fancied a ride. My eyes sparkled because naturally she could not go unaccompanied and I was sure she would prefer my company to Belter's.

Mellyora mounted her pony and I was on Cherry who was used for the pony cart. I hoped I should be seen by some of the St. Larnston people as I rode through the village, particularly Hetty Pengaster whom I had noticed more since I was aware of Johnny St. Larnston's interest in her.

However, we were only seen by a few children who stood aside as we passed; the boys pulled their forelocks and the girls curtsied—a fact which pleased me.

In a short time we were on the moor and the beauty of the scenery took my breath away. It was awe-inspiring. There was no sign of any dwelling, nothing but moor and sky and the tors which here and there rose up from the moorlands. The scene could, I knew, be somber in shadow; on this day it was sparkling, and as the sun caught the little rivulets, which here and there tumbled over the boulders, it turned them to silver; and we could see the moisture on the grass shining like diamonds.

Mellyora lightly touched her pony's flanks and broke into a canter; I followed and we left the road and went over the grass until Mellyora drew up before a strange formation of stone and as I came up behind her, for her pony was fleeter than mine, I saw that there were three slabs of stone standing upright in the ground supporting a slab which was resting on top of them.

"Eerie!" commented Mellyora. "Look round. There's not a sign of anyone. We're here, Kerensa, you and I, alone with *that*. Do you know what it is? It's a burial ground. Years and years ago . . . three or four thousands of years before Christ was born, the people who lived here made that grave. You couldn't move those stones if you tried for the rest of your life. Doesn't it make you feel . . . strange, Kerensa . . . to stand here, beside that and think of those people?"

I looked at her; with the wind tugging at her fair hair which fell in curls beneath her riding hat she was very pretty. She was earnest, too. "What *does* it make you feel, Kerensa?"

"That there isn't much time."

"Much time for what?"

"To live . . . to do what you want . . . to get what you want."

"You say strange things, Kerensa. I'm glad you do. I can't bear to know what people are going to say next. I do with Miss Kellow and even Papa. With you I'm never sure."

"And with Justin St. Larnston?"

She turned away. "He hardly ever notices me to speak to," she said sadly. "You say there isn't much time, but look how long it takes to grow up."

"You think so because you're fifteen and each year that passes seems long when you have only lived fifteen years and you've only got fifteen to compare it with. When you're forty or fifty—one year seems less because you compare it with the forty or fifty you've lived."

"Who told you?"

"My Granny. She's a wise woman."

"I've heard of her. Bess and Kit talk of her. They say she has 'powers,' that she can help people. . . ." She was thoughtful. Then she said: "This is called a quoit. Papa told me that

57

they were built by the Celts, the Cornish, who have been here much longer than the English."

We tethered our ponies for a while and sat leaning against the stones while they nibbled the grass and she talked to me of the conversations she had had with her father about the antiquities of Cornwall. I listened intently and I was proud of belonging to a people who had inhabited this island longer than the English and who had left these oddly disturbing monuments to their dead.

"We can't be far from the Derrise country," said Mellyora at length, rising to indicate that she wanted to mount. "Don't tell me you've never heard of the Derrises. They're the richest people in the neighborhood; they own acres and acres."

"More than the St. Larnstons?"

"Much more. Let's go. Let's get lost. It's always such fun to get lost and find your way after."

She mounted her pony and we were off, she leading.

"It's rather dangerous," she called over her shoulder, more concerned for me, who was not so expert, than for herself, and brought her pony to a standstill. I came up beside her and we walked our ponies over the grass.

"You can easily get lost on the moor because there is so much that looks alike. You have to find a landmark . . . like that tor over there. I think it's Derrise Tor and if it is I know where we are."

"How can you know where you are if you're not sure it's Derrise Tor?"

She laughed at me and said: "Come on."

We were climbing as we made our way to the tor; it was stony country now and the tor itself was on a hillock; a strange, twisted shape in gray stone that, from a distance, could be mistaken for a man of giant proportions.

We dismounted once more, tethered the ponies to a thick bush, and together we scrambled up the hillock to the tor. It was steeper than we had thought and when we reached the top Mellyora, looking like a dwarf beside a giant, leaned against the stone and cried excitedly that she was right. This was the Derrise country.

"Look!" she cried; and following her gaze I saw the great mansion. Gray stone walls, battlemented towers, a massive fortress looking like an oasis in a desert, for the house was surrounded by gardens; I glimpsed trees laden with fruit blossom, and the green of lawns. "Derrise Manor," she informed me.

"It's like a castle."

"It is, and though the Derrises are said to be the richest people in East Cornwall, they're doomed, some say."

"Doomed with a house like that and all those riches?"

"Ah, Kerensa. You always think in terms of worldly possessions. Don't you ever listen to Papa's sermons?"

"No, do you?"

"No, but I know without listening about treasures on earth and all that. In any case, for all their money the Derrises are doomed."

"What sort of doom?"

"Madness. There's madness in the family. It comes out every now and then. People say that it's a good thing there aren't any sons to carry on the line and that this generation will see the end of the Derrises and their curse."

"Well, that's a good thing."

"They don't think so. They want their name carried on and all that. People always do. I wonder why?"

"It's a sort of pride," I said. "It's like never dying, because there's always a part of you living on through your children."

"Why shouldn't daughters do as well as sons?"

"Because they don't have the same name. When they marry they belong to a different family and the line is lost."

Mellyora was thoughtful. Then she said, "The Martins will die with me. Think of that. At least the Carlees have your brother—the one who hurt his leg falling off a tree."

Because we had become close now and I knew I could trust her, I told her the truth of that incident. She listened intently. Then she said: "I'm glad you saved him. I'm glad Kim helped."

"You'll not tell anyone?"

"Of course not. But no one could do much about it now in any case. Isn't it strange, Kerensa? We live here in this quiet country place and tremendous things happen round us just as though we lived in a big city . . . perhaps more so. Just think of the Derrises."

"I'd never heard of them until this day."

"Never heard the story! Well, I'll tell you. Two hundred years ago one of the Derrises gave birth to a monster—it was quite frightful. They shut it up in a secret room and hired a strong man to look after it, and pretended to the world that the baby had been born dead. They smuggled a dead baby into the house and it was buried in the Derrise vault; meanwhile, the monster lived on. They were terrified of it because it was not only malformed but evil. Someone said that the

59

devil had been its mother's lover. They had other sons and in time one of these married and brought his new bride to the house. On the wedding night they played hide-and-seek and the bride went away to hide. It was Christmas time and the jailer wanted to join in the wassailing. So he drank so much that he went into a drunken sleep, but he had left the key in the door of the monster's room. When the new bride—who didn't know the house and that no one ever went into the wing which was said to be haunted because the monster made queer noises at night—saw the key in the lock, she turned it and the monster sprang at her. He didn't hurt her, because she was so fair and lovely, but she was shut in with him and she screamed and screamed so that those who were searching for her knew where she was. Her husband, guessing what had happened, snatched up a gun and bursting into the room shot the monster dead. But the bride went mad and the monster as he died cursed all the Derrises and said that what had happened to the young bride would recur every now and then in that family."

I listened spellbound to the story.

"The present Lady Derrise is half crazy, they say. She comes out onto the moor when the moon is full, and dances round the tor. She has a companion who's a sort of keeper. That's true enough; and it's the curse. They're the doomed, I tell you, so you shouldn't envy them their fine house and riches. But the curse will die out now, because this will be the end of the line. There's only Judith."

"The daughter of the lady who dances round the tor at full moon?"

Mellyora nodded.

"Do you believe the story of the Virgins?" I asked.

Mellyora hesitated. "Well," she said, "when I stand there amongst those stones they seem alive to me."

"To me, too."

"One night, Kerensa, when there's a full moon, we'll go down and look at them. I've always wanted to be there at full moon."

"Do you think there's something special about moon-light?"

"Of course. The ancient Britons worshiped the sun—and the moon, I expect. They made sacrifices and things. That day when I saw you standing in the wall I thought you were the seventh virgin."

"I guessed you did. You looked so odd . . . just the way you would look if you saw a ghost."

60

"And that night," went on Mellyora, "I dreamed that you were being walled up in the Abbas and I pulled away the stones till my hands were bleeding. I helped you escape, Kerensa, but I got terribly hurt doing it." She turned her back on the view spread out before us. "It's time we went home," she said.

At first we were very solemn as we rode back; then we both seemed to become obsessed by the desire to break the mood which had settled on us. Mellyora said that nowhere in the world were there so many legends as in Cornwall.

"Why should there be?" I asked.

"Because we're the sort of people things like that happen to, I suppose."

Then the frivolous mood came to us and we started telling wild stories about the stones and boulders which we passed, each trying to cap the other's story and becoming more and more ridiculous.

But neither of us was really attending to what we said; I believe Mellyora was thinking of that dream of hers; and so was I.

The time began to pass quickly because each day was like another. I had settled into my comfortable routine; and whenever I went to the cottage to see Granny I told her that being almost a lady was as wonderful as I had always thought it would be. She said that it was because I was constantly striving to reach a goal, which was a good way to live, providing it was a good goal. She herself was doing well—better than ever before, and could have lived well enough on the good things I brought to her from the parsonage kitchens and what Joe brought her from the vet's house; only yesterday the Pengasters had killed a pig and Hetty had seen to it that a fair-sized ham had come her way. She had salted it down and there was a meal for many a day to come. Her reputation had never been so fine. Joe was happy in his work; the vet thought highly of him, now and then gave him a penny or two when he had done some job particularly well. Joe said that he lived with the family and was treated as a member of it; but he wouldn't have minded how they treated him as long as he could be looking after his animals.

"It's strange how it's all turned out so well," I said.

"Like summer after a bad winter," agreed Granny. "Have to remember though, lovey, that winter can and will come again. Tain't natural to have summer all the time."

But I believed that I was going to live in perpetual summer. Only a few trivial matters darkened my pleasant existence. One was when I saw Joe riding through the village with the vet on the way to the Abbas stables. He was standing at the back of the trap and I felt it was an indignity for my brother to ride like a servant. I should have liked to see him riding like a friend of the vet's or an assistant. Better still if he could have ridden in the doctor's brougham.

I still hated those occasions when Mellyora went visiting in her best gown and long white gloves. I wanted to be beside her, learning how to enter a drawing room, how to make light conversation. But, of course, no one invited me. Then again Mrs. Yeo would let me know now and then that for all Miss Mellyora's friendliness I was only a superior servant in the house—on a level with her enemy Miss Kellow, almost, but not quite that. These were small pinpricks in my idyllic life.

And when Mellyora and I sewed our samplers—names and dates in the tiniest cross-stitches which were a trial to me, Miss Kellow allowed us to work our own motto and for mine I chose "Life is yours to make it as you will." And because it was my creed, I enjoyed every stitch. Mellyora chose as hers "Do unto others as you would they do unto you" because she said that if you followed that you must be a good friend to everyone, since you were your own best friend.

I often remember that summer: sitting by the open window as we worked at our lessons, or sometimes under the chestnut tree on the lawn while we stitched at our samplers and talked together to the background music of contented bees in sweet-scented lavender. The garden was full of good smells—the various flowers, the pine trees and warm damp earth mingled with occasional odors from the kitchen. White butterflies—there was a plague of them that summer—danced madly about the hanging purple of the buddleias. I would sometimes try to catch at a moment and whisper to myself "Now. This is *now!*" I wanted to keep it like that forever. But time was always there to defeat me—passing, inexorably passing; and even as I spoke, that "now" had become in the past. Beyond the hedge I was aware of the graveyard with its tombstones, a constant reminder that time will stand still for none of us; but I always contrived to turn my back on it, for how I wanted that summer to go on! Perhaps it was some intuition on my part, for that summer saw the end of the life in which I had found a comfortable niche for myself.

The year before, Justin St. Larnston had left the University and we saw more of him. Often I would encounter him riding through the village. It was his duty now to help with the estate in readiness for the day when he would become the squire. If Mellyora was with me he would bow courteously and even smile, but his was a rather melancholy smile. When we met him, that made Mellyora's day; she would become prettier and quieter as though occupied with pleasant thoughts.

Kim, who was a little younger than Justin, was still at the University; I thought with pleasure of the days when he would have finished; then perhaps we should see him more often in the village.

One afternoon we were sitting on the lawn with our samplers in our hands. I had finished my motto and had come to the full stop after "will" when Bess ran out onto the lawn. She came straight over to us and cried: "Miss, there be terrible news from the Abbas."

Mellyora turned a little pale and dropped her needlework onto the grass. "What news?" she demanded, and I knew that she was thinking something terrible had happened to Justin.

"Tis Sir Justin. He have collapsed like in his study, they do say. Doctor have been with him. He be terrible bad. Not expected to live, they do say."

Mellyora relaxed visibly. "Who says so?"

"Well, Mr. Belter he did have it from the head groom up there. He says they be in a terrible state."

When Bess went in we continued to sit on the lawn, but we could no longer work. I knew that Mellyora was thinking of what this would mean to Justin. He would be Sir Justin if his father died and the Abbas would belong to him. I wondered if she was sad because she didn't like to hear of illness or perhaps because Justin seemed more out of reach than ever.

It was Miss Kellow who had the next news first. She read the announcements each morning because as she implied she was interested to hear of the births, deaths, and marriages in the illustrious families she had served.

She came into the schoolroom, the paper in her hand. Mellyora looked at me and made a little grimace which Miss Kellow couldn't see. It meant "Now we shall hear that Sir Somebody is getting married or has died . . . and that she was treated as one of the family when she 'served' them—and how different her life was then before she had sunk to becoming a governess in the impecunious menage of a country parson."

"There's some interesting news in the paper," she said.

"Oh?" Mellyora always displayed interest. Poor Kelly! she said to me often. She doesn't get much fun out of life. Let her enjoy her honorables and nobles.

"There's to be a wedding up at the Abbas."

Mellyora didn't speak.

"Yes," Miss Kellow went on in that maddeningly slow way of hers which meant that she wanted to keep us in suspense as long as possible. "Justin St. Larnston is engaged to be married."

I didn't know I could ever feel someone else's distress so keenly. After all, it was nothing to me whom Justin St. Larnston married. But poor Mellyora, who had had her dreams! Even from this I could learn a lesson. It was folly to dream unless you did something about making a dream come true. And what had Mellyora ever done? Just smiled prettily at him when they passed; dressed with especial care when she was invited to tea at the Abbas! When all the time he had looked upon her as a child.

"Who is he going to marry?" asked Mellyora, speaking very distinctly.

"Well, it seems odd that it should be announced just now," said Miss Kellow, still eager to delay the dénouement, "with Sir Justin so ill and likely to die at any moment. But perhaps that is just the reason."

"Who?" repeated Mellyora.

Miss Kellow couldn't hold it back any longer.

"Miss Judith Derrise," she said.

Sir Justin didn't die, but he was paralyzed. We never saw him riding again to the hunt or striding to the woods, his gun over his shoulder. Dr. Hilliard was with him twice a day and the question most asked in St. Larnston was: "Heard how he is today?"

We were all expecting him to die, but he lived on; and then we accepted the fact that he wasn't going to die just yet although he was paralyzed and couldn't walk.

After she had heard the news Mellyora went to her room and wouldn't see anyone—not even me. She had a headache, she said, and wanted to be alone.

And when I did go in she was very composed though pale.

All she said was: "It's that Judith Derrise. She's one of the doomed. She'll bring doom to St. Larnston. It's that I mind."

Then I thought she couldn't have cared for him seriously. He was just the center of a childish dream. I had imagined that her feelings for him were as intense as mine were for rising out of that station in which I had been born.

It couldn't be so. Otherwise she would have cared as much whoever he had arranged to marry. That was how I thought, and it seemed sensible enough to me.

There was no reason why the wedding should be delayed— and six weeks after we saw the announcement it took place.

Some of the St. Larnston people went over to Derrise church to the wedding. Mellyora was on edge wondering whether she and her father would have an invitation but she need not have worried. There was none.

On the day of the wedding we sat in the garden together and were very solemn. It was rather like waiting for someone to be executed.

We heard news through the servants and it occurred to me what a good system of espionage we had. The servants from the parsonage, those from the Abbas and from Derrise Manor, formed a ring and news was passed on and circulated.

The bride had a magnificent gown of lace and satin, and her veil and orange blossom had been worn by numerous Derrise brides. I wondered if the one who had seen the monster and gone mad had worn the veil. I mentioned this to Mellyora.

"She wasn't a Derrise," Mellyora pointed out. "She was a stranger. That's why she didn't know where the monster was kept."

"Have you met Judith?" I asked.

"Only once. She was at the Abbas and it was one of Lady St. Larnston's At Homes. She is very tall, slender, and beautiful, with dark hair and big dark eyes."

"At least she is beautiful; and I suppose the St. Larnstons will be richer now, won't they. She'll have a dowry."

Mellyora turned to me and she was angry, which was rare with her. She took me by the shoulders and shook me.

"Stop talking about riches. Stop thinking of it. Isn't there anything else in the world? I tell you, she'll bring doom on the Abbas. *She's* doomed. They all are."

"It can't matter to us."

65

Her eyes were dark with something like fury.

"They are our neighbors. Of course, it matters."

"I can't see how. They don't care about us. Why should we about them?"

"They are my friends."

"Friends! They don't bother much about you. They don't even ask you to the wedding."

"I didn't want to go to his wedding."

"That doesn't make it any better for not asking you."

"Oh, stop it, Kerensa. It won't ever be the same, I tell you. Nothing will ever be the same. It's changed, can't you feel it?"

Yes I could feel it. It was not so much changed as changing; and the reason was that we weren't children any more. Mellyora would soon be seventeen; and I should be a few months after. We would put our hair up and be young ladies. We were growing up; we were already thinking with nostalgia of the long sunny days of childhood.

Sir Justin's life was no longer in danger and his elder son had brought a bride to the Abbas. This was a time for rejoicing and the St. Larnstons had decided to give a ball. It would take place before the summer was over and it was hoped that it would be a warm night so that the guests could enjoy the beauty of the grounds as well as the splendors of the house.

Invitations were issued and there was one for Mellyora and her father. The bride and groom had gone to Italy for their honeymoon and the ball was to celebrate their return. It was to be a masked ball; a very grand affair. We heard that it was the wish of Sir Justin, who would not himself be able to join in, that the ball should take place.

I wasn't quite sure how Mellyora felt about the invitation; she seemed to veer between excitement and melancholy. She was changing as she grew up; she had once been so serene. I was envious and couldn't hide it.

"How I *wish* you could come, Kerensa," she said. "Oh, how I should love to see you there. That old house means something to you, doesn't it?"

"Yes," I said, "a sort of symbol."

She nodded. It often happened that our minds were in tune and I didn't have to explain to her. She went about with a thoughtful frown for some days and when I mentioned the ball she shrugged the subject aside impatiently.

About four days after she had received the invitation she came out of her father's study looking grave.

"Papa's not well," she said. "I've known he hasn't been for some time."

I had known it, too; his skin seemed to be getting more and more yellow every day.

"He says," she went on, "that he can't go to the ball."

I had been wondering what sort of costume he would have worn because it was difficult to imagine him looking like anything but a parson.

"Does this mean that you won't go?"

"I can't very well go alone."

"Oh . . . Mellyora."

She shrugged impatiently and that afternoon she went out with Miss Kellow in the pony trap. I heard the trap from my window and when I looked out and saw them I felt hurt because she hadn't asked me to go with them.

When she came back she burst into my room, her eyes sparkling, her cheeks slightly flushed.

She sat on my bed and started to bounce up and down. Then she stopped and putting her head on one side said: "Cinderella, how would you like to go to the ball?"

"Mellyora," I gasped. "You mean . . ."

She nodded.

"You are invited. Well, not you exactly, because she hasn't the faintest notion . . . but I have an invitation for you and it's going to be such fun, Kerensa. Much more than going with Papa or some chaperone he might have found for me."

"How did you manage it?"

"This afternoon I called on Lady St. Larnston. It happens to be her At-Home day. That gave me an opportunity of speaking to her, so I told her Papa was unwell and unable to bring me to the ball, but I had a friend staying with me—so could his invitation be transferred to her? She was very gracious."

"Mellyora . . . but when she knows!"

"She won't. I changed your name just in case she might know you. She got the impression that you are my Aunt, although I didn't say so. It's a masked ball. She'll receive us at the staircase. You'll have to try to look of sober years . . . old enough to take a young lady to a ball. I'm so excited about it now, Kerensa. We'll have to decide what we're going to wear. Costumes! Just imagine it. Everyone will look glorious. By the way, you'll be Miss Carlyon."

"Miss Carlyon," I murmured. Then: "How can I get a costume?"

She put her head on one side. "You should have worked harder on your needlework. You see, Papa is worried about money so he can't give me very much to buy a gown; and we'll have to find two out of one."

"How can I go without a gown?"

"Don't be so easily defeated. 'Life is yours to make it as you will.' What about that? And here you are saying 'can't, can't, can't,' at the first obstacle." She put her arms round me suddenly and clung to me. "It's fun having a sister," she said. "What was that your old Granny said about sharing things?"

"That if you shared your joys you doubled them; if you shared your sorrows you halved them."

"It's true. Now that you're coming, I'm so excited." She pushed me away from her and sat down on the bed again. "The first thing to do is to decide what costumes we should like to wear; and then we'll see how near we can get to them. Picture yourself looking like one of those paintings in the gallery at the Abbas. Oh, you haven't seen them. Velvet, I think. You would make a fine Spaniard with your dark hair piled up high and a comb and a mantilla."

I was excited now. I said, "I have Spanish blood; my grandfather was Spanish. I could get the comb and mantilla."

"There, you see. Red velvet, I think, for you. My Mamma had a red velvet evening gown. Her things haven't been touched." She was up again, taking my hands and twirling me round. "The masks are easy. You cut them out of black velvet, and we'll do patterns on them with beads. We've got three weeks to get ready."

I was far more excited than she. It was true my invitation was a little oblique and would never have been given had Lady St. Larnston known who was receiving it; but still, I was going. I was going to wear a red velvet dress which I had seen and tried on. It had to be altered and reshaped, but we could do it. Miss Kellow helped, not very graciously, but she was an expert needlewoman.

I was pleased because my costume was costing nothing, and the money—not very much—which the Reverend Charles had given Mellyora could all be spent on her. We decided that her costume should be Grecian, so we bought white velvet and gold-colored silk on which we sewed gold sequins. It was a loose-fitting gown caught in by gold, and with her hair falling about her shoulders and in her black velvet mask she looked beautiful.

As the days passed we talked of nothing but the ball and Sir Justin's health. We were terrified that he would die and the ball have to be canceled.

I went to tell Granny Bee about it.

"I'm going as a Spanish lady," I told her. "It's the most wonderful thing that's ever happened to me."

She looked at me a little sadly; then she said: "Don't count on too much from it, lovey."

"I'm not counting on anything," I said. "I'm just reminding myself that I shall go in the Abbas . . . as a guest. I shall be dressed in red velvet. Granny, you should see the dress I'm to wear."

"Parson's daughter have been good to you, lovey. Be her friend always."

"Of course I shall. She's as glad to have me to go with her as I am to go. Miss Kellow thinks I shouldn't be going, though."

"'Tis to be hoped she don't find some way of telling Lady St. Larnston who you be."

I shook my head triumphantly. "She wouldn't dare."

Granny went to the storehouse and I followed and watched while she opened the box and took out the two combs and mantillas.

"I like to put mine on some nights," she said. "Then when I'm here alone I fancy Pedro's with me. For that's how he did like to see me. Come. Let me try this on you." Lightly she held up my hair and stuck the comb in the back. It was a tall comb set with brilliants. "You look just as I did at your age, lovey. Now the mantilla." She draped it about my head and stood back. "When it is done as it should be, there won't be one of 'em to touch you," she declared. "I'd like to dress your hair myself, Granddaughter."

It was the first time she had addressed me thus and I could sense her pride in me.

"Come to the parsonage on the night, Granny," I said. "Then you can see my room and dress my hair for me."

"Would it be allowed?"

I narrowed my eyes. "I'm not a servant there . . . not really. Only you can dress my hair, so you must."

She laid her hand on my arm and smiled at me.

"Take care, Kerensa," she said. "Always take care."

An invitation had arrived for me. It said that Sir Justin and Lady St. Larnston requested the pleasure of Miss Carlyon at the costume ball. Mellyora and I were almost hysterical with laughter when we read it, and Mellyora kept calling me Miss Carlyon in an imitation of Lady St. Larnston's voice.

There was no time to lose. When our dresses were finished we tried them on every day and I practiced wearing the comb and mantilla. We sat together making our masks, sewing shiny black bugle beads on them so that they glittered. Those days were some of the happiest of my life.

We practiced dancing. It was very easy when you were young and light on your feet, Mellyora said. You simply followed your partner; I discovered that I could dance well and I loved it.

During those days we did not notice that the Reverend Charles was growing more and more wan every day. He spent a great deal of time in his study. He knew how excited we were and I think—although this didn't occur to me until afterwards—that he didn't want to cast the slightest shadow over our pleasure.

At last the day of the ball arrived. Mellyora and I dressed in our costumes and Granny came to the parsonage to do my hair.

She brushed it and put some of her special concoction on it so that it gleamed and shone. Then came the comb and the mantilla. Mellyora clasped her hands in admiration when she saw the effect.

"Everyone will notice Miss Carlyon," she said.

"It looks well here in this bedroom," I reminded her. "But think of all the lovely costumes those rich people will be wearing. Diamonds and rubies. . . ."

"And all you two do have is youth," said Granny. She laughed. "Reckon some of 'em would be willing to barter their diamonds and rubies for that."

"Kerensa looks *different*," pointed out Mellyora. "And although they'll all look their best, no one will look quite like her."

We put on our masks and stood side by side giggling as we studied our reflections.

"Now," said Mellyora, "we look quite mysterious."

Granny went home and Miss Kellow drove us to the Abbas. The trap looked incongruous among all the fine carriages but that only amused us; as for me I was approaching the culmination of a dream.

I was overwhelmed as I stepped into the hall; I tried to see everything at once and consequently had nothing more than a hazy impression. A chandelier with what seemed like hundreds of candles; walls hung with tapestry; pots of flowers—— the scent of which filled the air; people everywhere. It was like straying into one of those foreign courts which I had read about in history lessons. Many of the ladies' dresses were fourteenth-century Italian I learned afterwards and several of them wore their hair caught into jewelled snoods. Brocades, velvets, silks and satins. It was a glorious assembly; and what made it all the more exciting were the masks we were all wearing. I was thankful for them; I could feel more like one of them when there was no danger of being discovered.

We were to unmask at midnight; but by then the ball would be over and this Cinderellalike condition cease to worry me.

A wide and beautiful staircase was at one end of the hall and we followed the crowd up this to where Lady St. Larnston, her mask in her hand, was receiving her guests.

We stood in a long and lofty room on either side of which were portraits of the St. Larnstons. Painted in their gorgeous silks and velvets they might have been members of the party. There were evergreen plants about the room and gilded chairs such as I have never seen before. I wanted to examine everything closely.

I was conscious of Mellyora beside me. She was very simply clad compared with most of the women, but I thought she was more lovely than any of the others, with her golden hair and the gold about her slim waist.

A man in green velvet doublet and long green hose came towards us.

"Tell me if I'm wrong," he said, "but I believe I've guessed. It's the golden locks."

I knew that voice to be Kim's, although I shouldn't have recognized him in that costume.

"You look beautiful," he went on. "And so does the Spanish lady."

"Kim, you shouldn't have guessed so soon," complained Mellyora.

"No. I should have pretended to be puzzled. I should have asked lots of questions and then, just before the stroke of midnight, guessed."

"At least," said Mellyora, "you've only guessed me."

He had turned to me and I saw his eyes through the mask; I could guess how they looked; laughing, with the wrinkles round them; they almost disappeared when he laughed.

"I confess myself baffled."

Mellyora sighed with relief.

"I had thought you would be here with your father," he went on.

"He is not well enough to come."

"I'm sorry. But glad it didn't prevent your appearing."

"Thanks to my . . . chaperone."

"Oh, so the Spanish beauty is your chaperone?" He pretended to peer behind my mask. "She seems too young for the role."

"Don't talk about her as though she's not here. She won't like that."

"And I'm so eager to win her approval. Does she speak only Spanish?"

"No, she speaks English."

"She hasn't spoken any yet."

"Perhaps she only speaks when she has something to say."

"Oh, Mellyora, are you reproaching me? Lady of Spain," he went on, addressing me, "I trust my presence does not offend you."

"It doesn't offend me."

"I breathe again. May I conduct you two young ladies to the buffet."

"That would be pleasant," I said, speaking slowly and guardedly, because I was afraid, now that I was here among the people with whom I had always longed to mix, that I might by some inflection of voice, some trace of accent or intonation betray my origins.

"Come then." Kim stood between us gripping our elbows as he piloted us through the crowd.

We sat at one of the little tables by the dais on which large tables laden with food had been set up. I had never seen so much food in my life. Pies and pasties being the main dish of rich and poor alike, there were more of these than anything else. But what pies and pasties! The pastry was a rich golden brown and some of the pies had been made into fantastic shapes. In the center was one which was a model of the Abbas. There were the battlemented towers and the arched doorway. People were looking at it and expressing their admiration. On the pies, figures of animals had been decorated to show what they contained; sheep for the muggetty and

72

lammy pies, pig for nattlins, tiny piglets for taddage to show that the pigs were stillborn; a bird for squab and curlew. There were great dishes of clotted cream, for the gentry, who could get it, always took cream with their pies. There were meats of all sorts; slices of beef and ham; there were pilchards served in various ways—in pies and in what we called fair maids and what Pedro had told Granny was really the Cornish way of pronouncing fumado. Pilchards served with oil and lemon and called by the Spaniards food fit for the grandest Spanish Don.

There were all kinds of drink; stirrup cup which we called dash-an-darras; there was metheglin and mead, gin, and other wines which came from foreign parts. It was amusing to see Haggety in charge of these, bowing obsequiously, looking very different from the self-important butler who had wanted to hire me at Trelinket Fair. When I thought of what he would say if he knew that he would now have to serve the girl he might have hired, I wanted to burst out laughing.

When you are young and have known hunger you can always eat with relish, however excited you might be, and I did justice to the lammy pie and fair maids which Kim brought to us while I sipped the mead poured by Haggety.

I had never tasted it before and I liked the flavor of honey; but I knew that it was intoxicating and I had no intention of dulling my senses on this most exciting evening of my life.

Kim watched us eat with pleasure and I knew he was puzzled about me. I sensed he recognized that he had met me before and was wondering where. I was delighted to keep him guessing.

"Look," he said as we sipped our mead, "here comes the Borgia boy."

I looked and saw him; he was dressed in black velvet, there was a little cap on his head and false mustaches. He looked at Mellyora and then at me. His gaze stayed on me.

He bowed and said in a theatrical manner: "Methinks I have met the fair Grecian in our St. Larnston lanes."

I knew at once that he was Johnny St. Larnston because I recognized his voice as I had Kim's.

"But I am certain I have never seen the Spanish beauty before."

"You should never be too sure of anything," said Mellyora.

"If I had seen her once I should never have forgotten her and now her image will remain with me all the days of my life."

73

"It's strange," said Mellyora, "that by merely wearing a mask you can't really hide your identity."

"The voice, the gestures betray," said Kim.

"And we three are known to each other," went on Johnny. "That makes me mighty curious about the stranger in our midst."

He drew his chair close to mine, and I began to feel uneasy.

"You're a friend of Mellyora's," he added. "I know your name. You're Miss Carlyon."

"You are not supposed to embarrass your guests," Mellyora told him primly.

"My dear Mellyora, the whole purpose of a masked ball is to guess the identity of your companions before the unmasking. Did you not know? Miss Carlyon, my mother told me that Mellyora was bringing a friend as her father could not come. A chaperone . . . an aunt, I think. That was what my mother said. Surely you are not Mellyora's aunt?"

"I refuse to tell you who I am," I answered. "You must wait for the unmasking."

"As long as I may be at your side at that exciting moment I can wait."

The music had started and a tall handsome couple were opening the ball. I knew the man in Regency costume was Justin and I guessed the tall, slim, dark-haired woman to be his newly married wife.

I could not take my eyes from Judith St. Larnston who, until recently, had been Judith Derrise. She was wearing a crimson velvet dress very similar in color to mine; but how much richer was hers! About her neck diamonds glittered; they were also in her ears and on her long, slender fingers. Her dark hair was worn in pompadour fashion which made her look slightly taller than Justin, who was very tall. She looked very attractive but what I noticed more than anything was a certain nervous tension about her. It was betrayed by the sudden movements of her head and hands. I noticed, too, how she clung to Justin's hand and even in the dance she gave the impression that she was determined never to let him go.

"How attractive she is!" I said.

"My new sister-in-law," murmured Johnny, his eyes following her.

"A handsome pair," I said.

"My brother is the handsome member of the family, don't you think?"

"It is difficult to say until the unmasking takes place."

"Oh, that unmasking! Then I shall ask for your verdict. But by that time I hope to have proved to you that Justin's brother has other qualities to make up for his lack of personal beauty. Shall we dance?"

I was alarmed, afraid that if I danced with Johnny St. Larnston I should betray that I had never danced with a man before.

If it had been Kim, I should have been less afraid, because I had already proved that in an emergency one could rely on him; I was unsure of Johnny. But Kim was already leading Mellyora out.

Johnny took my hand and pressed it warmly.

"Spanish lady," he said, "you are not afraid of me?"

I gave the kind of laugh I might have given years ago. Then I said in my slow, careful way, "I see no reason to be."

"That's a good start."

The musicians, who were in a gallery at one end of the ballroom, were playing a waltz. I thought of waltzing round the bedroom with Mellyora and I hoped that my dancing would not betray my lack of experience. But it was easier than I thought; I was skillful enough not to arouse suspicion.

"How well our steps fit," said Johnny.

I lost Mellyora in the dance and wondered whether Johnny had intended that I should; and when we sat together on the gilded chairs and I was asked to dance by someone else, I was rather relieved to escape from Johnny. We talked— or rather my partner did—of other balls, of the hunt, of the changing conditions of the country, and I listened, careful never to betray myself. I learned that night that a girl who listens and agrees, quickly becomes popular. But it was not a role I intended to play permanently. Then I was taken back to my chair where Johnny was impatiently waiting. Mellyora and Kim joined us and I danced with Kim. I enjoyed that very much, although it wasn't so easy as it had been with Johnny; I suppose because Johnny was a better dancer. And all the time I kept thinking: You're actually here in the Abbas. You, Kerensa Carlee—Carlyon for the night.

We had more food and wine and I didn't want the evening ever to end. I knew I should hate to take off my red velvet dress and let down my hair. I stored up in my mind every little incident so that I could tell Mellyora the next day.

I joined in the cotillion; some of my partners were paternal, others flirtatious. I managed them all with what I thought was great skill; and I asked myself why I had ever been nervous.

I drank a little of the dash-an-darras which Johnny and Kim had brought to our table with the food. Mellyora was a little subdued; I believe she was hoping that she might dance with Justin.

I was dancing with Johnny when he said: "It's so crowded here. Let's go outside."

I followed him down the staircase and out to the lawns where some of the guests were dancing. It was an enchanting sight. The music could be heard distinctly through the open windows and the dresses of the men and women looked fantastic in the moonlight.

We danced over the lawn and we came to the hedge which separated the Abbas lawns from the field in which stood the Six Virgins and the old mine.

"Where are you taking me?" I asked.

"To see the Virgins."

"I always wanted to see them in moonlight," I said.

A slow smile touched his lips, and I realized at once that I had given him a clue that I was not a stranger to St. Larnstons who had come for the ball, since I knew of the existence of the Virgins.

"Well," he whispered, "so you shall."

He took my hand and together we ran over the grass. I leaned against one of the stones and he came near to me pressing close. He tried to kiss me, but I held him off.

"Why do you plague me?" he said.

"I do not wish to be kissed."

"You're a strange creature, Miss Carlyon. You provoke and then become prim. Is it fair?"

"I came here to see the Virgins in moonlight."

He had put his hands on my shoulders and held me against the stone. "Six virgins. There might be seven here tonight."

"You've forgotten the story," I said. "It was because they weren't virgins. . . ."

"Precisely. Miss Carlyon, are *you* going to turn to stone tonight?"

"What do you mean?"

"Don't you know the legend? Anyone who stands here in moonlight and touches one of these stones is in danger."

"From what? Impertinent young men?"

He put his face close to mine. He looked satanic with the false mustaches and his eyes glinting through the mask. "You haven't heard the legend? Oh, but you don't come from these parts, do you, Miss Carlyon? I must tell you. If the question is asked 'Are you a virgin?' and you cannot answer 'Yes,' you'll be turned into stone. I'm asking you now."

I tried to wriggle free. "I wish to return to the house."

"You haven't answered the question."

"I think you are not behaving like a gentleman."

"Do you know so well the ways of gentlemen?"

"Let me go."

"When you answer my questions. I've already asked the first. Now I want an answer to the second."

"I shall answer no questions."

"Then," he said, "I shall be forced to satisfy my curiosity and impatience." With a swift gesture he snatched at my mask and as it came away in his hand, I heard the sudden gasp of amazement.

"So . . . Miss Carlyon!" he said. "*Carlyon.*" Then he began to chant:

> "Ding dong bell,
> Someone's in the well.
> Who put her in?
> Was it due to sin?"

He laughed. "I'm right, am I not? I *do* remember you. You are not a girl one easily forgets, Miss Carlyon. And what are you doing at our ball?"

I snatched the mask from him.

"I came because I was invited."

"H'm! And deceived us all very nicely. My mother is not in the habit of inviting cottagers to St. Larnston balls."

"I'm a friend of Mellyora's."

"Yes . . . Mellyora! Now who would have thought her capable of this! I wonder what my mother is going to say when I tell her?"

"But you won't," I said, and I was annoyed with myself because there seemed to be a note of pleading in my voice.

"But don't you think it is my duty?" He was mocking. "Of course, for a consideration I might agree to join in the deception."

"Keep away," I warned. "There is no question of a consideration."

He put his head on one side and regarded me with a puzzled look. "You give yourself airs, my cottage beauty."

"I live at the parsonage," I retorted. "I am being educated there."

"Tr la," he mocked. "Tr la la!"

"And now I wish to return to the ball."

"Maskless? Doubtless known by some of the servants? Oh, Miss Carlyon!"

I turned from him and started to run. There was no reason why I should return to the ballroom. The evening was spoilt for me in any case. I would go back to the parsonage and at least preserve my dignity.

He ran after me and caught my arm. "Where are you going?"

"As I am not returning to the ballroom, that is no concern of yours."

"So you are going to leave us? Now please don't do that. I was only teasing you. Don't you recognize a joke when you hear one? That's something you have to learn. I don't want you to leave the ball. I want to help. Could you repair the mask?"

"Yes, with a needle and thread."

"I will get them for you if you come with me."

I hesitated, not trusting him; but the temptation to go back was too great to be resisted.

He led me to a wall which was covered with ivy, and pushing this aside disclosed a door. When we passed through this we were in the walled garden and straight ahead of us was the spot in which the bones had been discovered. He was taking me to the oldest wing of the Abbas.

He opened a heavily studded door and we were in a dank passage. There was a lanthorn hanging on the wall which gave a feeble light. Johnny took this down and holding it high above his head turned to grin at me. He looked satanic and I wanted to run, but I knew that if I did I could not return to the ball. So when he said: "Come on!" I followed him up a spiral staircase, the steps of which were steep and worn down by the tread of feet over hundreds of years.

He turned to me and said in a hollow voice: "We are in that part of the house which was certainly the old convent. This is where our virgins lived. Eerie, don't you think?"

I agreed.

At the top of the staircase he paused. I saw a corridor in which were what appeared to be a row of cells, and when I followed Johnny into one of these, I saw the stone ledge cut in the wall which might have served as a bed for a nun; I saw a narrow slit unprotected by glass which could have been her window.

Johnny set down the lanthorn and grinned at me.

"Now we want a needle and thread," he said. "Or do we?"

I was alarmed. "I'm sure you won't find one here."

"Never mind. There are more important things in life, I do assure you. Give me the mask."

I refused and turned away, but he was beside me. I might have been very frightened if I hadn't remembered that this was only Johnny St. Larnston whom I regarded as a boy not much older than myself. With a gesture which took him completely by surprise, and using all my strength, I pushed him from me. He went sprawling backways, tripping over the lanthorn.

This was my opportunity. I ran along the corridor, clutching my mask in my hand, looking for the spiral staircase which we had ascended.

I could not find it, but came to another which led upwards; and although I knew I should not be going further into the house when what I wanted was to leave it, I daren't turn back for fear of meeting Johnny. There was a rope attached to the wall to serve as a banister because the stairs were so steep, and I saw that it could be dangerous not to use it. This was a part of the house which was rarely used, but on this night, presumably in case some of the guests should lose their way and find themselves in this wing, lanthorns had been placed at intervals. The light was dim and just enough to show the way.

I discovered more alcoves like those to which Johnny had taken me. I stood listening, wondering whether it would be wise to retrace my steps. My heart was racing; I could not help glancing furtively about me. I was prepared at any moment to see the ghostly figures of nuns coming towards me. That was the effect being alone in this most ancient part of the house had on me. The gaiety of the ball seemed far away—not only in distance but in time.

I had to get away quickly.

Cautiously I tried to retrace my steps, but when I came to a corridor through which I knew I had not passed before, I began to feel frantic. I thought: What if they never discovered me again? What if I remained locked away in this part of the house forever? It would be a kind of walling up. They would come for the lanthorns. But why should they? They would gradually go out one by one and no one would think of relighting them until there was another ball or house party at the Abbas.

This was panic. It was more likely that I should be discovered wandering about the house and recognized. They would be suspicious of me and accuse me of trying to steal. They were always suspicious of people like myself.

I tried to think calmly of what I knew of the house. The old wing was that part which looked down on the walled garden. That was where I must be . . . perhaps close to the spot where the nun's bones had been discovered. The thought made me shiver. It was so gloomy in the passages and there was no covering on the floor of the corridor which was cold stone like the spiral stairs. I wondered if it were true that when something violent happened to people their spirits haunted the scene of their last hours on earth. I thought of her being brought along these corridors from one of those alcoves which could have been her cell. What terrible despair there must have been in her heart! How frightened she must have been!

I took courage. My situation was comic compared with hers. I was not afraid, I told myself. If necessary, I should tell exactly how I came to be in this situation. Lady St. Larnston would then be more annoyed with Johnny than with me.

At the end of the stone corridor was a heavy door which I opened cautiously. It was like stepping into another world. The corridor was carpeted and there were lamps hanging at frequent intervals on the wall; I could hear the sound of music—though muted—which I had lost before.

I was relieved. Now to find my way to the dressing rooms. There would be pins there. I even believed I had seen some in a little alabaster bowl. I wondered I hadn't thought of it before; I had an uncanny feeling that thinking of the seventh virgin had helped me by calming my mind which was overexcited by the mingling of unaccustomed wine and strange events.

This was a vast house. I had heard it contained about a hundred rooms. I paused by a door and, hoping this might lead me towards that wing in which the ball was being held, gently turned the handle and opened it. I gasped with horror for in the dim light from the shaded lamp which stood by the bed, it seemed for those first seconds that I was looking at a corpse. A man was propped up by pillows; his mouth and one eye were drawn down on the left side. It was a grotesque sight and seeing it so soon after my fanciful thoughts in the

80

corridor, I believed I was seeing a ghost, for it was a dead face . . . almost. Then to my horror as I stood there something told me that I was seen, for there was a strange sound from the figure in the bed. I shut the door quickly, my heart pounding.

The man I had seen on the bed was a travesty of Sir Justin; I was horrified by the thought that someone who had been so robust, so arrogant, could become like that.

Somehow I must have reached the family sleeping quarters. If I met anyone now, I would say I was looking for the dressing rooms and had lost my way. I clutched again the torn mask in my hand and hesitated by a half-open door. Looking inside I saw a bedroom; two lamps on the wall gave a dim light. It suddenly occurred to me that on the dressing table there might possibly be some pins. I looked along the corridor; there was no sign of anyone, so I stepped into the room, and sure enough, on the mirror, looped by satin ribbons, was a pincushion with pins sticking in it. I took several and was about to make for the door when I heard voices in the corridor.

A sudden panic seized me. I had to get out of this room quickly. Old fears came back to me like those I had had on the night when Joe was missing. If Mellyora was found in one of these rooms and said that she had lost her way, everyone would believe her; if I were—and they knew who I was—that would subject me to the humiliation of suspicion. I must not be found here.

I looked about me and saw there were two doors. Without thinking I opened one and stepped forwards. I was in a cupboard in which clothes were hanging. There was no time to escape so I shut the door and held my breath.

In a few terrifying seconds I knew that someone had come into the room. I heard the door shut, and waited tensely for discovery. I must tell everything about Johnny trying to make love to me and who I was. I must make them believe me. I should open the door at once and explain. If I were caught I should look so guilty; and if I went out and explained right away, which was what Mellyora would have done, I should be more likely believed. But what if they didn't believe me?

I had hesitated too long.

A voice said: "But what is it, Judith?" A weary voice which I knew to belong to Justin St. Larnston.

"I had to see you, darling. Just to be alone with you for a few minutes. I had to be reassured. Surely you understand."

Judith, his wife! Her voice was what I would have expected. She spoke in short sentences as though she were breathless; and there was a feeling of tension which was immediately apparent.

"Judith, you must not get so excited."

"Excited? How can I help it when . . . I saw you and that girl . . . dancing together."

"Listen to me, Judith." His voice sounded slow and drawling almost, but perhaps that was in contrast to hers. "She's only the parson's daughter."

"She's beautiful. You think so, don't you? And young . . . so very young. . . . And I could see the way she looked . . . when you were dancing together."

"Judith, this is quite absurd. I've known the child since she was in her cradle. Naturally I had to dance with her. You know how one must at these affairs."

"But you seemed . . . you seemed. . . ."

"Weren't you dancing? Or were you watching me all the time?"

"You know how I feel. I was aware of you, Justin. Aware of you and that girl. You may laugh but there *was* something. I had to be reassured."

"But really, Judith, there is nothing to reassure you about. You're my wife, aren't you? Isn't that enough?"

"Everything. Just everything! That's why I couldn't bear . . ."

"Well then let's forget it. And we shouldn't be here. We can't disappear like this."

"All right, but kiss me, Justin."

Silence, during which I felt they must hear my heart beating. I had been right not to show myself. As soon as they had gone I would creep out and quickly repair my mask with the pins and then all would be well.

"Come on, Judith, let's go."

"Once more, darling, Oh, *darling*, how I *wish* we didn't have to go back to all those tiresome people."

"It'll soon be over."

"*Darling*. . . ."

Silence. The shutting of the door. I wanted to rush out but I forced myself to stay where I was while I counted ten. Then cautiously I opened the door, peered out at the empty room, sped to its door, and with a sigh of thankfulness reached the corridor.

I almost ran from that open door, trying to rid myself of the picture of one of them opening the door and finding me hiding in the cupboard. It hadn't happened, but, oh, it was a warning not to do anything so silly again.

The music was louder, as I had reached the staircase where Lady St. Larnston had received us. Now I knew my way. In my anxiety I had forgotten my mask until I saw Mellyora with Kim.

"Your mask!" cried Mellyora.

I held it up. "It's broken, but I've found some pins."

Kim said: "Well, I believe it is Kerensa."

I looked at him shamefacedly. Mellyora turned to him. "Why not?" she said fiercely. "Kerensa wanted to come to the ball. Why shouldn't she? I said she was a friend of mine and so she is."

"Why not indeed?" agreed Kim.

"How did it break?" asked Mellyora.

"My stitches weren't strong enough, I expect."

"Odd. Let me look." She took the mask. "Oh, I see. Give me the pins. Now I'll fix it. It'll last. Did you know that there's only half an hour to midnight?"

"I lost count of time."

Mellyora fixed the mask and I felt pleased to hide behind it.

"We've just been out into the gardens," said Mellyora. "The moonlight's wonderful."

"I know. I was out there, too."

"Let's go back to the ballroom now," said Mellyora. "There's not much time left."

We went back, Kim escorting us. A partner came to ask me to dance and I felt hilariously happy to be masked and dancing again, while I congratulated myself on my escape. Then I remembered that Johnny St. Larnston knew who I was, but I didn't really attach much importance to that. If he told his mother, I should quickly let her know how he had behaved; and I fancied she would not be any more pleased with him than with me.

I danced with Kim later and I was glad because I wanted to know what his reactions were. He was clearly amused.

"Carlyon," he said. "That's what puzzles me. I thought you were Miss Carlee."

"Mellyora gave me that name."

"Oh . . . Mellyora!"

I told him all that had happened while he was away at the University, how Mellyora had seen me at the fair and taken me home.

He listened intently.

"I'm glad it happened," he told me. "It's good for you and for her."

I glowed with pleasure. He was so different from Johnny St. Larnston.

"And your brother?" he asked. "How is he getting on with the vet?"

"You knew?"

He laughed. "I'm rather interested in his progress since it was I who mentioned to Pollent what an asset he would be."

"You . . . spoke to Pollent?"

"I did. Made him promise to give the boy a chance."

"I see. I suppose I should thank you."

"Don't if you'd rather not."

"But my Granny is so pleased. He's getting on well. The vet is pleased with him and . . ." I heard the note of pride in my voice. ". . . he's pleased with the vet."

"Good news. I thought that a boy who would risk so much for the sake of a bird must have a special gift. So . . . all goes well."

"Yes," I repeated, "all goes well."

"May I say that I think you have grown up just as I thought you would."

"And how is that?"

"You have become an extremely fascinating young lady."

What a number of emotions I experienced on that night, for dancing with Kim I knew absolute happiness. I wished it could have gone on. But dances quickly come to an end when you have the partner of your choice, and all too soon the clocks which had been brought into the hall to strike at the midnight hour began chiming at once. The music stopped. It was time to take off our masks.

Johnny St. Larnston passed near us; he grinned at me.

"It's no surprise," he said, "but still a pleasure."

And there was a purpose in his mocking smile.

Kim led me outside so that no one else would know that Miss Carlyon was really poor Kerensa Carlee.

As Belter drove us home to the parsonage neither Mellyora nor I spoke very much. We were both still hearing the music, caught up in the rhythm of the dance. It was a night we should never forget; later we would talk of it but now we were still bemused and enchanted.

We went soberly to our rooms. I was physically tired and yet had no desire to sleep. While I kept on my red velvet gown I was still a young lady who went to balls, but once I took it off life would become less exciting. In fact, Miss Carlyon would become Kerensa Carlee.

But obviously I could not stand before the mirror staring dreamily at my reflection all night, so by the light of two candles I reluctantly took the comb from my hair and let it fall about my shoulders, undressed, and hung up the red velvet gown. "You have become an extremely fascinating young lady," I said.

Then I thought of how exciting my life was going to be because it was true that life was yours to make as you wanted to.

It was difficult to sleep. I kept thinking of myself dancing with Kim, fighting with Johnny, hiding in the cupboard, and that horrified moment when I had opened the door of Sir Justin's room and seen him.

So it wasn't surprising that when I did sleep I had a nightmare. I dreamed that Johnny had walled me up and that I was suffocating while Mellyora was trying to pull away the bricks with her bare hands and I knew that she would not be able to save me in time.

I awoke screaming to find Mellyora standing by my bed. Her golden hair was about her shoulders and she had not put a dressing gown over her flannelette nightdress.

"Wake up, Kerensa," she said. "You're having a nightmare."

I sat up and stared at her hands.

"What on earth was it?"

"I dreamed I was walled up and that you were trying to save me. I was suffocating."

"I don't wonder at it, you were buried right under the bedclothes and think of all that dash-an-darras and mead."

She sat on my bed laughing at me; but I could still feel my nightmare hanging over me.

"What an evening!" she said, and clasping her knees stared before her. As the sense of nightmare faded I remembered what I had heard from the cupboard. It was Mellyora's dancing with Justin which had provoked Judith's jealousy.

I sat up. "You danced with Justin, didn't you?" I said.

"Of course."

"His wife didn't like his dancing with you."

"How do you know?"

I told her what had happened to me. Her eyes opened wide and she sprang up, took me by the shoulders and shook me. "Kerensa, I might have known that something would

85

happen to you! Tell me every word you heard when you were in the cupboard."

"I have . . . as far as I can remember. I was horribly scared."

"I should think so. What on earth made you?"

"I don't know. I just thought it was the only thing to do at the time. Was she right, Mellyora?"

"Right?"

"To be jealous."

Mellyora laughed. "She is married to him," she said; and I was not sure whether the flippancy hid a certain bitterness.

We were silent for a while, each preoccupied with her own thoughts. I was the one to break it. I said: "I think you have always liked Justin."

It was a time for confidences and indiscretions. The magic of the ball was still with us, and Mellyora and I were closer that night than we had been before.

"He's different from Johnny," she said.

"I should hope for his wife's sake that he is."

"No one would be safe with Johnny around. Justin doesn't seem to notice people."

"Meaning Grecians with long golden hair?"

"Meaning everybody. He seems remote."

"Perhaps he ought to have been a monk rather than a husband.

"What things you say!" She started to talk of Justin then: the first time she and her father had been invited to take tea with the St. Larnstons; how she had worn a sprigged muslin dress for the occasion; how polite Justin had been. I could see that she had a kind of childish adoration for him and I hoped that was all because I didn't want her to be hurt.

"By the way," she said, "Kim told me he was going away."

"Oh?"

"To Australia, I think."

"Right away?" My voice sounded blank in spite of my efforts to control it.

"For a long time. He's going to sail with his father but he said he might stay in Australia for a time because he has an uncle there."

The enchantment of the ball seemed to have disappeared.

"Are you tired?" asked Mellyora.

"Well, it must be very late."

"Early morning rather."

"We ought to get some sleep."

She nodded and went into her own room. Strange how we

both seemed suddenly to have lost our exhilaration. Was it because she was thinking of Justin and his passionately loving wife? Was it because I was thinking of Kim who was going away and had told her and not me?

It was about a week after the ball when Dr. Hilliard paid a visit to the parsonage. I was on the front lawn when his brougham drew up and he called good morning to me. I knew that the Reverend Charles had been seeing him recently and I guessed that he had come to discover how he was.

"The Reverend Charles Martin is not at home," I told him.

"Good. It is Miss Martin I have come to see. Is she at home?"

"Oh, yes."

"Then would you be so kind as to tell her I'm here."

"Certainly," I said. "Pray, come in."

I took him into the drawing room and went to find Mellyora. She was sewing in her room and seemed startled when I told her that Dr. Hilliard wanted to see her.

She hurried down to him at once and I went into my room, wondering if Mellyora was ill and had been consulting the doctor secretly.

Half an hour later the brougham drove away, and the door of my room was flung open and Mellyora came in. Her face was white and her eyes looked almost dark; I had never seen her like that before.

"Oh, Kerensa," she said, "this is terrible."

"Tell me what it's all about."

"It's Papa. Dr. Hilliard says he is gravely ill."

"Oh . . . Mellyora."

"He says Papa has some sort of growth and that he had advised him to have a second opinion. Papa didn't tell me. I didn't know he'd been seeing these doctors. Well, now they think they know. Kerensa, I can't bear it. They say he's going to die."

"But they can't know."

"They're almost certain. Three months, Dr. Hilliard thinks."

"Oh, no!"

"He says that Papa mustn't go on working because he's on the verge of collapse. He wants him to go to bed and rest. . . ." She buried her face in her hands; I went to her and put my arms round her. We clung together.

"They can't be sure," I insisted.

But I didn't believe that. I knew now that I had seen death in the Reverend Charles's face.

Everything had changed. Each day the Reverend Charles was a little worse. Mellyora and I nursed him. She insisted on giving him every attention and I insisted on helping her.

David Killigrew had come to the parsonage. He was a curate who was to take over the parson's duties until, as they said, something could be arranged. They really meant until the Reverend Charles died.

The autumn came and Mellyora and I hardly ever went out. We did few lessons, although Miss Kellow was still with us, because most of our time was spent in and out of the sickroom. It was a strangely different household; and I think we were all grateful for David Killigrew, who was in his late twenties and one of the gentlest people I had ever met. He went quietly about the house, making very little trouble; yet he could preach a good sermon and attend to parish affairs with an efficiency which was amazing.

He would often sit with the Reverend Charles and talk to him about the parish. He would talk to us, too; and in a short time we almost forgot what his presence meant in the house, for he seemed like a member of the family. He cheered us and made us feel that he was grateful for our company; as for the servants, they took to him as the people of the parish did; and for a long time it seemed as though this state of affairs would go on indefinitely.

Christmas came—a sad Christmas for us. Mrs. Yeo made some preparation in the kitchen because, as she said, the servants expected it; and she knew it was what the Reverend would wish. David agreed with her, and she set about making the cakes and puddings, just as she had every year.

I went out with David to get in the holly; and as he cut it I said: "Why do we do this? We none of us feel like making merry."

He looked at me sadly and answered: "It's better to go on hoping."

"Is it? When we can't help knowing that the end is near— and what that end will be?"

"We live by hope," he told me.

I admitted that this was true. I looked at him sharply. "For what do you hope?" I asked.

He was silent for a while; then he said: "I suppose what every man hopes for—a fireside, my own family."

"And you know that your hopes will be realized?"

He moved closer to me and answered, "If I should get a living."

"And not till then?"

"I have my mother to care for. My first duty is to her."

"Where is she now?"

"She is in the care of her niece who is staying in our little house until I return."

He had pricked his finger on the holly; he sucked it in a shamefaced way and I noticed that there was a warm flush under his skin.

He was embarrassed. He was thinking that when the Reverend Charles died he had a good chance of being offered the living.

On Christmas Eve the carol singers came to the parsonage and sang "The First Nowell," softly, below the Reverend Charles's window.

At the kitchen table Mrs. Yeo was making the Christmas bush by fastening two wooden hoops together and decorating them with furze and evergreens. She would hang it in the window of the sickroom, just to pretend that we were not too sad to celebrate Christmas.

David dealt with the services in a manner which gave satisfaction to everyone and I heard Mrs. Yeo commenting to Belter that if it had to happen, this was the best way.

It was on Twelfth Night that Kim called. I have always hated Twelfth Night since, telling myself often that it was because all the Christmas decorations were taken down then and that was the end of the festivities until next year.

I saw Kim riding up on the chestnut mare he always rode and I thought how fine and manly he looked—not wicked like Johnny, nor saintly like Justin—exactly as a man should look.

I knew why he had come, since he had told us that he would call to say good-bye. He had seemed sad as the time for departure grew near.

I went out to meet him because I believed that I was the one he regretted leaving.

"Why," he cried, "it's Miss Kerensa."

"I saw you arriving."

Belter had come to take his horse and Kim started towards the entrance. I wanted to delay him, to have him to myself before we joined Mellyora and Miss Kellow who, I knew, were in the drawing room.

"When are you leaving?" I asked, trying to hide the desolation in my voice.

"Tomorrow."

"I don't believe you want to go one bit."

"Just one bit does," he said. "The rest hates to leave home."

"Then why go?"

"My dear Kerensa, all the arrangements have been made."

"I see no reason why they shouldn't be canceled."

"Alas," he replied. "I do."

"Kim," I said passionately, "if you don't want to go . . ."

"But I want to go across the seas and make a fortune."

"What for?"

"To come back rich and famous."

"Why?"

"So that I can settle down, marry and raise a family."

These were almost exactly the same words David Killigrew had used. Perhaps this was a common desire.

"Then you will, Kim," I said earnestly.

He laughed and, leaning towards me, kissed me lightly on the forehead. I felt wildly happy and almost immediately desperately sad.

"You looked so like a prophetess," he told me, as though to excuse the kiss. Then he went on lightly: "I believe you are some sort of witch . . . the nicest sort, of course." For a moment we stood smiling at each other before he went on: "This cutting wind can't be good . . . even for witches."

He slipped his arm through mine and we went into the house together.

In the drawing room Mellyora and Miss Kellow were waiting and as soon as we arrived Miss Kellow rang for tea.

Kim talked mainly about Australia, of which he seemed to know a great deal. He glowed with enthusiasm and I loved listening to him, and saw vividly the land he described: the harbor with its indentations and sandy beaches fringed with foliage; the brilliant plumage of strange birds; the moist heat which made you feel as though you were in a steamy bath: it would be summer there now, he told us. He talked of the station to which he was going; how cheap land was; and labor, too. I thought with pain of a night when my brother had lain in a mantrap and this man had carried him to safety. But for Kim, my brother Joe might be "cheap labor" on the other side of the world.

Oh, Kim, I thought, I wish I were going with you.

But I was not sure that was true. I wanted to live in St. Larnston Abbas like a lady. Did I really want to live on some lonely station in a strange and uncultivated land, even with Kim?

It was my wild dream for Kim to stay, for Kim to own the Abbas instead of the St. Larnstons. I wanted to share the Abbas with Kim.

"Kerensa's thoughtful." Kim was watching me, quizzically. Tenderly? I wondered.

"I was imagining it all. You make it sound so real."

"You wait till I come back."

"And then?"

"I shall have some stories to tell you."

He shook hands with us as he was leaving, and kissed first Mellyora and then me.

"I'll be back," he said. "You'll see."

I went on remembering those words long after he had gone.

It was not that I overheard a precise conversation; it was little hints I caught now and then which made me understand what was in people's minds.

No one had any doubt that the Reverend Charles was dying. Sometimes he seemed a little better but he never really progressed and week by week we saw his strength slowly slipping away.

I wondered constantly about what would happen to us when he died, for it was clear that the state of affairs which now existed was only a compromise.

Mrs. Yeo gave me the first clue when she was speaking of David Killigrew. I realized that she accepted him as the new master of the house; she believed—and I realized that this had occurred to many others—that when the Reverend Charles died David Killigrew would have the living. He would become the parson here. And Mellyora? Well, Mellyora was a parson's daughter so it would be reasonable to suppose that she would make a good parson's wife.

It seemed to them right and reasonable, so they hinted that it was inevitable. Mellyora and David. They were good friends. She was grateful to him; and he must admire her. Suppose they were right, what would happen to me?

I shouldn't leave Mellyora. David had always shown the utmost friendliness towards me. I should stay on in the parsonage, making myself useful. In what capacity? Maid to Mellyora? She never treated me as maid. I was the sister she had always wanted and who had the same name as the one she had lost.

Some weeks after Kim's departure I met Johnny St. Larnston near the Pengaster farm. I had been to see Granny, to take her a basket of food, and I was preoccupied because—although she had talked animatedly about the day she had spent

91

at the vet's house, where she had been invited for Christmas Day—she looked thin and her eyes seemed less bright than usual. I noticed, too, that she still coughed too much.

My anxiety was due to the fact that I came from a house of sickness, I told myself. Because the Reverend Charles was ill, I was expecting everyone of his age to be threatened.

Granny had told me how much at home Joe was at the vet's house and how they treated him like one of the family. It was an excellent state of affairs for although the vet had four daughters he had no son, so he was pleased to have a boy like Joe to help him.

I was a little melancholy when I left the cottage; there were so many shadows threatening my life; the sickness in the house which I had come to regard as home; the apprehension over Granny's health; Joe, too, in a way, sitting at the vet's table instead of that of Dr. Hilliard.

"Hello!" Johnny was sitting on the stile which led to the Pengaster fields. He leaped down and fitted his step to mine. "I've been hoping we should meet."

"Is that so?"

"Allow me to carry your basket."

"There's no need. It's empty."

"And where are you going, my pretty maid?"

"You seem to have a fondness for nursery rhymes. Is that because you have not yet grown up?"

" 'My face is my fortune, sir, she said,' " he quoted. "It's true, Miss . . . er . . . Carlyon. But watch that sharp tongue of yours. By the way, why Carlyon? Why not St. Ives, Marazion. Carlyon! But it suits you, you know."

I quickened my steps. "I am really in a hurry."

"A pity. I was hoping we should be able to renew our acquaintance. I should have seen you before, don't doubt it. But I have been away and am only just back."

"You will soon be returning, I daresay."

"Do you mean you hope? Oh, Kerensa, why won't you be friends with me? I want to be, you know."

"You go the wrong way about making friends, perhaps."

"Then you must show me the right way."

He gripped my arm and pulled me round to face him. There was a light in his eyes which alarmed me. I thought of the way he had looked for Hetty Pengaster in church and how I had seen him on the stile. He had probably been coming from some rendezvous with her.

I twisted my arm free. "Let me alone," I said. "And not just now . . . always. I am not Hetty Pengaster."

He was startled; there was no doubt of that because I escaped with ease. I ran and when I looked over my shoulder he was still standing staring after me.

By the end of January the Reverend Charles became so ill that he was given sedatives by the doctor, which resulted in long hours of sleep. Mellyora and I would sit quietly talking as we sewed or perhaps read, and every now and then one of us would rise to look into the sickroom. David Killigrew was with us every moment he could spare and we both agreed that his presence soothed us. Sometimes Mrs. Yeo brought us food and she would always cast a fond eye on the young man. I had heard her declare to Belter that when this unhappy business was over her first task would be to build up the young parson. Bess or Kit would come in to make up the fire, and the glances they bestowed on him and Mellyora were significant to me, though perhaps not to him or to Mellyora. The latter's thoughts were occupied with her father.

A melancholy peace pervaded the house. Inevitable death was with us, but that had to pass; and then when it was over, we would grow away from it and nothing would be changed, inasmuch as those who now served one person would serve another.

Mellyora and David. It would be inevitable. Mellyora would settle down in time; she would cease to have dreams about a knight whose devotion had been given to another lady.

I looked up and caught David's eyes on me. He smiled when he realized that I had caught him. There was something revealing in that glance. Had I been mistaken?

I was disturbed. That was not how things were expected to work out.

During the next few days I knew that what I had suspected was a certainty.

I was sure after that conversation. It was not exactly a proposal of marriage because David was not the sort of man to propose marriage until he was in a position to afford to keep a wife. As a curate with an aged mother to support, he was not. But if, as he must believe since everyone else did, he acquired the St. Larnston living, that would be a different matter.

He and I were sitting by the fire alone, for Mellyora was at her father's bedside.

He said to me: "You regard this as your home, Miss Carlee?"

I agreed.

"I have heard how you came here."

I knew that was inevitable. As a subject of gossip it had ceased to be interesting, except of course when there was a newcomer who had not heard it before.

"I admire you for what you've done," he went on. "I think that you are most . . . most wonderful. I imagine that you hope never to leave the parsonage."

"I'm not sure," I said. He had made me wonder what I did hope for. To live at the parsonage had not been my dream. The night when I had dressed in red velvet and, masked, walked up the wide staircase to be received by Lady St. Larnston had been more like a dream coming true than living at the parsonage had ever been.

"Of course you are unsure. There are matters in life which require a great deal of thought. I myself have been reviewing my own life. You see, Miss Carlee, a man in my present position cannot afford to marry; but if that position should change. . . ."

He paused and I thought: He is asking me to marry him when the Reverend is dead and he has stepped into his shoes. He felt ashamed that he should be thinking of a future for which he must wait until another was dead.

"I think," he went on, "that you would make an excellent parson's wife, Miss Carlee."

I laughed. "I? I do not think so."

"But why not?"

"Everything would be wrong. My background, for one thing."

He snapped his fingers. "You are yourself. That is all that matters."

"My character."

"What is wrong with that?"

"It is hardly serious and pious."

"My dear Miss Carlee, you underrate yourself."

"You little know me." I laughed again. When had I ever underrated myself? Had I not always felt a power in myself that I believed would carry me wherever I wanted to go? I was as arrogant in my way as Lady St. Larnston was in hers. Truly, I thought, love is blind; for it was becoming increasingly clear to me that David Killigrew was falling in love with me.

"I am sure," he went on, "that you would succeed with anything you undertook. Besides . . ."

He did not finish for Mellyora came out then; her face was drawn and anxious.

"I think he is worse," she said.

It was Easter time and the church was decorated with daffodils when the Reverend Charles Martin died. Ours was a house of mourning, and Mellyora was inconsolable, for although we had known for so long that death was inevitable, when it came it was still a blow. Mellyora spent the day in her room and would see no one; then she asked for me. I sat with her and she talked of him, how good he had been to her, how lost she felt without him; she recalled instance after instance of his kindness, of his love and care; then she would weep quietly and I wept with her, for I had been fond of him, and I hated to see Mellyora so distressed.

The day of the funeral came and the tolling of the bell seemed to fill the house. Mellyora looked beautiful in her black clothes with the veil over her face; black was less becoming to my dark looks and the dress I wore under the black coat was too loose for me.

The prancing horses, the waving black plumes, the mutes, the solemnity of the burial service, the standing round that grave where I had stood with Mellyora when she had told me that she had had a sister named Kerensa, this was somber and melancholy.

Yet, even worse, was coming back to the parsonage which seemed empty because that quiet man, of whom I had seen very little, was gone.

The mourners came back to the parsonage, Lady St. Larnston and Justin among them; they made our drawing room, in which ham sandwiches and wine were served, seem small and simple—although I had thought it very grand when I had first seen it. Justin spent most of the time with Mellyora. He was gentle, courteous, and he seemed genuinely concerned. David was at my side. I believed that very soon he would definitely ask me to marry him; and I wondered what I could say, knowing as I did that others expected him to marry Mellyora. While the mourners ate their sandwiches and drank the wine which Belter had been called in to serve, I was seeing myself as mistress of this house, Mrs. Yeo and Belter taking their orders from me. A far cry, one might say, from the girl who had set herself up on the hiring stand at

Trelinket Fair. A long way indeed. In the village they would always remember. "Parson's wife, she came from the cottages she did." They would envy me and never quite accept me. But should I care?

And yet . . . I had dreamed a dream. This would not be its fulfillment. I did not care for David Killigrew as I did for Kim; and I was not even sure that I wanted to be with Kim who was so far from the Abbas.

When the mourners had left, Mellyora went to her room. Dr. Hilliard, who had made up his mind that I was a sensible young woman, called and asked to see me.

"Miss Martin is very distraught," he said. "I am giving you a mild sedative for her, but I don't want her to have it unless she needs it. She looks exhausted. But if she should be unable to sleep, give it to her." He smiled at me in his rather brusque way. He respected me. I began to dream then that I was able to talk to him, to interest him in Joe. I hated to find that my dreams even for others did not come true.

I went into Mellyora's room that night and found her sitting at the bedroom window looking out over the lawn to the graveyard.

"You'll catch cold," I said. "Come to bed."

She shook her head, so I put a shawl about her shoulders and drawing up a chair sat beside her.

"Oh, Kerensa, everything will be different now. Don't you feel it?"

"It must be so."

"I feel as though I am in a sort of limbo . . . floating between two lives. The old life is over; the new one is about to begin."

"For us both," I said.

She gripped my hand. "Yes, change for me means change for you. It seems now, Kerensa, that your life is entwined with mine."

I wondered what she would do now. I believed I could stay on at the parsonage if I wished. But what of Mellyora? What happened to the daughters of parsons? If they had no money they became governesses to children; they became companions to elderly ladies. What would Mellyora's fate be? And mine?

She did not seem to be concerned with her own future; her thoughts were still with her father.

"He is lying out there," she said, "with my mother and the baby . . . little Kerensa. I wonder if his spirit has flown to Heaven yet."

"You shouldn't sit there brooding. Nothing can bring him back, and remember he would not have wanted you to be unhappy. His great aim was to make *you* happy always."

"He was the best father in the world, Kerensa, yet I could wish now that he had been harsh and cruel sometimes, so that I did not have to mourn so much."

She began to weep silently and I put an arm about her. I led her to bed and gave her the sedative Dr. Hilliard had given me.

Then I stopped by her bed until she slept and I tried to peer into the future.

The future was not to be as we had imagined it. It was as though a mischievous fate were reminding us that man proposes and God disposes.

In the first place David Killigrew did not get the St. Larnston living. Instead, the Reverend James Hemphill with his wife and three daughters came to the parsonage.

David went sadly back to become a curate again, to shelve his dream of marriage and to share his life with his widowed mother. He said we must write to each other—and hope.

Mrs. Yeo and Belter were only really concerned—as were Bess and Kit—as to whether the Hemphills would require their services.

Mellyora seemed to have grown up in those weeks; I suppose I did, too, for we suddenly found that security had been swept away from us.

Mellyora took me to her bedroom where we could talk in peace. She looked grave; but her fear for her own future had at least superimposed itself on her grief for her father. There was no time for mourning.

"Kerensa," she said to me, "sit down. I've heard that my father has left so little that it will be necessary for me to earn my living."

I looked at her; she had lost weight and seemed frail in her black dress. She had put up her hair, which somehow made her look helpless. I pictured her in some stately mansion—the governess—not quite one of the servants and yet considered unfit to associate with the family. I shivered.

And what of my own fate? One thing I did believe; I should be more able to take care of myself than she would.

"What do you propose to do?" I asked.

"I want to talk it over with you. Because you see this affects you, too. You'll have to leave here."

"We shall have to find means of earning a living. I shall talk it over with Granny."

"Kerensa, I shan't like our being separated."

"Nor I."

She smiled at me wanly. "If we could be together somewhere. . . . I wondered if we could start a school . . . or something."

"Where?"

"Somewhere here in St. Larnston."

It was a wild plan and I could see that she didn't believe in it even as she spoke.

"When shall we have to leave?" I asked.

"The Hemphills are coming in at the end of the month. That gives us three weeks. Mrs. Hemphill is very kind. She has said I need not worry if I wanted to stay a little longer."

"She won't expect to find me here. I could go to my Granny, I suppose."

Her face puckered and she turned away.

I could have cried with her. I felt that everything I had gained was being snatched from me. No, not everything. I had come to the parsonage an ignorant girl; now I was a young woman almost as educated as Mellyora. I could be a governess even as she could.

That thought gave me confidence and courage. I would talk to Granny. I wouldn't despair yet.

A few days later Lady St. Larnston sent for Mellyora. I can only say "sent," because this was not like the invitations Mellyora had received previously; this was a command.

Mellyora put on her black cloak and black straw hat, and Miss Kellow, who was leaving at the end of the week, drove her to the Abbas.

They returned in about an hour. Mellyora went to her room, calling me to come to her.

"I've settled it," she cried.

I didn't understand her, and she went on quickly: "Lady St. Larnston has offered me a post and I've accepted it. I'm to be her companion. At least we won't have to go away."

"We?"

"You didn't think I would leave you?" She smiled and was like she had been in the old days. "Oh, I know we won't like it much . . . but at least it's something definite. I'm to be her companion and there's a job for you, too."

"What sort of job?"

"Lady's maid to Mrs. Justin St. Larnston."

"Lady's maid!"

"Yes, Kerensa. You can do it. You have to look after her clothes, do her hair . . . make yourself generally useful. I don't think it'll be very difficult . . . and you do like clothes. Think how clever you were with the red velvet dress."

I was too taken aback to speak.

Mellyora rushed on. "When she asked me she said it was the best thing she could do for me. She said she felt she owed something to us, and she couldn't let me be left penniless. I told her that you had been with me for so long that I regarded you as my sister and I wouldn't leave you. Then she thought for a while and said that Mrs. St. Larnston needed a maid, and that you would be taken on. I said I was sure you would be grateful. . . ."

She was breathless and there was an unmistakable gleam in her eyes. She wanted to go and live at the Abbas even as companion to Lady St. Larnston. I knew why. It was because she couldn't bear to think of leaving St. Larnston while Justin was there.

I went at once to Granny Bee and told her what had happened.

"Well, you always wanted to live in that house," she said.

"As a servant!"

"There's only one way as it could be aught else," she went on.

"How?"

"By marrying Johnny St. Larnston."

"As if . . ."

Granny laid her hand on my head, for I was sitting on a stool by her chair. "You be comely, my child."

"His sort don't want to marry mine—however comely we are."

"Not as a rule, tis true. But tain't the rule either that your sort be taken up and educated, now is it?"

I shook my head.

"Well, bain't that a sign? You don't expect things that happen to they ordinary folk to happen to 'ee, do 'ee?"

"No, but I don't like Johnny. Besides, he never would marry me, Granny. There's something in him that tells me he never would. He's different with me than with Mellyora, though perhaps he won't be now. He wants me. I know that, but he doesn't care for me one bit."

Granny nodded. "That's for now," she said. "Changes come. Be careful when you be in that house, lovey. Take special care of Johnny." She sighed. "I did hope you'd marry maybe a parson or a doctor like. That's what I could have wished to see."

"If it had all turned out as we thought, Granny, I don't know whether I'd have married David Killigrew."

She stroked my hair. "I know. Your eyes be fixed on that house. It have done something to 'ee, Kerensa. It have bewitched ye."

"Oh, Granny, if only the parson hadn't died."

"There comes a time when we all must die. He weren't a young man and his time had come."

"There's Sir Justin, too." I shuddered, remembering what I had seen when I had opened the wrong door. "Sir Justin and the Reverend Charles. That's two of them, Granny."

"'Tis natural. You've seen the leaves on the trees come autumn time. They shrivel and drop and dry. One by one they fall. That's because they be come to autumn. Well some of us be come to our autumn; then one after the other quickly we'll drop from the trees."

I turned to her in horror. "Not you, Granny. You mustn't die."

She laughed. "Here I be. Don't seem like my turn have come yet, do it?"

I was afraid in those moments—afraid of what the future held for me at the Abbas, afraid of a world which would not contain Granny Bee.

she were rather pleased to see us in this position, particularly me.

"I'll send one of my maids up to see if her ladyship is ready to receive 'ee," she said. She took us round to one of the back doors, emphasizing by a smirk that we had made the mistake of presenting ourselves at the great stone portico which led into the main hall. We should in future, Mrs. Rolt told us, not be expected to use that door.

Mrs. Rolt took us into the main kitchen, an enormous room with vaulted ceiling and stone floors; it was warm though, on account of an oven which looked—and I am sure was—big enough to roast an ox. Two girls sat at the table cleaning silver.

"Go up to her ladyship and tell her the new companion and maid has arrived. She wanted to see them herself."

One of the girls started for the door.

"Not you, Daisy!" cried Mrs. Rolt hastily. "My dear life! Going to her ladyship like that! Your hair do look like you've been pulled through a hedge backwards. You, Doll."

I noticed that the one addressed as Daisy had a plump, blank face—currant-eyed, with wiry hair that grew low down almost to the thick bushy eyebrows. Doll was smaller, more lithe and in contrast to her companion had an alert expression, which might have been crafty. She went through the kitchen into an adjoining room and I heard the sound of running water. When she emerged she was wearing a clean apron. Mrs. Rolt nodded her head with approval and, when Doll had gone, turned her attention to us.

"Her ladyship has told me that you will eat with us in the servants' hall." This was addressed to me. "Mr. Haggety will tell you your place." Then to Mellyora: "I understand you're to have meals in your own room, Miss."

I felt a rush of color to my cheeks and I knew Mrs. Rolt noticed it and was not displeased. I foresaw battles to come. I had to stop myself blurting out that I would take my meals with Mellyora; I knew this would be forbidden and I should be doubly humiliated.

I stared up at the vaulted ceiling. These kitchen quarters with their ovens and spits had been used from the earliest days and I discovered later that there were butteries, pantries, storerooms, and cooling houses attached.

Mrs. Rolt went on: "We be all sorry, Miss, about your bereavement. Mr. Haggety were saying as things won't be the same like what with the new Reverend at the parsonage and you, Miss, here at the Abbas."

102

"Thank you," said Mellyora.

"Well, we was saying—Mr. Haggety and me—as how we hoped you'd settle in well. Her ladyship needs a companion since Sir Justin was afflicted."

"I hope so too," answered Mellyora quietly.

"Of course you'll know how things be run in a big house, Miss." She glanced at me and that quirk played about her mouth. She was telling me that there was a world of difference between my position and that of Mellyora. Mellyora was the parson's daughter and a lady born and bred. I could see that she was thinking of me standing on the platform at Trelinket Fair and that was how she would always see me.

Doll came back to announce that her ladyship would see us now, and Mrs. Rolt told us to follow her. We mounted about a dozen stone stairs at the top of which was a green baize door which led to the main part of the house. We went along several corridors before we came to the main hall and ascended the staircase which I remembered from the night of the ball.

"Here be the part where the family do live," said Mrs. Rolt. She nudged me. "Why you be all pop-eyed, m'dear. Reckon you thinking how grand everything be, eh?"

"No," I retorted, "I was thinking how far it must be from the kitchens to the dining room. Doesn't the food get cold in transit?"

"Transit, eh? Who be 'e when he's out? Tain't going to worry 'ee, m'dear. You'll never be eating in they dining rooms." She gave a merry cackle. I caught Mellyora's eye and read a warning and a plea. Don't lose your temper, she was telling me. Give it a trial. It's our only chance of being together.

I thought that I recognized some of the corridors through which I had run in panic on the night of the ball. At last we stopped at a door and Mrs. Rolt knocked.

When she was told to come in, she said in a voice very different from that which she had used for us: "My lady, the new companion and maid is come."

"Bring them in, Mrs. Rolt."

Mrs. Rolt jerked her head and we entered the room. It was large and lofty, with huge windows looking over the lawns; a fire burned in the enormous fireplace; the room seemed to me luxuriously furnished but my attention was focused on the woman who sat upright in a chair near the fire.

"Come here," she said imperiously. Then, "That will do, Mrs. Rolt. Wait outside until you are summoned."

As we advanced Mrs. Rolt retired.

"Pray sit down, Miss Martin," commanded Lady St. Larnston. Mellyora sat while I remained standing because I was not invited to sit. "We did not discuss very fully what your duties would be, but that is something which you will, of course, discover as time goes on. I trust you read well. My eyes are not as good as they were and I shall need you to read to me each day. You will begin your duties without delay. Do you write a good hand? I shall need you to deal with my correspondence. These are matters which would ordinarily have been settled before you were engaged, but since we have been neighbors I felt a point could be stretched in your case. A pleasant room has been allotted to you. It is next to my bedroom so that you can be within call should I need you during the night. Has Mrs. Rolt told you where you are to have your meals?"

"Yes, Lady St. Larnston."

"Well, that seems to have taken care of everything. You shall be shown your room and unpack your bag."

She turned to me and lifted the lorgnette which hung from her waist and surveyed me coolly.

"And this is Carlee."

"Kerensa Carlee," I said as proudly as I had that day when I had stood in the wall.

"I have heard something of your history. I have taken you in because Miss Martin pleaded with me to do so. I trust you will not disappoint us. Mrs. Justin St. Larnston is not, I think, at home at the moment. You will be shown your room, and should wait there until she sends for you, which she will doubtless do on her return since she is aware that you are to arrive today. Now, tell Mrs. Rolt to come in."

I opened the door promptly, as Mrs. Rolt was hastily stepping back, having, I guessed, been crouching forwards, ear to the keyhole.

"Mrs. Rolt," ordered Lady St. Larnston, "show Miss Martin and Carlee to their rooms."

"Yes, my lady."

As we left, I was aware that Lady St. Larnston's eyes were on me, and I felt depressed. This was more humiliating than I had imagined it would be. All the spirit seemed to have been drained out of Mellyora. It should not be so with me. I made myself feel defiant and angry.

Soon, I promised myself, I should know my way about this house. Every room and corridor would be familiar to me. I remembered the night I had fled from Johnny and the panic I had suffered then. I was certainly not going to allow Johnny to humiliate me if, for the time being, I had to submit to his mother's insults.

"The family do have all their rooms in this part of the house," explained Mrs. Rolt. "This be her ladyship's and you'm next door, Miss Martin. Farther along the corridor, that be where Mr. Justin and his lady do have theirs." She nodded to me. "You be there too."

And so I was taken to my room—a maid's room—but not an ordinary maid, I reminded myself. A lady's maid. I was not like Doll or Daisy. I had special gifts and very soon I was going to make the kitchen staff aware of this.

In the meantime I must go slowly. I looked at my reflection in the mirror. I did not look like myself at all. I was wearing a black cloak and black bonnet. Black didn't suit me in any case, but the mourning bonnet hid my hair and was quite hideous.

Then I went to the window and looked out on the lawns and the Six Virgins.

That was when I said to myself, "You're here. You live here." And I couldn't help but feel this triumph because it was where I wanted to be. My melancholy left me. I was exultant and excited. I was in the house as a servant, but that in itself was a challenge.

As I stood at the window, the door opened, and I knew at once who she was. She was tall and dark—though not as dark as I—she was graceful and dressed in a pearl-gray riding habit and her skin glowed, presumably with her recent exercise. She was beautiful and she did not look unkind. I knew her for my employer, Judith St. Larnston.

"You're Carlee," she said. "I was told you had arrived. I'm glad you're here. My wardrobe is in a muddle. You'll be able to put it in order."

That staccato way of speaking immediately called to mind those panic-stricken moments in the cupboard.

"Yes . . . Madam."

I had my back to the window so that I was in shadow; the light was full on her face; I noticed the restless topaz-colored eyes; the rather flaring nostrils, the full sensuous lips.

"Have you unpacked your bag?"

"No." I wasn't going to call her Madam any more than was absolutely necessary. I was already congratulating myself because I believed my employer was going to be more lenient and more considerate than Mellyora's.

"Well, when you have done so, come to my room. Do you

know where it is? No, of course not. How could you? I'll show you."

I followed her out of my room and a few steps along the corridor.

"This door leads to my bedroom and the dressing room. Knock when you're ready."

I nodded, and went back to my room. I felt better in her company than I had in Mrs. Rolt's. I took off the hideous bonnet and felt better still. I tidied my hair which was dressed on top of my head, and the sight of those black gleaming coils reassured me. Beneath the black cloak I wore a black dress—one of Mellyora's. I longed to put a touch of scarlet or emerald green at the neck, but I dared not, for I was supposed to be in mourning. However, I should wear a white collar as soon as possible, I promised myself.

I went along to the room as instructed, knocked discreetly and was bidden to enter. She was sitting at her mirror looking idly at her reflection, and she did not turn round. I noticed the big bed with the brocade hangings, the long tapestry-covered stool at its foot; the rich carpet and curtains, the dressing table at which she sat, with its wood carving and the huge candelabra on either side of the mirror held up by gilded cupids. And of course the cupboard which I remembered so well.

She had seen my reflection in the mirror and she turned to stare at me, her gaze resting on my hair. I knew that taking off my bonnet had transformed me and that because of it she was not so pleased with me as she had been before.

"How old are you, Carlee?"

"Nearly seventeen."

"You are very young. Do you think you can do this work?"

"Oh yes. I know how to dress hair and enjoy caring for clothes."

"I had no idea . . ." She bit her lip. "I thought you were older." She came over to me, still looking at me. "I'd like you to go through my wardrobe. Make it tidy. I caught my heel in the lace of an evening gown. Can you mend lace?"

"Oh yes," I assured her, although I had never done so.

"It is very delicate work."

"I can do it."

"I shall need you to lay out my things every evening at seven. You will bring up the water for my bath. You will help me dress."

"Yes," I said. "Which dress do you wish to wear tonight?"

She had challenged me and I was going to prove my efficiency.

"Oh . . . the gray satin."

"Very well."

I turned to the wardrobe. She sat down by the mirror and began playing nervously with the combs and brushes while I went to the wardrobe and took out the clothes. I marveled at the dresses. I had never seen anything so magnificent. I couldn't resist stroking the velvets and satins. I found the gray satin, examined it, and was laying it out on the bed when the door opened and Justin St. Larnston came in.

"My darling!" It was like a whisper, but I heard the undertone of restless passion. She had risen and gone to him; in spite of my presence she would have embraced him had he given her some encouragement. "I wondered what had happened to you. I had expected you . . ."

"Judith!" His voice was cold, like a warning.

She laughed and said, "Oh, this is Carlee, the new maid."

We looked at each other. He hadn't really changed much from that very young man who had been present when they caught me in the wall. There was no recognition in his glance. He had forgotten that incident as soon as it was over, and the child from the cottages had made no impression on him.

He said: "Well, now you will have what you've been wanting."

"I don't want anything in the world but . . ."

He was almost willing her to silence. He said to me: "You can go now. Carlee, is it? Mrs. St. Larnston will ring when she needs you."

I bowed my head slightly and as I walked across the room I could feel her watching me and watching him at the same time. I knew what she was thinking because of what I had overheard when I was hidden in the cupboard in this very room. She was a violently jealous woman; she adored her husband; she could not bear him to look at another woman—even her own maid.

I touched the coils of hair on the top of my head; I hoped that the complacency I felt did not show. I was thinking as I went back to my room that money, position didn't necessarily make people happy. It was a good thing to remember when one was as proud as I was and found oneself suddenly in a humiliating position.

Those first days in the Abbas will stand out clearly forever in my mind. The house itself fascinated me even more than the people who lived in it. There was about it a brooding atmosphere of timelessness. It was so easy—when one was alone—to believe oneself to be in another age. Ever since I had heard the story of the Virgins my imagination had been captured; often I had pictured myself exploring the Abbas and this was one of those rare occasions when reality surpassed the imagination.

These lofty rooms with their carved and decorated ceilings—some painted, some inscribed in Latin or Cornish, were a delight to me. I loved to finger the rich stuff of curtains, to take off my shoes and feel the pile of carpet. I liked to sit on chairs and settees and imagine myself giving orders; and I sometimes talked to myself as though I were the mistress of the house. It became a game I enjoyed and I never lost an opportunity of playing it. But although I admired so much the luxuriously appointed apartments which were used by the family, I was drawn again and again to that wing of the house which was hardly ever used and which had obviously been part of the old convent. This was where Johnny had taken me on the night of the ball. There was about it an odor which both repelled and fascinated; a dank dark smell; a smell of the past. The staircases which seemed to appear suddenly and wind up for a few stairs and then stop at a door or a corridor; the stone which had been worn down by millions of steps; those strange little alcoves, with slitlike windows, which had been the nuns' cells; and underground were the dungeons, for the place had had its prison. I discovered the chapel—dark and chill—with its ancient triptych, its wooden pews, stone-flagged floor, its altar on which stood candles as though in readiness for the inhabitants of the house to come and worship. But I knew it was never used now because the St. Larnstons worshiped at St. Larnston Church.

In this part of the house the seven virgins had lived; their feet had trod the same stone corridors; their hands had clasped the rope as they climbed the steep stairs.

I began to love the house; and since to love was to be happy, I was not unhappy, in spite of petty humiliations, during those days. I had asserted myself in the servants' hall, and had rather enjoyed the battle which had had to be waged there, particularly as I assured myself I had been the victor. I was not beautiful with the finely chiseled features of Judith Derrise or with the delicate porcelain charm of Mellyora, but with my gleaming black hair, my big eyes which were very good at expressing scorn, and my pride, I was more startlingly attractive. I was tall and slender almost to thinness and possessed an indefinable foreign quality which, I was beginning to realize, could be used to my advantage.

Haggety was aware of it. He had put me at the table next to himself, a fact which I knew displeased Mrs. Rolt because I heard her protesting. "Oh come now, m'dear," he replied, "she's after all the lady's maid, you should know. A sight different from they maids of yours."

"And where be she come from, I'd like to know."

"That can't be helped. Tis what she be that we have to take account on."

What she be! I thought, smoothing my hands over my hips. Each day, each hour I was becoming more and more reconciled to my life. Humiliations, yes, but life in the Abbas would always be more exciting than anywhere else. And I lived here.

Seated at table in the servants' hall gave me an opportunity to study the members of the household who lived belowstairs. Mr. Haggety at the head of the table—little piggy eyes, lips inclined to slackness at the sight of a succulent dish or female, ruling the roost—the king of the kitchen, the Abbas butler. Next in importance Mrs. Rolt, the housekeeper, self-styled widow but very likely using Mrs. as a courtesy title, hoping that one day Mr. Haggety would put the question and Mrs. be hers by right when she had changed her name from Rolt to Haggety. Mean, sly, determined to keep her position—head of staff under Mr. Haggety. Then Mrs. Salt the cook, plump as became a cook, devoted to food and gossip; her disposition was a mournful one; she had suffered in her married life and had left her husband whom she talked of whenever possible as "him"; she had left him when she came to the Abbas from the very tip of Cornwall, west of St. Ives; and she expressed great fear that one day he would catch up with her. There was Jane Salt her daughter; a woman of about thirty who was a parlormaid, quiet, self-possessed, devoted to her mother. Then Doll, daughter of a miner, twenty or so, with crimped fair hair and a taste for electric blue which she wore when she had an hour or so off to go courting as she said. Simple-minded Daisy who worked with her in the kitchens, followed her round, imitated her and longed to be courting, and their conversation seemed to be confined to this subject. These servants all lived in the house, but there were also the outside servants who came in for meals. Polore and

Mrs. Polore, and their son Willy. Polore and Willy were attached to the stables while Mrs. Polore did housework in the Abbas. There were two mews cottages and the other was occupied by Mr. and Mrs. Trelance and their daughter Florrie. The opinion seemed to be that Florrie and Willy should marry; everyone but the couple concerned thought it an excellent idea; only Willy and Florrie held back. But as Mrs. Rolt said: "They'll come to it in time."

So it was a large party who sat round the great refectory table for meals, after the family had eaten. Mrs. Rolt and Mrs. Salt together saw that we lacked for nothing; and, if anything, we ate better than those who sat down in the stately dining room.

I began to enjoy the conversation which was very revealing, for there was little that remained unknown to these people, whether it concerned the house or village affairs.

Doll could always enliven the table with stories of her family's adventures in the mines. Mrs. Rolt declared that some of her talk fair gave her the creeps, and she would shiver and take the opportunity to move closer to Mr. Haggety for protection. Mr. Haggety was not very responsive; he was usually busy prodding my foot under the table, which he seemed to think was a way of letting me know he approved of me.

Mrs. Salt would tell hair-raising stories of her life with "him." And the Polores and Trelances would tell us how the new vicar was settling in and that Mrs. Hemphill was a real Nosy Parker and no mistake—prying here and prying there. She had a nose in the kitchen afore you had time to dust a chair for her to sit on. It was that very first night round the servants' table that I learned that Johnny was at his University and wouldn't be at the Abbas for some weeks. I was pleased. His absence would give me a chance to establish my position in the house.

I had fitted in to the rhythm of the days. My mistress was by no means unkind, indeed she was generous; during those first days she gave me a green dress of which she had tired; my duties were not arduous. I took pleasure in dressing her hair which was of a much finer texture than mine; I was interested in her clothes. I had long periods of freedom, and then I would go to the library, take a book and spend hours in my room reading while I waited for her bell to ring.

Mellyora's life was not so easy. Lady St. Larnston had determined to make the fullest use of *her* services. She must read to her for several hours a day; she must make tea for her often during the night; she must massage her head when she had a headache—which was frequent; she must deal with Lady St. Larnston's correspondence, take messages for her, accompany her when she went visiting in her carriage; in fact she was rarely free. Before the first week was out Lady St. Larnston decided that Mellyora, who had nursed her father, might be useful with Sir Justin. So that when Mellyora was not in attendance on Lady St. Larnston she was in the sickroom.

Poor Mellyora! In spite of meals in her room and being treated as though she were almost a lady, her lot was much harder than mine.

It was I who visited her in her room. As soon as my mistress went out—she had a habit of going for long rides, often alone—I would go to Mellyora's room in the hope of finding her there. We rarely had long together before the bell would ring and she had to leave me. Then I would read until she returned.

"Mellyora," I said to her one day, "how can you endure this?"

"How can you?" she reiterated.

"It's different for me, I haven't been used to much. Besides, I don't have to work as hard as you do."

"It has to be," she answered philosophically.

I looked at her; yes, it was satisfaction that I saw in her face. I marveled that she, the daughter of the parson, who had had her own way, who had been pampered and adored, should slip so easily into this life of servitude. Mellyora is a saint, I thought.

I liked to lie on her bed watching her, while she sat in a chair, ready to jump up at the first tinkle of the bell.

"Mellyora," I said, one early evening, "what do you think of this place?"

"Of the Abbas? Well, it's the most marvelous old house!"

"You can't help being excited about it?" I insisted.

"No. Nor can you, can you?"

"What do you think about when that old woman bullies you?"

"I try to make my mind a blank and not care."

"I don't think I could hide my feelings as you do. I'm lucky. Judith is not so bad."

"Judith . . ." said Mellyora slowly.

"All right: Mrs. Justin St. Larnston. She's a strange woman. She always seems overexcited as though life is terribly tragic . . . as though she's afraid. . . . There! I'm talking in that breathless way—as she does."

"Justin's not happy with her," said Mellyora slowly.

"I reckon he's as happy as he could be with anyone."

"What do you know about it?"

"I know that he's as cold as . . . a fish and she's as hot as a fiery furnace."

"You talk nonsense, Kerensa."

"Do I? I see more of them than you do. Don't forget my room is next to theirs."

"Do they quarrel?"

"He wouldn't quarrel. He's too cold. He doesn't care about anything and she cares . . . too much. I don't dislike her. After all, if he doesn't care about her why did he marry her?"

"Stop it. You don't know what you're saying. You don't understand."

"I know of course he's the bright and shining knight. You always felt like that about him."

"Justin's a good man. You don't understand him. I've known Justin all my life . . ."

The door of Mellyora's room was suddenly thrown open and Judith stood on the threshold, her eyes wild, her nostrils flaring. She looked at me lying on the bed and at Mellyora who had started up from her chair.

"Oh . . ." she said. "I didn't expect . . ."

I rose from the bed and said: "Did you want me, Madam?"

The passion had died out of her face and I saw an immense relief there.

"Were you looking for me?" I went on helpfully.

Now there was a flash of gratitude. "Oh yes, Carlee. I . . . I er thought you'd be here."

I went to the door. She hesitated. "I . . . I shall want you to come a little earlier this evening. Five or ten minutes before seven."

"Yes, Madam," I said.

She inclined her head and went out.

Mellyora looked at me in astonishment. "What did that mean?" she whispered.

"I think I know," I answered. "She was surprised, wasn't she? Do you know why? It was because she found me here when she was expecting to find . . ."

"Who?"

"Justin."

112

"She must be mad."

"Well, she's a Derrise. Remember that day when we were on the moors and you told me their story?"

"Yes, I remember."

"You said there was madness in the family. Well, Judith is mad . . . mad about her husband. She thought he was here with you. That was why she burst in like that. Didn't you see how pleased she was to find that I was the one you were talking to, not him."

"It's madness."

"Of a sort."

"You mean to say she's jealous of me and of Justin!"

"She's jealous of every attractive woman who comes within his vision."

I looked at Mellyora. She couldn't hide the truth from me. She was in love with Justin St. Larnston; she always had been.

I felt very uneasy.

There were no longer baskets of food to be taken for Granny. I could well imagine Mrs. Rolt or Mrs. Salt raising shocked voices if I had suggested doing so. But I still found time to visit her now and then; and it was on one of these occasions that she asked me if, on my way back to the Abbas, I would deliver some herbs to Hetty Pengaster. Hetty was waiting for them and Hetty, I knew, was one of Granny's best customers, so I agreed to go.

That was how I found myself one hot afternoon, making my way from Granny's cottage towards Larnston Barton, the Pengaster farm.

I saw Tom Pengaster at work in the fields and I wondered if it were true that he was courting Doll, as she had hinted to Daisy. It would be a good match for Doll. The Barton was a prosperous farm and Tom—not his piskey-mazed brother Reuben who did odd jobs—would inherit it one day.

I passed under the tall trees in which the rooks nested. Every May the shooting of rooks at Larnston Barton was quite a ceremony; and the rook pies, which were made by Mrs. Pengallon who was cook at the Barton, were considered a delicacy. A pie was always sent up to the Abbas and graciously accepted. Mrs. Salt had mentioned it recently—how she had served it with clotted cream and how Mrs. Rolt had eaten too much and suffered accordingly.

I reached the stables—there was stabling for about eight horses and two loose-boxes—and went on to the outbuildings.

I could see the pigeon loft and hear the cooing of the birds with their monotonous phrase which we said sounded like "Take two cows, Taffy."

As I was passing the mounting block, I saw Reuben Pengaster coming round by the pigeon loft holding a bird in his hands. Reuben walked in a queer, loping way. There must always have been something strange about Reuben. In Cornwall they say that in a litter there is often a "winnick," which means one not quite up to the standard of the others; and Reuben was the Pengaster winnick. I have always felt repulsed by the subnormal and although it was broad daylight with the sun shining brightly, I could not suppress a slight shiver as Reuben came towards me with that peculiar gait of his. His face was unlined like a very young person's; his eyes were porcelain blue and his hair was flaxen; it was the set of his jaw and the way in which his slack lips parted that betrayed him as piskey-mazed.

"Hello there," he called. "Where be to then?"

As he spoke he caressed the bird's head and I could see that he was far more aware of it than he was of me.

"I've brought some herbs for Hetty," I told him.

"Herbs for Hetty!" He laughed. He had high-pitched innocent laughter. "What 'er be wanting they for? To make her pretty?" His expression became bellicose. "Reckon our Hetty be pretty enough without." For a second his jaw was thrust forwards as though he were ready to attack me for suggesting she wasn't.

"It's for Hetty to say if she wants the herbs," I retorted sharply.

That innocent laughter rang out again. "Ay reckon so," he said. "Though Saul Cundy do think she be a rare fine 'un."

"I dare say."

"You might say she be spoke for," he went on almost shyly; and there was no mistaking his love for, and pride in, his sister.

"I hope they'll be happy."

"They'll be happy. Saul's a big fine man. Cap'en Saul . . . they miners have to mind their manners, eh . . . with Saul. If Saul do say go, they do go; and if Saul do say come, they do come. Mr. Fedder ain't no more important, I do reckon, than Cap'en Saul Cundy."

I was ready to let that point pass for I was anxious to deliver the herbs and be gone.

"Where is Hetty now?" I asked.

"Reckon her'll be in the kitchen with old Mother Pengallon."

I hesitated, wondering whether to give him the packet and ask him to take it to Hetty, but I decided against that.

"I'll go and find her," I said.

"I'll take 'ee to her," he promised and walked beside me. "Coop-coop, coooop, coop-coop," he murmured to the pigeon, and I was momentarily reminded of Joe, lying on the talfat mending a pigeon's leg. I noticed how big his hands were, and how gently they held the bird.

He led me to the back of the farmhouse and directed my gaze to the ridge tile which served as a decoration. There was a ladder propped up against the wall; he was doing a job on the farmhouse.

"Some of they tiles loose," he said, confirming this. "Twould never do. What if the Little People came a-footing it at midnight."

Again that high-pitched laughter which was beginning to irritate me. So much so that I wished Reuben would go.

I knew he was referring to what we called the piskey-pow—that ridge tile on which the piskeys were supposed to come and dance after midnight. If it was in a bad state of repair it was said this angered them and the piskeys' anger could bring bad luck on a house. It was natural, I suppose, that one who was said to be piskey-mazed should believe these legends.

"Tis all right now," said Reuben. "I see to that. Then I thought I'd take a look at my little birds."

He led me through a stone-floored washhouse into a flagged passage, where he threw open a door to show me an enormous kitchen with two large windows, an open fireplace as well as the cloam oven, red tiles, and huge refectory table; on the oak beams hung a ham, sides of bacon and bundles of herbs.

Seated at this table, peeling potatoes, was Mrs. Pengallon, who had been cook-housekeeper at the farm since the death of Mrs. Pengaster, a large comfortable-looking woman who at the moment seemed unusually melancholy. Hetty was in the kitchen, ironing a blouse.

"Well," said Hetty as we entered, "bless me if it ain't Kerensa Carlee. My dear life, we be honored. Come in. That's if you bain't too grand for the likes of we."

"Get along with 'ee," put in Mrs. Pengallon. "Tis only Kerensa Carlee. Come in, m'dear, and tell me if you've seen my Tabs about."

115

"You've lost your cat then, Mrs. Pengallon?" I asked, ignoring Hetty.

"These last two days, m'dear. Tis so unlike him. Out all day he's been before now, but always home come suppertime . . . always purring for his saucer of milk."

"I'm sorry. I haven't seen him."

"I'm worrit like, wondering what can have become of him. I can't but think he be caught in some trap like. Tis a terrible thing to have happened, m'dear, and I can't get it out of my mind. I've been wondering whether to come along to see your Granny. Maybe she could tell me something. She have done wonders like for Mrs. Toms. Her breathing be that much better and all her did was as your Granny said—took the webs of spiders, rolled 'em into a ball and swallowed 'em. Magic, I do reckon it to be and your Granny's a wonderful woman."

"Yes," I agreed, "she's a wonderful woman."

"And you tell her when you next see her that I've had no more trouble with that stye on my eye since I rubbed Tabs' tail on it as she did say. Oh, my poor little Tabs! Where he be to, I can't think; and it's no rest for me till he be found."

"Perhaps he's being fed somewhere else, Mrs. Pengallon," I suggested.

"I don't think so, m'dear. He knows his own home. He'd never stay away so long. Regular home lover, that's my Tabs. Oh my dear life, if he'd only come back to me!"

"I'll keep my eyes open," I told her.

"And ask your Granny if she can help me."

"Well, Mrs. Pengallon, I'm not going back there just now."

"Oh no," put in Hetty maliciously. "You be working up at the Abbas now, along of Doll and Daisy. Doll's pretty near courting our Tom, so she tells us all about it. My dear life, I wouldn't care to work for that family."

"I don't think it likely that you'll have the opportunity," I retorted.

Reuben, who had been standing watching us closely as we talked, joined in Hetty's laughter.

I said coldly: "I came to bring your herbs."

Hetty seized on them and thrust them into the pocket of her gown, and I turned to go.

"And don't 'ee forget to ask your Granny," said Mrs. Pengallon. "I don't rest o' nights wondering what have happened to my Tabs."

It was then that I intercepted the look between Hetty and Reuben. I was startled because it seemed to me . . . evil.

116

They were sharing some secret, and I fancied that while it was amusing to them it would not be so to others.

I had a great desire then to get out of the Pengaster kitchen.

I was too immersed in my own affairs to notice what was happening to Mellyora. I would often hear raised voices in the rooms near my own and I guessed that Judith was upbraiding her husband for some supposed negligence; these scenes were becoming a little monotonous and although I did not dislike my mistress, my sympathy—if my feeling went deep enough to be given such a description—was for Justin, even though he scarcely ever addressed me, and the only time he seemed conscious of my presence was when Judith embarrassed him by her excessive shows of affection. I did not believe he cared greatly for his wife and I could well imagine how tiresome it must be to have someone continually demanding affection.

Still, it was a state of affairs which I accepted and did not notice the rising tension, nor the effect it was having on the three people concerned: Justin, Judith and . . . Mellyora. Being so self-centered, I forgot temporarily that Mellyora's life could take as dramatic a turn as my own.

Two things happened which seemed of great importance. The first was my casual discovery of what had happened to Mrs. Pengallon's cat. It was Doll who betrayed the information. She asked me if Granny would make some complexion herbs for her like those she had given Hetty Pengaster. I said that I knew what they were and next time I went to see Granny I would bring some for her, and happened to mention that when I delivered Hetty's, Mrs. Pengallon was worried about her cat.

Doll started to giggle. " 'Er won't never see that cat again," she said.

"I expect he's found a new home."

"Yes, underground!"

I looked at Doll questioningly and she shrugged her shoulders. "Oh, twas Reuben killed him. I was there when he done it. Proper wild he were. The old cat got one of his pigeons . . . and *he* got the old cat. Killed it he did with his bare hands."

"And now he daren't tell Mrs. Pengallon!"

"Reuben says it serves her right. She knew the old cat was after his pigeons. You know the pigeon loft and house? There be a little square garden behind it, and he buried the

117

pigeon there . . . and the cat too. One the martyr, he did say. One the murderer. He were real mazed that day, I do declare."

I changed the subject but I did not forget; and that day I went to see Granny, and told her about the cat and what I had discovered. "He's buried at the back of the pigeon house," I told her. "So if Mrs. Pengallon asks you, you'll know."

Granny was pleased. She talked to me then of her reputation as a wise woman, and explained the importance of noticing everything that happened. No little detail in life should be ignored; because one never knew when it would be needed.

I did not take Doll's herbs with me on that occasion because I did not want her to think I had seen Granny; and the very next day Mrs. Pengallon called on Granny, begging her to use her magic and find the cat.

Granny was able to direct her to the little garden behind Reuben's pigeon house and when Mrs. Pengallon saw the recently disturbed ground and found the body of her beloved cat, she was filled with rage against his killer and grief for the loss of her pet. But when these emotions subsided a little, she was overwhelmed by admiration for Granny's skill; and for a few days the main topic in the cottages was the power of Granny Bee.

Gifts began to arrive on her doorstep and there was a real feast in the cottage. I went to see her and we laughed together over what had happened. I believed I had the wisest Granny in the world and I was determined to be like her.

I took back Doll's herbs and so great was her belief in them that they were completely effective and the spots on her back, for which she needed them, completely disappeared.

Granny was possessed of supernatural powers. Granny was aware of events which she could not possibly have witnessed; she could cure ailments. She was a person to be reckoned with; and as everyone knew how she doted on me, I must be treated with especial care.

And the fact that we ourselves had brought about this state, by turning a little good fortune to advantage, was doubly gratifying.

My dream of achieving all that I had set out to do was back with me. I believed that I could not fail.

We were seated at the table having supper. It had been an

exhausting day. Judith had been riding with Justin and they had set off in the early morning, she looking charming in her pearl-gray habit with the little touch of emerald green at the throat. When she was happy she looked very beautiful and she was contented on that day because Justin was with her. But I knew that she could not be contented for long; always she was watchful and some small gesture, some inflection of Justin's voice could set her wondering if he were growing tired of her. Then the trouble would start; she would ask interminable questions; she would demand passionately whether he loved her still, how much he loved her. I had heard her raised voice and his low one. The more intense she grew, the more remote he was. I did not think he handled her as well as he might; I believed he was aware of this, for sometimes I saw the relief in his face when she left a room.

But that morning they had set off in good spirits, and I was delighted because this meant that I would have some time to myself. I would go and see Granny; it was useless to hope for a little time with Mellyora, because Lady St. Larnston saw that she was kept busy all the day through. Poor Mellyora! My lot was easier than hers; yet at times I thought she looked supremely happy—at others I was not sure. But one thing I did know; she was growing more beautiful since we had come to the Abbas.

I spent the morning with Granny and in the early afternoon Judith came back alone. She was distraught, so much so that she confided in me—I suppose because she felt the need to talk to someone.

She and Justin had ridden over to her family for luncheon. Afterwards they had left together and, and. . . . She paused and I guessed that they had quarreled. I pictured them having luncheon in the gloomy house; perhaps her mother was there, a little vague—and they would be wondering all the time what she would do next. That house was full of shadows and the legend of the monster would be hanging over it. I imagined Justin wishing he had never married her, perhaps wondering why he ever had. I pictured him making some remark which upset her—then the passionate demands for him to show his affection, and the quarrels.

They would have left Derrise together and he angrily would whip up his horse and ride away from her—anything to escape; and she would weep. I could see she had been weeping. Too late she would try to follow him, would realize that she had lost him, and then begin to wonder where he was.

She had come back to the Abbas to find him and when he was not there she was overcome by jealous anxiety.

I was mending one of her gowns when she burst in on me.

"Kerensa," she said, for she had guessed that I objected to being called by my surname and this was one of the charms about her that she had a wish to please everybody, providing doing so made no great demands upon her. "Where is the companion?"

"Miss Martin?" I stammered.

"Of course. Of course. Where is she? Find her . . . at once."

"You wish to speak to her?"

"Speak to her. No. I wish to know if she is here."

I understood. I wondered fleetingly if Justin might be with Mellyora. What a calm and pleasant companion Mellyora would seem after this demanding, passionate woman. In that moment it did occur to me that a dangerous situation was arising—not for me, except that whatever touched Mellyora must touch me too, for our lives had become intermingled. I might have brooded on this—but for what was soon to follow and which affected me more personally.

I said quietly that I would see if I could find Mellyora. I took my mistress back to her room and made her lie down on her bed and left her.

It did not take me long to find Mellyora; she was in the garden with Lady St. Larnston who was picking roses. Mellyora walked beside her carrying the basket and the clippers. I could hear Lady St. Larnston's imperious orders and Mellyora's meek responses.

So I was able to go back to my mistress and tell her that Mellyora was in the garden with her employer.

Judith relaxed but she was exhausted. I was rather alarmed because I thought she was going to be ill. Her head ached, she told me, and I massaged her forehead and rubbed in eau de Cologne. I drew the curtains and left her to sleep but she did not rest for more than ten minutes before she needed me again.

I had to brush her long hair which, she said, soothed her, and every time we heard a movement below she would rush to the window hoping, I knew, that it was Justin returned.

This was a situation which could not go on. Something must happen sooner or later to change it. It was like the gathering of a storm; and it was natural that storms should break. I was beginning to be a little uneasy about Mellyora.

And that was how I was feeling when I went down to the hall to take supper with my fellow servants. I was tired because Judith's emotions had in some measure been communicated to me and Mellyora was a great deal in my thoughts.

I knew as soon as I sat down that Mrs. Rolt had some news which she was longing to tell us; but it was typical of her that she held back the titbit for as long as possible. When she was eating she would always leave the best pieces on her plate until the end and it amused me to watch her eying them with anticipation while she ate. That was how she looked now.

Mrs. Salt was talking in her low monotonous voice about her husband, and her daughter Jane was the only one who was really paying attention. Doll kept patting her hair in which she had tied a new blue ribbon and she was whispering to Daisy that Tom Pengaster had given it to her. Haggety sat down next to me, bringing his chair a fraction closer. He breathed onto my face and said: "Bit of trouble in high places today, eh, m'dear?"

"Trouble?" I asked.

"Him and her, of course."

Mrs. Rolt was watching us, her lips pursed, her eyes disapproving. She was telling herself that I was leading poor Mr. Haggety on; such a belief suited her better than the true one and she was a woman who would always delude herself into believing what she wanted to. And while she watched us she was smiling slyly, thinking of that titbit of news with which she was planning to startle us.

I did not answer Mr. Haggety because I disliked discussing Judith and Justin in the kitchen quarters.

"Ha," went on Haggety. "She comes in, in a rare paddy. I saw her."

"Well," put in Mrs. Rolt portentously, "it do go to show that money bain't everything."

Haggety sighed piously. "We'm a lot to be thankful, I'm thinking."

"Trouble comes to all sorts," went on Mrs. Rolt, giving me a clue to the news she was withholding, "be they gentry or the likes of we."

"You never spoke a truer word, me dear," sighed Haggety.

Mrs. Salt started to cut the great pasty which she had made that morning and Mrs. Rolt signed to Daisy to fill the mugs with ale.

"I reckon there's trouble coming," said Mrs. Salt. "And if

121

anyone knows trouble when they see it coming, that's me. Why I remember. . . ."

But Mrs. Rolt wasn't going to let the cook ramble back to her reminiscences. "It's what you might call a one-sided relationship, and them sort ain't good for nobody, if you were to ask me."

Haggety nodded in agreement and turned his rather bulging eyes on Mrs. Rolt while his foot touched mine under the table.

"Mind you," went on Mrs. Rolt, whose pleasure it was always to feign great knowledge of relationships between the sexes, "one thing, I'd say. Mr. Justin bain't the man to get himself into *that* sort of trouble."

"With another woman, you mean, me dear?" asked Haggety.

"That is exactly what I did mean, Mr. Haggety. That's the trouble if you ask me. One blowing hot and one blowing cold. Twould seem he don't want one woman, let be two."

"They're a wild family," put in Mr. Trelance. "I had a brother who worked over at Derrise."

"We do all know that story," Mrs. Rolt silenced him.

"And they say," put in Doll excitedly, "that last time when the moon was full . . ."

"That'll do, Doll," said Mrs. Rolt who would not allow the lower servants to discuss the family, it being a privilege of the higher ones to do that.

"I remember once," said Mrs. Trelance dreamily, "seeing that Miss Martin over here . . . that were when her father were alive. A real pretty creature. She were on her horse and Mr. Justin were helping her off it . . . and I said to Trelance here, I said, 'There's a pretty picture for you'; and Trelance he said that if parson's daughter were the mistress of Abbas one day we couldn't have a prettier nor a sweeter."

Mrs. Rolt turned an angry glance on Mrs. Trelance. "Well, her be the companion now and who ever heard of companions being the mistress."

"Well, she couldn't now . . . him being married," said Mrs. Salt. "Though men being men. . . ." She shook her head and there was a silence round the table.

Mrs. Rolt said sharply, "Mr. Justin bain't men, Mrs. Salt. And it ain't no good you're thinking all men is like that man of yours because I can tell you different." She smiled secretly and then went on in a voice portentous with promise. "And talk about trouble . . ."

We were all silent waiting for her to go on. She had come to the titbit; she had all our attention, and she was ready.

"Her ladyship sent for me this afternoon. She wanted me to see that a certain person's room be made ready. She weren't very pleased, I can tell 'ee. There have been terrible trouble. As soon as Mr. Justin come in, she sends for him. I was to watch out, she said, and the minute he come in he was to go to her. So I watched and I saw him come in. She was down there . . . Mrs. Justin . . . all tears and clinging to him. 'Oh, darling . . . darling . . . where have you been . . .?' "

There was a titter round the table but Mrs. Rolt was eager now to get on.

"I stopped all that. 'Her ladyship wants you to go to her at once, Mr. Justin,' I said. 'Her ladyship's orders that there shouldn't be any delay.' So he looks pleased like . . . anything to get away from her with her darling . . . darling . . . and he goes straight up to her ladyship. Now I knew what had happened because she'd told me, though she didn't tell me why, but as I was polishing in the corridor outside her ladyship's room I happened to hear her say: 'It's on account of some woman. This is *such* a disgrace. I thank God his poor father can't understand. If he could, it would kill him.' I says to myself trouble comes, be we gentry or the likes of we and it be true."

She paused and lifting her mug of ale to her lips drank, smacked her lips and regarded us triumphantly. "Mr. Johnny be coming home. They've sent him home. They don't want him there no more since he have disgraced himself over this woman."

I stared down at my plate; I did not want any of them to notice the effect those words had had on me.

Johnny's presence in the house changed it for me. I was aware that he was determined to be my lover and the fact that he now found me installed as a servant in the house amused and delighted him.

The very first day he returned he sought me out. I was sitting in my room reading when he walked in. I stood up angrily because he had not asked permission to enter.

"Well met, fair maid," he said, bowing ironically.

"Will you please knock if you want me?"

"Is it the custom?"

"It is what I expect."

"You will always expect more than you receive, Miss . . . Carlyon."

"My name is Kerensa Carlee."

"I shall never forget it, although you did adopt Carlyon on one occasion. You've grown beautiful, my dear."

"What did you want of me?"

His smile was mocking. "Everything," he retorted. "Just everything."

"I am maid to your sister-in-law."

"I know all about that. That's why I came down from Oxford. The news reached me, you see."

"I have an idea that it was for a very different reason that you came back."

"Of course you have! Servants listen at doors. And I'll swear there was some consternation when the news was brought."

"I do not listen at doors. But knowing you and knowing why young men are usually sent down . . ."

"So knowledgeable you have become. I remember a time. . . . But why hark back? The future promises to be so much more interesting. I'm looking forward to our future, Kerensa."

"I cannot see how yours and mine can have anything in common."

"Can you not. Then you do need educating."

"I am satisfied with my education."

"Never be satisfied, Kerensa, my dear one. It's unwise. Let us begin that education of yours without delay. Like this. . . ."

He was about to seize me but I held him off angrily. He shrugged his shoulders.

"There must be a wooing? Oh, Kerensa, such a waste of time! Don't you think we have wasted too much already?"

I said angrily: "I work here . . . unfortunately. But that does not mean I am your servant. Understand this . . . please."

"Why, Kerensa, don't you know that all I want is to please you."

"Then that is easy. If you will keep out of my way I shall willingly keep out of yours—and that will give me great pleasure."

"What words! What airs and graces! I shouldn't have thought it of you, Kerensa. So I am not to have even a kiss? Well, I shall be here now . . . and so shall you. Under the same roof. Is that not a delightful thought?"

He left me then but there was an ominous look in his eyes. There was no lock on my door, and I was alarmed.

The following evening Justin, Johnny and Lady St. Larnston retired to her ladyship's sitting room after dinner and there was a great deal of serious conversation. Haggety, who had served wine there, told us in the kitchen that Mr. Johnny was being put through his paces and they were seriously discussing his future. All were very concerned, it seemed, except Johnny.

I was putting Judith's clothes away when she came up. I brushed her hair as she commanded. It soothed her. She said I had magic in my fingers. I had discovered that I had a gift for hairdressing. It was my most successful accomplishment as a lady's maid. I tried different styles on her hair and sometimes I would copy them with my own. This delighted Judith and because she was generous by nature she often gave me some little gift and tried to please me, when she remembered it; but chiefly her thoughts were concerned with her husband.

Preparing her for bed was a ritual and this night there was an air of satisfaction about her. "You are aware of the trouble with Mr. Johnny, Kerensa," she said.

"Yes, Madam. I have heard it."

She shrugged her shoulders. "It's unfortunate. Inevitable though. He is not like . . . his brother."

"No, Madam. Two brothers could not be less alike."

She smiled; more at peace than I had ever seen her before.

I braided her hair and wound it round her head. She looked lovely in her flowing negligee.

"You are very beautiful tonight, Madam," I told her, because I felt a need to comfort her—perhaps after what I had heard in the kitchen.

"Thank you, Kerensa," she said.

Soon after that she dismissed me, saying she would want me no more that night.

I went along to Mellyora's room, and found her sitting by the window looking out on the moonlit garden. Her tray—symbol of her lonely life—was on a nearby table.

"So you are free for once," I said.

"Not for long." She grimaced. "I have to go along and sit with Sir Justin in a few minutes."

"They work you too hard."

"Oh, I don't mind it."

She looked radiant. The look, I thought, of a woman in love. Oh, Mellyora, I thought, you'd be very vulnerable, I'm afraid.

She went on: "Poor Sir Justin. It is dreadful to see him as he is and think of what he was. I remember Papa. . . ."

"It's unfair that you should have to help nurse him too," I said.

"It might be worse."

Yes, I thought. You might be a drudge in a house where there was no Justin. That's what you mean, isn't it?

Then I asked myself what had happened to my relationship with Mellyora. Once I should have said to her the things I was now thinking.

It was not that we had changed. It was just that this dangerous situation was too delicate a matter, too important to Mellyora for her to wish to discuss it or take advice, even from me.

"And now," I said, changing the subject. "Johnny is back."

"Oh . . . Johnny! It's not entirely unexpected. Johnny will always be Johnny."

She was almost smug. How different was Justin, she was implying. Then I thought of Judith who had said almost the same. Two women—both in love with the same man—deeply and passionately; for although Mellyora was calm and Judith was far from calm, both were the victims of a deep emotion.

"I wish he had not come back home," I said.

"You are afraid of him?"

"Not exactly afraid, but he can be a nuisance. Oh, never fear, I shall know how to handle him."

"I am sure you will." She turned to look out of the window and I knew that she was not thinking of Johnny and me because her thoughts were all for Justin, and it would be like that in the future. She was obsessed by her love even as Judith was; fortunately for Mellyora hers was a more balanced nature.

Some bond had snapped between us, for as her emotion deepened for one person so there became less time in her life for others.

I asked her then if she ever heard from Kim; she was startled and for a few seconds seemed as though it were an effort to remember him.

"Kim . . . oh no. He wouldn't write. He always said he was no letter writer, but that he would come back one day."

"You think he will?"

"Of course. He was certain of it. It was a sort of promise and Kim always keeps promises."

I felt great pleasure. I pictured him coming back to St. Larnston, walking into the Abbas one day. I could imagine his voice, 'Why, Kerensa, you've become a fascinating young lady.' And when he saw Mellyora, obsessed by Justin, he would become more my friend than hers. I was certain that you could make life go the way you wanted it, but was it possible to bring the people you wanted back to you? I must ask Granny.

Mellyora said that it was time she went to Sir Justin, so I left her and returned to my room. I stood at the window for some time, thinking of Kim and the night of the ball. Then I went to my mirror and lighted the candles there. Had I changed much since that night? I had become older, wiser, more accomplished. I had read a great deal. I was making myself worthy . . . of Kim? No. Of the person I intended to be.

I took the pins out of my hair and shook it about my shoulders. Thick, luxuriant, it was more beautiful than Judith's. Deftly I began to coil it high on my head. Where was my Spanish comb? Where was my mantilla? I adjusted them and stood enraptured by my own reflection. Narcissus! I mocked. In love with yourself.

I went to the window. Out there were the ring of stones that never seemed to be far from my thoughts. I had always promised myself a visit by moonlight. Why not? I was free. I believed Johnny was closeted with his brother, and there was no danger of his being around. Now was the time.

I was soon there. How exciting they seemed by moonlight. Alive! The Six Virgins! And I made a seventh. Did it really happen as the legend said? Did they in truth dance here? Were they struck down in their defiance and turned to stone, to stand on this spot as the centuries passed? How fortunate they were! Sudden death was preferable to a lingering one. I thought of the seventh—the one who had been dragged to the hollow wall, the one who was shut in to die; and I was filled with a momentary melancholy.

Footsteps! The sound of a low whistle. I leaned against one of the stones, waiting, some instinct telling me who had followed me here.

"So the seventh is here tonight?"

I felt furious with myself for coming. Johnny had seen me leave the house after all. In that moment I hated him.

He had stepped into the circle of stones and was grinning at me.

"Miss Carlyon in person!" he cried. "The Spanish lady."

"Is there any reason why I should not dress my hair as I wish?"

"There's every reason why you should since it so becomes you."

"I wish you would not follow me."

"Follow you? But why should I not visit the Virgins if I wish? They are not exclusively yours, are they?"

"Since you have come to see the Virgins, I will leave you."

"There's no hurry. I prefer the seventh to all the six put together. Ladies of stone are not to my fancy. Yet the seventh would have me believe she is composed of the same unyielding material. I'm going to prove to her that she is not."

"Is it impossible for you to believe that I do not want your advances?"

"Quite impossible."

"Then you are more arrogant than I imagined."

"I'll tell you something, my Spanish lady. You would not reject my advances in some circumstances."

"I don't understand you."

"You have always had a mighty high opinion of yourself. If I said to you, 'Kerensa, will you marry me?' you would consider my proposal very seriously and I'll warrant it wouldn't take you long to recognize its merits. It is merely because you think I would treat you like any serving girl that you are so haughty."

I caught my breath for his words had conjured up a picture of myself living at the Abbas as I had always longed to. It had seemed an impossibility but if I married Johnny my dream would come true. With a shock I realized that this was the only way in which it could. But almost immediately I knew that he was teasing me.

I said haughtily: "I do not wish to listen to any suggestions you make."

He laughed. "Only because you know that the one you want to hear is the one I should never offer."

I turned away and he caught my arm. "Kerensa . . ." he began. He put his face close to mine and the blaze of desire in his eyes alarmed me. I tried not to show my fear by slapping off his arm; but he would not release me; he kept his face close to mine, grinning at me. "I," he said, "can be as determined as you."

"You don't know how determined I can be when it is a matter of ridding myself of you."

"Then," he said, "we shall see, shall we not?"

In spite of my efforts I could not free myself. He caught me to him and I felt his teeth against mine. I kept mine firmly clenched and I hated him. I hated him so fiercely that I found a certain pleasure in my hatred. In that moment Johnny St. Larnston aroused an emotion in me that I had never felt before. It was not without desire. Perhaps, I thought later when I was alone and trying to analyze my feelings, the desire I felt was for a house, for a different station of life than that into which I had been born, for a fulfillment of a dream. My desire for these things was so fierce that perhaps another kind of desire could be aroused by anyone who could give me them; and Johnny's words about marriage had put an idea into my mind.

One thing I was sure of; he must not guess for one moment that he aroused anything in me but contempt and a longing to be rid of him.

Holding myself away from him, I said: "You had better be careful. I shall complain if you attempt to persecute me and in view of your reputation I do not think I shall be disbelieved."

I knew then that he had been aware of some change in my feelings and that he was expecting me to give way; thus I took him off his guard and with a little push as I had on another occasion, I freed myself. I turned and walked haughtily towards the house.

When I reached my room I looked in the mirror.

Is it possible? I asked myself. Would Johnny St. Larnston consider marrying me? And if he did, would I accept?

I was trembling. With hope? With fear? With pleasure? With repulsion?

I was not sure which.

My room was touched by moonlight. I sat up with a start. Something had awakened me.

I was in danger. An extra sense seemed to be telling me this. I stared in dismay, for someone was in my room. I saw the outline of a figure seated in an armchair, watching me.

I gave a stifled cry, for the figure had moved. I thought, I have always thought the Abbas was haunted. Now I know.

I heard a low laugh and then I knew that my visitor was Johnny, as I should have guessed.

"You!" I cried. "How dare you!"

He sat on the edge of my bed looking at me.

"I'm very daring, Kerensa, particularly where you're concerned."

"You had better go . . . without delay."

"Oh no. Don't you think I'd better stay?"

I sprang out of bed. He stood up but did not come towards me. He merely stood staring at me.

"I always wondered how you wore your hair at night. Two long plaits. Most demure! I should like to see it loose though."

"If you do not leave at once I shall shout for help."

"I shouldn't do that, Kerensa, if I were you."

"You are not me, and I tell you, I shall."

"Why cannot you be reasonable?"

"Why cannot you behave like a gentleman?"

"To you . . . who are scarcely a lady?"

"I hate you, Johnny St. Larnston."

"Now that sounded like the little girl from the cottages. But I'd rather you hated me than were indifferent."

"I have no feelings for you . . . none at all."

"You have no feeling for the truth. You know you hate me and you're longing for me to make love to you, but you feel that the lady you are trying to become should insist on marriage before entertaining a lover."

I ran to the door and flung it open. I said: "I will give you ten seconds, Johnny St. Larnston. If you are not outside by then, and if you attempt to touch me, I shall scream to wake your brother and his wife."

He could see I meant what I said, and was temporarily defeated. He walked past me and into the corridor; his eyes were angry and malevolent. I was horrified because I realized that he really believed I would have become his mistress that night.

I went into my room and shut my door. I leaned against it, trembling. How, I asked myself, was I going to rest in peace, knowing that at any hour of the night he could walk into my room?

I could not go back to bed. I went to the window and looked out. The moonlight showed me the lawn and beyond it the meadow with the ring of stones.

I stood there for some time. I heard a clock strike midnight. And then I saw Johnny. He was walking purposefully

130

away from the house. I stood still watching him as he skirted the field and took the road towards the village. It led also to Larnston Barton.

Some instinct told me that, having failed with me, Johnny was going to Hetty Pengaster.

I crept along the corridor to Mellyora's room and knocked gently on the door. There was no reply so I went in. Mellyora was asleep.

I stood for a few seconds looking down at her. So beautiful and innocent she looked, lying there. Mellyora, too, I thought, was defenseless in this house. But Justin would never come uninvited into her room. Even so, Mellyora was more vulnerable than I.

"Mellyora," I whispered. "Don't be alarmed. It is I . . . Kerensa."

"Kerensa!" She started up alarmed. "Whatever is wrong?"

"It's all right now. But I don't want to go back to my room."

"What do you mean? Something's wrong?"

"Johnny came in. I don't feel safe when he can come walking in when he likes."

"Johnny!" she said contemptuously.

I nodded. "He is trying to seduce me, and I'm afraid of him. . . ."

"Oh . . . Kerensa!"

"Don't be alarmed. I only want to come in with you."

She moved over and I slipped into the bed.

"You're shivering," she said.

"It was rather horrible."

"You don't think . . . you ought to go away?"

"Away from the Abbas? Where to?"

"I don't know . . . somewhere."

"To work in some other house, to be at the beck and call of someone else?"

"Perhaps, Kerensa, it would be best for us both."

It was the first time she had admitted her own difficulties, and I was afraid. In that moment I was certain I would never willingly leave the Abbas.

"I can manage Johnny," I said.

"But this latest affair. . . ."

"Will make everyone understand whose fault it is if I should have to tell on him."

"Kerensa, you're so strong."

131

"I've had to look after myself all my life. You had your father to look after you. Don't worry about *me*, Mellyora."

She was silent for a while. Then she said, "Perhaps for us both, Kerensa. . . ."

"We couldn't 'go farther and fare worse,' " I quoted.

I felt the relief in the little sigh she gave.

"Where would we find posts together?" she asked.

"Ah, where?"

"And St. Larnston is, after all, home to us."

We were silent for a while. Then I said: "May I share your room in future, while he is here?"

"You know you may."

"Then," I said, "there'll be nothing for *me* to fear."

It was a long time before either of us slept.

Judith knew, of course, that I was sleeping in Mellyora's room and when I hinted at the reason made no objection.

During the weeks that followed, Mellyora and I grew close again, for sharing a room meant sharing confidences, and our relationship was more as it had been in the parsonage than it had been since we came to the Abbas and her feeling for Justin had set us a little apart.

I received a letter from David Killigrew during that time. He thought of me constantly, he wrote; his mother was as strong as ever physically, but growing a little more forgetful every day; he was kept busy but he saw no hope of getting a living which, he implied, he must do before asking me to marry him.

I could scarcely remember what he looked like. I felt guilty because he was so earnest and at one time I had contemplated marrying him as now, deep down in my heart I was contemplating marrying Johnny St. Larnston.

What sort of a woman was I, I asked myself, who was ready to turn this way and that for the sake of expediency?

I tried to make excuses for myself. I had fabricated a dream; and the fulfillment of that dream was the most important thing in my life. I wanted a position for myself that I might suffer no more humiliation; I wanted to give Granny comfort in her old age; I wanted to make a doctor of Joe. It was ironical that Johnny, whom I told myself I hated, was the only one who held the key to all that. It was a key he would be reluctant to relinquish; but perhaps if he were hard pushed . . . ?

Johnny was watching me with smoldering eyes. He was eager for me as he ever was, and yet he made no move. I suspected that he had been to my room and found it empty.

He would guess where I was, but he dared not come to Mellyora's.

I continued to hear Judith's raised voice in the apartments she shared with Justin; and I knew that she was growing more and more restless.

As for Mellyora, she seemed to be living in a state of exultation. I believed I knew why, because I had seen her and Justin together one day from my window. They had met accidentally and exchanged only a word; but I watched him look after her as she passed; I saw her turn to look at him, and for a few seconds they stood still, gazing at one another.

They had betrayed themselves. Judith's suspicions had some foundation.

They loved each other; and they had admitted it, if not in words, by a look.

We were seated at the table when the clanging of the bell from Sir Justin's room started up. For a few seconds we stared at each other, then Haggety, followed by Mrs. Rolt, hurried upstairs.

We all looked at each other, for the bell went on clanging until they reached the room, and we knew that this was no ordinary call.

In a few moments Haggety returned to the kitchen. Polore was to go at once for Dr. Hilliard.

When he had gone we sat at the table but we did not eat.

Mrs. Salt said mournfully: "This'll be the end, you see. And if you were to ask me it'll be a happy release."

Dr. Hilliard was fortunately at home and within half an hour he came back with Polore. He spent a long time in Sir Justin's room.

A tension had fallen on the house; everyone spoke in whispers, and when Dr. Hilliard left, Haggety told us that Sir Justin had had another stroke. He was still alive but, in his opinion, he wouldn't last the night.

I went up to Judith to prepare her night things; I found her quieter than usual; she told me that Justin was with his father; the whole family were there.

"This is not entirely unexpected, Madam," I said.

She shook her head. "It had to happen sooner or later."

"And is it . . . the end, Madam?"

"Who can say? He is not dead yet."

Soon, I thought, she will be Lady St. Larnston and Justin will be the head of the house. It would make no difference to me. But Mellyora? I believed Justin hated to see his mother bullying Mellyora. When he was Sir Justin what would he do to prevent it? Would he betray his feelings?

Life never remains stationary, I thought. A little change here, a little change there . . . and what was safe and normal becomes no longer so. I thought of the seventh virgin of the legend who had meditated not far from where I was standing, who had taken her vows and no doubt believed she would live the rest of her life in peaceful security. Then she loved and she submitted to love; and the result was lingering death in the convent wall.

Dr. Hilliard came twice a day and each morning we believed that Sir Justin would be dead before the day was over. But for a week he lingered on.

Mellyora was constantly in attendance. She was excused her duties of reading and flower gathering. I went back to my own room for she was needed in the sickroom, and since I was alone there was no point in being in hers.

She had little rest during those six days, but she did not seem to need it. She had lost a little weight which was rather becoming, and there was a shine about her. I, who knew her so well, understood that just for a while she was content to bask in the knowledge that Justin loved her.

Perhaps, I thought, they could go on like that for the rest of their lives. Theirs would be a relationship of ideals, unsullied by any physical need. Justin would never be a passionate man and Mellyora would be ready to adapt herself to his ways. It would be a sublimated love; they would be kept apart always by the flaming sword of propriety and convention.

What a contrast was this profane attraction which Johnny had for me and I, perhaps, for him.

Sir Justin was dead, and there was a lightening of the atmosphere as preparations for the funeral began. At all the windows blinds were drawn; we moved about the house in somber gloom. There was no real sadness though, for no one had loved Sir Justin and his death had been expected for so long.

It was a question of: "Sir Justin is dead. Long live Sir Justin." The servants slipped naturally into the new form of address. Judith had become "my lady," and almost imperceptibly the Dowager Lady St. Larnston moved slightly into the background.

Everyone attached to the house wore black crape bands

about their arms—for "respect," said Mrs. Rolt. A collection was made in the kitchens, to which both Mellyora and myself were invited to add our share and there was great excitement when the wreath arrived—"The Gates of Heaven Ajar," which had been Mrs. Rolt's choice.

When I asked if they thought Sir Justin would go to Heaven, since, from what I had heard, his life had not been exemplary, I was regarded by shocked eyes and Doll gave a little squeal as she looked over her shoulder, half expecting, she explained, Sir Justin's shade to come into the kitchen and strike me dead with the copper stick which Daisy had brought in from the washhouse and had forgotten to take back.

Didn't I know that it was dangerous to speak ill of the dead? Didn't I know that the dead were sanctified? No matter if Sir Justin had taken unwilling maidens; no matter if he had sent men, women and young children to the hulks or transportation for no greater sin than trespassing on his estates; he was dead now and therefore a saint.

I felt impatient with them; nor was I afraid of the ghost of Sir Justin. But it was no use trying to explain.

The black mutes had done their duty; the velvet-caparisoned horses had carried their sacred burden away and the funeral was over.

I was no longer afraid of Johnny. In fact I was rather eager for more encounters with him. I had been to see Granny while Sir Justin was so ill and I had talked to her about Johnny.

She was very thoughtful; then she said: "The fact that he talked of marriage would seem to show that he had it in his mind."

"Only," I replied, "as something which could not possibly take place."

Granny shook her head and regarded me fondly. "Why, Kerensa," she said, "I'd be ready to swear that if you were dressed up like a lady and taken where no one knew you, they'd think you were one."

I knew it was true for I had worked with all my strength towards this end. It was the first and essential step.

"Granny," I said, "he would never marry me. His mother would never allow it. Nor would his brother."

I narrowed my eyes, thinking of Justin who would be from now on the head of the house. He had a secret—his love for Mellyora. But was it a secret? Wasn't it already suspected in

135

the servants' hall? Still, he was vulnerable; and, with such a secret, was he in a position to harm me?

"So you think now, my love. But who's to say what the future holds? Who'd have thought you'd ever read and write and talk like one of they?"

"Who'd have thought it!" I echoed. Then I seized her hand: "Granny," I said, "could you give me some potion . . ."

She snatched her hand away, laughing with mockery. "And I thought you be educated! Have you forgotten that I did tell 'ee? The future is for you to make. You can have what you want . . . if you're ready to pay the price for it. Everyone can. But you must never forget that the price has to be paid and it's sometimes more than you've bargained for, Kerensa!" She was very serious. "Listen to what I be saying. And don't 'ee forget it."

I lay on Mellyora's bed. When the house was quiet I would go back to my own room.

"But do you want to, Kerensa?" she had said. "Do you feel safe?"

"Safe from Johnny!" I was scornful. "Don't worry on my account. I know how to handle Johnny."

She clasped her hands behind her back and looked up at the ceiling. Again I could only describe her expression as exalted.

"Mellyora," I said, "you should tell me."

"Tell you?"

"Something's happened, hasn't it?"

"You know well enough what's happened. There has been a death in this house."

"It was hardly unexpected."

"Death is always a shock, expected or not."

"I would not say that you are shocked."

"No?"

I could see the confidences trembling on her lips. She wanted to tell me; but this was not her secret alone. I was determined that she should tell me. I seemed to hear Granny's voice in my ear: It is important to learn everything. . . ."

"You can't deceive me, Mellyora. Something *has* happened."

She turned to look at me and I saw that she was startled. She reminded me of a dainty gazelle who has heard a rustle in the undergrowth and while wanting to satisfy curiosity knows it is wiser to run away.

But she was not going to run away from me.

"And," I went on firmly, "it has something to do with Justin."

"Sir Justin," she said softly.

"He is Sir Justin now, I agree, and head of the house."

"How different he will be from his father! The tenants will love him. He will be kind and as just as his name implies. . . ."

I made an impatient gesture. I did not want a eulogy of the new Sir Justin.

"He will be perfect in every way," I said, "except that he has been foolish enough to marry the wrong woman."

"Kerensa, what are you saying?"

"You heard me perfectly and I am only saying what has been in your thoughts for a long time—and perhaps his, too."

"You must never say that to anyone else, Kerensa."

"As if I should. This is between us two. You know that I would always be on your side, Mellyora. You are close to me . . . we're as close as sisters . . . no, closer because I shall never forget that you took me from the hiring stand and made me as your sister . . . in a way you made me what I am, Mellyora. The bond between us is stronger than a blood tie, even."

She turned to me suddenly and threw herself against me; I held her tightly while her body heaved with silent sobs.

"You should tell me," I said. "You know that everything that happens to you is my concern. You love Justin . . . Sir Justin. I have known it a long time."

"How could anyone help loving such a man, Kerensa?"

"Well, I manage very well, which is fortunate. It would not do for everyone to be in love with him. I have known for a long time what your feelings were . . . but what of his?"

She withdrew herself and lifted her face to mine. "He loves me, Kerensa. He thinks he has always loved me. Only he did not know . . . until it was too late."

"He has told you this?"

"He would not have done so. But it was when we were both sitting by his father's bedside. It was after midnight. The house was so quiet and there was a moment when it was impossible to hide the truth."

"If he always loved you, why did he marry Judith?" I demanded.

137

"You see, Kerensa, he looked upon me as a child. He seemed so much older, and because when he knew me first I was only a child, he went on thinking of me as one. And then there was Judith."

"Ah, Judith! He married her, you know."

"He didn't want to, Kerensa. It was against his will."

"And what sort of man is he to marry against his will?"

"You don't understand. It is because he is good and kind that he married her."

I shrugged my shoulders and I could see that she was battling with herself, wondering whether she should tell me. She could not bear my unspoken criticism of Justin, so she decided to.

"His father wanted the marriage before he was ill, but Justin refused because he did not want to marry until he was in love. His father was furious; there were many scenes, and it was during one of these that he had his first stroke. Justin was horrified, you see, because he felt responsible. And when his father was so ill he thought it would help him to recover if he did what he wanted. So he married Judith. He soon knew what a terrible mistake it was."

I was silent. I believed Justin had told her the truth. They were two of a kind, she and Justin. How admirably suited they were. I thought, if she had married Justin, I should have come here in a very different capacity. Oh why hadn't Mellyora married Justin!

I pictured them—one on either side of that dying man who had played such a part in their lives—their whispered confidences, their longings.

"Mellyora," I said, "what are you going to *do?*"

She opened her eyes incredulously. "Do? What can we do? He is married to Judith, is he not?"

I did not speak. I knew that for a while it was enough for her to know he loved her; but how long would she—or he—be content with that?

The blinds were up at all the windows. I felt that everywhere there was a subtle change. Nothing could be quite the same again. Old Lady St. Larnston had talked halfheartedly of going to the Dower House, but when Justin had urged her to remain at the Abbas she had been delighted to do so.

A new Sir Justin. A new Lady St. Larnston. But those were merely names. I saw Justin's eyes follow Mellyora, and I knew that confession of theirs had changed their relationship, however much they believed it had not. How long, I wondered, did they think they could keep their secret from such as Mrs. Rolt, Haggety and Mrs. Salt.

There would soon be more gossip in the kitchens. Perhaps it had already started. And how long before Judith was aware—she, who watched her husband every second he was in her company! Already she suspected that his feelings towards Mellyora were dangerously strong.

This atmosphere was filled with danger . . . tense and quiet, waiting for disaster.

But it was my own affairs which were absorbing me, because Johnny's passion for me was increasing, and the more aloof became, the more determined he was. He never attempted to come to my bedroom again but whenever I went out I would find him walking by my side. Sometimes he cajoled, sometimes he blazed; but his conversation was all on one theme.

Again and again I told him that he was wasting his time; he retorted that I was wasting our time.

"If you are waiting for marriage, you will wait a long time," he said angrily.

"You happen to be right. I am waiting for marriage, but not with you. David Killigrew wants to marry me as soon as he gets a living."

"David Killigrew! So you plan to be a parson's wife! What a joke."

"Your feeling for humor is rather childish, of course. There is nothing funny in this, I assure you. It is a very serious matter."

"Poor Killigrew!" he snorted and left me.

But he was uneasy. I knew then that to possess me had become an obsession with him.

Whenever possible I went to see Granny. There was nothing I enjoyed more than stretching out on the talfat and talking to her as I used to when I was a child. I knew that my affairs were as important to her as they were to me and she was the only person in the world with whom I could be absolutely frank.

We discussed the possibility of a marriage with David Killigrew. Granny shook her head over it. "It would be good, lovey, for some, but I reckon you'd always be a-hankering."

"You're not going to say that Johnny St. Larnston's the man for me?"

"If you married him you'd be marrying a dream, Kerensa."

"And that would not be good?"

"Tis only you can make it good or bad, lovey."

"In that case I could make a marriage with David good or bad?"

She nodded.

Then I went on to tell her about my last encounter with Johnny and from that to talk of life at the Abbas. I never stopped talking of the Abbas. I liked to make her see it as I did—the odd winding staircases and stone cells where the nuns had lived; it was the old part of the Abbas which interested me most; but I loved it all; and when I thought of marriage with David Killigrew I thought of leaving the Abbas and that felt like parting with a lover.

"You're in love with a house," said Granny. "Well, tis safer perhaps to love a house than a man. If it be yours, then tis yours and you need have no fear of its betraying you."

Judith had gone to bed early on account of a headache and had dismissed me for the night. It was nine o'clock and because I had a yearning to see Granny I slipped out of the house and went down to the cottage.

She was sitting smoking her pipe and, as always, was glad to see me. We sat and talked; I told her that Johnny's attitude seemed to be changing and that I could not understand him. He had been a little cool lately and there were times when I thought he was abandoning the chase; yet at others he seemed more determined than ever.

Granny lighted two candles, for the twilight was on us and my conversation, as usual, had turned to the house itself, when I was suddenly startled by a movement at the window. I was just in time to see a dark shape move quickly away. Someone had been looking in at us!

"Granny," I cried. "Someone's outside."

Granny rose rather slowly, for she was no longer nimble, and went to the door.

She turned to me and shook her head. "There's no one there."

"But someone was looking in at us." I followed her to the door and peered into the dimness. "Who's there?" I called.

There was no answer.

"Who could it have been?" I asked. "Who could have

140

stood out there peering in at us? And I wonder for how long?"

"It were likely someone as wanted to see me if I were alone," was Granny's comfortable explanation. "They'll come back . . . that's if they want to see me bad enough."

The uneasy feeling of having been spied on stayed with me; I could not settle down to talk and as it was growing late I realized it was time I went back to the Abbas.

I said good night to Granny and left her. But I kept wondering who it was who had looked through the window and decided not to come in.

I had no opportunity of seeing Granny again until I had made my decision. In a way, I told myself, that was a good thing because it had to be my decision. I had to take it with my eyes wide open; I had to bear the entire responsibility myself.

Judith had been tiresome. I was discovering facets of her character which I had not known before. She had a violent temper which when it was manifested was the more fierce for having been kept in check. I guessed that the future in this house was going to be very stormy. Judith would not tolerate Mellyora's presence in the house much longer.

And when Mellyora went . . . what of me?

However, that was not the concern of the immediate future. Judith had one of her headaches; I must brush her hair; I must massage her forehead. Sometimes I hated the smell of the eau de Cologne she used. It would always remind me of my servitude to this woman.

"How clumsy you are, Carlee." It was a sign of her irritation that she should use my surname. She was deliberately trying to hurt me because she was hurt. "You are pulling my hair. You are useless, useless. Sometimes I wonder why I employ you. When I come to think of it, I did not engage you. You were found for me. What am I in this house . . . ?"

I tried to soothe her. "My lady, you are not feeling well. Perhaps you should rest."

I hated calling her my lady. If Mellyora had been my lady I should have boasted of my friendship with Lady St. Larnston but she would be Mellyora, not my lady, to me.

Mellyora, however, could never be Lady St. Larnston while this woman was alive.

"Don't stand there like a fool. Braid my hair. And don't pull. I warned you before."

She took the brush from me and, as she did, the bristles

tore the skin of one of my fingers, making it bleed. I looked at it in dismay while she flung the brush across the room.

"Oh, you *have* been treated brutally!" she mocked. "And serve you right." Her eyes were wild. I thought: Shall we in a few years' time have Lady St. Larnston going out on the moor to dance when the moon is full?

They were doomed, these Derrises—doomed to madness by a monster. And Judith was one of the doomed.

A bitter anger was in me that night. I hated those who humiliated me, and Judith was humiliating me. I had better take care, she told me. She would get rid of me. She would choose her own maid. She was Lady St. Larnston now and there was no reason why she should be dictated to by any-one.

I suggested she have one of the soothing powders which Dr. Hilliard had prescribed for her and to my surprise she agreed. I gave it to her and the effect—in about ten minutes—was apparent. The storm was passing; docilely she allowed me to get her to bed.

I went back to my room and although it was late I dressed my hair in the Spanish fashion, putting in my comb and mantilla. This always soothed me and had become a habit with me. With my hair thus I would remember the ball and dancing with Kim and how he had told me I was fascinating. At the back of my mind was a dream that Kim came back and was fond of me. By some miracle he was the owner of the Abbas and we married and lived there happy ever after.

As I sat at the window looking out on the moonlight, I felt a desire to go out to the stones but I was tired. I took a book in order to soothe myself by reading, and propped myself up on my bed, fully dressed, because I wanted to leave the comb in my hair; reading never failed to comfort me, it reminded me how far I had come, and that I had achieved what most people would have said was impossible.

I read on and on and it was past midnight when I heard the sound of footsteps creeping to my room.

I sprang off the bed and blew out my candles. I was standing behind the door when Johnny opened it and came in.

This was a different Johnny. I did not know what had changed him, I only knew that I had never seen him like this before. He was quiet, serious; and there was a strange deter-mination about him.

"What do you want?" I demanded.

He lifted a finger, warning me to keep quiet.

"Get out or I shall shout," I told him.

"I want to talk to you. I've got to talk to you."

"I have no desire to talk."

"You've got to listen. You've got to stand by me."

"I don't understand you."

He stood close to me and all the truculence had gone from him; he was like a child, pleading with me; and this was strange with Johnny.

"I'll marry you," he said.

"What!"

"I said I'd marry you."

"What game are you playing?"

He took me by the shoulders and shook me. "You know," he said. "You know. It's the price I'm ready to pay. I tell you I'll marry you."

"And your family?"

"They'll raise hell. But I say: To hell with the family. I'll marry you. I promise."

"I'm not sure that I will marry you."

"Of course you will. It was what you were waiting for. Kerensa, I'm serious . . . never more deadly serious in my life. I don't want to marry. There'll be trouble. But I tell you I'll marry you."

"It's not possible."

"I'm going to Plymouth."

"When?"

"Tonight. . . . No . . . it's already morning. Today, then, I'm catching the first train. I'm leaving at five. Are you coming with me?"

"Why this sudden decision?"

"You know. Why pretend?"

"I think you're mad."

"I've always wanted you. And this is the way. Are you coming with me?"

"I don't trust you."

"We've got to trust each other. I'll marry you. I'll get the special licence. I swear it."

"How do I know . . . ?"

"Look. You know what's happened. We'll be together. Once it's done, it's done. I'll marry you, Kerensa."

"I want time to think about it."

"I'll give you till four. Be ready. We're leaving then. I'm going to pack some things. You do the same. Then we'll take the trap to the station . . . in time for the train."

"This is madness," I said.

He caught me to him and I could not understand the embrace he gave me; it was made up of desire, passion, and perhaps hatred. "It's the way you want it. It's the way I want it."

Then he left me.

I sat by the window. I thought of the humiliation of the evening. I thought of the fulfillment of my dream. It could come true the way I had dreamed it.

I wasn't in love with Johnny. But some sensuality in him touched something in me. I was meant to marry and bear children—children who would be St. Larnstons.

Already the dream was becoming more ambitious. Justin and Judith had no child. I saw my son: Sir Justin. I, the mother of the heir to the Abbas!

Anything was worth while for that. Marriage with Johnny—anything.

I sat down and wrote a letter to Mellyora; I enclosed one which I asked her to give to Granny.

I had made up my mind.

So I left on the five-o'clock train for Plymouth.

Johnny was as good as his word, and shortly afterwards I became Mrs. Johnny St. Larnston.

4

The days that followed our flight from the Abbas still seem
something like a dream to me; and it was only weeks afterwards when I returned to the Abbas as Mrs. St. Larnston,
needing all my strength to fight for the place I intended to
have, that life took on reality.

I was not afraid on the day we returned; there was
scarcely any room for any feeling but triumph. It was
Johnny who was afraid; I was to learn that I had married a
weakling.

During that early morning journey to Plymouth I had
made my plans. I was determined not to return to the Abbas
until I was Mrs. St. Larnston, and I was determined to return
to the Abbas. I need not have worried. Johnny made no
attempt to evade his promise; in fact he seemed as eager for
the ceremony as I was, and was even prepared to keep his
distance until it was over; and then we had a few days'
honeymoon in a Plymouth hotel.

Honeymooning with Johnny was an experience I do not
particularly care to recall even now. Ours was a partnership
purely of the senses. I had no real love for him, nor he for
me. Perhaps he had a grudging admiration for my tenacity;
there were times when I believed he was glad of my strength;
but ours was a physical relationship which for those first
weeks was satisfying enough for us not to examine too
closely the situation in which we had put ourselves.

For me this was the culmination of my most cherished dream; and out of these dreams had grown a new and more ambitious one—I longed passionately for a child; my whole body cried out for a child! A boy who would be the heir of St. Larnston—my son, a baronet. During those days and nights in the Plymouth hotel, when for Johnny and me there seemed to be no meaning in life beyond our passion, I was wildly and hilariously happy because I sensed a growing power within me. I could make my dreams come true. I was determined to conceive without delay; I could not wait to hold my son in my arms.

I did not tell Johnny of this; aware of my need which equaled his for me, he completely misconstrued my passion; but it ignited his and he repeated to me often his pleasure in me. "I regret nothing . . . nothing," he cried; and he laughed, reminding me of my aloofness towards him. "You're a witch, Kerensa," he told me. "I always believed you were. That Grandmother of yours is one and you're the same. All the time you were as mad for me as I was for you although you treated me as if you loathed me. What about that parson now, eh?"

"Don't be too sure of yourself, Johnny," I warned him.

And he laughed at me and made love to me and I would never hold back because I would say to myself: Perhaps my son will be conceived now.

Johnny could abandon himself to the moment without thought of the future; I understood later that this characteristic was the source of all his troubles. During those weeks in Plymouth we were the newly married couple reveling in the possession of each other; he did not give a thought to our return until the day before we left for the Abbas.

Johnny had written to his brother telling him that we were returning and asking that Polore be sent to the station to meet us.

I shall never forget stepping out of the train. I was wearing a traveling suit of green velours cloth trimmed with black braid; and my bonnet was of a matching green with black ribbons. Johnny had bought these clothes for me and he declared that in the appropriate garments, which he intended I should have, I should put Judith in the shade.

Johnny seemed to hate his family, but I understood that was because at this time he was afraid of them. It was typical of Johnny to hate what he feared. Sometimes he would make allusions to our relationship which baffled me. I had forced him to this step, he told me, but he didn't think

146

he was going to be sorry after all. We understood each other. We would stand by each other; and we had learned, had we not, that we were necessary to each other?

Polore's manner was subdued as he greeted us. After all, what did one say to a woman who had sat at the servants' table and suddenly become one of the ladies of the house? Polore was quite at a loss.

"Good day, Mr. Johnny, sir. Good day . . . er . . . Ma'am."

"Good day, Polore." I had set the tone. "I hope all is well at the Abbas?"

Polore gave me a sidelong glance. I could imagine him repeating the incident over supper tonight; I could hear Mrs. Rolt's "My dear life" and Mrs. Salt's "I ain't been so shook, m'dear, since 'e come home in a mood one night. . . ."

But the gossip at the servants' table was no longer my concern.

We clop-clopped along the road and there was the Abbas looking more wonderful than it ever had before because I now had a share in it.

When he pulled up before the portico, Polore told us that old Lady St. Larnston had ordered that as soon as we arrived we were to be taken to her.

Johnny was a little tense but I held my head high. I wasn't afraid. I was Mrs. St. Larnston now.

Sir Justin and Judith were with her; they looked at us in astonishment as we entered.

"Come here, Johnny," said Lady St. Larnston; and as Johnny walked across the room to her chair I was beside him.

She was quivering with indignation and I could imagine how she had felt when she had first heard the news. She did not look at me but I knew she had to fight hard to prevent herself from doing so. In my new clothes I felt ready to face them all.

"After all the trouble you have caused," she went on, her voice quavering, "and now . . . this. I can only be glad that your father is not here to see this day."

"Mother, I . . ." began Johnny.

But she held up a hand to silence him.

"Never in my life has a member of my family so disgraced the name of St. Larnston."

I spoke then. "There is no disgrace, Lady St. Larnston. We are married. I can prove that to you."

"I was hoping it was another of your escapades, Johnny," she said, ignoring me. "This is worse than I expected."

Sir Justin had come to stand beside his mother's chair; he laid a hand on her shoulder as he said calmly: "Mother, what is done is done. Let us make the best of it. Kerensa, I welcome you into the family."

There was no welcome in his face; I could see he was as horrified by the marriage as his mother was. But Justin was a man who would always choose the peaceful way. By marrying a servant in his mother's house Johnny had created a scandal but the best way of subduing that scandal was to pretend it didn't exist.

I almost preferred Lady St. Larnston's attitude.

Judith came to support her husband. "You are right, darling. Kerensa is a St. Larnston now."

Her smile was warmer. All she wanted from the St. Larnstons was Justin's complete and undivided attention.

"Thank you," I said. "We are rather tired after our journey. I should like to wash. The trains are so dirty. And, Johnny, I should like some tea."

They were all looking at me in astonishment and I believe that I had Lady St. Larnston's grudging admiration and that while she was furious with Johnny for marrying me, she could not help admiring me for forcing him to it.

"There's a great deal I shall have to say to you." Lady St. Larnston was looking at Johnny.

I put in: "We can talk later." Then I smiled at my mother-in-law. "We do need that tea."

I slipped my arm through Johnny's and because they were all so astonished I had time to draw him from the room before they could reply.

We went to his room and there I rang the bell.

Johnny looked at me with the same expression I had seen on the faces of his family, but before he had time to comment Mrs. Rolt had arrived. I guessed she had not been far off during that interview with the family.

"Good day, Mrs. Rolt," I said. "We should like tea sent up at once."

She gaped at me for a second and then she said: "Er . . . yes . . . Ma'am."

I could picture her returning to the kitchen where they would be waiting for her.

Johnny leaned against the door; then he burst out laughing.

"A witch!" he cried. "I've married a witch."

148

I was longing to see Granny, but my first interview was with Mellyora.

I went along to her room; she was expecting me, but when I opened the door she merely stared at me with something near horror in her eyes.

"Kerensa!" she cried.

"Mrs. St. Larnston," I reminded her with a laugh.

"You really *have* married Johnny!"

"I have the marriage lines if you wish to see them." I held out my left hand on which the plain gold band was evident.

"How could you!"

"Is it so hard to understand? This changes everything. No more Carlee, do this . . . do that. I am my ex-mistress' sister-in-law. I'm her ladyship's daughter-in-law. Think of that. Poor little Kerensa Carlee, the girl from the cottages. Mrs. St. Larnston, if you please."

"Kerensa, sometimes you frighten me."

"I frighten you?" I looked boldly into her face. "There is no need for you to be afraid for me. *I* can look after myself."

She flushed, for she knew I was hinting that perhaps she could not.

Her lips tightened and she said: "So it would seem. And now you are no longer a lady's maid. Oh, Kerensa, was it worth it?"

"That remains to be seen, doesn't it?"

"I don't understand."

"No, you wouldn't."

"But I thought you hated him."

"I don't hate him any more."

"Because he offered you a position you could accept?"

There was a tinge of sarcasm in her voice which I resented.

"At least," I said, "he was free to marry me."

I flounced out of the room but after a few minutes I went back. I had caught Mellyora off her guard; she was lying on her bed with her face buried in the pillow. I threw myself down beside her. I could not bear that we should not be friends.

"It's like it used to be," I said.

"No. . . . It's quite different."

"The positions are reversed, that's all. When I was at the parsonage you looked after me. Well, now it will be my turn to look after you."

"No good will come of this."

"You wait and see."

"If you loved Johnny. . . ."

"There are all sorts of love, Mellyora. There's love . . . sacred and profane."

"Kerensa, you sound so . . . flippant."

"It's often a good way to be."

"I can't believe you. What has happened to you, Kerensa?"

"What has happened to us both?" I asked.

Then we lay still on the bed and we were both wondering what the outcome of her love for Justin would be.

I could scarcely wait to see Granny and ordered Polore to drive me to the cottage the next day. How I enjoyed alighting, dressed in my green and black. I told him to return for me in an hour.

Granny looked anxiously into my face.

"Well, my love?" was all she said.

"Mrs. St. Larnston now, Granny."

"So you've got what 'ee do want, eh?"

"It's beginning."

"Oh," she said, opening her eyes very wide; but she did not ask me to explain. Instead she took me by the shoulders and looked into my face. "You look happy," she said at length.

Then I threw myself into her arms and hugged her. When I released her she turned away and I knew she didn't want me to see the tears in her eyes. I took off my hat and coat and mounted to the talfat and I lay there and talked to her while she smoked her pipe.

She was different, sometimes so absorbed in her own thoughts that I believed she didn't hear all I said. I didn't mind. I just wanted to open my heart and talk as I could talk to no one else.

I would have a child soon, I was certain of it. I wanted a boy—a St. Larnston he would be.

"And, Granny, if Justin doesn't have any children, my son will inherit the Abbas. He'll be a sir, Granny. How do you like that? Sir Justin St. Larnston, your great-grandson."

Granny stared intently at the smoke from her pipe.

"There'll always be a new goal for 'ee, lovey," she said at length. "Maybe that's how life were meant to be lived. Maybe tis all for the best the way things has worked out. And you love this husband of yours?"

"Love, Granny? He's given me what I wanted. It's from

him I'll get what I want now. I remember that it couldn't have been . . . without Johnny."

"And you think that's a substitute for love, Kerensa?"

"I'm in love, Granny."

"In love with your husband, girl?"

"In love with the present, Granny. What more can one ask?"

"No, us couldn't ask more than that, could us? And who be we to question the means when the ends give us all we could wish for? I'd die happy, Kerensa, if you could go on as you be at this moment."

"Don't talk of dying," I ordered; and she laughed at me.

"Not I, my beauty. That were an order from one as gives orders now."

Then we laughed as only we could laugh together; and I fancied that Granny was less uneasy than she had been when I first arrived.

How I enjoyed my new position! I suffered no embarrassment. I had schooled myself for the role so many times in my imagination that now I was perfectly rehearsed and could play it to perfection. I amused myself and Johnny by imitating the sort of conversation which I knew was going on in the kitchen. I could give orders as coolly as old Lady St. Larnston and a great deal more so than Judith. Judith and I were actually friends. Sometimes I would dress her hair for her because she was now without a maid, but I clearly let her understand this was a sisterly gesture. I think the fact that I had married Johnny pleased her because she could not stop herself believing that every woman was after Justin. To have me paired off with Johnny was therefore a comfort; although had it been Mellyora who had eloped with Johnny she would have been really delighted.

She was inclined to relax with me and I was certain that soon she would be confiding in me.

With Judith's acquiescence I had ordered that a new suite of rooms be prepared for Johnny and me and had had furniture moved from other parts of the house to our apartments. The servants whispered behind my back but this I was prepared for. I knew that the Dowager Lady St. Larnston talked of upstarts and the tragedy of Johnny's marriage but I cared nothing for her. She was old and would soon be of little consequence. I was looking to the future.

I was waiting my time, eagerly watching for the first signs

of pregnancy. I was certain that I would soon have my son; and when I could announce that I was expecting a child, my position in that household would change. Above everything, old Lady St. Larnston wanted a grandchild and she despaired of Judith's giving her one.

One day I rode out to the vet's to call on my brother. I wanted to talk to him for I had made Johnny promise that my brother should train as a doctor and I could scarcely wait to tell Joe the good news.

Mr. Pollent's house, which had once seemed so grand, now looked modest; but it was a comfortable dwelling, standing back from the road in an acre of ground, most of which was occupied by stables, kennels and outbuildings. At the windows clean dimity curtains hung and when I alighted I saw these move, so I knew that my arrival was being watched.

One of the Pollent girls came into the hall to greet me.

"Oh come into the hale, *do,*" she cried, and I was sure she had hastily put on a clean muslin dress in which to receive me.

I followed her into the hale—another name for parlor—which was clearly only used on special occasions. This was gratifying and I took the chair which was offered me—glancing at the china dogs on the mantelpiece.

"I've come to see Joe," I said.

"Oh yes, Mrs. St. Larnston. I'll be going and telling him. If you'll excuse me for a minute or two."

I smiled graciously as she went out. I guessed that the story of my marriage had been the main topic throughout the countryside and that Joe had become more important because of his connection with me. I was gratified (I was always pleased when I could bring honor to my family).

I was studying the silver and china in the corner cupboard and, on assessing its value, telling myself that the Pollents were, if not rich, comfortably off, when Miss Pollent returned to tell me that Joe had asked her to take me to where he was working as he was busy.

I was a little deflated by this indication that Joe did not share the Pollents' respect, but I hid this and allowed myself to be taken to a room where I found him standing at a bench mixing a liquid in a bottle.

His pleasure was real as I went to him and kissed him.

He held up the glass bottle to show me. "A new mix," he explained. "Mr. Pollent and I reckon we've got something as has never been used before here."

"Have you?" I said. "I've got news for you, Joe."

He laughed. "Oh yes, you be Mrs. St. Larnston now. We all heard along of how you run off to Plymouth with Mr. Johnny."

I frowned. He would have to learn to express himself like a gentleman.

"My word," he went on, "what a to-do! You and Mr. St. Larnston and Hetty Pengaster all going off on the same day."

I was startled. "Hetty Pengaster!"

"Hadn't 'ee heard? She went away too. Regular how-do-'ee-do, I can tell 'ee. The Pengasters was in a rare state, and Saul Cundy were going to murder, that he were. But . . . there it be. Doll reckoned she'd gone all the way to London. She'd allus said that's where her did want to go."

I was silent momentarily, forgetting the importance of my mission to Joe. Hetty Pengaster! How strange that she should have chosen to leave home the very same day that Johnny and I had left.

"So she's gone to London," I said.

"Well, no one's heard yet, but that's what they do say. There was a young fellow from London who was here in the summer and Doll says he were friendly like with Hetty. Doll reckons they did plan it while he were here . . . though Hetty didn't tell her exactly like."

I looked at Joe and his contentment with his life irritated me.

"I've wonderful news for you, Joe," I told him.

He looked at me then and I went on: "Everything is different now. There's no need for you to continue in this humble position."

He wrinkled his eyebrows and looked foolish.

"I've always meant to do something for you, Joe, and now I'm in a position to. I can help you to become a doctor. You can tell Mr. Pollent tonight. There'll be a lot of studying to be done, and I'm going along to ask Dr. Hilliard's advice tomorrow. Then . . ."

"I don't know what you be talking about, Kerensa," he said, and a flush spread slowly across his face.

"I'm a St. Larnston now, Joe. You know what that means?"

Joe put down the bottle he was holding and limped over to one of the shelves; there he picked up a jar containing some liquid and began shaking this absent-mindedly. I felt emotional watching him, thinking of the night when Kim and I had rescued him from the mantrap and I had a great longing to see Kim now.

"I can't see what difference it do make to me," he said. "And I'm going to stay here along of Mr. Pollent. Here's where I belong to be."

"A vet? When you could be a doctor!"

"This is where I belong to be," he repeated.

"But you'll be educated, Joe. You could be a doctor."

"I couldn't be so. I be a vet and here's where . . ."

"Where you belong to be!" I finished impatiently. "Oh Joe, don't you want to get on?"

He looked at me and his eyes were colder than I had ever seen them.

"I do want to be let alone, that's what," he said.

"But Joe . . ."

He limped towards me and when he was close he said, "The trouble with you, Kerensa, be that you want to be like God. You do want to make the rest of we dance to your tune. Well, I won't, see? I be here with Mr. Pollent. And that's where I belong to be."

"You're a fool, Joe Carlee," I told him.

"That be your opinion, but if I be a fool, well then, tis a fool I like to be."

I was angry. Here was my first real obstacle. I had known so well what I had wanted. Mrs. St. Larnston of the Abbas; her son heir to the title; her brother the local doctor, her Grandmother installed in . . . say, the Dower House. I wanted every detail of the dream to come true.

And Joe, who had always been so meek, was opposing me.

Angrily I turned away, and when I abruptly opened the door I almost fell over one of the Pollent girls who had quite clearly been listening at the keyhole. I ignored her and she ran into the room.

I heard her say: "Oh Joe, you bain't going away, be you?"

I waited and Joe replied: "Nay, Essie. You do know I'd never go away. Tis here with you and the work where I belong to be."

I hurried away then, disgusted.

I had been married two months and I was certain I was to have a child.

I told no one but Granny when I first suspected this; it was only when I was sure that I let it be known.

My triumph exceeded my expectations.

The first person at the Abbas to be told was my mother-in-law. I went to her room and knocked at the door. She was alone and none too pleased to be disturbed.

"I am not free to see you now," she said. She had never addressed me by name up to that time.

"I wanted you to be the first to hear my news," I replied coolly. "If you do not wish to do so, it is of little importance to me that you are kept in ignorance."

"What news is this?" she asked.

"Shall I sit down?" I asked.

She nodded, not very graciously.

"I am going to have a child," I said.

She lowered her eyes but not before I had seen the excitement there.

"Doubtless it was for this reason that marriage was necessary."

I stood up. "If it is your intention to insult me, I would prefer to go when I have told you that your assumption is incorrect. The birth of my child will prove that, and I suppose you will need proof before you believe me. I am sorry I believed it was right to tell you first. It was stupid of me."

I walked haughtily from the room, and as I shut the door I thought I heard her whisper: "Kerensa." I went to the rooms I shared with Johnny.

I would go to see Granny and soothe my wounded vanity in her company. But while I was putting on my coat there was knock at the door.

Mrs. Rolt stood there. "Her ladyship says she would be pleased if you would go to her . . . Ma'am."

"I was about to go out," I replied. I hesitated, then shrugged my shoulders. "Very well. I'll look in on my way down. Thank you, Mrs. Rolt."

Knowing Mrs. Rolt so well, I could see the words trembling on her lips. "The airs! Like she was born to it."

I opened the door of Lady St. Larnston's sitting room and stood there, waiting.

"Kerensa," she said and her voice was warm, "come in."

I approached her and stood waiting.

"Do please sit down."

I sat on the edge of a chair, showing her by my manner that her approval meant little to me.

"I am pleased by this news," she said.

I couldn't hide the pleasure which flooded over me. "It is what I want . . . more than anything in the world," I answered. "I want a son."

155

In that moment our relationship changed. She deplored my marriage, but I was young and strong; I was even presentable and it was only the people in the neighborhood (the lower orders) who need know whence I had come. I had been married two months and had already conceived a child—a grandchild for her. And all this time there had been nothing from Judith. Old Lady St. Larnston was a woman who had had most of what she wanted in life. She must quickly have come to terms with her husband's incontinence. Perhaps she accepted that as part of the needs of a gentleman and as long as his wife's power in the house remained absolute she was content. I could not imagine what her married life had been like, but I did know that some quality in her, some love of power, the desire to manage her own life and those of the people around her, was shared by me; and because each recognized this in the other we were essentially allies.

"I am glad of this," she said. "You must take care of yourself, Kerensa."

"I intend to do everything to ensure having a healthy boy."

She laughed. "Let us not be too sure that the child will be a boy. If it is a girl we shall welcome her. You are young. Boys will come."

"I long for a boy," I said fervently.

She nodded. "We shall hope for a boy. Tomorrow I myself will show you the nurseries. It is long since there were babies at the Abbas. But I am a little tired today and I should like to show them to you myself."

"Tomorrow then," I said.

Our eyes met. This was conquest. This proud old woman who a short time before had been deploring Johnny's marriage was now becoming quickly reconciled to a daughter-in-law in whom she recognized a kindred spirit.

A son for St. Larnston! It was what we both wanted more than anything else in the world, and it was in my power to give it to her—more, it seemed only mine.

When a woman becomes pregnant she undergoes a change. There is often nothing for her but the child which, as the weeks pass, she is aware of, growing steadily within her. She senses the changes in the child, the development of that small body.

I was living for the day when my child should be born.

I became serene, contented; my manner was more gentle;

156

Dr. Hilliard called often to see me and he would find me with Mellyora in the rose garden sewing some small garment, for I asked that she should help me with the layette.

Lady St. Larnston put nothing in my way. I was not to be crossed. If I wanted Mellyora, I should have her. I must be cosseted and humored. I was the most important person in the household.

Sometimes the situation would strike me as so comic, that I would be overcome with silent laughter. I was happy. I told myself that never had I been so happy in my life.

Johnny? I cared nothing for him. His attitude had changed too because for the first time in his life, it seemed he had the approval of his family. He had sired a child—something which Justin had failed to do.

When we were alone together he would jeer at Justin.

"So perfect he has always been. I have suffered from Justin all my life. It is irritating to have a saint for a brother. But there is one thing sinners can evidently do more effectively than saints!" He laughed and embraced me. I pushed him away, telling him to be careful of the child.

Johnny stretched himself out on our bed, his head supported by his arms, watching me.

"You never cease to amaze me," he said. "Nothing will convince me that I haven't married a witch."

"Remember it," I warned. "Don't offend her or she might cast a spell on you."

"She already has done that. On me . . . and the whole household, including our dear Mamma. Kerensa, you witch, how did you manage that?"

I patted my swollen body. "My ability to bear a child without delay."

"Tell me this, do you ride out on a broomstick and practice fertility rites with your Grandmamma?"

"Never mind what I do," I retorted. "It is the result which is important."

He jumped up and kissed me. I pushed him away. I was no longer interested in Johnny.

I sat stitching under the trees with Mellyora.

She looked so pretty with her head slightly bent as she watched the dainty progress of her needle. I was transported back in my thoughts to those days when I had peeped at her in the parsonage garden sitting with Miss Kellow. How our positions were reversed! I remembered, too, what I owed to her.

Dear Mellyora, to whom I should be grateful for the rest of my life.

I wished that she could be as happy as I was. But even as I thought that, I felt a clutch of fear at my heart. Happiness for Mellyora would mean marriage with Justin. But how could she marry Justin when he had a wife? Only if Judith died could Mellyora marry Justin; and if she did, if they had children . . . sons . . . her sons would take precedence over mine!

My son: Mr. St. Larnston; Mellyora's Sir Justin.

It was unthinkable. But there was no cause for anxiety. Mellyora could never marry Justin and some instinct told me that Judith was a barren woman.

I was longing for the time to pass; I could only be content when I held my son in my arms. At times I was overcome by a fear that the child would be a girl. I should have loved to have a daughter, a girl for whom I could plan, perhaps as Granny had planned for me; but my dream would not be complete until I had a son. My son, mine, should be owner of the Abbas; I should have given it to him; and all the future generations would have my blood in them.

So I must have a son.

Granny, who was wise in such matters, believed that I would; the way I carried the child indicated it, she told me. As the months passed she became more and more sure and so my happiness increased.

I scarcely noticed what was going on about me; it did not occur to me that my good fortune must have its effect on one as near to me as Mellyora. Not even when she said: "Who would have believed all this could have happened to you when you stood at the hiring stand at Trelinket!" did I understand that she was thinking: If this can come to you, why shouldn't my life change miraculously?

But during those months of my child's gestation, the love which had been conceived by Justin and Mellyora was growing too. Their very innocence made it all the more apparent and none would be more aware of it than Judith.

She had not engaged a lady's maid after my marriage. Doll did certain duties for her and often I went along to dress her hair for some special occasion. One day when she and Justin were dining with the Hemphills I went to her room, as I had promised, to do her hair for her.

I knocked gently on the door but there was no answer, so I opened the door and called "Are you there, Judith?"

There was no reply; then I saw her: she was lying on the bed, on her back, her face turned up to the ceiling.

"Judith," I said. Still she did not answer; and for a second or so I believed she was dead and the first thought which came to my mind was: Now Justin will be free to marry Mellyora. They will have a son and he will take precedence over mine.

Now I had an obsession too: my son.

I approached the bed and I heard then a heavy sigh. I saw that her eyes were open.

"Judith," I said. "You remember I promised to come to do your hair."

She grunted and going close I bent over her. I saw that her cheeks were wet.

"Oh . . . Kerensa," she murmured.

"What has happened?"

She shook her head.

"You're crying."

"Why shouldn't I?"

"Something is wrong?"

"Something is always wrong."

"Judith, tell me what has happened."

"He doesn't care for me," she murmured in a slurred whisper and I guessed that she was scarcely aware of me; she was talking to herself. "It has been worse since she came. Does he think I don't see? It's clear, isn't it? They're crying out for each other. They would be lovers . . . only they're such *good* people. How I loathe good people, yet . . . if they were, I'd kill her. Yes, I would. Somehow I would. She's so meek and mild, is she not? Such a quiet inoffensive little lady. So much to be pitied. Fallen on hard times. Her father dies and, poor young lady, she had to go out into the cruel world and earn her living. Poor poor Mellyora! Such a hard life! Such a need to be protected. *I* would protect her."

I said, "Hush, Judith. Someone will hear you."

"Who's there?" she asked.

"It is only Kerensa . . . come to do your hair as promised. Have you forgotten?"

"Kerensa." She laughed. "The lady's maid who will now give us the heir. That is something else against me, don't you see? Even Kerensa, the girl from the cottages, can give St.

Larnston an heir and I'm a barren barren woman. The barren fig tree! That is Judith. It is all dear Kerensa. We must take care of Kerensa. Is Kerensa in a draft? Remember her condition. It is funny, don't you see? A few months ago she was Carlee . . . she was here on sufferance. And now she is holy, the mother-to-be of the sainted heir of St. Larnston."

"Judith," I said earnestly. "What is wrong? What has happened?"

And as I bent over her I knew, because I could smell the spirits on her breath.

Judith . . . intoxicated, attempting to forget her misery in the whiskey bottle!

"You've been drinking, Judith," I reproached her.

"What if I have?"

"It is foolish."

"And who are you, pray?"

"Your sister-in-law, Kerensa, your friend."

"My friend! You're her friend. No friend of hers is a friend of mine. Kerensa, the sainted mother! It's been worse since you married Johnny."

"Have you forgotten you are dining with the Hemphills— you and Justin?"

"Let him take *her*. He'd rather."

"You are being foolish. I am going to order some black coffee. Pull yourself together, Judith. You are going to the Hemphills' with Justin. He will be here in an hour and if he finds you like this, he will be disgusted."

"He is already disgusted."

"Then do not disgust him further."

"He is disgusted by my love for him. He is a cold man, Kerensa. Why do I love a cold man?"

"I cannot tell you that, but if you want to turn him away from you, you are going the right way about it."

She clutched my arm. "Oh Kerensa, don't let him be turned away . . . don't let him be."

She began to cry quietly and I said to her, "I'm going to help you. But you must do as I say. I shall order coffee for myself and bring it to you. It would not do for the servants to see you in this state. They gossip too much as it is. I shall be back soon; then I shall have you ready by the time you leave for the Hemphills'."

"I hate the Hemphills . . . silly Hemphills."

"Then you must pretend to like them. That is the way to please Justin."

160

"There is only one way of pleasing him. If I could have a child, Kerensa . . . if only I could have a child."

"Perhaps you will," I said, hoping with all my being that she never would.

"He is such a cold man, Kerensa."

"Then you must make him warm. You will not do so by getting drunk. That much I can tell you. Now lie there until I come back."

She nodded. "You're my friend, Kerensa," she said. "You promised you were."

I went to my room and when I rang the bell, Doll answered.

"Bring me some coffee please, Doll. Quickly," I ordered.

"Coffee . . . er, Ma'am?"

"I said coffee, Doll. I have a fancy for it."

She went away then and I imagined them discussing my fancies in the kitchen. Well, a pregnant woman was supposed to have fancies.

She came back with it and left it in my room. When she had gone I hurried along with it to Judith. It was unfortunate that as I went in, Mrs. Rolt should suddenly appear in the corridor.

If they suspected then for what purpose I wanted the coffee, they already knew that Judith was drinking. It was very likely that they did, for how could she take whiskey from the house supplies without Haggety's knowing? He would eventually have to tell Justin if only to protect himself. It seemed, therefore, that she had only just begun drinking. In which case it might be possible to stop her.

As I poured out the coffee, as I made Judith drink it, I asked myself: How much do the servants know of our lives? How can we keep any secrets from them?

May was hot that year, a beautiful month as was fitting, I thought, for the entry of my child into the world. The hedgerows were ablaze with wild flowers and the blossom everywhere was wonderful.

Mine was not an easy labor, but I stoically welcomed the excruciating pain. I welcomed it because it meant that my child would soon be born.

Dr. Hilliard and the midwife were at my bedside while it seemed to me that the entire house was tense, waiting for the cry of a child.

I remember thinking that the agony of the walled-up nun

161

could not have been greater than mine. Yet I exulted in my agony. How different it was from hers which was the pain of defeat, while mine was that of glory.

At last, it came. The long-awaited cry of a child.

I saw my mother-in-law with my baby in her arms; she was crying, that proud woman. I saw the tears glistening on her cheeks and I was afraid that something was wrong. My baby was crippled, a monster, dead.

But they were tears of pride and joy; she came to the bed and hers was the first voice I heard proclaiming the glad news.

"A boy, Kerensa, a lovely healthy boy!"

Nothing can go wrong, I thought. I have but to make my plans and my dreams become realities.

I am Kerensa St. Larnston and I have borne a son. There is no other male child to replace him. He is the heir of St. Larnston.

But I could be defeated in small matters.

I was lying in bed, my hair falling about my shoulders, wearing a white lacy jacket with green ribbons—a present from my mother-in-law.

The baby was in his cradle and she was bending over him, her face so soft with love that she was like a different woman.

"We'll have to think of a name for him, Kerensa."

She came to the bed and sat down, smiling at me.

I said: "I thought of Justin."

She turned to me in some surprise. "But that's out of the question."

"Why? I like Justin. There have always been Justin St. Larnstons."

"If Justin has a son he will be Justin. We must save that name for him."

"Justin . . . have a son!"

"I pray every night that he and Judith will be blessed as you and Johnny have been."

I forced myself to smile. "Of course. I merely thought that there ought to be a Justin in the family."

"So there should. But the son of the eldest son."

"They have been married some time."

"Oh yes, but there are years ahead of them. I hope to see a house full of children before I die."

I felt deflated. Then I assured myself that the name wasn't important.

162

"What other name did you have in mind?" she asked.

I was thoughtful. I had been so sure that my son would be Justin that I had not considered another name for him.

She was watching me and knowing her to be a shrewd old woman, I did not want her to understand how my thoughts ran.

I said spontaneously: "Carlyon."

"Carlyon?" she repeated.

No sooner had I said it than I knew that was the name I wanted for my son if I could not have Justin. Carlyon. It held a significance for me. I saw myself mounting the steps to the portico in my red velvet gown. It was the first occasion when I had been absolutely certain that dreams could come true.

"It's a good name," I said. "I like it."

She repeated it, rolling it over on her tongue. "Yes," she said. "I like it. Carlyon John—the last after his father. How's that?"

Johnny for his father. Carlyon for his mother.

Yes, since he could not be Justin, that was what he should be.

I was a different woman. For the first time in my life I loved someone better than I loved myself. The only thing that mattered was my son. I have often made excuses for the wicked things I did by telling myself: They were for Carlyon. I kept assuring myself that to sin for the sake of one you love is not the same as sinning for yourself. Yet deep in my heart I knew that Carlyon's glory was mine; and that my love for him was so fierce because he was part of *me*, bone of my bone, flesh of my flesh, as the saying goes.

He was a beautiful child, big for his age, and the only feature he had inherited from me were his enormous dark eyes; yet there was a look of serenity in them which mine had never had. And why, I asked myself, should they not be serene, with a mother such as I to fight for him? He was a contented baby; he would lie in his cradle accepting the homage of the family as his right—yet not imperiously; he was just happy to be loved. Carlyon loved everybody and everybody loved Carlyon; but, I assured myself, there was a special contentment in his lovely face when I picked him up.

Lady St. Larnston discussed the question of a nanny for him. She enumerated a few of the likely village girls, but I rejected them all. A sense of guilt had come to me because of the absurd fear which I had—almost a premonition—that something might happen to Judith and enable Justin and Mellyora to marry. I did not want that to happen. I wanted Judith to live and remain Justin's barren wife, for only thus could my son become Sir Carlyon and inherit the Abbas. I pictured the dreary waste Mellyora's life must be, but I shrugged aside my guilt. Was it not a choice between my friend and my son; and what mother would not always choose her son to a friend, however close?

All the same I wanted to help Mellyora and I had conceived a plan for doing so.

"I do not want him speaking with a village accent," I told my mother-in-law.

"But we have all had these girls for nurses," she reminded me.

"I want the best for Carlyon."

"My dear Kerensa, so do we all."

"I had thought of Mellyora Martin." I saw the astonishment beginning to dawn on my mother-in-law's face, and I hurried on: "She is a lady. She is fond of him and I believe she would be good with children. She could teach him as he grows older; she could be his governess until he is ready to go to school."

She was considering the inconvenience of relinquishing Mellyora. She would miss her; and yet she realized the good sense of what I was saying. It would be difficult to find a nurse of the caliber of the parson's daughter.

That day I discovered that the imperious old lady was ready to make sacrifices for her grandson.

I went along to Mellyora's room; she was very tired, having had an exhausting afternoon with Lady St. Larnston. She was lying on her bed, and I thought she looked like a daffodil which has been left too long out of water.

Poor Mellyora, the strain of her life was becoming too much for her!

I sat on the edge of her bed and studied her intently.

"Has it been a very tiring day?" I asked.

She shrugged her shoulders.

"I'll be back," I told her; and I went to my room and returned with some of the eau de Cologne which I had used during my pregnancy and which I had learned from Judith could soothe a headache.

I patted it on Mellyora's forehead with a pad of cotton wool.

"What luxury to be waited on!" she murmured.

"Poor Mellyora! My mother-in-law is a tyrant. But life is going to be better in future."

She opened wide her lovely blue eyes in which a hint of sadness was beginning to be apparent.

"You are to have a new employer, a new job."

She struggled up, fear coming into her eyes. I thought: Don't fret. You are not to be taken away from Justin, never fear. And that devil in me whispered: No, while you are here and there is this hopeless love between you and Justin he is even less inclined for his wife's company. And the less he is inclined towards her the less likelihood there is of their having a child who could replace my Carlyon.

When such thoughts came to me I always wanted to be especially kind to Mellyora, so I said quickly, "*I* am going to be your employer, Mellyora. You are going to be Carlyon's nurse."

We were hugging each other and for a few moments we were like those two young girls in the parsonage.

"You will be as his aunt," I said. "There will be no question of anything else. We are sisters, are we not?"

We were silent for a while and then she said: "Life is awe-inspiring sometimes, Kerensa. Do you see a pattern in ours?"

"Yes," I answered, "a pattern."

"First I help you . . . then you help me."

"There are invisible cords binding our lives together. Nothing will ever break them, Mellyora. We couldn't, even if we tried."

"We will never try," she assured me. "Kerensa, when I knew my mother was going to have a child I prayed for a sister. I prayed fiercely, not just at night, but all through the day, every waking moment! My life was a prayer. I created a sister in my imagination, and her name was Kerensa. She was like you . . . stronger than I, always there to help me, although there were times when I helped her too. Do you think God was so sorry to have to take my sister from me that he gave me you?"

"Yes," I said, "I think it was meant that we should be together."

"Then you believe as I do. You always used to say that if you want something, pray for it, live for it . . . it comes."

"My Granny says it comes but there are so many forces which we cannot understand. Perhaps your dream is fulfilled but you must pay for it. . . . Perhaps you will get your sister but she may not be all you hope she is."

When she laughed she was like the old Mellyora who had not yet suffered the humiliations which a proud woman like my mother-in-law could not help inflicting on those she considered to be in her power.

"Oh come, Kerensa," she said, "I am well aware of your faults."

I laughed with her and I thought: No, Mellyora, you are not. You would be surprised if you could look into this black heart of mine. Black? Perhaps not entirely so. But not shining bright and pure. Tinged with gray.

I was determined that I would make Mellyora's life easier for her.

What a change Carlyon had wrought at the Abbas. There was not one of us who was unaffected by his presence. Even Johnny had dropped some of his cynicism and had become a proud parent. My child was the whole meaning of life to me, of course. Mellyora was more at peace than she had been for a long time. She was devoted to the baby and there were times when I feared he might grow to love her as much as he loved me. Lady St. Larnston would soften visibly at the sight of her grandson, and the servants adored him; when he was in the garden I knew they all made excuses to go out to him. I guessed he was the only one in the house of whom they were not critical.

There was however one person, perhaps two, who were less happy for his coming. To Judith he was a continual reproach, and I suspected to Justin too. I had seen Justin look with yearning at my son and I could read his thoughts; as for Judith she could not hide hers. There was a wild resentment in her heart as though she were demanding of fate: Why cannot I have a child?

Strangely enough she allowed me to become her confidante. Why she should have chosen me, I could not imagine; perhaps it was because she felt I understood her more than anyone else in the house.

Sometimes I would go and sit with her and I had a way of making her talk which excited me and which she found soothing. I continually remembered Granny's saying that it was wise to discover all one could because every scrap of knowledge might at some time prove useful.

I would feign sympathy; I would lure her to confidences;

and when her mind was dulled by whiskey she talked the more readily. Every day she rode out alone. Her purpose, I knew, was to buy whiskey from the various inns in the neighborhood. She had evidently realized the danger of using the house supplies.

When Justin discovered the empty bottles in the cupboard, he was horrified by her secret drinking.

At first she was elated. "He was so angry, I have rarely seen him so angry. He must care, mustn't he, Kerensa, to be so angry? He said I would ruin my health. Do you know what he did. He took my whiskey away so that I shouldn't ruin my health."

But the elation did not last. I knew then how much she had come to rely on her whiskey. I went into her room once and found her sitting at a table, crying over a letter.

"I'm writing to Justin," she said. I looked over her shoulder and read 'My darling, What have I done that you should treat me so? Sometimes I think you hate me. Why do you prefer that girl with her silly meek face and her baby-blue eyes. What can she give you that I can't . . .' "

I said: "You are not going to send that to Justin?"

"Why not? Why shouldn't I?"

"You see him every day. Why do you want to write to him?"

"He avoids me. We have separate rooms now. Did you know? It is because I am a nuisance. He prefers to forget me. Things have changed since you were my maid, Kerensa. Clever Kerensa! I wish I knew how to manage my life as you do yours. You don't care much for Johnny, do you? But he cares for you. How strange! It's sort of turnabout. The two brothers and their wives. . . ."

She began to laugh wildly and I said warningly: "The servants will hear."

"They're far away in the kitchen."

"They're everywhere," I replied.

"Well, what would they discover? That he neglects me? That he wants the parson's daughter? They know that already."

"Hush."

"Why should I?"

"Judith, you are not yourself."

"I am dying for a drink. He has taken away my one comfort, Kerensa. Why shouldn't I have my comfort? He has his. Where do you think he and that girl have gone, Kerensa?"

"You are being foolish. You are imagining this. They are

167

both too . . . " I paused and added, "too conscious of convention to be anything but friends."

"Friends!" she jeered. "Waiting for the moment when they will be lovers. What do they talk about together, Kerensa? The days when I shall no longer be here?"

"You are overwrought."

"If I could have a drink I should be better. Kerensa, help me. Buy some whiskey for me . . . bring it to me. Please, Kerensa, you don't know how I need a drink."

"I couldn't do it, Judith."

"So you won't help me. No one will help me. . . . No . . ." She stopped and smiled slowly.

A thought had evidently occurred to her, but I did not discover what it was until a few days later.

That was when she rode over to her old home and brought Fanny Paunton back with her. Fanny had been a nursery maid at Derrise and had worked there in another capacity when there was no longer a place for her in the nursery.

Fanny was to be Judith's new lady's maid.

The affairs of Judith and Justin were suddenly of no more interest to me. My son was ill. One morning I leaned over his cradle and found him in a fever. I was terrified and sent at once for Dr. Hilliard.

Carlyon was suffering from measles, the doctor told me, and there was no cause for alarm. It was a normal childish complaint.

No cause for alarm! I was beside myself with anxiety.

I was with him night and day; I would not allow anyone else to nurse him.

Johnny remonstrated with me. "It's what happens to all children."

I gave him a scornful look. This was my son who was different from all other children. I could not bear that he should run the slightest risk.

My mother-in-law was extraordinarily gentle to me.

"You'll make yourself ill, my dear. Dr. Hilliard assures me it is just an ordinary childish complaint and dear Carlyon's attack is a mild one. Get some rest, I do assure you that I shall look after him myself while you do."

But I would not leave him. I was afraid that others would not give him the care that I could. I would sit by his cradle and visualize his death, the little coffin being carried to the St. Larnston vault.

Johnny came to sit beside me.

"Do you know what's the matter with you?" he said. "You want more children. Then you won't have all these alarms over one. What would you say to half a dozen little sons and daughters? You were meant to be a mother. It's done something to you, Kerensa."

"Don't be flippant," I commanded.

But when Carlyon was better and I could think more reasonably, I thought of a large family and the years ahead when I should be the grand old lady of the Abbas with not only Sir Carlyon and his children, but others . . . my children, my grandchildren. I would be to them what Granny Bee had been to me.

It was an expansion of my dream.

Johnny had given me a glimpse into a future which seemed good to me.

Carlyon suffered no ill effects and was soon himself again. He was walking and talking now. It gave me the utmost joy to watch him.

Johnny and I had slipped into a new relationship. We were as we had been during those early days of our marriage. There was passion between us as fierce as there had been then. On my side it grew out of a desire to fulfill a dream; on his, for a woman whom he was half convinced was a witch.

In the rose garden, Carlyon was playing with a wooden hoop, guiding it with a wooden stick, as he bowled it along. Mellyora was sitting on a seat near the Virgin's wall, sewing, when I came into the garden.

Carlyon was now nearly two years old and big for his age; he was rarely out of temper, and always happy to play by himself, although he would share the game with any who wished to join him. I often marveled that a man like Johnny and a woman like myself could have produced such a child.

I was at this time twenty-one and I often felt as I went about the Abbas that I had lived there all my life.

Lady St. Larnston was visibly aging; she suffered from rheumatism which kept her in her room a great deal, and had not employed another companion to take Mellyora's place because she no longer had much correspondence, nor did she wish to be read to as she had in the past. She wanted to rest more and occasionally Mellyora or I would sit with her. Mellyora sometimes read to her; when I did, she would always interrupt and we would find ourselves talking, mostly about Carlyon.

This meant that I was gradually becoming mistress of the house, a fact which the servants realized and only occasionally did I see an expression flicker over one of their faces which told me they were remembering that time when I had been one of them.

Judith did not stand in my way at all. She would sometimes spend days in her room with no one but her maid—"that Fanny from over Derrise," as the servants called her.

Granny was not as well as I should have liked but I was not worried about her as I had once been. It was my plan to set her up in a little house of her own near the Abbas, with a servant to look after her. It was a subject I had not yet broached with her for I knew that, at the moment, it would not be well received.

Joe was engaged to Essie Pollent and Mr. Pollent was to make him a partner on the day of the marriage. I felt piqued by Granny's glee in this state of affairs. She said: "Both of my little 'uns have done well for themselves." I did not see how Joe's rise could be compared with mine; and I still felt a nagging irritation that he was not studying to be a doctor.

My desire for other children had not yet been satisfied, but Granny had assured me that it was normal enough to have a gap of two or three years, and better for my health too. I had all my life before me. So I was content enough. I had the perfect son; and with each passing month, I became more and more sure that Judith would never bear a child. Thus Carlyon would inherit the title and the Abbas, and I would one day be the grand old lady of the Abbas.

That was the state of affairs that morning when I joined Mellyora and Carlyon in the rose garden.

I sat down by Mellyora and for a few seconds gave myself up to contemplating my son. He had been immediately aware of my coming into the rose garden and stood still to wave to me; then he trotted after his hoop, picked it up, sent it bowling, and glanced at me to see if I was watching. This was another of those moments which I should have liked to capture and preserve forever; moments of pure happiness, and when one grows older one learns that happiness—complete and unadulterated happiness—comes only in moments, and must be recognized and savored to the full, for even in the happiest life, the complete joy is not always present.

I saw then that Mellyora was uneasy and immediately the moment was passed, for joy had become tinged with apprehension.

"Something is on your mind?" I asked.

She was thoughtful; then she said: "It's Judith, Kerensa."

Judith! Of course it was Judith. Judith was the cloud which hid the sun. Judith stood across her path like a colossus preventing her passage along the river to love and contentment.

I nodded.

"You know she is drinking far too much."

"I know she has a fondness for the bottle, but I believe Justin is aware of this and won't let her drink to excess."

"She *is* drinking too much in spite of . . . Justin."

Even the way in which she said his name was a revelation. The little pause; the hushed reverence. Oh, Mellyora, I thought, you betray yourself in a hundred ways.

"Yes?" I said.

"I was passing her room yesterday; the door was open and I heard her . . . groaning, so I thought. I went in. She was lying across the bed in a drunken stupor. It was awful, Kerensa. She didn't recognize me. She was lying there with a dazed look in her eyes, groaning and mumbling. I couldn't hear what she said. I was so worried I went along to find Fanny. Fanny was in her room . . . the room you used to have. She was lying on the bed and she didn't get up when I went in. I said to her: 'I think Lady St. Larnston needs you. She seems ill.' And she lay there looking at me in a horrid, sneering sort of way. 'Is that so, Miss Martin?' she said. I went on: 'I heard her moaning and I went in to see. Pray go and do something for her.' She laughed. 'Her ladyship's all right, Miss Martin,' she said. Then: 'I didn't know it was her ladyship you were interested in.' It was horrible. It's a great pity that woman ever came here. I was so angry, Kerensa. . . ."

I glanced at Mellyora, remembering how she had fought for me when she had brought me to the parsonage from Trelinket. Mellyora could fight when the need arose. She would fight now. Any slur on the relationship between her and Justin was a slur on Justin. That was how she would see it. I knew there had been no consummation of this love between her and Justin, that there never would be while Judith was alive to stand between them.

Mellyora went on: "I said to her 'You are insolent.' And she lay there laughing at me. 'You give yourself airs, Miss Martin,' she said. 'You might be your ladyship by the way you act. But you ain't that . . . not by a long chalk you ain't.' I had to stop her because I was afraid she was going to say something dreadful, something which I wouldn't be able

171

to ignore, so I said quickly: 'Someone is supplying Lady St. Larnston with whiskey and I believe it is you.' She jeered again and as she did so, her eyes went to the cupboard. I went over and opened it and I saw them . . . bottles and bottles . . . some full, some empty. She is getting them for Judith when . . . Justin has tried to stop her drinking."

"What can you do about it, Mellyora?"

"I don't know. It worried me."

"These sneers about you and Justin make me more anxious than Judith's drinking."

"We are innocent," she said proudly, "and the innocent have nothing to fear."

I did not answer and she turned to me fiercely. "You do not believe me," she accused.

"I believe what you tell me always, Mellyora. I was thinking of your words: 'The innocent have nothing to fear.' I was wondering how true they were."

The next day Johnny went to Plymouth on the family business. It was strange how he had seemed to have become respectable since our marriage; I could believe that in twenty years' time he would have lived down his reputation. Life was extraordinary. Justin, who had made the marriage his parents had chosen for him, was losing his reputation, for there was no doubt that the main interest in the servants' hall was now the affair of Justin, Judith, and Mellyora. Johnny, who had disgraced the family by marrying the servant, was proving himself to have chosen wisely. It was indeed an ironic turn of events.

I wondered whether Johnny was unfaithful to me. I didn't greatly care. My position was assured. I had had all I wanted from Johnny.

When he returned he brought with him the elephant. It was made of gray cloth and there were wheels on its feet so that it could be pulled along. I have seen bigger and better elephants since, but at the time it seemed magnificent. It stood about twelve inches from the ground; it had two boot buttons for eyes, a magnificent trunk, a correspondingly grand tail, and a pair of soft ears. About its neck was a thin red leather band and to this was attached a red cord.

Johnny came into the nursery calling for Carlyon. Solemnly our son undid the wrapping about the box which seemed as big as himself; his little hands pulled at the tissue-paper wrapping and there, revealed in all its glory, was the elephant.

Carlyon stared at it, touched the gray cloth, put his finger on the boot-button eyes.

Then he looked from me to Johnny.

"It's an elephant, darling," I said.

"Nellyphant," he repeated, wondering.

Johnny took it out of its box and put the string into our son's hand. He showed him how to pull it along. Silently Carlyon pulled the toy round the room; then he knelt down and put his arms about its neck.

"Nellyphant," he whispered wonderingly. "My Nellyphant."

I was conscious of a momentary jealousy because Johnny had given him something that he liked so much. I wanted always to be first in his affections. It was a trait I deplored, but I couldn't help it.

Carlyon loved his elephant. The toy stood by his bed at night; he pulled it along wherever he went. He continued to call it his Nellyphant and it was natural that this was shortened to Nelly. He talked to Nelly; he sang to Nelly; it was a joy to see his delight in the thing.

My only regret was that it had not been my gift.

There were disturbing undercurrents at the Abbas that summer. The situation had worsened since the coming of Fanny who was not only supplying Judith with drink but was working on her suspicions. She hated Mellyora and between them, she and Judith were trying to make Mellyora's position at the Abbas intolerable.

Mellyora did not tell me of all the insults she had to endure, but there were occasions when she was so upset that she could not keep them to herself.

I had never liked Justin because I knew he had never liked me. He believed I had tricked Johnny into marrying me and he was too much of a patrician to accept me willingly into the family; while he was always coolly polite he never showed the least friendliness towards me, and I was inclined to think that he did not entirely approve of Mellyora's friendship with me.

For him I had little sympathy; but I loved Mellyora and I did not want to see her humiliated. Moreover, she loved Carlyon and he was fond of her; she was an excellent nurse and would be a good governess for him. I think really what I wanted was for things to go on as they were, with myself virtually mistress of the Abbas; Mellyora in a position which she owed to me and which put her in continual need of my protection; Justin, melancholy, in love with a woman who was forbidden to him, the victim of a loveless marriage;

Johnny my husband fascinated by me still, realizing that there was a great deal about me which he did not understand, admiring me more than any woman he had ever known; myself powerful, in possession of the strings which jerked my puppets.

But Judith and the odious Fanny were planning to get rid of Mellyora.

People in love are apt to play the ostrich. They bury their heads and think because they see no one, no one sees them. Even such a cold-blooded man as Justin could fall in love and be foolish. He and Mellyora decided they must meet in some place where they could be alone and occasionally they would ride out—not together—and meet, though never twice in the same place. I pictured them walking their horses, talking earnestly before they parted to come home separately. But of course it was noticed that they both disappeared on the same afternoons.

This was their only indulgence. I was as certain as I was of anything that they had never been lovers in fact. Mellyora might have been tempted had her lover been of a more fiery temperament. The restraint would be on Justin's part.

But such a situation, however determined the chief actors were to preserve their honor and do their duty, was like sitting on top of a barrel of gunpowder. At any moment there could be an explosion and Fanny—perhaps Judith too—was determined that there would be.

One morning when I went down to the kitchens to give orders for the day I overheard a remark which disturbed me. It was Haggety who made it and Mrs. Rolt tittered her appreciation. Fanny had seen them together. Fanny knew. Parsons' daughters were the same as any village sluts given half the chance. Fanny was going to find out the truth, and when she had, someone was going to be sorry. You could trust Fanny. There wasn't much she missed.

There was silence when I walked into the kitchen; and mingled with my apprehension for Mellyora was my pride in the manner in which my presence could subdue them.

I gave no hint that I had heard what they were saying, but merely proceeded to give orders.

But when I went upstairs I was thoughtful. If Fanny did not go soon, there was going to be trouble which might result in Mellyora's being obliged to leave the Abbas. What would happen then? Would Justin let her go? Often a decision could be forced and when it was, how could one be sure in what way people would act? Fanny must go; but how could *I* dismiss Judith's maid?

I went to Judith's room. It was early afternoon and I knew that after luncheon she retired to her room to drink herself drowsy.

I knocked lightly at the door and when there was no answer knocked again more loudly. I heard the clink of glass and the shutting of a cupboard door. She still kept up the pretense that she was not drinking.

"Oh," she said, "it's you."

"I came in for a chat."

As I came close to her I could smell the spirits on her breath and noted the glazed look in her eyes; her hair was untidy.

She shrugged her shoulders and I set a chair before the mirror. "Let me dress your hair, Judith," I said. "I always liked doing it. It's what I call good-tempered hair. It does what you want it to."

She sat down obediently and as I took out the pins and her hair fell about her shoulders, I thought how vulnerable she looked.

I massaged her head as I used to and she closed her eyes.

"There's magic in your fingers," she said in a soft slurred voice.

"Judith," I said softly, "you're very unhappy."

She did not answer, but I saw that her mouth drooped.

"I wish there was something I could do."

"I like you to do my hair."

I laughed. "I mean something to help you to be happier."

She shook her head.

"Is it wise . . . all this drinking?" I went on. "Fanny gets it for you, I know. It's wrong of her. You've been worse since she came."

"I want Fanny here. She's my friend." Her mouth was obstinate.

"A friend? Who smuggles drink to you when Justin is so anxious that you shouldn't drink, when he wants to see your health improved?"

She opened her eyes and they flashed momentarily. "Does he? Perhaps he would rather I were dead."

"What nonsense. He wants you to be well. Get rid of Fanny. I know she is bad for you. Get well . . . and strong.

175

If your health were better you might have a child which would give Justin so much pleasure."

She turned round and gripped my arm. Her fingers burned my skin.

"You don't understand. You think you do. Everybody thinks they do. They think it is my fault there are no children. What if I were to tell you that it is Justin's?"

"Justin's. You mean . . . ?"

She released me and, shrugging her shoulders, turned back to the mirror. "What does it matter? Just brush it for me, Kerensa. That soothes me. Then tie it back and I'll lie down and sleep awhile."

I picked up the comb. What did she mean? Was she suggesting that Justin was impotent?

I felt a great excitement. If this were so, there could never be any danger of anyone's displacing Carlyon. The problems of Mellyora and Justin were forgotten before such an important issue.

But how much trust could I put into Judith's wild statements? I considered Justin—so cool and aloof; the love for Mellyora which I was certain had never been consummated. Was this due to inability rather than morality?

I had to find out.

Then I remembered the history of the Derrise family; the story of the monster and the curse. I wanted to know more about that family.

"Judith . . ." I began.

But her eyes were closed and she was already half asleep. I could get little out of her now, and then I should not be sure how true it was.

I remembered that, when I had been her maid, she had often talked of her old nurse, Jane Carwillen, who had been with her family for years, and had been nurse to Judith's mother. I had heard Judith say that she had left the family now but lived in a cottage on the Derrise estate. I made up my mind that if I rode over to Derrise and had a talk with Jane Carwillen, I might learn something of importance.

The next day I left Carlyon with Mellyora and rode out to the moor.

At Derrise Tor I paused to look down at the house—a magnificent mansion built in Cornish stone, surrounded by its park in which I caught a glint of sunshine on the fishponds. I could not help comparing myself with Judith who had been born to all that luxury and was now one of the most miserable women on earth, while I, born to poverty in a fisherman's

176

cottage, had become Mrs. St. Larnston. I was continually making comparisons, continually congratulating myself on my achievements. I told myself that my character was strengthening; and if it was hardening too, well, hardness was strength.

I rode down towards the Derrise estate and on my way met some workmen whom I asked to direct me to Miss Carwillen's cottage. In a short time I found it.

I tied my horse to a fence and knocked at the door. There was a short silence before I heard slow footsteps; then the door was opened by a little woman.

Her back was bent and she walked with the aid of a stick; her face was as wrinkled as the skin of a stored apple, and she peered up at me through overhanging unkempt brows.

"Forgive my calling," I said. "I'm Mrs. St. Larnston from the Abbas."

She nodded. "I know. You be Kerensa Bee's girl."

"I am Judith's sister-in-law," I said coolly.

"What do you want with me?" she demanded.

"To talk to you. I'm anxious about Judith."

"Come in, then," she said, becoming slightly more hospitable.

I stepped down into the room and she led me to the highbacked settle in front of a turf fire. The fireplace was like a cave in the wall, and there were no bars to keep in the fire. It reminded me of the fireplace in Granny's cottage.

I sat down beside her and she said: "What be wrong with Miss Judith?"

I decided that she was a forthright woman, so I must pretend to be forthright too. I said bluntly: "She's drinking too much."

That remark shocked her. I saw her lips twitch; then she pulled thoughtfully at the long stiff hair which grew out of a wart on her chin.

"I've come because I'm so anxious about her, and I thought you might be able to advise me."

"How so?"

"If," I said, "she could have a child, I believe it would help her, and if she would not drink so much, her health would improve. I've spoken to her about it. She seems to despair and think it isn't possible for her to have a child. You know the family well. . . ."

"They'm a barren family," she answered, "and there have always been this trouble. They don't get children easy. There's some as is cursed that way."

177

I dared not look at her; I was afraid the shrewd old woman would read the satisfaction in my eyes and understand the reason.

"I've heard there's a curse on the family," I ventured. "I've heard it said that long ago a Derrise gave birth to a monster."

She blew with her lips. "There be wild tales in all these old families. The curse be no monster. It be this barrenness and . . . the drink. The one do go with the other. Tis a sort of despair in them like. They say tis in the family not to bear sons . . . and tis like they've made up their minds to be barren, and they be so. They say . . . there be some on us as can't resist the drink. . . . Then they don't resist it."

"So that's the family curse," I said. And after a short pause, "You think it's unlikely that Judith can have a child?"

"Who can say? But her have been married some time and far as I know there be no sign. Her grandmother did have two—reared one and lost the other. He were a boy, but not strong. My young lady's mother were a Derrise. Her husband took the name when he did marry her—to keep the family alive, you see. It gets harder for them, it do seem. My young lady were so much in love. I remember how excited she were when he rode over. We said, Surely love like that will be fruitful. But it don't look like it."

No, I thought, she will have no sons. Her relationship with Justin has turned sour now. It will be my Carlyon who will have the Abbas.

I was glad I had ridden over to see Jane Carwillen. No one could say definitely that Judith and Justin would not have a son; but my spirits were high because I knew it was unlikely that they would.

"And this drinking . . ." murmured the old woman shaking her head. "It don't do no good."

"It's been worse since Fanny Paunton came to her."

"Fanny Paunton's with her?"

"Yes. She came as lady's maid. Didn't you know?"

She shook her head sadly. "I don't like that. I never could abide Fanny Paunton."

"Nor I. I am certain that she smuggles spirits into the house."

"Why didn't her come to me? I would have told her. Tis long since I have seen her. Tell her I be missing her. There was a time when she'd ride over regular. But lately . . ."

"It may be since Fanny has come. I should like to send her away. Judith won't hear of it though."

"She were always loyal to them that served her. And you do say she have been worse since Fanny came! That ain't to be wondered at, seeing as how . . ."

"Yes?" I prompted.

Jane Carwillen leaned nearer. "That Fanny Paunton be a secret drinker," she said.

My eyes sparkled. Let me find her the worse for drink and I should have my excuse.

"Tain't often you'd find her drunk like," went on Jane. "Though there be times when her do let go. I could always see 'un coming. A slyness. . . . A look in the eye. A slackness. . . . Oh, I did know it. I tried to catch her at it, but I were always too late. She'd shut herself in her room . . . saying her wasn't well. Then her'd drink herself silly, I do believe. But in the morning, she'd be up and right as rain. A sly one, Fanny Paunton . . . and bad . . . bad for my young lady. For there be a way these drinkers do have. They want everyone to be like 'em."

"If I found her drunk I should dismiss her," I said.

The old woman gripped my hand; her fingers scraped my skin lightly; she was like a repulsive bird, I thought.

"You watch for the signs," she whispered. "If you be smart, you may catch 'un. You be on the watch."

"How often do these drinking bouts take place?"

"I don't believe she'd hold out longer than a month or six weeks."

"I shall keep watch. I know it will be the best thing possible for my sister-in-law if I can rid her of this woman."

The old woman said she would give me a glass of her elderberry wine.

I was about to refuse but I could see that would be unwise. We were sealing a pact. We were in agreement about the undesirability of Fanny.

I took the glass and drank the stuff. It was warming and, I was sure, very potent. That and the turf fire made my face burn; and I knew the old woman was watching me closely, Kerensa Bee's girl, who must have given the neighborhood even as far as Derrise something to talk about.

"And ask my young lady to come and see old Jane," she begged me as I left.

I said I would; and as I rode back to the Abbas I was pleased with my journey. I felt certain that Judith could not bear a son and that very shortly I should find a reason for dismissing Fanny.

As I came past Larnston Barton I saw Reuben Pengaster. He was standing leaning against a gate and in his hands he held a pigeon.

I called good day to him as I rode past.

"Why," he said, "it be Mrs. St. Larnston. A very good day to 'ee, Ma'am."

He came loping towards me so that I had to stop.

"What do 'ee think of 'un?" he asked, holding up the bird which was docile in his hands; the sun shone on the iridescent wing and I was struck by the contrast of that sleek beauty and Reuben's spatulate black-rimmed fingers.

"She looks like a show bird to me."

Proudly he showed me the silver-colored ring about her leg. "She be a homing bird."

"Wonderful."

He peered up at me and his jaw wagged slightly as though he were overcome by secret silent laughter.

"No matter where this bird do fly to, 'er'll come home."

"I've often wondered how they find their way."

The thick fingers tenderly touched the bird's wing, all gentleness, all softness. I thought of those fingers about the throat of the cat.

"This be a miracle," he said. "Do 'ee believe in miracles, Mrs. St. Larnston, Ma'am?"

"I don't know."

"Oh, there be miracles. Pigeons is one of them." His face darkened suddenly. "Our Hetty went away," he said, "but 'er'll come back. Our Hetty be a homing bird, I reckon."

"I hope so," I answered.

His face creased pathetically. " 'Er went away. 'Er didn't tell I. 'Er ought to have told I." Then he was smiling again. "But 'er'll be back. I know it. Same as I know when I sends out a bird. 'Er'll come back, I says. 'Er be a homing bird. Our Hetty were a homing bird."

Lightly I touched my horse's flanks. "Well, good day, Reuben. I hope you're right."

"Oh, I be right, Miss. I do know. Piskey-mazed, they say I be, but I do have a little more in some ways to make up for it. Our Hetty won't stay away forever."

That June, Mr. Pollent had an accident when out riding; Joe took over the practice completely and there seemed to be no reason why his marriage to Essie should be delayed.

This might have been a little awkward had I allowed it to

180

be. If Joe had done as I wished and become a doctor, the awkward situation would never have arisen; and I could not quite forgive Joe for being the one person to stand out against me. But for him I could have achieved all I set out to do. Joe however was clearly very happy and imagined himself to be the luckiest man alive and when I was with him I always softened towards him. The sight of him dragging his left leg slightly as he walked, brought back memories of that terrible night and how Kim had helped me; that softened me always and set me thinking of Kim and wondering whether he would ever come back.

On the wedding day Mellyora and I drove to the church in one of the Abbas carriages. Granny had been staying at the Pollents' house for the night. The respectability of her grandchildren was even having its effect on Granny, and I believed that before long I should have her living the life of a genteel old lady in some small house on the St. Larnston estate.

As we drove along I noticed that Mellyora looked pale but I did not mention the fact. I could imagine the strain she was undergoing and I promised myself that before long I should have Fanny out of the house.

The church had been decorated for the wedding because the Pollents were a highly respected family. There was a little stir when I took my place with Mellyora for it was rarely that a St. Larnston was a guest at such a wedding. Would they be reminding themselves, I wondered, that I was only Kerensa Bee's granddaughter after all. I fancied, too, that many covert glances were directed towards Mellyora, the parson's daughter who was now nurse to my son.

The wedding ceremony, performed by the Reverend Mr. Hemphill, was soon concluded; and Essie and Joe came out to the vet's carriage which was to take them back to the Pollents' where a feast was waiting for them and the guests.

The traditional rice was flung and the old pair of shoes attached to the carriage. Essie, blushing and giggling, clung to Joe's arm. As for Joe he managed to look both sheepish and proud.

I shrugged my shoulders impatiently, imagining how different this could have been if Joe had been marrying the doctor's daughter.

As we drove back, Mellyora watched me quizzically and asked me of what I was thinking.

"Of the night Joe was caught in the trap," I replied. "He

might have died. This wedding would never have taken place but for Kim."

"Dear old Kim!" murmured Mellyora. "How long ago it seems since he was with us."

"Do you never hear from him, Mellyora?" I asked wistfully.

"I've told you that he never writes letters."

"If he ever did . . . you would let me know?"

"Of course. But he never will."

The reception was typical of such occasions. The guests filled the Pollent parlor, the living room, and the kitchen. The kitchen table was laden with food which the Pollent girls must have been preparing for weeks: cakes and pies— hams, beef, and pork; there were homemade wines—blackberry, elder, gillyflower, parsnip, cowslip, and sloe gin.

The party would be very merry before it was over. There were the usual sly jokes; the expected comments; and several of the men whispered their intention to begin the shallal— without which few weddings in our part of Cornwall were celebrated. This was a so-called band, the sole object of which was to create as much noise as possible. Pans, kettles, tea trays—any implement on which hands could be laid, and with which the maximum noise could be made was brought into use. This was to proclaim to the neighborhood for miles round that two people had married that day.

Joe and Essie accepted all this fuss with pleasure. Essie, threatened with the usual horseplay when it was time to retire, giggled with feigned horror.

At least *I* should not be present when they dragged her and Joe from their bed and beat them with a stocking filled with sand. *I* should not be one of those who thought it such a great joke to put a furze bush in the bed.

It was while I sat with Granny and Mellyora and ate the food which the Pollent girls carried round to the guests that I learned of the growing concern in the neighborhood.

Jill Pengert, a housewife with a husband and three sons who were all miners, took a seat beside Granny and earnestly asked her whether there was any truth in the rumors which were going around.

"Be they going to close down the Fedder mine, Mrs. Bee?" asked Jill.

Granny said she hadn't looked that far into the future but knew there was a fear the lode might be running out.

"Where shall we be *to* if Fedders should close?" demanded Jill. "Think on all the men who'll be without work."

Granny shook her head and as Saul Cundy was standing nearby talking to Tom Pengaster, Jill called out: "Do 'ee know ought about these rumors, Cap'en Saul?"

Saul replied: "You've heard that the lode be running out, have 'ee? Well, you bain't the first."

"But is it true, Cap'en?"

Saul stared into his sloe gin. He looked as though he knew more than he thought it wise to tell. "Tis the same story all over Cornwall," he said. "These mines have been worked for years. They say there be only so much richness under the soil. Down St. Ives way one or two have already closed down."

"My dear life and soul!" cried Jill. "And what's to become of the likes of we?"

"Reckon every bit of tin 'ull have to be taken out of they mines afore we'll let 'em close," said Saul. "We won't let any mine be turned into an old scat bal till we be sure every scrap of ore be brought to the surface."

"Bravo!" growled one of the men; and the cry was taken up.

Saul was a man who would fight for his rights, and those of others. I wondered if he had recovered from the shock of Hetty Pengaster's flight to London when he had planned to marry her. He would, I imagined, be the kind of man who was more interested in fighting for the rights of the miners than settling down and marrying.

Thinking of Hetty I did not hear his next comment until the words "St. Larnston mine" attracted me.

"Ay," he went on, "we'll have no idle mine. If there be tin in Cornwall, hungry men will want to bring it up."

I could feel eyes turning towards me and was aware of the signs which were being flashed to Saul.

He put down his glass suddenly and walked away.

"I hadn't heard this rumor about the possibility of Fedders closing down," I whispered to Granny.

"I've been hearing rumors since I was so-size," answered Granny, holding her hand about a foot above the ground.

That pronouncement of hers and my presence seemed to put an end to the subject—or at least I did not hear it mentioned again.

After Joe's wedding, events began to crowd one on another leading up to that climax which would haunt me for the rest of my days.

I watched Fanny constantly so that I should not lose my opportunity of catching her.

The day came when I was successful.

Dinner was always a rather formal meal at the Abbas. We dressed, not elaborately, but in what we called semievening dress. I had bought a few simple dresses, subduing my natural love of color; I always enjoyed these meals because they gave me a chance to show how easily and naturally I had adjusted myself since my rise from the kitchen to the dining room.

Justin sat at one end of the table; Judith at the other. But I would often sign to Haggety when dishes should be served. Old Lady St. Larnston was too fatigued to care that I had assumed these duties; as for Judith she wouldn't notice that I did. I always fancied that Justin was irritated by my arrogance; as for Johnny he was amused, half cynically, half delightedly. He enjoyed watching me with my cool manners which were so different from Judith's. I don't think he ever grew tired of trying to draw the comparison between us and showing how much more brightly I could shine than Judith; and in fact as I became more polished, more sure of myself, more the lady of the house, so Judith deteriorated. Her drinking habits were having the inevitable effect, her hands would shake as she lifted her glass to her lips; how eagerly she took her wine, how surreptitiously she filled it again and again.

It was not a happy state of affairs between the brothers—but I was not responsible for that. In fact, it was gratifying to know that I had given Johnny his new dignity and importance in the house.

On this particular night Judith looked worse than I had ever seen her before. Her dress was not properly buttoned, and her hair, insecurely pinned, was beginning to fall down at the back.

A sudden thought struck me. She had dressed herself this evening.

It excited me. Could it be that this was the day?

Justin was saying: "I met Fedder this afternoon. He's concerned about the mine."

"Why?" asked Johnny.

"There are signs that the lode is giving up. He says they've been working at a loss and he's already dispensing with some of his people."

Johnny whistled. "That's bad."

184

"Going to be very bad for the neighborhood," went on Justin.

He frowned. He was different from Johnny. He would be a good squire, caring about the neighborhood. These thoughts passed lightly through my mind because I was longing for the moment when I could go up to Fanny's room and see what had happened to her.

"Fedder was hinting that we ought to open up the St. Larnston mine."

Johnny was looking at me. I saw the anger in his face, and was mildly surprised that he should care so much.

I heard his voice then; it sounded strangled with fury. "You told him that we should do no such thing, I suppose."

"The idea," said Justin, "of having a working mine so close to the house does not appeal to me."

Johnny laughed a little uneasily. "I should think not."

"What's that?" asked my mother-in-law.

"We were talking about the mine, Mother," said Justin.

"Oh dear," she sighed. "Haggety, a little more of the Burgundy."

That meal seemed interminable. But at last we had left Johnny and Justin over their port and on the way to the drawing room, I made an excuse to go upstairs and straight to Fanny's room.

I stood for a few seconds outside, listening. Then cautiously I opened the door and looked in.

She was lying on her bed, completely intoxicated. I could smell the whiskey fumes as I approached her.

I hurried back to the dining room where the men were sitting over their port.

"I'm sorry," I said, "but I must speak to you both without delay. Fanny must be told to go at once."

"What's happened?" asked Johnny, with a flicker of amusement in his eyes which was always there when he imagined I was playing the mistress of the house.

"We must be frank among ourselves," I said. "Judith has been worse since Fanny came here. I am not surprised. Fanny encourages her to drink. The woman is lying on her bed now—drunk."

Justin had grown pale; Johnny gave a little laugh.

I ignored my husband and appealed to Justin. "She must go at once. You must tell her to go."

"Certainly she must go," said Justin.

"Go to her room now and you will see for yourself," I said.

He did. He saw.

The next morning he sent for Fanny; she was told to pack her bags and leave without delay.

The subject of Fanny's dismissal was being discussed in the kitchen. I could imagine the excitement, and what was being said round the table.

"Was it Fanny who led her ladyship astray or t'other way about, do 'ee think?"

"Well, tis small surprise her ladyship do take a little nip now and then . . . when you think of what 'er has to put up with."

"Do 'ee think Miss Martin put'un up to it?"

" 'Er? Well, it may be. Parson's daughter can be as sly as any other, I reckon."

Judith was desolate. She had come to rely on Fanny. I talked to her and tried to persuade her to pull herself together, but she remained melancholy.

"She was my friend," said Judith. "That was why she went. . . ."

"She went because she was discovered drunk."

"They wanted her out of the way because she knew too much."

"Too much about what?" I asked sharply.

"About my husband and that girl."

"You must not say such things . . . nor even think such things. They are quite untrue."

"They are not untrue. I talked to Jane Carwillen . . . and she believed me."

"So you have been to see her."

"Yes, you told me to, didn't you? You told me she asked for me. I told her how he wanted that girl . . . how he wished he hadn't married me. And she believed me. She said she wished I'd never married. She said she wished we were together as we used to be."

"But she was glad, wasn't she, that Fanny had been dismissed?"

Judith was silent. Then she burst out: "You're against me . . . all of you."

It was a week after Fanny had left when Judith went looking for whiskey with a lighted candle. I did not come onto the scene until the drama was at its height, but discovered

186

later that Judith, after searching in vain for the bottles which Fanny had kept in her cupboard and which had been removed at the time of her dismissal, had set down the lighted candle in Fanny's old room and left it. An open door, a sudden draft, and the curtains were alight.

Justin was accustomed to taking lonely rides. I had guessed that there were occasions when he wanted to be alone with his uneasy thoughts. I often wondered whether during those lonely rides he made wild plans which he knew—being the man he was—he would never put into execution. Perhaps he found some relief in planning even though he knew the plans would never come to anything.

Returning from one of these drives I imagined that after stabling his horse he would walk to the house, unable to prevent his eyes straying to the window of the room which was Mellyora's.

And on this night he saw smoke coming from that side of the house in which she slept and what more natural than that he should rush to her room.

She told me afterwards that she had awakened and smelt the smoke, had put on her dressing gown and was about to investigate when the door burst open and there was Justin.

In such a moment how could they hide their feelings? He must have embraced her, and Judith, wandering in search of her solace, came upon them thus as she had so often sought to find them; Mellyora in her dressing gown, her fair hair loose; Justin, his arms about her, caught displaying that affection for which Judith had longed so passionately.

Judith began to scream and awoke us all.

The fire was soon put out. It wasn't even necessary to call the brigade; only the curtains and some of the walls were damaged. But greater damage had been done.

I shall never forget that scene, with the servants all assembled in their nightclothes, with the acrid smell in our nostrils, and Judith. . . .

She must have had a small secret store of her own for she had certainly been drinking, but she was sober enough to choose a moment when we were all present so that we should all know. She began to shout.

"This time I've caught you. You didn't know I saw you. You were in her room. You were holding her . . . kissing her. . . . You think I didn't know. Everybody knows. Ever since she came here it's been going on. That's why you had her here. You wished you'd married her. But that makes no

187

difference. You'll not let a little matter like that stand in your way. . . ."

"Judith," warned Justin, "you've been drinking."

"Of course I've been drinking. What else have I? Wouldn't you drink . . . ?" She stared at us glassily, waving her arms. "Wouldn't you . . . if your husband had his mistress here in the house . . . if he made every excuse to get away from you . . . to go to her. . . ."

"We must get her to her room quickly," said Justin. He was looking at me almost pleadingly so I went to Judith and took her arm.

I said very firmly: "Judith, you are not well. You have imagined something which does not exist. Come, let me take you to your room."

She began to laugh wildly, demoniacally. She turned towards Mellyora and for a moment I thought she was going to fly at her; I quickly placed myself between them and said: "Mrs. Rolt, Lady St. Larnston is unwell. Please help me to take her to her room."

Mrs. Rolt took one of Judith's arms, I the other, and although Judith tried to free herself we were too strong for her. I caught one glimpse of Mellyora's face; it was quite stricken; I saw the pain and shame in Justin's. Never, I imagined, had there been such a scene in the history of the Abbas—the shocking element being of course that it was happening in the sight of all the servants. I saw Johnny; his smile was sly; he was delighted at his brother's discomfiture and at the same time proud because I—the lady's maid—was the one who had taken charge of the situation, the one on whom Justin was relying to end it as quickly as it could be ended.

Between us, Mrs. Rolt and I dragged the hysterical Judith to her room. I shut the door and said, "We'll just get her to bed, Mrs. Rolt."

We did so and covered her up. "Dr. Hilliard gave her some sedatives," I went on. "I think she should have one now."

I gave it to her and to my surprise she meekly took it. Then she began to cry weakly. "If I could have a child it would be different," she murmured. "But how can I? He's never with me. He doesn't care for me. He only cares for her. He never comes to me. He shuts himself in his room. The door's locked. Why is the door locked? Tell me that. Because he doesn't want me to know where he is. I know, though. He's with her."

Mrs. Rolt clicked her tongue and I said: "I'm afraid, Mrs. Rolt, that she has been drinking."

"Poor soul," murmured Mrs. Rolt. "Can you wonder at it?"

I raised my eyebrows to imply that I wanted no confidences and Mrs. Rolt immediately recoiled.

I said coldly: "She will be quiet in a moment. I don't think there is any need for you to stay now, Mrs. Rolt."

"I'd like to help all I can, Ma'am."

"You have been a great help," I told her. "But there is nothing else to be done. I'm afraid Lady St. Larnston is sick . . . very sick."

She had lowered her eyes: I knew that there would be sly knowledge in her eyes.

Mellyora was in distress.

"You must see, Kerensa, that I can't stay here now. I'll have to go."

I was thoughtful, wondering what my life would be like without her.

"There must be something we can do."

"I can't endure it. They are whispering about me. All the servants. I know it. Doll and Daisy chatter together; they're all silent as soon as I appear. And Haggety. . . . He's looking at me in a different way as though . . ."

I knew Haggety and I understood.

"I must find some way of keeping you here, Mellyora. I'll dismiss Haggety. I'll dismiss all the servants. . . ."

"How could you? Besides, it wouldn't help. They're talking all the time about us. And it's untrue, Kerensa. Say you believe it's untrue."

"That you and he are lovers? I can see he loves you, Mellyora; and I know you have always loved him."

"But they are suggesting . . ."

She could not look at me and I said quickly: "I know you would never do anything of which you were ashamed . . . you or Justin."

"Thank you, Kerensa. At least you believe that of us."

But what help was it to be innocent when everyone believed you guilty?

She turned to me suddenly, "You are clever. Tell me what to do."

"Be calm. Be dignified. You are innocent. Therefore behave as though you are innocent. Convince people. . . ."

"After that dreadful scene. How?"

"Don't panic. Let things drift. Perhaps I'll think of something."

But she was desperate. She did not believe that I or anyone could help her.

She said quietly: "It is all over. I must go from here."

"What of Carlyon? He'll be brokenhearted."

"He'll forget me. Children do."

"Not Carlyon. He's not like other children. He's so sensitive. He'll grieve for you. And what of me . . . ?"

"We shall write to each other. We shall meet now and then. Oh Kerensa, this isn't the end of our friendship. That'll never end until one of us dies."

"No," I said fervently. "It'll never end. But you mustn't despair. Something will happen. It always does. I'll think of something. You know I never fail."

But what could I think of? There was nothing I could do. Poor grief-stricken Mellyora! Poor Justin! I believed they were the sort who would accept their fate however unendurable. They were not of my kind.

Mellyora studied the papers. She wrote for several posts. A parson's daughter with some experience as a lady's companion and a nursery governess should not find a post difficult to come by.

Each year a small circus came to St. Larnston; the big top was set up in a meadow just outside the village and for three days we heard the sounds of music and voices floating through the country lanes. For a week or so before the arrival of the circus, and for some time after, there was no talk of anything else; and it was a tradition that all the servants of the Abbas should have a free half day to visit the circus.

Promptly on the appointed day the vans came trundling along the lanes. I was never more glad of the diversion which I hoped would turn the conversation away from Justin, Mellyora, and Judith.

But that very morning there was a letter for Mellyora. She called me to her room to read it to me. It was a reply from one of the posts for which she had written—a revealing letter, I called it, clearly betraying the kind of woman who had written it. She would be prepared to see Mellyora and if her qualifications and references were acceptable give her a trial. There were three children in the household and Mellyora's duties, it seemed, would be to be their governess, their nurse and their slave. All this she would do for a minute salary; she would be expected to keep to the nurseries; her youth was against her but for a smaller salary than the gracious lady would have paid a more experienced governess she might be given a trial provided the interview was satisfactory.

"Tear that one into shreds," I commanded.

"But Kerensa," she said, "I've got to do something. It's no worse than the others."

"She sounds impossible. The most fearful snob. You'll hate it."

"They are all the same and I shall hate everything—so what difference does it make? I've got to do something. Kerensa, you know I've got to get away."

I looked at her and realized how much I was going to miss her. She was so much a part of my life. I couldn't let her go.

"You're not going, Mellyora. I can't let you go. In fact, I won't."

She smiled sadly. "You've become accustomed to giving orders, Kerensa. But I've come to the end. I've got to go. Since that awful night, I can't stay here. When I met Haggety on the stairs this morning he barred my way. It was awful. The way he looked at me. His fat hands . . . I pushed him away and ran. But that's not the end of it. It's the same everywhere. Tom Pengaster at the back door for Doll. The way his eyes followed me. I saw Reuben in the lane. His jaw wagged as though he were laughing . . . secretly. Don't you see?"

I knew then how desperate she was, that she had made up her mind and that I wasn't going to find it easy to stop her going.

Mellyora would go out of my life as Joe had gone; and Mellyora was important to me.

"You can't go," I said, almost angrily. "You and I belong together."

"Not any more, Kerensa. You've become the respectable married woman whereas I . . ."

I remember that moment even now. The silence in the room and the sudden roar of the caged lion as the circus cavalcade passed through St. Larnston.

It was a moment of uneasiness. Life was not moving as I wanted it. I could not bear to lose Mellyora; she was part of my life; every time we were together I was aware of the change in our positions and compared the past with the present. I could not help but feel satisfaction in Mellyora's presence, yet at the same time I deplored her unhappiness. I was not all bad up to that time.

"Something will happen to stop this," I said, clenching my fists.

Something would happen. I was sure of my power to control our fates.

Mellyora shook her head. Heartbroken, she was passively accepting hers.

Carlyon came in with Doll who had taken him to the end of the lane to see the cavalcade. His eyes were brilliant, his cheeks scarlet. I could never look at him without marveling at his beauty.

"Mamma," he said, running to me and throwing his arms about my knees, "I have seen the lions."

I picked him up and laid my cheek against his. I thought: What does anything matter while I have him?

But all was not well with him; he withdrew himself slightly to peer anxiously into my face.

"Mamma," he said, "I saw a nellyphant. Two nelly-phants."

"That was lovely, my darling."

He shook his head.

I understood when I took him to the nursery. He went straight to his toy and knelt down beside it; he put a cautious finger on the black boot buttons. He said: "You've got your eyes on, Nelly."

He gave the toy a little push and it rolled across the floor until it reached the wall. Then he turned to me and the tears were streaming down his cheeks.

"Nelly's not a real live nellyphant," he sobbed.

Mellyora had written asking for an interview. I was certain that if she went she would get the post, for her prospective employer would pay her less than was usual and congratulate herself on having acquired a parson's daughter.

The servants seemed absent-minded; I could hear them continually whispering and giggling together. Even Mrs. Salt and her daughter seemed excited. The circus brought strangers to the place and perhaps there was an added thrill for them in case the terrible Mr. Salt might be among them. Haggety would accompany Mrs. Rolt, Doll would go with

Tom Pengaster and perhaps they would let Daisy go with them. Lunch was to be served half an hour earlier so that they could clear up and get away in good time.

Johnny had gone to Plymouth, as he said, on estate duty. Justin rode off alone immediately after luncheon. I always spent a part of the afternoon with Carlyon so Mellyora had a few hours of freedom; and when I saw her come downstairs in her riding habit that afternoon, I guessed that she was meeting Justin.

They were very sad, both of them, because there would not be many more occasions when they could be together.

"Mellyora," I said, "I hope Justin will persuade you not to go."

She flushed and in those moments looked very lovely. "He knows, as well as I do," she answered, "that this is the only way."

She pressed her lips firmly together as though she feared the suppressed sobs would escape while she hurried past me.

I went straight up to the nursery where I found Carlyon talking about the animals. I had told the servants not to mention to him that they were going to the circus because I knew that he would then want to go too and I was afraid of the circus, afraid that he might be harmed in some way. So many unclean people who might give him some disease; he might be lost; I could picture a hundred mishaps. Perhaps next year, I'll take him myself, I thought.

We went out to the rose garden where old Lady St. Larnston was sitting in a wheel chair; she had been suffering from rheumatism in the last months and used the chair a good deal. The last year or so had brought great changes in this house. Her eyes brightened at the sight of Carlyon and he went straight to her and stood on tiptoe as she bent creakily forward to receive his kiss.

I sat on the wooden seat near her chair while Carlyon sprawled out on the grass absorbed in the progress of an ant which was climbing a blade of grass.

While he played, my mother-in-law and I talked desultorily.

"This wretched circus." She sighed. "It has been the same for years. My hot water was five minutes late this morning and my tea was cold. I told Mrs. Rolt and she said: 'It's the circus, my lady.' I remember when I was first married . . ."

Her voice trailed off as it often did when she started some reminiscence and she would be silent while she relived the past in her thoughts. I wondered whether her mind was beginning to fail as her body was.

"It's one of the great days in their lives," I remarked.

"The empty house . . . the servants . . . quite impossible." Her voice quavered.

"Fortunately it only happens once a year."

"Everyone gone . . . just everyone. . . . Not a servant in the house. If anyone should call. . . ."

"No one will. Everyone knows it is the day of the circus."

"Kerensa, my dear . . . Judith. . . ."

"She's resting."

Resting! That significant word. We used it when we meant to imply that Judith was not quite presentable. When visitors called we would say: "She is a little indisposed. She is resting."

Her condition had improved since the departure of Fanny. It was true that she was drinking less; but there was a continual craving which seemed to be turning to a madness. When her mother went out onto the moors and danced by moonlight was it because she was drunk? Was it, as Jane Carwillen had said, that drink was the monster that haunted the Derrise family?

We were silent, each occupied with our separate thoughts; and suddenly I noticed that Carlyon was stretched out on the grass, his little body shaking with sobs.

I went over to him at once and picked him up. "What is it, my darling?" I asked.

He clung to me and it was some time before he could speak.

"It's Nelly," he said. "I was a wicked one."

I smoothed the thick hair back from his forehead and murmured endearments; but I couldn't comfort him.

"I didn't like her any more because she wasn't a true nellyphant."

"And you like her again?"

"She's Nelly," he said.

"Well, she'll be happy now you like her again," I soothed.

"She's gone."

"Gone?"

He nodded.

"Where?" I asked.

"I don't know."

"But, darling, if she's gone away you must know where."

"I looked and looked. She's gone because I told her she wasn't a true nellyphant."

194

"She's in the nursery waiting for you."

He shook his head. "I looked."

"And she wasn't there?"

"She's gone right away. I didn't like her any more. I said she wasn't a true nellyphant."

"Well," I said, "she isn't."

"But she's crying. I said I don't want her any more. I wanted a true nellyphant."

"And now do you want her?"

"She's my Nelly, even though she's not a true nellyphant. I want Nelly to come back and she's gone."

I rocked him in my arms. Bless his tender heart! I thought. He believes he has hurt poor Nelly and wants to comfort her.

"I'll go and find her," I told him. "You stay here with Grandmamma. Perhaps she'll let you count her carnelians."

One of his greatest pleasures was examining the stone necklace which my mother-in-law invariably wore during the day; it was composed of carnelian stones of golden brown, rather roughly hewn. Carlyon had always been fascinated by them.

He brightened at the prospect and I put him on my mother-in-law's lap; she smiled for the counting of the carnelians was, I believed, as great a pleasure for her as for him. She would tell him about the necklace and how her husband had given it to her and how his mother had given it to him for his bride; it was a St. Larnston necklace and the stones themselves had been found in Cornwall.

I left Carlyon considerably comforted, listening to his Grandmother's sleepy voice recounting the history as she had many times before, he watching the movement of her lips, telling her when she used a word which had not been in the previous tellings.

As soon as I entered the Abbas, I tell myself now, I felt an odd foreboding. But perhaps I imagined that afterwards. Yet I was very susceptible to what I called the moods of the house. The house was a living thing to me; I had always felt my destiny was wrapped up in it. It certainly was that afternoon.

Such a silence. All the household away. It was rare that there were not some servants present. But this was the special day of the year when it was agreed that all should be absent.

Only Judith would be lying in her room, her hair tousled, her face already bearing that misshapen vague look of the dipsomaniac, the eyes a little wild and bloodshot. I shivered, although it was a warm afternoon.

I longed to be out in the rose garden with my son. I smiled thinking of him sitting on Lady St. Larnston's lap, his eyes close to the carnelian stones, perhaps tracing the streaks in them with a plump finger.

My darling child! I would die for him. Then I laughed at the sentiment. Of what use would I be to him, dead? He needed me to plan for him, to give him the life of which he was worthy. Did I sense in him already a softness, a sentimentality which might let his heart rule his head.

How happy he would be when I put his toy elephant into his arms. Together we would explain that he loved her still, and the fact that she was not a true elephant was unimportant.

I went along first to the nursery, but the toy was not there. I had seen him with it that morning. I smiled, remembering how he had dragged it along in a dejected sort of way. Poor Nelly! She was in disgrace. When had I seen him? It was when Mellyora had brought him to my room on their way out. They had gone together along the corridor and down by the main staircase.

I followed the direction, guessing that his attention had been distracted and he had relinquished the strap and left the toy somewhere on the way. I would descend the stairs and go out to one of the front lawns where he had played that morning.

When I reached the top of the staircase I saw the elephant. It was lying on the second stair from the top and caught in it was a shoe.

I went closer. A high-heeled shoe caught in the cloth of the elephant's coat! Whose shoe?

I stood up holding the toy in one hand, the shoe in the other, and as I did so I saw a form at the bottom of the staircase.

My heart was beating as though it would burst out of my body as I ran down the stairs.

Lying at the foot of the stairs was Judith.

"Judith," I whispered. I knelt beside her. She was very still. She wasn't breathing and I knew that she was dead.

It seemed now that the house was watching me. There I was alone in it . . . with death. In one hand I held the shoe—in the other the toy elephant.

I could see it all so clearly. The toy lying at the top of the stairs; Judith coming down, slightly tipsy, not seeing the toy.

I could picture her stepping on it, her heel catching in the cloth—her balance lost; the sudden descent, down the great staircase which I had mounted once so proudly in my red velvet dress . . . down to death.

And this because my son had left his toy on the stairs—a death trap innocently set.

I closed my eyes and I thought of the whisperings! The little boy was responsible for her death in a manner of speaking. . . . It was the sort of story they loved, that lived on for years.

And he would know it, and even though none could say it was his fault, it would cloud his happiness to know that he was responsible for her death.

Why should his bright future be clouded because a drunken woman had fallen down the stairs and broken her neck?

The great silence of the house was unnerving. It was as though time had stopped—the clocks had stopped and there was no sound whatever. Great events had taken place within these walls over the centuries. Something told me that I was now facing one of those occasions.

Then time seemed to begin again. I heard the ticking of the grandfather clock as I knelt down by Judith. There was no doubt that she was dead.

I laid the shoe on the stairs; but I took the elephant back to the nursery and left it there. No one was going to say that Judith had died because of my son's action.

Then I ran out of the house, as fast as I could to Dr. Hilliard's.

5

Death in the Abbas. A hushed atmosphere. The blinds drawn to shut out the sun. The servants creeping about on tiptoe, speaking in whispers.

In that bedroom where I had so often dressed her hair, Judith lay in her coffin. The servants hurried past the closed door, eyes averted. I was oddly moved to see her lying there, in the white frilled cap and the white nightdress, looking more at peace than she ever had in life.

Justin shut himself in his room and was seen by no one. Mrs. Rolt took trays up to his room but she brought them all down again, the food untouched. There was a grim look about her mouth. I guessed that in the kitchen she said: "It's on his conscience. Poor lady! Can you wonder at it?" And they would all agree because of their unwritten law that the dead were sanctified.

The events of that day stand out clearly in my mind. I remember running along the road in the hot sun, finding Dr. Hilliard asleep in his garden, a newspaper over his head to protect him from the sun, blurting out that there had been an accident, and going back to the Abbas with him. The house was still silent; the shoe lay on the stairs; but the elephant was in the nursery.

I stood there beside him as he touched her poor face.

"This is terrible," he murmured. "Terrible."

Then he looked up the stairs and at her shoe. "She'd been drinking," he went on.

I nodded.

He stood up. "There's nothing I can do for her."

"Would it have been instantaneous?" I asked.

He lifted his shoulders. "I should think so. No one heard her fall?"

I explained that the servants were all at the circus. It was the one occasion of the year when the house was empty.

"Where is Sir Justin?"

"I don't know. My husband has gone to Plymouth on estate duty and Lady St. Larnston is in the garden with my son."

He nodded. "You look shaken, Mrs. St. Larnston."

"It was a great shock."

"Exactly. Well, we must try and get hold of Sir Justin as soon as possible. Where would he be at this time of day?"

I knew where he was . . . with Mellyora; and then the fear struck at me for the first time. He was free now . . . free to marry Mellyora. In a year—which would be a respectable time—they would marry. Perhaps in another they would have a son. I had been so intent on arranging that Carlyon's toy should not be involved in the accident that I had not realized that what I dreaded might after all happen.

Dr. Hilliard was talking, giving instructions; but I merely stood still and it was as though the house itself were mocking me.

Later that day Judith's parents arrived at the Abbas. Her mother was very like Judith—statuesque with the same tortured eyes. They were indeed tortured on this occasion.

She went to the room where Judith lay on her bed, for they had not yet made her coffin. I heard her wild sobbing and her reproaches.

"What have you done to my daughter? Why did I ever let her come to this house?"

The servants heard. I met Mrs. Rolt on the stairs and she lowered her eyes so that I should not see the excitement there. This was a situation the servants loved. Scandal in high places. While they talked of the death of Judith, they would speak in the same breath of her unhappiness and that last scene when she had betrayed before them all her jealousy of Mellyora.

Jane Carwillen called at the Abbas, having arranged for

one of the Derrise grooms to drive her over. Doll received her and tried to prevent her from entering the house but she thrust the girl aside and demanded: "Where be my young lady? Take me to her."

I heard the commotion and came into the hall. As soon as I saw her I said: "Come with me, I will take you to her."

And I led the way to that room where Judith lay in her coffin.

Jane Carwillen stood beside it, looking down at Judith. She did not weep; she did not speak but I saw the grief in her face and I knew that a hundred little incidents of Judith's childhood were passing through her mind.

"And her so young," she said at last. "Why did it have to be?"

I whispered gently: "These things happen."

She turned on me fiercely. "There was no need. She were young. Her whole life were before her."

She turned away and as we left the room of death together we encountered Justin. The look of hatred Jane Carwillen flashed at him startled me.

Mrs. Rolt was waiting in the hall. She eyed Jane Carwillen eagerly. "I was thinking Miss Carwillen might take a glass of wine for comfort," she said.

"There bain't be no comfort you nor any can give me," answered Jane.

"There be always comfort in a sorrow shared," put in Mrs. Rolt. "You open your heart to us . . . and we'll open ours to 'ee."

Was that a message? Did it mean we have something to tell you which we think you ought to know?

Perhaps Jane thought so because she agreed to go to the kitchen and take a glass of wine.

Half an hour later, knowing she had not left the house I made an excuse to go down to the kitchens.

I knew that the servants were telling Jane about that occasion when Judith had accused her husband and Mellyora of being lovers. For the first time it was being said Judith's death was not an accident.

The verdict at the inquest was accidental death. Judith, it seemed, had been in a state of semi-intoxication; and thus had missed her footing on the stairs and plunged down to her death.

I gave evidence, since I had found her, explaining how I had come to the house to look for my son's toy; then I had seen Judith lying at the bottom of the staircase, her shoe on

200

one of the lower stairs. No one doubted me, although I was afraid my nervousness would betray me. It was presumed that I was upset, which was natural.

Sir Justin seemed to have aged ten years. I could see how he was reproaching himself. As for Mellyora, she looked like a ghost. I knew that she hated meeting any of the servants. She had forgotten all about the interview which she was supposed to have had and was too numbed by what had happened even to think very clearly. How different she was from me! Had I been in her place, I assured myself, I should have been exulting now, seeing the future clear before me. I should have snapped my fingers at the servants' gossip. What was there to worry about when soon one would be mistress of the house, with the power to dismiss any of them. They would know this and adjust their attitude accordingly. But at the moment they were not sure which turn events would take.

But perhaps one of the most uneasy people in the house was myself. My son's future was at stake. He was everything to me now. I did not care to look too closely at my own life. My marriage was not satisfactory, and there were times when I disliked Johnny. I wanted children and that was the only reason I tolerated him. I did not love him; I had never loved him; but there was a bond of sensuality between us which served as love. I had often dreamed of a love which would give me all I wanted from life and more especially so now. I wanted a husband to whom I could turn; who would comfort me and make my life worth while, even if my ambitious dreams were thwarted. Never had I felt as lonely as I did at this time because I had been shown how by one thrust of fate dreams could be destroyed. I had felt myself to be powerful, able to will destiny to give me what I wanted; but had not Granny told me, time after time, that fate was more powerful than I. I felt weak and helpless; and feeling thus, I wanted a strong arm about me. I thought increasingly of Kim. That night in the woods had been significant in more ways than one. It had decided my future as well as Joe's.

In my strange and devious way I was in love with Kim, in love with an image perhaps; but because my desires always went deep, because when I wanted something I wanted it passionately and wholeheartedly, I knew that was how I should love a man, deeply, passionately. And that night when I was young and inexperienced so that I did not fully understand my feelings, I had chosen Kim; and I had gone on building his image. There was a belief in the back of my mind that one day Kim would come back and he would come back for me.

And now, because I believed I could lose all I had wanted for Carlyon, I wished that I had a strong man beside me to comfort me; and it saddened me to know that man was not my husband and that this marriage of mine was a sordid bargain—a marriage without love, a marriage of a desire on one side so fierce that it had forced this step, and on the other a desire as fierce, but in my case for power and position.

I waited uneasily for what would happen next; and then I began to see that fate was giving me another chance.

The rumors had begun.

I was aware of this when I overheard one single remark from the kitchen. Mrs. Rolt had a penetrating voice.

"One law for the rich, one for the poor. Accidental Death. Accidental . . . *if* you please. And where was he? And where was she? Bessie Culturther did see them . . . walking in Trecannon Woods . . . horses tethered . . . holding hands they were. That were days afore. Planning? Maybe? And where were they when her ladyship was having her *accidental* death. Well, don't do to ask, do it, because these be the gentry."

Rumors. Gossip. They could grow big.

They did grow. There was gossip, endless gossip. It was too fortuitous, said the whispers. Events could not work out so neatly. Justin in love with Mellyora! Mellyora about to go away! The sudden death of the one who stood between them! Was it natural to suppose that Lady St. Larnston had had an accident at precisely the right time to prevent her husband losing his mistress?

How obliging fate could be to some people! But why should this be so? Did fate say "Oh, but this is Sir Justin and he must have what he wants!" Fate must give events a little push to make everything come right for Sir Justin St. Larnston. A little push? Those were the well-chosen words!

Where had Sir Justin been at that moment when his wife had fallen down the stairs? At the inquest he had explained that he had been exercising one of his horses. They did not ask Mellyora where she had been. If they had, she would have had to reply that she too had been exercising one of the horses. I could imagine the big table in the servants' quarters; they would be sitting round it like so many detectives, piecing the story together.

The time had been cleverly chosen; the house quiet; the servants at the circus; Mr. Johnny away on business; Mrs. St. Larnston with her son and the old lady in the garden. Had Sir Justin come back to the house? Had he led his wife along the corridor to the top of the stairs, had he thrown her from top to bottom?

The servants were saying it; they were saying it in the village. In the little post office Miss Penset knew that Miss Martin had been writing letters to addresses in various parts of the country; and in view of that little scene when one of the rooms had caught fire at the Abbas and she had been seen—in her night clothes—with Sir Justin, and her poor ladyship had said just what was in her mind, there was little doubt as to what her ladyship had insisted on. Miss Penset would have had an account of that scene from several quarters. There was always Mrs. Rolt and Mrs. Salt, as well as Mr. Haggety to lean over the counter and stare at Miss Penset's bosom beneath her black bombazine bodice; to smile knowingly, implying that she was a fine woman. She could worm any secret out of a man who admired her as much as Mr. Haggety did. Then there was Doll who was never very discreet, and Daisy who thought it so clever to imitate Doll. And hadn't the postman told her he'd taken a letter to Miss Martin with a postmark on it which showed it came from one of the addresses she'd written to?

Miss Penset had her finger on the pulse of the village; she could tell that a girl was pregnant almost before the girl herself knew. All the dramas of village life were of the utmost interest to her; and as postmistress she was in a special position to be aware of them.

So I knew that in the post office, people talked to Miss Penset; when I went in there would be a hushed silence. I was regarded with more favor than ever before. I was an upstart perhaps; but at least I was not wicked like some people. Moreover my affairs had become of secondary importance now.

It was the day of the funeral. Flowers kept arriving and the smell of lilies pervaded the house. It was like the smell of death.

We were all dreading the ordeal. As I put on my bonnet, the face which looked back at me from the mirror seemed scarcely like my own. Black didn't suit me; I had parted my hair in the center and wore a heavy knot on the nape of my neck, and long jet earrings in my ears and a necklace of jet about my throat.

My eyes looked enormous; my face thinner and more pale. I had been sleeping badly since Judith's death and I had bad dreams when I did sleep. I kept dreaming of the hiring platform at Trelinket Fair and Mellyora coming over to take my hand. I dreamed once that I looked down at my feet and saw that I had grown a cloven hoof.

Johnny in his black top hat and black jacket looked more dignified than he usually did. He came and stood beside me by the mirror.

"You look . . . regal," he said, and bending, so that he did not disturb my bonnet, kissed the tip of my nose.

He laughed suddenly. "By God," he said, "there's talk in the neighborhood."

I shivered. I hated his look of complacence.

"He was always held up as an example . . . my holy brother. Do you know what they're calling him now?"

"I don't want to."

He raised his eyebrows. "That's not like you, my sweet wife. You usually like to pry into everything. There can only be one reason why you don't want me to tell you. You know already. Yes, my love, they are saying that my sainted brother murdered his wife."

"I hope you told them how absurd this was."

"Do you think my words would have carried any weight?"

"Who's saying this? The postmistress? Scandalmongers like her?"

"I've no doubt the answer to that is yes. That old vixen would repeat any scandal she could get her filthy tongue round. That's to be expected. But it's in higher places. My brother is going to find it hard to live this one down."

"But everyone knew she was drinking."

"Everyone knew that he wanted to be rid of her."

"But she was his wife."

He repeated my words mockingly. "What has come over my clever little wife? Now, Kerensa, what do you think?"

"That he is innocent."

"You have a pure mind. You're the only one who thinks that."

"But the verdict. . . ."

"Accidental death. That covers a lot. I can tell you this; no one will ever forget, and when Justin marries Mellyora Martin, which he will after a respectable interval, that rumor will persist. You know how it is in these parts. Stories are handed down from generation to generation. It'll be there forever . . . the skeleton in the cupboard and no one will ever be sure when some mischievous person is going to open the cupboard door."

He was right. I must tell the truth.

I shivered. I had not told all the truth at the inquest. How could I come forward now? Yet how could I not do so when even his own brother believed Justin might well be a murderer.

Johnny sat on the edge of the bed, studying the tips of his boots.

"I don't see how they can ever marry," he said. "The only way to kill this rumor is for them not to."

How my eyes shone—unnaturally so. If they did not marry—if Justin never married—there could be no threat to Carlyon's future.

The bell from the church began to toll.

"It's time we were going," said Johnny. He took my hand. "How cold you are! Cheer up. It's not my funeral."

I hated him. He didn't care for his brother's trouble. He was only smug and complacent because he could no longer suffer by comparison, for no one could ever hold Justin up as an example again.

What sort of man had I married? I asked myself; and that question was immediately replaced by another and more disquieting one.

What sort of a woman was I?

It was an even greater ordeal than we had feared. Not only St. Larnston village but the entire neighborhood for miles round seemed to have come out to see the burial of Judith.

It was stifling in the church; the scent of lilies was overpowering, and the Reverend James Hemphill seemed as though he would go on forever.

Justin with his mother and Judith's parents sat in the first of the St. Larnston pews, Johnny and I in the second row. I kept staring at Justin's shoulders and I wondered what he would do. I could not bear to look at the coffin, weighed down by flowers and set up on trestles; I couldn't keep my mind on what the Reverend James Hemphill was saying; I could only look at the parsonage pew in which Mrs. Hemphill and her three daughters were now sitting, and think of sitting there with Mellyora and how proud I was because she had given me a gingham dress and straw hat to wear.

My mind would keep wandering back to the past, reminding me of all Mellyora had done for me.

Now the service was over; now we would go out to the vault in the graveyard. The Reverend James Hemphill was coming down from the pulpit. Oh, that funeral scent!

Then I saw Jane Carwillen. It was an extraordinary sight—this old woman, bent almost double, slowly making her way to the coffin. We all sat so still that the sound of her stick tapping in the aisle echoed through the church. Everyone was so surprised that no one attempted to stop her.

She stood by the coffin; then she lifted her stick and pointed it towards the St. Larnston pews.

"Her's gone, my little lady," she said quietly; then, raising her voice: "I curse them as harmed her."

Mrs. Hemphill—always the efficient parson's wife, had moved swiftly from her pew and put an arm through Jane's.

I heard her voice cool, clipped. "Now, come along. We know how upset you are. . . ."

But Jane had come to the church to make a public protest and was not so easily disposed of.

She stood for some seconds staring at the St. Larnston pews. Then she shook her stick menacingly.

As Mrs. Hemphill drew her away to the back of the church the sound of loud sobbing was heard and I saw Judith's mother bury her face in her hands.

"Why did I let her marry. . . ." The words must have been audible to many; and in that moment it seemed as though everyone was waiting for some sign from Heaven, some denunciation from above, some vengeance on those they believed to be Judith's murderers.

Judith's father put an arm about his wife; Justin was moving out of his pew when from behind me, where the Abbas servants were seated, there came a new disturbance.

I heard the words: "She's fainted."

I knew who before I turned.

It was I who went to her; it was I who loosened the neck of her bodice. She lay there on the floor of the church, her hat falling back, her fair lashes still against her pale skin.

I wanted to cry out: "Mellyora. I don't forget. But there's Carlyon . . ."

The servants were watching. I knew what their expressions meant.

Guilty in a holy place!

Back in the Abbas. Thank heaven, the bells had ceased their dismal tolling! Thank heaven the blinds were drawn up to let in the light!

We drank the sherry and ate the food which had been prepared for the funeral. Justin was calm and remote. Already he was gaining his composure. But how unhappy he looked—stricken, as a bereaved husband should look.

Judith's mother had been taken home. It was feared that there would be a hysterical scene if she remained. We tried to talk of anything but the funeral. The rising prices; the state of the government; the virtues of young Mr. Disraeli; the shortcomings of Peel and Gladstone. There were problems more especially our own. Was the Fedder mine really going to close down and what effect would this have on the community?

I was the hostess. Had Judith been here I should still have been, but now I was accepted as such, and should be until Justin had a wife.

But Justin must never have a wife!

There, I had faced it. The determination in my heart. Justin should never have a legitimate son and before he could, he must have a wife.

Justin must never have a son who could take Carlyon's place.

But he would marry Mellyora. Could he? Only if they were prepared to face perpetual scandal.

Would Justin face that?

As soon as I could I went to Mellyora's room which was in semidarkness, for no one had drawn up her blinds.

Her fair hair was unbound and she was lying on the bed, looking young and helpless, reminding me so much of the days of our childhood.

"Oh, Mellyora," I said; and there was a break in my voice. She held out her hand to me and I took it. I felt like Judas. "What now?" I asked.

"It's the end," she answered.

I hated myself. I whispered: "But why? Now . . . you are free."

"Free?" she laughed bitterly. "We have never been less free."

"This is ridiculous. She no longer stands between you. Mellyora, we can speak frankly together."

"Never did she stand more firmly between us."

"But she is gone."

"You know what they are saying."

"That he—perhaps with your help—killed her."

She raised herself on her elbows and her eyes were wild. "How dare they! How can they say such things of Justin."

"It seemed as though she died just at that moment when. . . ."

"Don't say it, Kerensa. You don't believe it."

"Of course I don't. I know he had nothing to do with it."

"I knew I could trust you."

Oh, don't, Mellyora, don't, I wanted to cry; I couldn't speak for a moment because I was afraid that if I did, I should blurt out the truth.

She went on: "We have talked together. It is the end, Kerensa. We both know it."

"But. . . ."

"You must understand. I couldn't marry him. Don't you see that would confirm everything . . . at least, so they would think. There is only one way of proving that Justin is innocent."

"You will go away?" I asked.

"He won't let me go. He wants me to stay here with you. He says you are strong and my friend. He trusts you to look after me."

I buried my face in my hands. I couldn't hide the sneer which played about my mouth. I was sneering at myself and she must not know that. She, who had once known me so well, might know me now.

"He says life would be too hard for me . . . away from here. He says he knows what a wretched existence a governess or a companion can have. He wants me to stay here . . . to look after Carlyon as I am doing now . . . to keep you for my friend."

"And in time . . . when they have forgotten . . . he will marry you?"

"Oh no. We shall never marry, Kerensa. He is going away."

"Justin going away!" There was a lilt in my voice. Justin resigning his rights. The field clear ahead for me and mine.

"It's the only way. He thinks it's best. He will go to the East . . . China and India."

"He cannot mean it."

"He does, Kerensa. He cannot bear to stay here and that we should remain apart. Yet he would not marry me, for he knows the insults that would be levied at me. He wants me to stay with you . . . and in time perhaps. . . ."

"You will go to him?"

"Who shall say."

208

"And he is determined to do this? He can't mean it. He will change his mind."

"There is only one thing that could make him change it, Kerensa."

"What could do that?"

"If something could be *proved*. If someone had seen. . . . But we know no one did. You see, there is no way of proving that we are innocent except this one way . . . by going away from each other, by renouncing what they believe we committed this crime for."

Now was the time. I must confess to her. Judith tripped over Carlyon's toy. He had left it there near the top stair. She didn't see it. It is obvious what happened because her shoe was caught in the cloth. I took the toy away because I didn't want Carlyon's action to have caused her death. I didn't want any shadow to touch my son.

But there was a new issue.

I could clear Justin and Mellyora; they could marry; they could have a son.

No, I could not. That Abbas was for Carlyon. Sir Carlyon. How proud I should be on the day the title was his. I had made a loveless marriage; I had fought hard for what I wanted; I had endured much. Was I going to throw it away for the sake of Mellyora?

I was fond of Mellyora. But what sort of love was hers and Justin's? Had I been Mellyora, would I have allowed my lover to leave me? Would I have loved a man who could so easily accept defeat?

No, a love such as theirs was not worth the sacrifice.

I must keep on reminding myself of that.

If they really loved, they would be ready to face anything for each other.

I was fighting for my son's future and nothing must stand in the way.

6

One can forget the unpleasant episodes of life for days, weeks, months at a stretch and then some incident occurs to revive them in all their disturbing clarity. I was the kind of person who could make excuses for my sins, who could force myself to see the excuses as the truth. I was becoming more and more that kind of person. But truth is like a specter which will haunt you all your life and appear suddenly when you are off your guard to disturb you, to remind you that no matter how many pleasantly colored wrappings you can put over the truth, they can be discarded in a moment by one rude gesture.

There was I sitting at my bureau planning the dinner party of that evening. The Fedders were coming. They had business to discuss with Johnny. Johnny was not pleased, but he had to invite them. I knew very well that Johnny and business did not suit each other.

There was no denying the fact that estate matters were not managed so skillfully as they had been when Justin was at the Abbas. I knew that if Johnny received letters which he found disagreeable he thrust them into a drawer and tried to forget about them. There were complaints from several sources. The farmers said that in Sir Justin's day this and that, which was neglected now, had been carried out. Repairs of cottages which should have been done were left undone; and the fact that Johnny was prepared to promise anything that was asked did not help matters, since he had no intention of keeping his promises. In the beginning he had been very popular, now they knew they couldn't trust him.

It was two years since Justin had gone away. He was in Italy now and wrote rarely. I was always expecting that one day there would be a letter for Mellyora asking her to join him there.

When you have wronged someone deeply your feelings towards them must change. There were times when I almost hated Mellyora; I was really hating myself, but as it is always difficult for a person of my nature to do that, the only outlet is to hate the one who has made you hate yourself. When these moods were on me I tried to be more gentle with her. She would be Carlyon's nurse and governess, until he was old enough to go to school, but I had insisted that she should be treated like a member of the family, taking meals with us, and even coming to dinner parties; people met her as Miss Martin, the daughter of the late parson, rather than the nursery governess at the Abbas. I had taught Carlyon to call her Aunt Mellyora. There were times when there was little I wouldn't have done for Mellyora.

She had changed; she looked older; she was quieter. It was strange, but as I grew more flamboyant she seemed to grow more colorless. She wore her lovely yellow hair in smooth braids about her head; mine were coiled high and elaborately so as not to lose one bit of its beauty. She wore quiet grays and blacks—which were becoming to her fair skin—but so quiet. I wore black rarely; it did not suit me and when I did, I would always have with it a touch of flaming color—scarlet or my favorite jade green. I had evening dresses of scarlet chiffon and jade silk; sometimes I wore lavender and a combination of dark blue dominated by pink.

I was the lady of the Abbas now; there was no one to stand in my way and in the two years since Justin had gone away I had stabilized my position. The disaffection of Justin had helped me considerably. I almost believed that Haggety and Mrs. Rolt forgot for long periods at a time that I was not born and bred to the role which I played so perfectly.

Lady St. Larnston had died the previous year, quietly in her sleep, so there had been another funeral at the Abbas. But how different this one from that of Judith! Calmly and conventionally as she had lived her life, so the old lady passed out of it.

And since her going, my position had become even more secure.

There was a knock at the door.

"Come in," I said, with the proper touch of authority, not arrogant, not condescending, merely giving an order naturally. Mrs. Rolt and Mrs. Salt entered.

"Oh Ma'am, it's about the dinner tonight," said Mrs. Salt.

"I have been thinking of it." I looked up at them, conscious of myself—white hands on the table, the pen held lightly; my wedding ring and the square-cut emerald above—the one which was a St. Larnston ring and which Lady St. Larnston had given me after Justin had gone away. My feet in black leather slippers showing beneath the skirt of my mauve morning gown which was trimmed with satin ribbons; my hair in a chignon on the top of my head—simply and elegantly clad in the morning attire of a great lady.

"A clear soup to begin with, Mrs. Salt. Then I think sole with a sauce which I shall leave to you. Partridge . . . or chicken . . . and the roast beef. We must keep it simple because I gather from Mrs. Fedder that Mr. Fedder's digestion is giving him a little trouble."

"It's not to be wondered at, Ma'am," said Mrs. Rolt. "It's all this talk about the mine. Not that I suppose they'm got much to worry about—them Fedders. Reckon they've been feathering their nests all this time. But have you heard, Ma'am, if it be true the mine be closing down?"

"I have heard nothing," I said coolly and turned to Mrs. Salt. "A soufflé, I think, and let us have apple pie with cream."

"Very good, Ma'am," said Mrs. Salt.

Mrs. Rolt put in: "And Haggety were wondering about the wines, Ma'am."

"He should see Mr. St. Larnston about the wines," I replied.

"Well, Ma'am . . ." began Mrs. Rolt.

I inclined my head. This was one of those mornings when they were becoming too talkative. On most occasions I could subdue them completely.

I haughtily inclined my head and picked up my pen. They exchanged glances and murmuring: "Thank you, Ma'am!" went out; I heard their voices, low, whispering as the door closed.

I frowned. It was as though their prying fingers had opened a cupboard door which I preferred to keep shut. What was it Johnny had once said about skeletons in cupboards? Justin's and Mellyora's? Well, I was ready to admit I had my skeletons too.

I tried to dismiss the memory of those two mischievous old faces, as I picked up my pen and started going through the last month's account which Haggety had put on my desk a few days before in accordance with my orders.

Another knock.

"Come in."

This time it was Haggety himself.

A curse on memories! I thought of his foot touching mine under the table. That little light in his eyes which meant: We must understand each other. I pay lip service to Mrs. Rolt but you're the one I really fancy.

I hated him when I remembered; and I must force myself to regard him as the butler merely, quite efficient if one shut one's eyes to his shortcomings—too much freedom with the women servants, a little bribery to suppliers, a little adjustment of accounts so that they came out in his favor. The sort of failings one might have with any butler.

"Well, Haggety?" I went on writing just because I had remembered.

He coughed. "Er, Ma'am . . . er . . ."

Now I must look up. There was no disrespect on his face, only embarrassment. I waited patiently.

"It's about the wine, Ma'am."

"For tonight, yes. You must see Mr. St. Larnston about it."

"Er . . . Ma'am. It's that we'll just about have enough for tonight, Ma'am, and then . . ."

I looked at him in astonishment. "Why haven't you seen that the cellar is well stocked?"

"Ma'am. The merchant, Ma'am . . . he wants a settlement."

I felt a faint color in my cheeks. "This is extraordinary," I said.

"No, Ma'am. There's a large amount outstanding . . . and . . ."

"You had better let me see the account, Haggety."

A smile of relief touched his face. "Well, Ma'am, I've what you might say anticipated that. Tis here. If, Ma'am, you'll settle it, there'll be no trouble, I do assure you."

I did not look at the statement he handed me.

I said: "Such treatment is most disrespectful. Perhaps we should change our wine merchant."

Haggety fumbled and brought out another bill. "Well, Ma'am, in a manner of speaking we have two . . . and things is the same with the both."

It had always been a tradition at the Abbas that wine bills were the affair of the man of the house. Although I dealt with

213

other expenditure, since the departure of Justin, the cellar had been a matter between Haggety and Johnny.

"I will see that this has Mr. St. Larnston's immediate attention," I said, and I added: "I do not think he will be pleased with these merchants. It may be necessary to find others. But the cellars, of course, should not be allowed to be depleted. You should have brought this matter to light before this."

Haggety's face puckered as though he were about to cry.

"Ma'am, I have told Mr. Johnny . . . Mr. St. Larnston . . . nigh on a dozen times."

"Very well, Haggety, I understand. It has slipped his memory. I see that you are not to blame."

Haggety went out and immediately I looked down at the wine merchants' accounts. To my horror I saw that between the two we owed some five hundred pounds.

Five hundred pounds! No wonder they refused to supply us with more until we paid. How could Johnny have been so careless.

A sudden fear had come to me. What was Johnny doing with the money which was coming in from the estate? I had my allowance with which I settled household accounts and bought what I needed. Why did Johnny go so often to Plymouth—far more often than Sir Justin had gone? Why were there continual complaints about the estate?

It was time I had a talk with Johnny.

That was an uneasy day.

I carefully put away the wine bills but I couldn't forget them. Those figures kept dancing before my eyes and I thought of my life with Johnny.

What did we know of each other? He still admired me; I still attracted him, not with the same passionate fire as in the beginning, not with that abandonment which had made him risk his family's displeasure to make me his wife; but there was physical passion there. He still found me different from other women. He told me so again and again. What other women? I asked once, wondering what other women there were in Johnny's life. "All other women in the world," he answered. And I didn't care enough to pursue that point. I always felt I must repay Johnny for my position, the fulfillment of a dream, all that he had given to me. And most of all he had given me Carlyon, my blessed son, who, thanks to Johnny was a St. Larnston and could one day be Sir Carlyon. For this I must be grateful. I remembered this always and tried to repay him by being the sort of wife he needed. I believed I was. I shared his bed; I ran his house; I was a credit

214

to him when people could forget my origins which were like a shadow, visible on some days when the bright sun discovered it, but often out of sight and out of mind. I never asked questions about his life. I suspected that there might be other women. The St. Larnstons—with the exception of Justin—were like that; his father had been, and there was his Grandfather who had played his part in Granny's story.

Johnny could lead his own private life, but the management of the estate was something he could not keep to himself. If there were debts I must know.

I suddenly realized how lax I had been. The St. Larnston estate was important because one day it was going to be Carlyon's.

What had I heard about the days of uneasiness, years ago when the Abbas and all its lands had almost passed into other hands. Then tin had been discovered in the meadow near the Six Virgins and that tin had saved the family fortunes. I remembered how, at Joe's wedding, there had been talk of our mine. Perhaps I could speak to Johnny. I must discover whether the wine bills had been left unpaid through carelessness or for other more alarming reasons.

Those figures continued to dance before my eyes, jerking me out of my complacence. I had been too content with my life. For the last year it had run too smoothly. I even believed that Mellyora had become resigned and was not yearning so much for Justin; once or twice I had heard her laugh as she used to when we were both together at the parsonage.

I had seen everything turning out as I had planned it should. I was reconciled to Joe's lack of ambition; Granny had left her cottage and lived with the Pollents now. I knew that it was the most satisfactory arrangement and yet I was sad in a way because she must live with Joe instead of with me. Granny would never have fitted in at the Abbas with her potions and cures and her Cornish accent; but at the Pollents' she was very welcome. There was Joe working on his cures for animals and Granny continuing with her work. It fitted somehow. But it wasn't quite what I had wanted for her; and I often felt sad when I visited her there. When we talked together I knew that our relationship had not changed and I was as important to her—and she to me—as we had ever been.

Yes, indeed I had been too complacent; I must not remain any longer in ignorance of our financial position.

I put away my papers and shut the desk. I would go to the nursery to see Carlyon who could always soothe me. He was growing up fast and was advanced for his age. He was not a bit like Johnny, nor like me; I often marveled that we could have had such a child. He was already reading and Mellyora said that he had practically taught himself; his attempts at drawing seemed to me astonishing; and he had his own little pony because I had wanted him to ride at an early age. I never allowed him to ride without me—I wouldn't trust anyone else, not even Mellyora; and I myself would lead him round the meadow. He had a natural aptitude and was quickly at home in the saddle.

There was only one characteristic in him which I should have liked to change. He could be reduced to tears very quickly when he thought something was hurt. There had been one occasion more than a year earlier during the very hot weather when he had come in crying because there was a crack in the brown earth and he thought it was broken. "Poor, *poor* ground! Mend it, Mamma," he said, looking at me with tear-filled eyes as though he had thought me an omnipotent being. So it was with animals—a mouse in a trap, a dead hare he had seen hung in the kitchen, a cat who had been hurt in a fight. He suffered acutely because his heart was too tender and I often used to fear that when he grew older he would be too easily hurt.

On that morning I hurried along to the nursery, guessing that Mellyora would be getting him ready to take out and thinking that we would go together.

I could shelve all disturbing fears while I was with Carlyon. I threw open the nursery door. It was empty. When old Lady St. Larnston was alive I had had the nurseries redecorated and she and I had become very friendly while that operation was in progress. We had chosen the wallpaper together—a wonderful wallpaper, blue and white with the willow-pattern story repeated over and over again. Everything was blue and white; a white pattern on blue curtains, a blue carpet. The room was full of sunshine, but there was no sign of Carlyon or Mellyora.

"Where are you?" I called.

My eyes went to the window seat where propped up against the window was Nelly. I could never look at the thing without a shock. I had said to Carlyon: "This is a baby's toy. Do you want to keep it? Let's find some big boy's toys."

He had taken it firmly from me, his face puckered in grief; I believe he fancied that the thing could hear my words and be hurt.

"It's Nelly," he said, with dignity, and opening a cupboard door he put it inside as though he feared for its safety.

Now I picked it up. The torn cloth had been neatly mended

216

by Mellyora. But it was visible like a scar. If she had known. . . .

This was an unpleasant morning because too much that should be forgotten was coming back to leer at me.

I put Nelly back on the window seat and opened the door into the adjoining room where Carlyon had his meals.

As I did so I came face to face with Mellyora.

"You've seen him?" she said and I noticed how anxious she was.

"What?"

"Carlyon? He's with you?"

"No. . . ."

"Then where . . . ?"

We stared at each other in dismay and I was conscious of that feeling of sickness, numbness, and desperation which the thought of any harm overtaking Carlyon could give me.

"I thought he must be with you," she said.

"You mean . . . he's not here?"

"I've been looking for him for the last ten minutes."

"How long have you missed him?"

"I left him here . . . after breakfast. He was making a drawing of his pony. . . ."

"We must find him," I commanded. "He must be here somewhere."

I went roughly past her. I wanted to upbraid her, to accuse her of carelessness. That was because seeing the toy elephant on the window seat had reminded me vividly how I had wronged her. I called sharply: "Carlyon. Where are you?"

She joined me; and we had soon made sure that he was nowhere in the nursery.

Now the dreadful sick fear was a certainty. Carlyon was lost. In a short time I had the whole household searching for him. Every nook of the Abbas must be searched, every servant questioned. But I was not satisfied that they would search properly. I must search myself, so I went through the house . . . through every room, calling for my son to come out if he were hiding, begging him not to frighten me any more.

I thought of all the things that could have harmed him. I pictured him trampled to death by galloping horses, kidnaped by gypsies, caught in a trap . . . maimed as poor Joe had been. And there I was in the old part of the house where the nuns had lived, meditated, and prayed; and I seemed to feel despair close in on me and that I was shut in with grief. A horrible suspicion came to me then that some harm had befallen my child. It was as though the spirit of the nun was beside me,

217

that she identified herself with me, that her grief was my grief; and I knew then that if my son were taken from me it would be as though I were walled in by grief which would be as enduring as stone walls.

I fought to throw off the spell of evil which seemed to wrap itself about me.

"No," I cried out aloud. "Carlyon, my son. Where are you? Come out of your hiding place and stop frightening me."

As I ran out of the house, I met Mellyora and glanced hopefully at her but she shook her head.

"He's not in the house," she said.

We began searching the grounds, calling his name.

Near the stables I saw Polore.

"The little master be lost?" he asked.

"Have you seen him?" I demanded.

"Just about an hour ago, Ma'am. He were talking to me about his pony. Took sick it were, in the night, and I were telling him."

"Was he upset?"

"Well, Ma'am. He were always fond of that pony. Talked to 'er he did. Said to never mind. 'Er'd soon be better. Then he did go back to the house. I watched 'un."

"And you haven't seen him since?"

"No, Ma'am. I ain't seen him since."

Everyone must join in the search, I commanded. Everything must be left. My son must be found. We had established that he was not in the house; he could not be far away because Polore had seen him only an hour before in the stables.

I cannot explain all that I suffered during the search. Again and again hope was raised and dashed. I felt as though I lived through years of torment. I blamed Mellyora. Was she not supposed to look after him? If anything has happened to him, I thought, I shall have paid in full for everything I did to Mellyora.

She was white and harassed and I had not seen her so unhappy since Justin went. I reminded myself that she loved Carlyon; and it seemed to me that my grief would always be hers. We shared our troubles . . . except on one occasion when her loss was my gain.

I saw Johnny riding into the stable and called to him. "What the devil . . . ?" he began.

"Carlyon's lost."

"Lost! Where?"

"If we knew, he wouldn't be lost." My grief was so great

I had to release some of it in anger. My lips were working and I couldn't control them. "I'm frightened," I said.

"He's playing somewhere."

"We've searched the house and grounds. . . ." I looked wildly about me and I caught the glint of the sun on the Virgins.

Then a sudden fear struck me. I had shown him the stones the other day; he had been fascinated by them. "Don't go near the old mine, Carlyon. Promise." He had given his ready promise and he was not a child to break his word. But suppose my very words had aroused some curiosity; suppose he had become so fascinated that he could not resist the temptation to examine the mine; suppose he had forgotten his promise? After all he was little more than a baby.

I turned to Johnny and clutched at his arm. "Johnny," I said, "suppose he went to the mine. . . ."

I had never seen Johnny so frightened and I warmed to him. There had been times when I had reproached him for his lack of interest in our son. Oh God, I thought. He is as frightened as I am.

"No," said Johnny. *"No."*

"But if he did . . . ?"

"There's a warning there. . . ."

"He couldn't read it. Or if he did, it might have made him want to explore."

We stared at each other wildly.

Then I said: "We'll have to find out. They'll have to go down."

"Go down the mine! Are you mad . . . Kerensa?"

"But he might be there. . . ."

"It's madness."

"At this very moment he might be lying hurt. . . ."

"A fall down there would kill him."

"Johnny!"

"It's a mad idea. He's not there. He's playing somewhere. He's in the house. . . . He's . . ."

"We've got to search the mine. There's no time to be lost. Now . . . now."

"Kerensa!"

I threw him off and started to run towards the stables. I would summon Polore and some of the men. They must prepare without delay. This new terror obsessed me. Carlyon had fallen down the old mine shaft. I visualized his fear if he were conscious; the horror of his not being.

"Polore!" I called. "Polore."

Then I heard the sound of horse's hoofs and my sister-in-law Essie came riding into the stable yard.

I scarcely looked at her. I had no time for her on an occasion like this. But she was shouting at me. "Oh, Kerensa, Joe said to come and tell 'ee without delay because you'd be anxious like. Carlyon, he be with his uncle."

I nearly fainted with relief.

"He did come over fifteen minutes since. Some tale about his pony needing Joe. Joe said to ride over right away and tell 'ee where he be. He said you'd be nigh fit to drop with the worry of it."

Johnny was standing beside me.

"Oh, Johnny," I cried, because I saw that he was as happy as I was.

Then I threw myself into his arms and we clung together. I had never felt so close to my husband.

It was an hour later when Joe brought Carlyon back to the Abbas. Carlyon was standing up with Joe in the trap; Joe had allowed him to hold the reins with him so that Carlyon believed that he himself was driving the trap.

I had rarely seen him look so happy.

Joe was happy too. He loved children and longed for a son of his own; so far there was no sign that Essie was going to produce one.

"Mamma!" called Carlyon as soon as he saw me, "Uncle Joe's come to mend Carpony."

Carpony was his own name for the pony, derived from Carlyon's pony. He found his own special name for everything he loved.

I stood by the trap looking at him, great thankfulness in my heart to see him, alive, unmaimed. I could scarcely keep the tears from my eyes.

Joe noticed my emotion. "I sent Essie over the minute he come," he said, gently, "knowing how you'd feel."

"Thank you, Joe," I answered briskly.

"A proper little man 'e be . . . a-driving my trap now. What next?"

"Driving the trap now," repeated Carlyon happily. "Coming to mend Carpony now, Uncle Joe?"

"Yes, reckon we'd be better getting along to see how that little old pony be."

Carlyon said: "We'll soon mend him, eh, Uncle Joe?"

"That's one thing I reckon we can be pretty sure on."

There was a camaraderie between them which disturbed me. I had not meant the future Sir Carlyon to become too friendly with the vet. He must acknowledge him as his uncle, it was true, but there were not to be too many meetings. If Joe had been the doctor it would have been different.

I lifted Carlyon out of the trap. "Dearest," I said, "another time, don't go off without telling us first."

The happiness died out of his face. Joe must have told him how worried I should be. He put his arms about my neck and said softly: "Tell next time."

How adorable he was! It hurt me to see him so friendly with Joe and yet at the same time I was pleased. This was my own brother who had once been very dear to me—and still was, although I was disappointed in him.

I watched Joe go into the stables. His limp always softened me towards him, always reminded me of that night when Kim had carried him back to the cottage; somehow there was an ache in my heart—but not for the past. How could I, who was so successful now, want to be back there? But there was a feeling of longing to know what Kim was doing now.

Joe examined the pony. "Not much wrong with her, I reckon."

Joe scratched his head thoughtfully.

"Not much wrong with her, I reckon too," repeated Carlyon, scratching his head.

"Nothing that we can't put right, seems to me."

Carlyon smiled. His eyes all for his wonderful Uncle Joe.

The dinner party that night was scarcely a success. I had not had an opportunity of speaking to Johnny about the wine bills during the day and while we sat at dinner I remembered them.

The Fedders were not a very interesting couple. James Fedder was in his late fifties, his wife a few years younger. I had nothing in common with her.

Mellyora dined with us, although I had not invited an extra man to make us an even number, since the Fedders were with us, because James wanted to talk business with Johnny, and after the meal the men would be left to talk at the dinner table over their port.

I was glad when Mellyora, Mrs. Fedder, and I could retire to the drawing room, although I found it a very boring evening and was even more delighted when the time arrived for the Fedders to leave.

It had been an exhausting day: first the shock about the bills, then Carlyon's escape, and after that a dinner party which was not in the least stimulating.

221

In our bedroom I decided to open the subject of the bills with my husband.

He looked tired, I thought, but the matter could be shelved no longer: it was too important.

"Haggety has disturbed me, Johnny," I began. "Today he showed me two demands from wine merchants. He says they won't supply us with any more wine until the bills are paid."

Johnny shrugged his shoulders.

"It's . . . it's insulting," I said.

He yawned, feigning an indifference which I suspected he did not feel. "My dear Kerensa, people like us don't feel we have to pay bills as soon as they're submitted."

"So people like you are in the habit of having tradespeople refuse to supply you?"

"You're exaggerating."

"I've had it straight from Haggety. This sort of thing didn't happen when Justin was here."

"All sorts of things happened when Justin was here which don't happen now. For instance, wives mysteriously fell down staircases to their deaths."

He was changing the issue; just as I liked to justify myself when feeling guilty, so did he.

"The bills should be paid, Johnny."

"What with?"

"Money."

He shrugged his shoulders. "You find it and I'll pay the bills."

"We can't entertain our guests if we can't give them wine to drink."

"Haggety must find someone who *will* supply us."

"And run up more bills?"

"You've got a cottage mentality, Kerensa."

"I'm glad of it if it means I pay my debts."

"Oh, don't talk to me of money."

"Johnny, tell me frankly, are we in difficulties . . . financial difficulties?"

"There are always money troubles."

"Are there? Were there in Justin's day?"

"Everything was perfectly arranged in Justin's day. He was so clever in every way . . . until his cleverness caught up with him."

"Johnny, I want to know everything."

"To know all is to forgive," he quoted lightly.

"Are we short of money?"

"We are."

"And what are you doing about it?"

"Hoping and praying for a miracle."

"Johnny, how bad are things?"

"I don't know. But we'll pull through. We always do."

"I must go into these matters with you . . . soon."

"Soon?" he said.

A sudden thought struck me. "You haven't been asking James Fedder for money?"

He laughed. "The shoe is on the other foot, my sweet wife. Fedder is looking for a kind friend who'll come to his aid. He chose the wrong one tonight."

"He wanted to borrow money from you?"

Johnny nodded.

"And what did you say?"

"Oh I gave him a blank check and told him to help himself. There was so much in the bank, I wouldn't miss a few thousand."

"Johnny . . . seriously."

"Seriously, Kerensa, I told him I was in a low state. The Fedder mine's running out, in any case. It's no use trying to bolster things up."

"The mine," I said. "Of course, the mine!"

He stared at me.

"I know we shan't like it but if it's the only way . . . and if there's tin there as people say there is."

His lips were tight; his eyes blazing.

"What are you saying?" he demanded.

"But if it's the only way . . ." I began.

He cut me short. "You . . ." he said so low that I could scarcely hear. "*You* . . . to suggest such a thing. What do you think?" He took me by the shoulders and shook me roughly. "Who are you . . . to think you can rule the Abbas?"

For the moment his eyes were so cruel that I believed he hated me.

"Open the mine!" he went on. "When you know as well as I do. . . ."

He lifted his hand; he was so angry that I thought he was going to strike me.

Then he turned abruptly away.

He lay at one side of the bed; I at the other.

I knew that he did not sleep until the early hours of the morning. It had been a strange disturbing day and its events would not be dismissed from my mind. I saw Mrs. Rolt and

223

Mrs. Salt standing before me; I saw Haggety with the wine bills; Carlyon riding with Joe, holding the reins of Joe's horse in plump beloved fingers; and I saw Johnny, his face white with anger.

A bad day, I thought. The stirring of ghosts; the opening of cupboards and disclosing old skeletons best forgotten.

From then on my days were disturbed. My attention became focused on Johnny because I had suddenly realized that he was no fit person to handle the estate and that his mismanagement could have its effect on Carlyon's future.

I knew little of business matters but I did know how easily inefficient people could get into trouble. I went to see Granny, taking Carlyon with me. My son was delighted when he heard where we were going. I myself drove the little trap I used for such short journeys and Carlyon stood before me, holding the reins as he had with Joe. All the time he was chattering about his Uncle Joe. Uncle Joe says horses have feelings just like people. Uncle Joe says all animals know what you're saying, so you have to be careful not to hurt them. Uncle Joe says. . . .

I should be pleased that I had given him an uncle whom he admired so much.

Essie came out to meet us—as always, a little shy in my company. She took us into Granny's room. Granny was in bed; it was not one of her good days, she told me.

Her black hair was in two plaits and she looked older; she had always seemed out of place in the Pollents' house, although I knew that Essie had done her utmost to make her welcome and at home. The room with the neat dimity curtains and the starched counterpane was not Granny's style; and there was about her an air of resignation, as though, I thought with alarm, she had come here to await the end.

Carlyon climbed onto the bed to embrace her and for a few minutes she talked to him. He remained passively polite in her arms, watching her lips with some concentration, but I knew that he was longing to be with Joe. Essie had told Joe that we were here and when he came in at the door Carlyon was off the bed and rushing at my brother. Joe lifted him in his arms and held him above his head.

"So you be come along to give a hand, have 'ee?"

"Yes, Uncle Joe, I've come to give a hand."

"Well I got to go along to Farmer Pengaster this morning. One of his horses. I be thinking that a bran mash'll be all she's needing. What do 'ee think, partner?"

Carlyon put his head on one side. "Yes, I *do* think all she be needing is a bran mash, partner."

"Well, look 'ee here, how'd it be if you was to come along with me and have a look at her? I'd get your Aunt Essie to wrap up a pasty for us in case we was to feel a bit peckish."

Carlyon had thrust his hands in his pockets; he was standing with his weight on one leg as Joe stood; he hunched his shoulders which I knew to be a sign of joy.

Joe was glancing at me, his eyes alight with pleasure. There was only one thing I could say.

"You'll bring him back this afternoon then, Joe."

Joe nodded. "Reckon our rounds'll bring us that way. I've got to look in at the Abbas stables. . . ."

Carlyon gave a sudden laugh. "Better be going partner," he said. "It's a heavy morning."

When they had gone, Essie going with them to wrap up the pasties, Granny said to me: "Tis good to see them together." She laughed. "But you don't think so, lovey. Your brother's not good enough for you now."

"No, Granny, that's not true. . . ."

"You don't like to see the little one playing the vet, eh? And Joe so happy to have him and he's so happy to be with Joe! I trust Joe'll have a son one day, but till that day, lovey, don't grudge him a little share in yours. Remember how you used to love your brother. Remember how you were going to have all the best for him as well as yourself. You were born to love, Kerensa my girl; you do it with all your heart and soul. And tis good to do what you do with all your power, for then you do it well. And the boy's worthy of your devotion, but don't 'ee try to force him, girl. Don't 'ee do that."

"I'd never force him to do anything."

She laid her hand over my own. "You and I understand each other, Granddaughter. I know your mind because it works as mine does. You're uneasy. You've come to talk to me about it."

"I've come to see *you*, Granny. Are you happy here?"

"My bones is old. They creak, lovey. When I stoop to pick my herbs there's a stiffness in my joint. I'm not young any more. I'm too old to live alone, they tell me. My life is done; now I be lucky to have a comfortable bed where I can rest my old bones while I'm waiting."

"Don't talk like that, Granny."

"'Tain't no use shutting your eyes to truth. Tell me, what brought ye here for a talk with your old Granny?"

"It's Johnny."

"Ah!" A film seemed to pass across her eyes. It was often so when I talked of my marriage which was a painful subject to her. She was delighted that my dream had come true, that I was mistress of the Abbas, but I sensed that she wished it could have come about through some other means.

"I'm afraid he's wasting money . . . money that should be Carlyon's."

"Don't 'ee look too far ahead, lovey. There be the other one."

"Justin. He's safe . . . for a while."

"How can 'ee be sure? He might make up his mind to marry."

"If he were thinking of marriage he would have said so by now. He rarely writes to Mellyora and when he does he never mentions marriage."

"I'm sorry for parson's daughter. She were good to you."

Granny was watching me but I could not meet her eye. I had not told even her what I had done that day when I had found Judith at the bottom of the stairs.

"And you and Johnny?" she asked. "There's a severance between you?"

"Sometimes I feel I don't know much about Johnny."

"There's few of us—however close we be—who can see down deep into another's heart."

I wondered if she knew my secret, if those special powers of hers had revealed it. I said quickly: "What should I do, Granny? I've got to stop him wasting money. I've got to save Carlyon's inheritance."

"Can you make him do as you say, Kerensa?"

"I'm not sure."

"Ah!" She gave a long drawn-out sigh. "I fret about you, Kerensa. I wake sometimes in this room of mine and it do all seem so strange at night, and I fret about you. I wonder about that marriage of yours. Tell me this, Kerensa, if you could go back . . . if you could be a maiden once more and the choice were yours, what would it be? Single and fighting your way in the world, a governess or companion—for you had the education to be that—and freedom; or the Abbas and the marriage that had to go with it?"

I turned to her in astonishment. Give up the Abbas, my position, my pride, my dignity . . . my son! And for the sake

226

of being an upper servant in someone else's house! There was no need to consider my answer to that. My marriage was not all that one hoped for in a marriage; Johnny was no ideal husband and I was not, and never had been, in love with him; but I did not have to consider for one moment.

"When I married Johnny I made the right choice," I said, and I added: "for me."

A slow smile touched Granny's lips.

"Now I be content," she said. "No more fretting over you, lovey. Why did I doubt? You knew what you wanted right from the time you was a little one. And this new trouble? Don't you fret yourself. You'll see all's well. You'll make Mr. Johnny St. Larnston dance to your tune."

I felt better after that talk with Granny. I drove back to the Abbas alone, assuring myself that I would insist on Johnny's sharing the burdens of the estate with me. I would discover how deeply in debt we were. As for the mild irritation of Carlyon's interest in Joe and his work, all children had these enthusiasms; he would grow out of that when he went away to school and on to the University.

It wasn't easy to tie Johnny down. When I tried to discuss business with him he became flippant; and yet at the same time I sensed a lack of ease in his manner and I knew that deep down he was concerned.

"What do you propose to do?" he demanded. "Wave your witch's wand?"

I retorted that I should like to know exactly how matters stood, and that we might get advice.

"It's not advice we need, sweet wife. It's money."

"Perhaps we could cut down expenses."

"Brilliant idea. You begin."

"We'll both begin. Let us see if we can find means of economizing."

He laid his hands on my shoulders. "The clever little woman!" Then he frowned. "Be more clever still, my love, and keep your nose out of my affairs."

"But Johnny . . . I'm your wife."

"A position you secured through bribery and corruption."

"What?"

He laughed aloud. "You amuse me, Kerensa. I never saw anyone more able to play a part. All the lady of the manor now. Even my mother never had quite such an air of the

227

grande dame. I'm not sure that you ought not to be at Court
—we're too simple for you here in St. Larnston."

"Can't we be serious?"

"That's what I want to be. I'm asking you to keep out."

"Johnny, if there's a way I'm going to find it. There's
Carlyon's future to think of."

He shook me then. "I'm warning you, Kerensa. I don't
want your advice. I don't want your help."

"But this concerns us both."

He threw me from him and stalked away.

I had an uneasy feeling that it was more than the lack of
money which was worrying Johnny. He wouldn't confide in
me; at times he gave me the impression that he hated me; but
I was determined to find out.

There were afternoons when he went into Plymouth and
did not return until late at night. Another woman? A sudden
suspicion came to me that it was she who was ruining him;
for myself I did not care, but I cared for Carlyon.

Johnny was a careless man; there were occasions when he
forgot to lock his desk.

I told myself that everything I did was for Carlyon and although I did not enjoy going through his private papers I was
prepared to do so for the sake of my son.

The morning Johnny left his desk unlocked I learned what
I wanted to know.

Johnny was gambling. That would explain his visits to
Plymouth. He was deeply in debt, and the majority of his
liabilities were gambling debts.

I was going to put a stop to this.

Johnny was not at home. I guessed that he was at the
gambling club in Plymouth for he had ridden off that afternoon. I was enraged against him. I had blazed at him, telling
him that I knew what he was doing, demanding to know if
he had some crazy idea of winning a fortune. I could see that
was exactly what he hoped for.

And there was nothing I could do to stop him.

Mellyora and I dined alone together. She knew I was worried because she had always been able to sense my moods;
and she guessed that my anxieties were concerned with the
estate.

"Things have been going wrong ever since . . ." she began.

I did not answer. I could never bear her to refer to Justin.

She was silent, her eyes lowered; I knew that she was

228

thinking of all that might have been. Was she seeing, as I was, herself sitting at this table, Justin smiling at her, a happy Justin, content in his marriage? Was she thinking of the son —the future Sir Justin—who might at this time be asleep in the nurseries?

I felt angry with her. I said sharply: "Things have not been going well at the Abbas for some time."

She played with her knife and fork. "Kerensa, there's going to be a lot of poverty hereabouts."

"You mean when the Fedder mine closes?"

She looked up then and her eyes were full of pity. She nodded.

"It can't be long now," she went on. "And then . . ."

"It seems to me that we're all falling on hard times." I couldn't help it but I had to know what was in her mind, so I went on: "Mellyora, have you heard from Justin lately?"

"Not for two months," she answered, and her voice sounded tranquil. "His letters have changed."

"Changed?" I wondered whether she noticed the fear in my voice as soon as I had spoken.

"He seems . . . more at peace. Reconciled."

"There is . . . someone else?"

"No. It is just that he is at peace . . . spiritually."

I said harshly: "If he had really loved you, Mellyora, he would never have left you."

She regarded me steadily. "Perhaps there are several kinds of love, Kerensa. Perhaps it is difficult for you to understand them all."

I felt contemptuous of them both—Justin and Mellyora. I need not reproach myself. They were not capable of deep and passionate love. Love for them had to be right and conventional. That was no way to love. What I had done need not haunt me. After all, if they had really loved, they would not have allowed themselves to be parted. The only worth-while love was one which was ready to cast aside all worldly considerations for its sake.

We were suddenly aware of unusual sounds. The tramp of feet, the sound of voices.

"What's happening?" I asked, and we were silent, listening, as the voices came closer. I heard the loud clanging of the doorbell, followed by silence and Haggety's footsteps. Then the sound of voices and Haggety was coming to the dining room.

I looked up as he entered. "Yes, Haggety?"

He cleared his throat. "Tis a deputation, Ma'am. They want to see Mr. St. Larnston."

"Did you tell them that he was not at home?"

"Yes, Ma'am, but I don't rightly think they believed me."

"What deputation is this?"

"Well, Ma'am. It be some of the men from Fedder's, I do think, and there's Saul Cundy with 'em."

"And they've come here?" I asked. "Why?"

Haggety looked discomfited. "Well, Ma'am, I did tell them . . ."

I knew why they had come. They wanted the St. Larnston mine to be examined for tin. If it were possible that it could provide work, they wanted it provided. And why not? Might it not be the solution to our problems? The mine had saved the Abbas once. Why not again?

I said: "*I* will see the men, Haggety. Bring them into the library."

Haggety hesitated; I looked at him coldly and he turned away to do my bidding.

In the library I faced the men. Saul Cundy looked big and powerful. A grim man, a leader, I thought; and I wondered once more what he had seen in Hetty Pengaster.

Saul was the spokesman, so I addressed myself to him.

"You have come to see my husband but he is not at home. He consults me in business matters, so if you care to tell me why you have come here I shall be able to pass on your message to him."

They hesitated; I could see skeptical looks on some of the faces. Perhaps they didn't believe that Johnny wasn't at home; perhaps they didn't care to talk to a woman.

Saul Cundy and I took each other's measure. I was sure he was remembering that I was Granny Bee's daughter. He decided to talk to me.

"Well, Ma'am," he said, "tis a certain fact that the Fedder mine be closing down and that will bring real hardships to many on us. We believe there be good tin in St. Larnston mine and us wants a chance to find out, and if we be right to get it working."

"That seems fair enough," I answered.

I could see the relief on their faces and I went on: "As soon as my husband returns I will tell him of your visit and the matter will be looked into."

Saul Cundy went on: "Well, Ma'am, there shouldn't be no delay like. Reckon it 'ud put everyone's mind at rest if we did start getting the boryers ready."

"What makes you so sure there is tin in St. Larnston mine?"

"Well, our grandfathers did tell our fathers and our fathers did tell we how it were closed down sudden like. For a whim, ye might say. Reg'lar lot of hardship it caused too. Well, hard times is coming and hard times is no times for gentlemen to flaunt their whims."

There was a threat there and I did not like threats, but I realized the wisdom of their reasoning. "I will certainly tell my husband that you have called," I assured them.

"And tell him, Ma'am, that we'll be calling again."

I bowed my head and they filed out respectfully.

I went back to Mellyora. She was quite pale.

"Kerensa," she said, her eyes showing her admiration, "is there nothing you will not do?"

I retorted that I could not see that I had done anything extraordinary, and I thought: This is the answer. The mine will be worked again. The Abbas will be saved for Sir Carlyon.

I was awake when Johnny came in that night. I saw before I spoke that there was a look of desperation in his eyes; it was what I had come to recognize as the losing look.

So much the better. He would now be as eager for the investigations into the possibility of working the mine as everyone else.

I sat up in bed, and as soon as he entered I cried: "Johnny, there has been a deputation."

"A what?"

"Saul Cundy and some of the miners have been here. They want you to open the St. Larnston mine."

He sat down on the bed and stared at me.

"I know you don't like it. But it's a way out of our difficulties. What worked once can work again."

"Are you mad?" he demanded. He rose unsteadily and went over to the window; he drew back the curtains and stood there looking out.

"You've been drinking," I accused. "Oh, Johnny, don't you see that something *has* to be done? These men are going to open up the mine whether you like it or not."

"If I find them on my property, I'll have them up for trespassing."

"Listen, Johnny. Something will have to be done. There's going to be a lot of hardship here when the Fedder mine closes. You can't let our mine stand idle when it could provide work. . . ."

He turned then, his mouth was twitching. I had not realized he was in such a bad state.

231

"You know very well that the mine can't be interfered with."

"I know that we've got to do something about it, Johnny."

"What?"

"We've got to show these people that we're willing to open up the mine. What will they think of us if we refuse?"

He looked at me as though he could have killed me. "The mine is not being touched," he said.

"Johnny."

He went out of the room. He didn't come back, but spent the night in his dressing room.

Johnny was adamant. He would not open the mine. I had never known him so stubborn. He had changed; he had always been lighthearted and careless and I could not understand this change in him. Why should he be so sternly against it? He had never cared so much for the family pride as Justin had.

Justin! I had the idea of writing to Justin. After all, Justin was the head of the house still. If he gave his permission for investigations to begin, that was enough.

I hesitated. I pictured Justin's receiving the letter, deciding this was a good enough reason for his return. I saw him winning the approval of the village. Perhaps they would be ready to forget the circumstances which had led to his departure if he returned and opened the mine.

No, I couldn't write to Justin.

Everything was changing in the village. Disaster was threatening; forelocks were pulled with a sullen gesture. We, the St. Larnston family, might have provided work and refused to do so.

A stone was once thrown at Johnny as he rode through the village. He did not know who had thrown it and it did not hit him; but it was a sign.

I had never felt so uneasy.

I did not try remonstrating with him because I had an idea that that made him more stubborn. He was hardly ever at home; he would come in quietly at midnight and creep into the dressing room. He was clearly avoiding me.

I had retired to bed early. I kept telling myself that things couldn't go on in this way. Something would happen. Johnny would give way.

I lay sleepless. I guessed Johnny would not be home until midnight . . . or later still. Then I must have another talk with him, no matter how angry I made him. I must remind him of his duty to our son. What foolish family pride this was which made him hold out against the inevitable.

I rehearsed the words I would use, and as I lay there some impulse made me get out of bed and go to the window.

It was a habit of mine often to stand at that window because from it I could see the ring of stones and they fascinated me now as they ever had. None of my problems, I always told myself, were as great as theirs had been. Perhaps that was why I could always draw comfort from them.

I stood very still, for one of the stones had moved. One of the Virgins had come to life! No. It was someone else there . . . someone with a lanthorn! There was more than one lanthorn . . . and lights moved eerily about the stones. A figure stood out clearly for a moment; he was wearing a helmet of some sort. I watched him intently; then I saw other figures. They were standing within the circle of stones and they all wore helmets.

I had to know who they were, and what they were doing, so I hastily put on some clothes and left the house. Over the lawns I went to the meadow but when I arrived there was no one there. In the starlight I saw the stones, ghostly, looking like women caught and petrified in the dance. And not far distant the old mine which was causing such controversy.

A sudden thought came to me. Could it have been Saul and his friends meeting to discuss what they would do next? What more appropriate spot to choose for such a meeting!

But they were gone now. I stood within the circle of the stones and while I was wondering what Saul and his friends would do next I could not help thinking of the Six Virgins and chiefly of the seventh who had *not* come dancing on that fatal night.

Shut in, built in, and left to die!

Stupid fanciful thoughts; but what could one expect when one stood in the center of a ring of stones in starlight?

I didn't hear Johnny come in that night—I must have been asleep when he did—so I didn't have a chance to talk to him.

He rose late next morning and went out. He rode into Plymouth and went to his club there. He must have spent the afternoon gambling.

We afterwards found out that he left the club round about midnight. But he did not come home.

Next morning I saw that the single bed in the dressing room

233

had not been slept in, and I waited all day for him to come in because I had made up my mind that I couldn't delay talking to him any longer.

The next night he did not come either. And when another night and day passed and he had still not returned we began to suspect that something had happened to him.

We made inquiries and it was then we discovered that he had left his club at midnight two nights before. We thought at first that he might have been seen to win money, followed and robbed; but he had lost heavily and had had little money with him when he left.

The search began; the inquiries started.

But no one could trace Johnny. And when a week passed and there was still no news I began to realize that he had indeed disappeared.

7

I was a woman without a husband, yet I could not call myself a widow. What had happened to Johnny? It was a mystery as baffling as that which Judith had provided when she fell down the stairs.

I tried to remain calm. I told Carlyon that his father had gone away for a while and that satisfied him; he had, I suspected, never been very fond of Johnny. I tried to brace myself for two possibilities: his return, or a life spent without him.

There was no immediate talk of opening the mine. That would come later, I suspected. I was being given a short respite on account of the shock of my husband's disappearance.

As I had in the old days, I took my problems to Granny. She scarcely ever left her bed now and it grieved me to see her growing a little more frail every time we met. She made me sit by her bed while she looked searchingly into my face.

"So you've lost your Johnny now," she said.

"I don't know, Granny. He may come back."

"Is that what you want, lovey?"

I was silent for I could never lie to Granny.

"You'm wondering what will happen next, eh? This 'ull like as not bring the other home."

I nodded.

"And parson's daughter?"

"Mellyora thinks of me before herself."

Granny sighed.

"This 'ull decide him," she said. "If this don't bring him back, nothing will."

"We can wait and see, Granny."

She leaned forward and gripped my hand. "Do you want your husband back, lovey?"

She wanted a straightforward answer; and she was very anxious.

"I don't know," I said.

"Kerensa," she went on, "do you remember . . . ?"

Her voice had sunk to a whisper and she gripped my hand still more firmly. I sensed that she was on the point of telling me something which was of the utmost importance.

"Yes, Granny?" I softly prompted.

"I've been turning over in my mind . . ."

Again she paused and I looked at her intently.

She closed her eyes and her lips moved soundlessly as though she were talking to herself.

"Do you remember," she said at length, "how I dressed your hair, set it up in coils and we put in the comb and mantilla Pedro gave to me?"

"Yes, Granny. I shall always keep it. I dress my hair that way often and wear the comb and mantilla."

She sank back on her pillows and a puzzled look came into her eyes.

"Pedro would have liked to see his Granddaughter," she murmured. But I knew that was not what she had been on the point of saying.

Mellyora and I sat alone in my sitting room.

How like the old days it was, those days when we had been together in the parsonage. We both felt this and it drew us closer together.

"This is a waiting time, Mellyora," I said. "Life will change soon."

She nodded, her needle poised; she was making a shirt for Carlyon and she looked daintily feminine and helpless working there.

"No news of Johnny . . . day after day," I mused. "When do you think they will give up the search?"

"I don't know. I suppose he will be listed as a missing person and will remain so until we have some news of him."

"What do you think has happened to him, Mellyora?"

She did not answer.

"There was a lot of feeling against him in St. Larnston," I went on. "Do you remember how angry he was that day when someone threw a stone at him? The people of St. Larnston might have killed him because he would not open the mine. Their livings were at stake. They knew I would be willing to open it."

"*You* . . . Kerensa."

"I shall be the mistress of the Abbas now . . . unless. . . ."

"The Abbas belongs to Justin, Kerensa; and it always did."

"But he has gone away and Johnny administered everything in his absence. Until he comes back . . . ."

"I do not think he will ever come back. I haven't told you this before but he is trying to come to a decision now. He believes that he will stay in Italy and enter a religious order."

"Is that so?" I wondered if I succeeded in keeping the joy out of my voice. Justin a monk! Never to marry!

I suddenly remembered Mellyora, sitting at home, patiently waiting like Penelope. I looked at her sharply. "And you, Mellyora? You loved him so much. Do you still?"

She was silent. "You are so practical, Kerensa. You would never understand me. I should seem so foolish to you."

"Please try to make me understand. It is important to me . . . your happiness I mean. I have grieved for you, Mellyora."

"I know you have." She smiled. "Sometimes you have been angry when Justin's name was mentioned. I knew it was because you were so sorry for me. Justin was a hero of my childhood. It was a child's adoration I had for him. Picture it. He was the heir to the big house; and the Abbas meant something to me as it did to you. To me he seemed just perfect; and I suppose my most cherished dream was that one day he would notice me. He was the prince of the fairy tale who should have married the woodcutter's daughter and made her a queen. It grew out of a childish fantasy. Do you understand?"

I nodded. "I thought you would never be happy again when he went away."

"So did I. But ours was a dream idyll. His love for me and mine for him. If he had been free we should have married and perhaps it would have been a good marriage; perhaps I should have gone on adoring him. I should have been a good meek wife to him; he would have been a courteous tender husband; but there would always have been this dream quality about our relationship, this bloodlessness, this unreality. *You* have shown me that."

"I? How so?"

"With your love for Carlyon. That fierce passion of yours. That jealousy I have seen when you think he cares too much for me or Joe. It is a wild all-consuming thing, your love; and that is real love, I have come to believe. Think of this, Kerensa, if you had loved Justin as I thought I did, what would *you* have done? Would you have said farewell? Would you have allowed him to go? No. You would have gone away with him, or you would have stayed here and fought defiantly for the right to live together. That is love. You never loved Johnny in that way. But you once loved your brother like that; you loved your Granny: and now all your love is for Carlyon. One day, Kerensa, you will love a man and that will be the fulfillment of your being. I believe I too shall love that way. We are young yet, both of us; but I took longer to grow up than you did. I am grown up now, Kerensa, and we are neither of us fulfilled. Do you understand me? But we shall be."

"How can you be sure?"

"Because we have grown together, Kerensa. There is a bond between us, a line of fate which we cannot break."

"You have an air of wisdom this morning, Mellyora!"

"It is because we are both free . . . free from the old life. It is like a beginning again. Johnny is dead, Kerensa. I am sure of it. I believe what you say is right. Not one but several people killed him because he stood between them and their living. They murdered him that they and their wives and children might live. You are free, Kerensa. The hungry men of St. Larnston have freed you. And I am free . . . free of a dream. Justin will enter a religious order; no longer shall I sit and dream as I sew, no longer wait for a letter, no longer start up at the sound of arrival. And I am at peace. I have become a woman. It is like gaining freedom. You too, Kerensa, for you haven't deceived me. You married Johnny, you suffered him for the sake of this house, the position he gave you, for the sake of being a St. Larnston. You have what you want and all the installments are paid. It is a new beginning for you as well as for me."

I looked at her and I thought: She is right. No more reproaches. I need never shudder when I look at Nelly; the scar on her back is no longer a scar on my soul. I did not ruin Mellyora's life when I saved the Abbas for Carlyon. There need be no more regrets.

On impulse I went to Mellyora and put my arms about her. She smiled up at me, and I bent and kissed her forehead.

"You are right," I said. "We are free."

I made two discoveries within the next few weeks.

The family solicitor came to the Abbas to see me. He had depressing news. For some years the St. Larnston fortunes had been on the wane and several economies were needed.

Judith Derrise had bolstered up the position with her dowry, but it was to have been paid over a number of years and as she was dead and there were no children of the marriage, the remainder of the dowry would not be paid. Johnny's gambling had expedited the disaster which, with careful economies, would have to be staved off and, had Judith lived, would never have occurred.

Johnny had heavily mortgaged certain properties to pay for his gambling debts; in a few months capital would have to be raised. There seemed to be no alternative but to sell the Abbas.

The situation was similar to that which had threatened the family some generations back. Then the tin mine had proved a source of wealth and the family retained the old mansion.

Some action within the next few months was vital.

What action? I demanded to know.

The solicitor looked at me kindly. He was sorry for me. My husband had disappeared. Large sums of money belonging to the estate could not be accounted for, but they had passed through Johnny's hands, probably lost in gambling. In any case, Johnny had disappeared and I was left to salvage what I could for my son. Justin was about to renounce the world and all his possessions except a small private income which would go to the monastery where he would spend the rest of his days.

"I think, Mrs. St. Larnston," the solicitor said, "that you should leave the Abbas for the Dower House which is vacant just now. If you lived there you would considerably reduce your expenses."

"And the Abbas?"

"You might find a tenant. But I doubt whether that would solve your difficulties. It may be necessary to sell the Abbas. . . ."

"Sell the Abbas! It has been in the possession of the St. Larnston family for generations."

He lifted his shoulders. "Many estates like this one are changing hands nowadays."

"There is my son. . . ."

"Well, he is young and it is not as though he has spent a great number of years in the place." Seeing my distress he softened. "It may not come to that."

"There is the mine," I said. "It saved the Abbas once. It will save it again."

I asked Saul Cundy to come and see me. I could not understand why the agitation to open the mine had stopped. I had made up my mind I was going to set work in motion at once, and the first and all-important discovery to make was whether or not there was tin in the mine.

I stood at the library window, waiting for Saul, looking out across the lawns to the meadow and the ring of stones. What a different scene there would be when the sound of the tinners' voices would be heard and I should see them going to work with their horn picks and wooden shovels. We should need machines. I knew little of the industry except what I had picked up from Granny but I did know that a certain Richard Trevithick had invented a high-pressure steam engine which hoisted out the ore and crushed and stamped it on the surface.

How strange it would be—all that noise, all that activity so near the ring of ancient stones. Well, it had happened before and it was the modern industry which was going to preserve the ancient house.

Tin meant money and money could save the Abbas.

I was growing impatient when at last Haggety announced that Saul Cundy was outside.

"Bring him in at once," I cried.

He came, hat in hand, but I fancied he found it difficult to meet my eye.

"Sit down," I said. "I think you know why I have asked you to call."

"Yes, Ma'am."

"Well, you are aware that there is no news of my husband and that Sir Justin is far away and not in a position to manage affairs here. You headed a deputation some time ago and I did all I could to persuade my husband that you were right. Now I am going to give permission for an investigation to be made. If there is tin in the St. Larnston mine, then there will be work for all those who want it."

Saul Cundy twirled his hat round and round in his hands and stared at the tips of his boots.

"Ma'am," he said, "twouldn't be no good. St. Larnston mine be nothing but an old scat bal. There bain't be no tin there and there won't be no work for us here in this district."

I was aghast. All my plans for saving the Abbas were being destroyed by this slow-speaking giant.

"Nonsense," I said. "How can you know?"

"Because Ma'am, us have already made the investigation. We made 'un before Mr. Johnny was . . . before Mr. St. Larnston went."

"You made it?"

"Yes, Ma'am. Us had our livings to think on. So a few on us got working on it at nights and I went down so I be certain sure there bain't no tin in the St. Larnston mine."

"I don't believe it."

"Tis so, Ma'am."

"You went down alone?"

"I thought it was best like, there being a danger of collapse —seeing it were my idea in the first place."

"But . . . I . . . I shall get the experts to look into this."

"Cost you a mint of money, Ma'am . . . and us tinners do know tin when we see it. Us have worked all our lives in the mine Ma'am. There bain't no fooling we."

"So that's why there's been no more agitation about opening the mine."

"Tis so, Ma'am. I and us tinners be going out to St. Agnes. There be work there for we. The best tin in Cornwall do come from St. Agnes way. We be leaving by the end of the week and we be taking the women and children with us. There be work for us there."

"I see. Then there is nothing more to be said."

He looked at me and I thought his eyes were like those of a spaniel. He seemed to be asking me for forgiveness. He would know of course that I needed the rich tin, for that all was not well at the Abbas would be common knowledge. It was Haggety and Mrs. Rolt and our servants who would now be wondering how *they* were going to live.

"I be sorry, Ma'am," he said.

"I wish you good fortune at St. Agnes," I answered. "You and everyone who goes there."

"Thank 'ee, Ma'am."

It was only after he had gone that I saw the double significance of this.

I knew, of course, that the men I had seen from my window were the tinners. They had been down the mine that very night and discovered it to be sterile. Then the thought hit me: that was before Johnny died. So they knew the mine had nothing to offer them. Why then should they kill Johnny? What was the point?

Then it was not these men who had killed him. Who then? Could it be that Johnny was not dead?

I discussed the future with Mellyora. She was becoming gay again; it was as though she had escaped from a spell Justin had put on her. This was the Mellyora who had championed me at the fair. Her adoration for Justin had made her meek, a patient Griselda; now she was recovering her own personality.

"You see yourself as a benevolent god, ruling us all," she told me. "The rest of us are like little kings whom you have put in charge of our kingdoms. If we do not rule as you think we should, you want to take over and rule for us."

"What a fantastic notion!"

"Not when you consider. You wanted to manage Joe's life . . . Johnny's . . . Carlyon's. . . ."

I thought with a twinge of remorse: Yours too, Mellyora. If you did but know it, I *have* governed your life too.

I should tell her one day because I should not be completely at rest until I did.

I decided that we must move to the Dower House. Haggety and the Salts found other employment. Tom Pengaster at last married Doll, and Daisy came with us to the Dower House. The solicitors took over the management of the estate and the Polores and Trelances stayed in their cottages and continued their work, while Mrs. Rolt remained at the Abbas as housekeeper—Florrie Trelance coming in from the cottages to help her.

The Abbas was to be let furnished, which could mean that, with care, by the time Carlyon was of age he might be able to afford to live in it himself. It seemed as satisfactory as a temporary arrangement could be. Each day I went to the Abbas to make sure that everything was being kept in order.

Carlyon was content with the Dower House; together Mellyora and I taught him. He was a docile pupil, though not a brilliant one and often I would see him looking wistfully out of the windows when the sun was shining. Every Saturday he accompanied Joe on his rounds and they were his red-letter days.

We had had only two prospective tenants. One had found the Abbas far too big; the other considered it eerie. I began to think it would remain empty, waiting for us to return.

It had always amazed me how important events burst suddenly upon one. I feel there should be some warning, some little premonition. But there rarely is.

I rose that morning rather late as I had overslept, and when I dressed and went down to breakfast I found a letter awaiting me from the agents who were dealing with the house. They were sending a client along that afternoon, and hoped three o'clock would be a convenient time.

I told Mellyora as we sat at breakfast.

"I wonder what will be wrong this time," she said. "Sometimes I think we are never going to find a tenant."

At three o'clock I walked over to the Abbas, thinking that I should be wretched when I could not go in and out as I wished. But perhaps we should become friendly with the new tenants. Perhaps we should receive invitations to dine. How strange—to go to dine in the Abbas as a guest. It would be like that occasion when I had gone to the ball.

Mrs. Rolt was unhappy, sadly missing the old days and, I was sure, all the gossip round the table.

"I don't know what we are coming to," she would say every time I saw her. "My dear life, the Abbas be a quiet sad place these days. I never knew the like."

I knew she was wishing for a tenant, someone to spy on, to gossip about.

Soon after three there was loud knocking on the main door.

I stayed in the library and Mrs. Rolt went to let in the visitor. I felt melancholy. I did not want anyone to live in the Abbas, and yet I knew someone must.

There was a knock on the door, and Mrs. Rolt appeared with a look of blank astonishment on her face; and then I heard a voice; Mrs. Rolt stepped aside and I thought I must be dreaming, for it was like a dream—a long cherished dream—coming true.

Kim was coming towards me.

Those were, I believe, the happiest weeks of my life. It is difficult now to record exactly what happened. I remember his picking me up in his arms; I remember his face close to mine, the laughter in his eyes.

"I wouldn't let them mention my name. I wanted to surprise you." I remember Mrs. Rolt standing in the doorway; the distant murmur of "My dear life!" and I wanted to repeat "My dear life . . . my dear *dear* life!" because it had suddenly become very precious.

He hadn't changed much, I told him. He looked at me.

"You have. I used to say you were becoming a very fascinating woman. Now you've become one."

How can I describe Kim? He was gay, full of high spirits, teasing, mocking yet at the same time tender. He had wit but it was never used to hurt others; I think that was what made him a very special person. He laughed with people, never at them. He made you feel that you were important to him—as important as he was to you. Perhaps I saw him in a rosy glow because I was in love with him, and I knew as soon as he returned that I was in love with him, and had been ever since that night he had carried Joe to safety.

His father was dead, he told me; when he had retired from the sea, they had settled together in Australia and had bought a ranch there. They had bought it cheaply and made money raising cattle; then suddenly he had decided that he had made enough money; he sold out at a high figure and had come home with a fortune. What did I think of that for a success story?

I thought it was wonderful. I thought everything was wonderful—life, everything—because he had returned.

We talked so much that the time fled by. I told him all that happened since his departure—how Mellyora and I had worked at the Abbas, how I had married Johnny.

He took my hands and looked at me with concentration.

"So you married, Kerensa?"

I told him about Johnny's disappearance, how Justin had gone away when Judith had died, how we had fallen on hard times and that was why the Abbas was to let.

"So much happening at home!" he said. "And I not knowing it!"

"But you must have thought of us. Otherwise you wouldn't have wanted to come back."

"I've thought of you continually. I've often said 'I wonder what's happening back home. One day I'll go and see . . .' And there was Kerensa marrying Johnny; and Mellyora . . . Mellyora, like me, never married. I must see Mellyora. And your son, I must see him. Kerensa with a son! And you called him Carlyon! Oh, I remember Miss Carlyon. Well, Kerensa, if that is not just like you."

I took him to the Dower House. Mellyora had just returned from a walk with Carlyon. She stared at Kim as though she were seeing a vision. Then laughing—and almost crying I believe—she was in his arms.

I watched them. They were greeting each other like the old friends they were. But already my love for Kim was beginning to take possession of me. I did not like his attention to stray for one moment from me.

I visited Granny Bee every day because something told me that I should not be able to do so for much longer. I would sit there by her bed and she would talk to me of the past, which was what she loved to do. There were occasions when she seemed to get lost in the past like someone wandering in a maze; at others she would be lucid and very perceptive.

One day she said to me: "Kerensa, you have never been so beautiful as you are now. Tis the beauty of a woman in love."

I flushed. I was afraid to talk of this feeling I had for Kim. I felt superstitious about it. I wanted to forget what had gone before; I wanted a different kind of life, governed by different emotions.

I felt frustrated because each day it was becoming clearer to me that I wanted to marry Kim. And how could I, when I did not know whether or not I had a husband living.

Granny wanted to talk about Kim and was determined to.

"So he's back then, lovey. I'll never forget the night he carried Joe home from the woods. He were our friend from that night on."

"Yes," I said. "How afraid we were then, but we need not have been."

"He's a good man and twere he who spoke to Mr. Pollent. When I think what our Joe owes to him I bless him with all my strength, I do."

"I too, Granny."

"I can see it. There's something else I'd like to see, Granddaughter."

I waited and she went on softly: "There was never barriers between we two. Nor should there ever be. I'd like to see you married happy, Kerensa, which is something you haven't had yet."

"To Kim?" I said quietly.

"Aye. He be the man for you."

"I think so too, Granny. But perhaps I'll never know whether I'll be free to marry."

She closed her eyes and just as I thought she might have gone meandering into the past, she said suddenly: "T'as been on the tip end of my tongue to tell 'ee these many times and I've said, 'No, better not.' But I don't say 'No,' no longer, Kerensa. I don't think I'll be with 'ee much longer, child."

"Don't say it, Granny. I couldn't bear it if you weren't."

"Oh, child, you've been a regular comfort to me. I've often thought of the day you walked in with your little brother . . . come to look for Granny Bee! That were one of the happy days of my life and I've had many. It's a great thing to marry the man you love, Kerensa, and have children by him. Reckon that be one of the real reasons for living. Not rising above what you was born, not getting big houses. I'd like 'ee to know the sort of happiness I've had, Kerensa, and you can find it inside of four cob walls. You should know it now, girl, because now you've got the shine of love on you; and if I be right, you'm free."

"Granny, you *know* that Johnny is dead?"

"I didn't see him die. But I know what goes on and I think I be right. . . ."

I leaned close to the bed. Was she dreaming? Was she really thinking of Johnny or had her mind lost itself in the past?

She read my thoughts, for she smiled gently and said: "No, I be clear in the mind, Kerensa, and I shall tell you now all that happened and led up to this. I didn't tell 'ee before because I weren't sure it were good for 'ee to know. Can you cast your mind back to a night when you come to me from the Abbas. You was lady's maid then to her that fell down the stairs and while you was here you saw a shadow at the window? Do 'ee remember, Kerensa?"

"Yes, Granny, I remember."

"Twas someone looking in as wanted to see me and wanted to make sure none see her come. It were Hetty Pengaster—five months with child and frightened. She was afraid of discovery, she says, and her father so strict and her spoken for by Saul Cundy and it couldn't be his. She were frightened, poor girl. She wanted to wipe out all sign of what she'd been up to, and start again. Learned, she had, that Saul were the man for her; and she wished she hadn't listened when the other came courting."

I said quietly: "Her child was Johnny's?"

Granny went on: "I said to her, 'Tell I who be the father,' and her wouldn't tell. Said she mustn't tell. He'd told her not. He was going to do something for her, she said. He'd have to. She were meeting him the next night and she was going to make him see that he'd got to do something for her. She believed he might marry her, but I could tell she were fooling herself. Then she went away, fair mazed she were. Her father being so strict and her being spoken for by Saul. She were frightened of Saul. Saul weren't the sort to let another take what were his. . . ."

246

"And she didn't tell you Johnny was the man?"

"No, she didn't tell, but I feared it. I knew how he were after you, and that made me determined like to find out if he were the man. I said to her bain't you feared someone will see you meeting like, and Saul or your father'll come to hear on it? She said No, they did always meet in the meadow by the Virgins and the old mine and twere safe enough there, for people didn't like to be there after dark. I can tell 'ee, I was worried. I wanted to know if it were Johnny. I had to know on account of you."

"And it was, Granny. Of course it was. I always knew he had a fancy for her."

"I was worried all that day, and I said to myself, Kerensa'll work out her destiny, same as you did. And I thought of how I'd gone to Sir Justin and deceived my Pedro and how I'd tell myself now twere all for the best. And thinking of Pedro I dressed my hair with my comb and mantilla and I sat wondering what I was going to do when I found out Johnny were the father of Hetty's child. I had first to be certain, so that night I went to the meadow and I waited there. I hid myself behind the biggest Virgin and I saw them meet. There were a crescent moon and the stars were bright. Twas enough to show me. Hetty, she were crying and he were pleading with her. I couldn't hear what were said, for they didn't come near enough to the stones. I think she were frightened of them. Maybe she thought like one of they Virgins she'd be turned to stone. Close to the mine shaft they were. And I think she were threatening to throw herself down if he didn't marry her. I knew her wouldn't. Her was only threatening. But he were frightened. I guessed he were trying to persuade her to leave St. Larnston. I moved away from the stones to try to hear what they were saying and I heard her say: 'I'll kill myself, Johnny. I'll throw myself down there.' And he said, 'Don't be silly. You'd do no such thing. You don't fool me. Go back to your father and tell him. He'll get you married in time.' Then she was real angry; she stood for a moment poised there on the edge. I wanted to shout to him: Leave her be. She won't do it! But he didn't leave her be. He caught her arm . . . I heard her cry out suddenly and then . . . he were there alone."

"Granny, he killed her!"

"I couldn't say for certain sure. I couldn't see clear enough . . . and even if I had, I couldn't be sure. One second she was there, poised on the edge, threatening to throw herself down; the next she were gone."

Events slipped neatly into place: the strangeness of his conduct; his desire to get away; his fear that the mine would be reopened. Then I stared at Granny, remembering that he must have come straight back and asked me to marry him.

Granny went on slowly: "For a second or so he stood there as though like one of the maidens as were turned into stone. Then he looked wildly round him and he saw me standing there in the light of that crescent moon, my dark hair piled high, my mantilla, my comb. He said: 'Kerensa.' Quiet . . . like a whisper almost, but it came to me in the stillness of the night. Then he looked back at the mine and down into the darkness; and I ran, I ran as fast as I could through the circle of stones and across the meadow. I had reached the road when I heard him call again: 'Kerensa. Kerensa, come here!'"

"Granny," I said, "he thought I was the one who was standing there. He thought I was the one who saw."

She nodded. "I went back to the cottage and I sat up all night thinking on what I should do. And then, in the morning, Mellyora Martin brought me your letter. You had run away to Plymouth to marry Johnny St. Larnston."

"I see," I said slowly. "He asked me to marry him as a bribe, to say nothing. And I thought it was because he could not do without me. What sort of a marriage was it?"

"On his side for protection lest he should be charged with murder; on yours a big house you'd always craved to be mistress of. You made a big dream, Kerensa, and you paid dear for it."

I felt numbed by this knowledge. My life seemed to have a different meaning. Chance had shaped my life as much as my own maneuverings, and Hetty Pengaster, whom I had always despised, had played as important a role as myself. And Johnny had not wanted me so desperately, only my silence.

"You never told me, Granny," I said half reproachfully.

"Not after you were married. What good could it do? And when there was a child coming I knew I was right to keep silent."

I shuddered. "It was horrible. Johnny thinking that I wanted marriage in exchange for silence. I should never have married him if I had known."

"Not even for the St. Larnston name, lovey?"

We looked at each other and I answered truthfully as I always must to Granny. "In those days I would have done anything for the St. Larnston name."

"It was a lesson you had to learn, Granddaughter. Perhaps

you've learned it now. Perhaps you know that there's as much happiness to be found inside of four cob walls as in a mansion. If you learned that it don't matter greatly what you had to pay for the lesson. And now you can start again."

"Is it possible?"

She nodded. "For listen here. Johnny wouldn't open the mine and Saul Cundy was determined he should. Saul were going to find out whether there was tin in the mine. He were going down to find out and he did. But he found Hetty too. He'd know why she were down there, and he'd know too that Johnny were responsible, for he'd have heard the whispers. And Johnny going off and marrying you the day she disappeared . . . well, it do speak for itself."

I caught my breath. "You think that Saul murdered Johnny because of what he found down the mine?"

"Tis something I can't say, not having been seen. But Saul didn't say nothing about finding Hetty and I know she were down there. Why didn't he say he did find her there? Twere because he be a man who was born dead-set against the gentry and he were determined as Johnny should pay in full. Johnny could withhold the right of men to work for their livings; Johnny could rob a man of his bride. He were not going to trust the law, for he did say often enough there was one for rich and one for poor. Saul did take the law into his own hand. He waylaid Johnny coming home from his gambling, and killed him, I reckon; and where should he be most likely to put him but down the mine shaft. To keep Hetty company! Then away he goes . . . to St. Agnes . . . far away from St. Larnston."

"It's a terrible story, Granny."

"Twas a bitter lesson but I knew from the first you'd be one who must learn your own lessons. Tweren't no good my trying to teach you. Find your man, Kerensa; love him as I loved my Pedro, bear his children . . . and never you mind whether you live in a mansion or a cob-walled cottage. Happiness don't ask to see who you be afore her sits down at your table. 'Er comes and sits with them as know how to welcome her and keep her the willing guest. Tis done with, my love; and happy I be to go now. All be set fair for you. I've seen love in your eyes for a man, Kerensa. I've seen love for me, love for Joe, love for Carlyon, and now for a man. That's a powerful lot of love for one person to give, lovey. But Joe have his own wife to cleave to and so will Carlyon one day; and I can't be with 'ee forever. So I be glad that there be a man you love, and now I shall go happy. . . ."

"Don't talk of going, Granny. You mustn't. Do you think I'll ever be able to do without you?"

"'Tis a good thing to hear said, my sweet Granddaughter, but I'd be sad if I believed it were true. You'll do without me, because the man you love will be beside you and you'll grow in love and wisdom. Peace and love . . . that be the meaning of our names, girl; tis the meaning of the good life too. You've grown mellow, girl. You ain't reaching out for what ain't good for you. Love and be happy . . . tis time you came to that. Forget what be past. The woman you are today is not the same one you were yesterday. Tis well to remember that. Never mourn for the past. Never say that were a tragedy. Say that were experience. Because of that I be what I am today—and all the better because I have passed through the fire."

"But Johnny is missing. . . ."

"Open up the mine, girl. You'll find him there. I be sure on it. Him and Hetty. There'll be the old scandal revived, but tis better than being tied to a missing man all your life."

"I'll do it, Granny," I said. But as I spoke, a thought struck me which made me catch my breath in horror. Granny was looking at me expectantly and I cried out: "I can't do it. There's Carlyon."

"What of Carlyon?"

"Don't you see. They'd say he was the son of a murderer."

Granny was silent for a while. Then she said: "You'm right. It would never do. Tis something that would cast a shadow over him all his life. But what of you, my dear? Are you never to be free to marry then?"

It was like a choice between Kim and Carlyon; but I knew Carlyon's sensitive and gentle nature and I couldn't let him ever be called the son of a murderer.

Granny began to speak slowly. "There be a way out, Kerensa. It's coming to me. They'd not be able to tell by now when Hetty died. If they went down the mine they'd find her there . . . and they'd find Johnny. I reckon Saul Cundy killed Johnny and I reckon Saul be miles away by now. Leave things be awhile; then open the mine. There's many comes to see me still. I'll put it about that Hetty have been back, that she have been seen. What if it were to see Hetty, Johnny went to Plymouth, and Saul found out . . . and caught 'em. Well, he knew there were no tin in the mine, why shouldn't he have killed 'em both and put their bodies down there?"

I was staring at her incredulously, and I thought: You make life go the way you want. That was her creed. Well, why not?

She seemed more vital than she had for a long time. She was not ready to die yet, not while she could be of help to me.

How I loved her! How I relied on her! When I was with her she made me feel that everything was possible.

"Granny," I said firmly, "I don't believe Johnny killed Hetty. It was an accident."

"It was an accident," she soothed. She understood. My Carlyon's father *must* not be a murderer.

Nor must he be suspected of being one.

It was like old times. We drew strength from each other. I knew that I was going to be free and at the same time we would make sure that there would be no danger of the taint of murder touching Carlyon.

We waited for a month. During that time I made a trip to St. Agnes to see if I could find out anything about Saul Cundy. He was not there; he had, I learned, been there for a few days but not to work. It was believed that he and his family had left the country for good, for they had disappeared completely and none knew where they had gone.

This was triumph indeed. I went back and told Granny.

"Don't wait no longer," she said. "You're not one for waiting. I've not much time, and I'd like to see 'ee settled afore I go."

I shut myself in my bedroom. All the morning the experts had been at work. I had heard that safety must be ensured before the descent was made; a mine disused so long could present certain dangers—flooding, falls of earth, and other disasters. It would be a costly matter to discover whether or not the mine would be a business proposition.

Kim came riding over to the Dower House. I was glad that Mellyora was out with Carlyon. Daisy came up to tell me that he was downstairs, and I said I would shortly be with him. I looked at myself in the mirror. I was a young woman, many would say in my prime. In my lavender morning dress with the lace at the throat and sleeves and the satin ribbons I was beautiful. Granny was right: being in love put a shine on one. My hair had more luster. I wore it piled high on my head; the brilliance of my eyes made them look bigger. I was pleased with myself as I went down to greet Kim; and I knew that perhaps this very day would prove me a free woman.

As I opened the door of the sitting room I saw him standing by the fireplace, legs apart, his hand in his pocket; there was a tender smile about his lips which I felt sure was for me.

He came towards me, took both my hands, his eyes smiling, faintly amused.

"Kerensa!" He even said my name as though it amused him.

"It was good of you to call."

He put his head on one side, and smiled. "You are amused?" I asked.

"Pleasantly so."

"I'm glad I can pleasantly amuse you."

He laughed and drew me to the window.

"What a noise they are making in the meadow today."

"Yes. At last they're getting to work."

"And the outcome means a lot to you, Kerensa."

I flushed, afraid for the moment that he knew the real reason. Kim's eyes seemed to have become more penetrating while he had been away, there was an air of wisdom about him which I found attractive but which alarmed me faintly.

"It's important that we should be able to work the mine again."

I summoned Daisy to bring wine and the special biscuits which had always been kept for visitors at the Abbas—a custom, like many others, which I had brought to the Dower House.

We sat at a small table sipping the wine, and looking round the room he said: "It's a warmer place than it was when I lived here. It's a strange feeling, Kerensa, to come back to a house that has been home to you and to find it is someone else's home, different furniture, different faces, different atmosphere. . . ."

"I always used to envy your living at the Dower House."

"I know. I saw it in your face. You had the most expressive face in the world, Kerensa. You could never hide your feelings."

"How alarming. I hope that's not the case now."

"Such scorn! Such pride! I never saw anyone so scornful nor so proud."

"I was an angry child."

"Poor Kerensa." He laughed. "I remember your standing in the wall . . . the broken wall. The Seventh Virgin. Do you remember how taken we were with the story at that time."

"Yes. That was why I came to look."

"We all came. We all met there."

I saw it all clearly. Myself, Mellyora, Justin, Johnny and Kim.

"We teased you horribly, I'm afraid. We made you very angry. I can see you now . . . turning to put out your tongue. I've never forgotten."

"I wish you had something more pleasant to remember!"

"There was Miss Carlyon at the ball. Magnificent in red velvet. And there was that night in the woods. . . . You see, Kerensa, I remember so much of the past. You and Mellyora at the ball! Mellyora having brought you without the knowledge of the hostess!" He laughed. "It made the ball for me. I'd always found them a bore. But that ball . . . I've never forgotten. I've often laughed about the way Mellyora secured your invitation. . . ."

"We've always been like sisters."

"I'm glad of it." He looked into his glass and I thought: If I only knew that I was free. When he knows that I am free he will tell me he loves me.

He wanted to talk of the past. He made me tell him about the day I had stood up to be hired at Trelinket Fair and how Mellyora had come along and hired me. I went on to explain how sadly the Reverend Charles Martin had died and how we had found ourselves penniless.

"Neither Mellyora nor I could be separated, so I became the lady's maid and Mellyora the lady's drudge."

"Poor Mellyora!"

"Life was hard for both of us."

"But you would always be able to take care of yourself."

We laughed together.

It was his turn to talk. He spoke of the lonely life in the Dower House. He had been fond of his father but the fact that he was always away at sea had meant that he was left to the care of the servants.

"I never felt I had a real *home*, Kerensa."

"And you wanted a home?"

"I didn't know it, but I did. Who doesn't? The servants were kind to me . . . but it wasn't the same. I was at the Abbas a great deal. I was fascinated by the place. I know how you felt about it . . . because in a way I felt the same. There's something about it. Perhaps it's the legends that attach themselves to such houses that intrigue us? I used to say to myself, when I grow up I'm going to make a fortune, I'm going to live in a house like the Abbas. It wasn't so much that I wanted the house as all that went with it. I longed to be a member of a

253

big family. You see, I'm a lonely man, Kerensa. Always have been, and my dream was to have a big family . . . that would grow in all directions."

"You mean that you want to marry, have children, and be a grand old man . . . with grandchildren and great-grand-children always near you?"

I smiled for was this not my dream? Did I not see myself, the grand old lady of the Abbas? Now I pictured us to-gether; Kim and myself, grown old. Serene and happy, we would watch our grandchildren at play. Then instead of look-ing forward I would be looking back . . . back on a life which had given me all I had asked of it.

"It's not a bad ambition," he said almost sheepishly.

Then he told me how lonely it had been on the station; how he had longed for home. "And home, Kerensa, was all this . . . the Abbas . . . the people I had known."

I understood. I told myself his dream was mine.

We were interrupted by the return of Mellyora and Carl-yon. Carlyon was laughing and shouting to her as they came across the lawn.

We both went to the window to watch them. I saw the smile on Kim's lips and I believed that he envied me my son.

It was later that day that Kim came riding over to the Dower House.

I saw him coming, and noticed the bewildered expression on his face. As he came into the hall I was waiting there for him.

"Kerensa." He strode towards me, took my hands and looked long into my face.

"Yes, Kim."

"I've bad news. Come into the drawing room and sit down."

"Tell me quickly, Kim. I can bear it."

"Where's Mellyora?"

"Never mind. Tell me now."

"Kerensa . . ." He put his arm about me and I leaned against him, conscious of playing the weak woman, eager to lean on him because his concern for me was so sweet.

"Kim, you're keeping me in suspense. It's the mine, isn't it? It's no good."

He shook his head.

"Kerensa, you're going to be shocked. . . ."

"I must know, Kim. Don't you see . . ."

He gripped my hands tightly. "They've made a discovery in the mine. They've found . . ."

I lifted my eyes to his, trying to read the triumph behind the anxiety. I could see nothing but his concern for me.

"It's Johnny," he went on. "They've found Johnny."

I lowered my eyes. I gave a little cry. He led me to a sofa and sat there supporting me. I leaned against him; I wanted to cry out in triumph: I'm free!

Never had there been such excitement in St. Larnston. The bodies of Johnny and of Hetty Pengaster were found in the mine; and it was recalled that there had been whispers lately that Hetty Pengaster had been seen in Plymouth and even nearer to St. Larnston. People remembered that Johnny had once been sweet on her and that he had often gone to Plymouth. Hetty had left St. Larnston suddenly when he had married me. Well, what more natural than that Johnny should set her up in Plymouth to get her out of the way when he married?

It all seemed so simple. Saul Cundy had suspected, had lain in wait, had found Johnny and Hetty together, and had taken his revenge. Saul had always been one for justice, and he had made sure of it this time by taking the law into his own hands. Knowing there was no tin in the mine, because he was the one who had been down to see, he had felt it safe to throw his victims' bodies down there.

Hetty's body was only recognizable by a locket she was wearing and which the Pengasters identified as one Saul Cundy had given her; Johnny's was in a better state of preservation which was baffling for a while. Then a story was put forward that in falling, Johnny's body could have dislodged some earth which it had carried to the bottom of the shaft with it and thus could have become partially sealed off. This was generally accepted and the difference thus explained.

The investigations went on. The police wanted to interview Saul Cundy and went to St. Agnes to look for him, but when he could not be traced and it seemed he had left the country, his destination unknown, this strengthened the conjecture, and the story the villagers had pieced together was accepted as the true one.

It was an anxious period while the search for Saul went on; but as time went by it seemed more and more certain that he would never be found.

No one would ever know the truth—although Granny and I could make a fair guess at it. But even we did not know whether or not Johnny had killed Hetty. Indirectly, I suppose he was responsible, but we could not say whether he had actually sent her to her death. We were certain that Saul had killed Johnny. His discovery of Hetty's body and his flight both pointed to it.

But the secret was safe. My Carlyon could never be called the son of a murderer.

There was not enough tin in the mine to make the working of it a profitable proposition; but the mine had given me what I wanted. It had proved that I was a widow and free to marry the man I loved.

On the day Granny heard the news she seemed to grow suddenly weaker. It was as though she had done her work, had seen the results she looked for, and was ready to go in peace.

A terrible sadness came to me, for no matter what joy or happiness was mine I believed it could never be complete for me if I lost her.

I spent the last days with her. Essie made me very welcome and Joe was glad to have me there too. Carlyon was with him, and as I did not wish him to be in the sickroom he spent all his time with Joe.

I remembered the last afternoon of Granny's life.

I sat by her bed and the tears were on my cheeks—I, who could not remember crying, except in anger.

"Don't grieve, my sweet Granddaughter," she said. "Don't mourn for me when I am gone. For I'd as lief you forgot me for evermore than rememering me should make you grieve."

"Oh, Granny," I cried, "how could I ever forget you?"

"Then remember the happy times, child."

"Happy times. What happy times can there be for me when you are gone?"

"You're too young to want your life linked with an old woman's. I've had my day and you'll have yours. There'll be happiness and pleasure ahead of you, Kerensa. Tis yours. Take it. Keep it. You've had your lesson, girl. Learn it well."

"Granny," I said, "don't leave me. How can I get along without you?"

"Is this my Kerensa speaking? My Kerensa, who be ready to fight the world?"

"With you, Granny—not alone. We've always been together. You can't leave me now."

"Listen, lovey. You ain't got no need of me. You love a man and that's how it should be. There's a time when the birds leave the nest. They fly alone. Ye've a strong pair of wings,

Kerensa. I bain't feared for you. You've flown high but you'll fly higher. You'll do what's good and right now. Your life be all before you. Don't fret, my sweetheart, I be glad to go. I'll be with my Pedro, for some says as we live on after death. I didn't always believe it but I want to believe it now . . . and, like most, I believes as I wants. Now don't 'ee weep, my sweet one. I must go and you must stay, but I leave 'ee happy. You're free, my love. There's the man of your heart awaiting for 'ee. Never 'ee mind where you be, as long as you be together. Don't fret for poor old Granny Bee when you have the man you love."

"Granny, I want you to live and be with us. I want you to know our children. I can't lose you . . . because something tells me it'll never be the same without you."

"Ah, there was a time when you were so proud and happy when you was first Mrs. St. Larnston. . . . Then I don't think 'ee had a thought in the world save playing the lady. Well, lovey, now, you'll be the same again, only this time it won't be for a house and the sake of being a fine lady, it'll be for love of your man—and there bain't no happiness in the world to compare with that. Now, my dear, there be little time left to us, so we should say what should be said. Unbind my hair, Kerensa."

"It would disturb you, Granny."

"Nay, unbind it, I say. I want to feel it round my shoulders."

I obeyed.

"Still black it be. Though I've been too tired of late for the treatment. Yours must stay the same, Kerensa. You must stay beautiful, for he loves you partly for that. The cottage be just as I left it, bain't it?"

"Yes, Granny," I said, for it was true. When she had gone to live with Essie and Joe, she had been anxious to keep her cottage. In the beginning she had gone there often and still used her herbs there to make her concoctions. Later she had sent Essie to get what she wanted or sometimes she had asked me to call in for it.

I had never liked going to the cottage. I had hated my memories of the old days because one of my greatest desires had been to forget I had ever lived in humble conditions. It had been necessary, I had told myself, if I were to play my role of great lady with success.

"Then go there, my dear, and in the corner cupboard you will find my comb and mantilla which be yours and there'll be, too, the recipe for your hair that'll keep it black and glossy all

257

the days of your life. Tis easy to make, with the proper herbs; look, my love, there's never a gray hair, old as I be! Promise me you'll go there, lovey?"

"I promise."

"And I want ye to promise something else, my darling child. Not to grieve. Remember what I said. There comes a time when the leaves wither on the trees; and I be but a poor brown leaf about to fall."

I buried my face in her pillow and began to sob.

She stroked my hair and like a child I implored her to comfort me.

But death was in the room and it had come for Granny Bee; and there was no power in her, no ready potion to hold off death.

She died that night; and when I went to her the next morning she looked so peaceful lying there, her face grown younger, her black hair neatly braided, like a woman who is ready to go in peace because her work is done.

It was Kim, with Carlyon and Mellyora, who comforted me after the death of Granny Bee. They all did their best to rouse me from my melancholy; and I was comforted because during those days I became certain that Kim loved me; and I believed that he was waiting until I had recovered from the shock of the discovery of Johnny's body and the death of Granny.

I would find him and Mellyora talking together about me, planning how to divert my thoughts from recent events. As a result we were often entertained at the Abbas and Kim was frequently at the Dower House. There was never a day when we did not meet.

Carlyon did his best, too. He had always been gentle, but during those days he was my constant companion; among the three of them I felt surrounded by love.

Autumn had set in with the usual southwest gales and the trees were being rapidly denuded of their leaves. Only the stubby firs bent and swayed in the wind and glistened as brightly green as ever; the hedges were draped with spiders' webs and on the narrow threads the dewdrops glistened like crystal beads.

The wind dropped and the mist drifted in from the coast. It hung in patches that afternoon when I went along to Granny's cottage.

I had promised her that I would go and find the formula

which she had been so anxious for me to have; I would take it with the mantilla and comb and cherish them in memory of her. Joe had said that we ought not to allow the cottage to stand idle. We shall put it in good order and let it. Why not? I thought. It was pleasant to own a little property, however small, and the cottage which had been built in a night by Grandfather Bee was of some sentimental value.

The cottage, being some little distance from the rest in the village and surrounded by its little copse of fir trees, had always seemed to stand apart. I was glad of that now.

I was steeling myself because I had not visited the cottage since Granny's death and I knew it was going to be a painful experience.

I must try to remember her words. I must try to do what she would want. That was forget the past; not to brood; to live happily and wisely as she would have wanted me to.

Perhaps it was the stillness of the afternoon; perhaps it was my mission; but I suddenly had a feeling of uneasiness, a strange awareness that I was not alone; that somewhere, not far off someone was watching me . . . with evil intentions.

Perhaps I heard a sound in that still afternoon; perhaps I had been too deep in my thoughts to recognize it as a footfall; but nevertheless I had an uneasy feeling that I was being followed and my heart began to beat fast.

"Is anyone there?" I called.

I listened. Absolute stillness all about me.

I laughed at myself. I was forcing myself to visit the cottage which I did not want to do. I was afraid, not of something evil, but of my own memories.

I hurried on to the cottage and let myself in. Because of that sudden scare in the copse I drew the heavy bolt. I stood leaning against the door looking about me at those familiar cob walls. The talfat where I had spent so many nights! What a happy place that had seemed during my first days in the cottage when I had brought Joe to find a refuge with Granny.

The tears were blinding me. I should not have come so soon.

I would try to be sensible. I had always been impatient of sentiment and here was I weeping. Was this the girl who had forced her way from the cottage to the big house? Was this the girl who had refused Mellyora the man she loved?

But you are not crying for others, I told myself. You are crying for yourself.

I went into the storehouse and found the formula as Granny

had said I would. The ceiling was damp. If the cottage were to be lived in, that would have to be repaired. No doubt there would have to be certain renovations. I had an idea of building on to it, making it a pleasant little house.

Then suddenly I stood very still because I was sure that the latch of the door was being tried . . . stealthily.

When you have lived in a house for many years you know all its sounds—the creak of the talfat with its own special creak, the floorboard which is loose, the peculiar sound of the latch being lifted, the creak of the door.

If someone was outside why did he . . . or she . . . not knock? Why did they try the door so stealthily?

I left the storehouse and came into the cottage room and went swiftly to the door and waited there for the latch to move. Nothing happened. And then suddenly the window was momentarily darkened. I, who knew that cottage so well, was instantly aware that someone was standing there looking in.

I did not move. I was terrified. My knees had begun to tremble and a cold sweat was on my skin, though I did not know why I should have been so frightened.

Why did I not run to the window and look for whoever was peering in? Why did I not shout as I had in the copse? Who is there?

I could not say then. I could only stand cowering against the door.

The room was suddenly light and I knew that whoever had been looking in at the window was there no longer.

I was very frightened. I did not know why, because I was not timid by nature. I must have stood there not daring to move for what seemed like ten minutes, but it could not have been more than two. I was clutching the formula, the comb and the mantilla as though they were a talisman which could protect me from evil.

"Granny," I was whispering, "help me, Granny."

It was almost as though her spirit was there in the cottage, as though she were telling me to pull myself together, to be my old brave self.

Who could have followed me here? I asked myself. Who could want to harm me?

Mellyora for ruining her life? As if Mellyora would ever harm anyone.

Johnny? Because he had married me when he need not have done. Hetty? Because he had married me when it was so important that he should marry her.

I was afraid of ghosts!

This was nonsensical. I opened the door of the cottage and stepped out. There was no one in sight.

I called: "Is anyone there? Does anyone want me?"

No answer. I locked the door hastily and ran through the copse to the road.

I did not feel safe until I came within sight of the Dower House; but as I crossed the lawn I saw that there was a fire in the drawing room and Kim had called.

Mellyora and Carlyon were with him; they were all talking animatedly.

I rapped on the window and they all looked towards me—pleasure apparent in their faces.

As I joined them by the fire I was able to tell myself that I had imagined the uncanny episode in the cottage.

The weeks began to pass. It was for me a time of waiting—and there were times when I believed Kim felt the same. Often I fancied he was on the point of speaking to me. Carlyon had become his friend, although no one could replace Joe in Carlyon's affections and esteem. But he was allowed to make free with the Abbas stables and for him it was as though he still lived there. That was how Kim wanted it to be and this attitude gave me a great deal of pleasure because it seemed an indication of his intentions. Haggety had come back to his old position and Mrs. Salt and her daughter followed. It then seemed as though we had merely moved into the Dower House for convenience and that the Abbas was as much our home as ever.

We were like a cozy family—Kim and myself, Carylon and Mellyora. And I was the center of it because they were concerned for me.

One morning Haggety brought me a note from Kim. He stood waiting while I read it because he told me there would be an answer.

My dear Kerensa,

I have something to say to you. I have been meaning to say it for some time but in the circumstances thought you would not yet be ready to make a decision. If it is too soon, you must forgive me and we will forget about it for a while. Where can we talk best? Here at the Abbas, or would you prefer me to come over to the Dower House? Would three this afternoon suit you?

Affectionately,
Kim.

I was jubilant. Now! I said to myself. This is the moment. And I knew that nothing in my life had ever been so important to me.

It should be at the Abbas, I decided—that place of destiny. Haggety stood by me while I wrote:

Dear Kim,

Thank you for your note. I am most interested to hear what you have to say and should like to come to the Abbas at three o'clock this afternoon.

Kerensa.

As Haggety took the note and went out, I wondered if he, Mrs. Rolt, and the Salts were discussing me and Kim; I wondered whether they were laughing together, telling themselves that there would soon be a new mistress at the Abbas —the old mistress.

I went to my room and studied my reflection. I did not look like a woman who had recently heard that her husband had been murdered. My eyes were brilliant; there was the faintest color in my cheeks—rare with me, but how becoming as it went well with the shine in my eyes. It was now only eleven o'clock. In a short time Mellyora and Carylon would come in from their walk. They must not guess how excited I was, so I should have to be careful during luncheon.

I decided what I would wear. A pity I was in mourning. One should not be in mourning when one received a proposal of marriage. Yet I should have to make a pretense of mourning for one year; the marriage could not take place before that was out. A year since Johnny's death or discovery? What would be expected of me. Was I supposed to endure a year of widowhood? I would count from the night Johnny had disappeared.

What a gay widow I should be. But I must hide my happiness, as I had managed to do successfully so far. No one had guessed how joyful I was when they had found Johnny's body.

A touch of white on my black dress? What about the lavender silk? It was half mourning; and if I covered it with a black coat and wore my black bonnet with the flowing widow's weeds, I could remove cloak and bonnet while I took tea—for surely I should take tea. We would make our plans over the tea table. I would pour the tea as though I were already the mistress of the house.

The lavender, I decided. No one would see it. I would go

across the meadow from the Dower House to the Abbas, past the Virgins and the old mine. Now that the mine was proved to be useless we would have all sign of it removed, I decided. It would be dangerous for our children.

At luncheon both Carlyon and Mellyora noticed the change in me.

"I have never seen you look so well," Mellyora told me.

"You look as though you've been given something you wanted for a long time," added Carlyon. "Have you, Mamma?"

"I haven't received any presents this morning if that's what you mean."

"I thought perhaps you had," he told me. "And I wondered what."

"You're settling in," added Mellyora. "You're coming to terms with life."

"What terms?" asked Carlyon.

"It means that she likes things as they are."

When I come back, they will know, I thought.

As soon as luncheon was over I put on the lavender silk and dressed my hair very carefully, using the Spanish comb. That added to my height and made me look regal—a worthy chatelaine of the Abbas. I wanted him to be proud of me. I couldn't wear the bonnet because of the comb, so I put on my cloak which adequately covered my gown and was ready. I was early. I must wait, so I sat by the window and looked out to where I could just see the tower of the Abbas through the trees and I knew that it was where I wanted to be more than anywhere else in the world—there with Kim and the future.

Granny was right; I had learned my lesson. To be in love was the very meaning of existence. And I was in love—not with a house this time, but with a man. If Kim had said he wanted to wander round the world, if he had said that he wanted me to return with him to Australia, I should have done so . . . willingly. I should have felt a nostalgia for the Abbas all through my life, but I should not have wanted to return to it without my family.

But there was no need to think of that. Life was offering me perfection in Kim *and* the Abbas.

At last I could leave. It was a mild afternoon and an autumnal sun made the feathery branches of the firs glisten. Being in love heightened the senses, every one. Never had the earth seemed to offer so much—the rich scent of pines, grass and damp soil; the warmth of the sun was caressing, so was the faint southwest breeze which seemed to carry exotic smells from over the sea. I was in love with life that afternoon as I never had been before.

I must not be too early; so I went into the meadow to stand within that ring of stones which had somehow made themselves a symbol in my life. They had loved life too but they were the unwise virgins. They were like butterflies awakened to the sun; they had danced too madly in its rays and had dropped to death. Turned into stone. Poor sad creatures. But it was the absent one—the seventh—who always took first place in my thoughts when I stood here.

Then I thought of myself standing in the wall and all of us being gathered there. It was like the start of a drama . . . all the main characters gathered together. Some of the actors had found tragedy, others happiness ever after. Poor Johnny who had met a violent death; Justin who had chosen to shut himself away; Mellyora who had been buffeted by fate because she had not been strong enough to fight for what she wanted; and Kerensa and Kim, who would give the story its happy ending.

I prayed then that my marriage would be fruitful. I had my beloved son and I would have others—Kim's and mine. For Carlyon there would be the title and the Abbas, for he was a St. Larnston and the Abbas had been the property of the St. Larnstons as long as anyone could remember; but I would plan brilliant futures for the sons and daughters Kim and I would have.

I went across the lawns to the Abbas.

I stood in the great portico and rang the bell. Haggety appeared.

"Good afternoon, Ma'am. Mr. Kimber is waiting for you in the library."

Kim came towards me as I entered. I could sense his excitement. He took my cloak and he showed no surprise to see that I had discarded my mourning. He was looking at my face, not at my gown.

"Shall we talk first and have tea after?" he asked. "There'll be a good deal to discuss."

"Yes, Kim," I answered eagerly. "Let's talk now."

He slipped his arm through mine and led me to the window where we stood side by side looking out across the lawns. I could see the ring of stones in the meadow, and I thought this was the perfect setting for his proposal.

"I've been thinking a great deal about this, Kerensa," he said, "and if I've spoken too soon after your tragedy . . . you must forgive me."

"Please Kim," I told him earnestly, "I am ready to hear what you have to say."

He still hesitated; then he went on: "I knew a great deal about this place in the past. You know I used to spend most of my school holidays here. Justin was my greatest friend and I think the family took pity on a lonely boy. I often went round the estate with Justin's father. He used to say that he wished his own sons had my interest in the place."

I nodded. Neither Justin nor Johnny had given the Abbas the care it deserved. Justin would never have retreated as he did if he had really loved the place. As for Johnny, to him it merely meant the provision of funds with which to gamble.

"I used to wish that it could be mine. I'm telling you all this because I want you to know that I am very much aware of the state into which it has fallen. A big estate like this soon begins to suffer without the proper attention. It hasn't had that care for a long time. It needs capital and hard work . . . I could give it what it needs. I have the capital but most of all I have love for it. Do you understand me, Kerensa?"

"Completely. I have been aware of all this. The Abbas needs a man . . . a strong man . . . who understands it and loves it and is ready to devote time to it."

"I'm that man. I can save the Abbas. If something isn't done, it will fall into decay. Did you know that the walls need attention, that there is dry rot in one wing, that the woodwork needs replenishing in a score of places? Kerensa, I want to buy the Abbas. I know this is a matter for the lawyers. I don't quite know yet what Justin's position is, but I wanted to talk with you first to know how you feel about it, because I know you love the house. I know you would be very sad to see it become derelict. I want your permission to start negotiations. How do you feel, Kerensa?"

How did I feel! I had come to hear a proposal of marriage and was confronted by a business proposition.

I looked into his face. It was flushed, and in his eyes was a faraway look as though he was not aware of this room nor of me, as though he were looking into the future.

I said slowly: "I had thought the place would one day be Carlyon's. He will inherit the title if Justin does not marry and have a son—and that is scarcely likely now. This is a little unexpected. . . ."

He took my hand and my heart leaped with sudden hope. He said: "I'm a tactless fool, Kerensa. I should have broached the matter differently . . . not blurted it out like this. I've all

265

sorts of schemes going round and round in my head. It's not possible to explain everything to you now . . ."

It was enough. I believed I understood. This was only the beginning of a plan. He would buy the Abbas and then ask me to be its mistress.

"I'm a bit dull-witted just now, Kim," I said. "I loved Granny so much and without her . . ."

"My dearest Kerensa! You must never feel lost and lonely. You know I'm here to look after you . . . I . . . Mellyora, Carlyon. . . ."

I turned to him and laid my hand on his coat; he took it and kissed it swiftly. It was enough. I knew. I had always been impatient. I wanted everything settled as soon as I knew how much I desired it.

Of course it was too soon to ask me yet. That was what Kim was telling me. First he would buy the Abbas; he would put it in order; and when it was restored to its old dignity he would ask me to be its mistress.

I said gently: "Kim, I am sure you are right. The Abbas needs you. Please go ahead with your plans. I am certain that it is the best thing that can happen to the Abbas . . . and to us all."

He was delighted. I thought for one glorious moment that he was going to embrace me. He desisted however and cried happily: "Shall we ring for tea?"

"I will." I did so and he stood smiling at me.

Mrs. Rolt answered the bell. "Tea please, Mrs. Rolt," he said, "for Mrs. St. Larnston and me."

And when it was brought it was like having come home. I sat at the round table, pouring out from the silver teapot just as I had imagined myself doing. The only difference was that I would not be engaged to marry Kim until after a suitable lapse of time.

But I was certain that it was only a postponement, that he had made his intentions clear; and all I had to do was be patient until my dreams became realities.

Kim was going to buy the Abbas and the St. Larnston estate. It was a complicated negotiation but while we were waiting for it to be finalized he was going ahead with certain repairs.

He never failed to consult me about these, which meant that there were many meetings between us. Afterwards Mellyora and Carlyon would join us at the Abbas—usually for tea —or he would come back with me to the Dower House.

Those were pleasant days—each one shortening the period of waiting.

There were workmen in the Abbas and one day when Kim took me round to show me what work was in progress I saw Reuben Pengaster working there.

I felt sorry for Reuben and all the Pengasters because I guessed what a blow it was to them when Hetty's body had been found; Doll had told Daisy that Farmer Pengaster had shut himself into his bedroom for three days and nights without a mite passing his lips when he had heard the news. It had been a house of mourning. I knew that Reuben had loved his sister dearly, but when I saw him working at the Abbas he looked happier than he had appeared to be for some time.

He was planing wood and his jaw was shaking as though he were enjoying a secret joke.

"How's it progressing, Reuben?" asked Kim.

"Pretty good, sir, I reckon."

His eyes slewed round to me and his smile was almost radiant.

"Good afternoon, Reuben," I said.

"Good afternoon to 'ee, Ma'am."

Kim started to explain to me what was happening and we moved off. Then I remembered that I wanted certain renovations done at the cottage and I mentioned this to Kim.

"Ask Reuben to go along and give you an estimate. He'll be pleased to."

I went back to Reuben.

"I want some repairs done to the cottage, Reuben," I said.

"Oh ay!" He went on planing but I could see that he was pleased.

"Could you come along and have a look?"

"Oh ay," he said.

"I'm thinking of building on to the cottage to make it into a small house. The foundations are good. Do you think that would be possible?"

"Reckon so. I'd have to have a good look like."

"Well, will you come along sometime?"

He stopped work and scratched his head.

"When would 'ee like me to, Ma'am. After I've finished work here tomorrow?"

"That would be excellent."

"Well then . . . six o'clock like."

"It'll be getting dark. You'd want to see it in daylight."

267

He scratched his head again. "Reckon I could be there at five. That'd give us an hour of daylight, eh?"

"All right then, Reuben, five o'clock tomorrow . . . at the cottage. I'll be there."

"Very good, Ma'am."

He went back to his work, his jaw wagging with the secret mirth.

It showed he was not fretting, and I was glad. Reuben was simple and Hetty had been away so long; he had probably forgotten what she looked like.

I rejoined Kim.

"Well," he asked, "have you made your appointment?"

"Yes, he seemed pleased about it."

"Reuben's happiest when he's working."

Kim looked at his watch. "Let's get back to the library. Mellyora and Carlyon will be here in a few minutes."

As I made my way to the cottage I remembered the last occasion when I had visited it and I felt a return of my uneasiness.

As I entered the copse I kept looking over my shoulder, fancying that I might be followed. I was in good time. I should be there exactly at five o'clock. I hoped Reuben would be punctual. Once he arrived, my fancies would be dispersed.

I had never before regretted the isolation of our cottage, but welcomed it. But when Granny was there everything had seemed so safe. For a moment I was overcome by sadness and a knowledge that the world would never be quite the same for me now that Granny had left it.

The cottage seemed different. Once it had been refuge and home; now it was four cob walls, isolated from the other cottages, a place where the latch could be alarmingly lifted, where a shadow could appear at the window.

I reached the door and unlocking it, stepped inside, glancing anxiously about me. The cottage had always been dark because of the smallness of the window. I wished that I had waited for a bright morning to ask Reuben here. Still, I should be able to show him what I wanted done, I supposed, and that was all that was necessary at this stage.

Hastily I looked round the cottage and went into the storehouse to assure myself that no one was hiding there. I laughed at myself; but all the same I locked the door.

I had convinced myself that it was probably some gypsy or tramp who had tried the door and looked in at the window

268

on that other occasion, perhaps seeking some place to return to at night to use for a shelter. Finding the door locked and seeing someone there, the intruder had rapidly retired.

I examined the ceiling of the storehouse. It certainly needed attention. If I had more rooms built on—perhaps preserving the main room with its talfat—I should have quite an interesting place.

My heart leaped in terror. It was the same as before. Someone was lifting the latch. I ran to the door and as I leaned against it there was the shadow at the window.

I stared. Then I began to laugh. "Reuben!" I cried. "So it's you. Wait a moment, I'll let you in."

I was laughing with relief as he stepped into the cottage— pleasant, familiar Reuben, not a sinister stranger.

"Well," I said briskly, "it's not the best time of day for our business."

"Oh, it be a good enough time of day, Ma'am."

"Well, perhaps for our purpose. You'll have to come again one morning. You see there'll be lots of repairs needed . . . but I'm thinking of building on. We'll have a plan. There's one thing I do want though . . . this room must be left just as it is. I always wanted it to remain like this . . . with the old talfat round the wall. You see, Reuben?"

He was watching me as I talked but he said: "Oh, I do see, Ma'am."

"We'll build up and on. I don't see why we shouldn't have a nice little house here. It'll mean cutting some of the trees down. That's a pity but we shall need extra ground."

"Oh yes, Ma'am," he said. He didn't move but stood still, looking at me.

"Well," I went on, "shall we take a look round while there is some daylight? There's not much left, I'm afraid."

"There's none left for our Hetty," he said.

I turned and glanced at him sharply. His face was puckered and he looked as if he were about to weep. "'Tis long since her have seen the light of day," he went on.

"I'm sorry," I said gently. "It was terrible. I can't tell you how sorry I am."

"I be going to tell ye how sorry I be, Ma'am."

"We must make the most of the light. It'll soon be dark."

"Ay," he said, "it'll soon be dark for 'ee like it is for our Hetty."

Something in his voice, something in the manner in which he kept looking at me, began to alarm me. I remembered that Reuben was unbalanced; I remembered that occasion when I had seen him exchange a glance with Hetty in the Pengaster kitchen after he had killed a cat. I remembered too that the cottage was lonely, that no one knew I was here; and I remembered that other occasion when I had been alone and frightened in this cottage and I wondered if it were Reuben who had followed me here then.

"Now the roof?" I said briskly. "What do you think of the roof?"

For a second he looked up. "Reckon something'd have to be done to the roof."

"Look here, Reuben," I said. "It was a mistake to come at this time. It's not even a bright day, which would have helped. What I am going to do is give you the key of the cottage and I want you to come one morning and make a thorough examination of the place. When you have done that, you can give me a report and I'll decide what we can do. Is that all right?"

He nodded.

"I'm afraid it's too dark to do anything now. There was never much light here on the sunniest day. But morning will be best."

"Oh no," said Reuben. "Now is the best. The hour have struck. This be the time."

I tried to ignore that and moved towards the door. "Well, Reuben?" I murmured.

But he was before me, barring my way.

"I do want to tell 'ee," he began.

"Yes, Reuben."

"I do want to tell 'ee about our Hetty."

"Some other time, Reuben."

His eyes were suddenly angry. "Now," he said.

"What then?"

"Her be cold and dead, our Hetty." His face puckered. "She were pretty . . . like a little bird, our Hetty were. Tweren't right. He did belong to marry her, and you made him marry you instead. Can't do naught about that. Saul took care of 'em."

"It's over now, Reuben," I whispered soothingly and I tried to pass him; but still he stopped me.

"I mind," he said, "when the wall did fall. I did see her. There one minute she were . . . and the next no more. She reminded me of someone."

"Perhaps you didn't really see anything, Reuben," I said, glad that he had stopped talking of Hetty and spoke instead of the Seventh Virgin.

"She were there one minute," he muttered, "and she were

gone the next. If I hadn't taken away the stones her'd be there to this day. Walled up her were, all on account of her terrible sin. Her did lie with a man, and her taken holy vows! And she'd be there now . . . but for I!"

"It was no fault of yours, Reuben. And she was dead. It didn't matter that she was disturbed when she was dead."

"All along a me," he said. "She had a look of someone . . ."

"Who?" I asked faintly.

His crazy eyes looked full into my face. "She had a look of you," he said.

"No, Reuben, you imagined it."

He shook his head. "Her sinned," he said. "*You* sinned. Our Hetty sinned. She paid . . . but you didn't."

"You mustn't worry, Reuben," I urged, trying to speak calmly, "you must try and forget all about that. It's over. Now I must go."

"No," he said, "bain't over yet. Twill be . . . but not yet."

"Well, don't worry any more, Reuben."

"I bain't worried," he answered, "for twill soon be done."

"That's all right then. I'll say good night. You can keep the key. It's on the table there."

I tried to smile, straining every effort. I must dash past him; I must run. I would go to Kim and tell him that what we had always feared about Reuben was happening. The tragedy of his sister's disappearance and the discovery of her body had sent his poor brain tottering. Reuben was no longer slightly, but completely mad.

"I'll take the key," he said and as he glanced at the table I took a step to the door. But he was beside me and when I felt his fingers on my arm, I was immediately aware of his strength.

"Don't 'ee go," he commanded.

"I must, Reuben. They'll be waiting for me . . . expecting me. . . ."

"Others be waiting," he said. "Others be expecting."

"Who?"

"They," he said. "Hetty and her . . . her in the wall."

"Reuben, you don't know what you're saying."

"I do know what I have to do. I've promised 'un."

"Who? When?"

"I've said, Hetty don't 'ee worry my little 'un. You've been done wrong. He'd have married you stead of murdering you, but there was 'er you see. . . . She'd come out of the wall and she'd done you harm and I were the one as let her out.

271

She be bad . . . she do belong to be back in the wall. Don't 'ee worry. You'll be at peace."

"Reuben, I'm going now. . . ."

He shook his head. "You'm going where you belong to be. I'm taking 'ee."

"Where's that?"

He put his face close to mine and began to laugh that horrible laughter which would haunt me for the rest of my life. "You do know, m'dear, where you belong to be."

"Reuben," I said, "you followed me here to the cottage before this."

"Aye," he said. "You did lock yourself in. But twouldn't have done. I weren't ready. I had to be ready. I be ready now. . . ."

"Ready for what?"

He smiled and again that laughter filled the cottage.

"Let me go, Reuben," I pleaded.

"I'll let 'ee go, my little lady. I'll let 'ee go to where 'ee do belong to be. Tain't here . . . in this cottage. Tain't on this earth. I be going to put 'ee back where you was when I disturbed 'ee."

"Reuben, listen to me, please. You've misunderstood. You didn't see anyone in the wall. You imagined it because of the stories . . . and if you did, she had nothing to do with us."

"I let 'ee out," he said. "It were a terrible thing to do. Look what 'ee did to our Hetty."

"I did nothing to Hetty. Whatever happened to her was due to what she did herself."

"She were like a little bird . . . a little homing pigeon."

"Listen, Reuben. . . ."

"Tain't time for listening. I have your little nest all awaiting for 'ee. There you'll rest, cozy like you was till I disturbed 'ee. And then you can't hurt no one no more . . . and I can tell Hetty what I done."

"Hetty's dead. You can't tell her anything."

His face puckered suddenly. "Our Hetty's dead," he murmured. "Our little homing bird be dead. And he's dead. Saul see to that. Saul always said there be one law for them and one for the likes of we . . . and he was one to see justice done. Well, so be I. Tis for you, Hetty. Don't 'ee fret no more. She be going back where she do belong."

As he released me, I moved towards the door but there was no escape. I heard his laughter filling the cottage and I saw his hands—his strong capable hands; I felt them about my throat . . . pressing out the life.

The cold night air revived me. I felt sick and ill and there was a pain in my throat. My limbs were cramped and I was fighting for my breath.

Enveloped in darkness as I was, I became aware of jolting uncomfortably; I tried to cry out but no sound came. I knew I was being carried somewhere, for every now and then a pain would jerk through my body. I tried to move my arms but I could not and the sudden understanding came to me that they were tied behind my back.

Memory returned. The sound of Reuben's laughter; the sight of his half-crazed face near my own; the gloom of the cottage which had for so long been my home and my refuge; the horror that had turned it into a sinister place.

I was being taken somewhere and Reuben was taking me. I was trussed up and helpless like an animal being taken to the slaughterhouse.

Where am I going? I asked myself.

But I knew.

I must shout for help. I must let Kim know that I was in the hands of a madman. I knew what he was going to do. In his crazy mind he had identified me with a vision—real or imaginary, who could say?—and to him I *was* the Seventh Virgin of St. Larnston.

This could not be so. I had imagined it. This could not happen to me.

I tried to call Kim, but there was only a strangled sound and I realized that my body was covered by a piece of rough substance, probably sacking.

We had come to a halt. The covering was removed and I was looking up at the stars. So it was night and I knew where I was, for now I could see the walled garden, and the wall . . . as it had been on that day when we had all been there together, Mellyora, Johnny, Justin, Kim and me. And now I was here alone . . . alone with a madman.

I heard his low laughter, that horrible laughter which would always be with me.

He had wheeled me close to the wall. What had happened to it? There was the hole as there had been on that other occasion; there was the hollow.

He had dragged me out of the wheelbarrow in which he had brought me from the cottage; I could hear his heavy breathing as he forced me into the hollow.

"Reuben . . . !" I breathed. "No . . . for God's sake, Reuben. . . ."

"I feared 'ee'd be dead," he said. "Twouldn't have been right. I be powerful glad you be alive still."

I tried to speak, to plead with him. I tried to call. My bruised throat felt constricted and although I exerted all my will I could not produce a sound.

I was there . . . standing there as I had stood that day. He was but a dark shadow and as though from far off I heard him laugh. I saw the brick in his hand and I knew what he was going to do.

As I fainted I thought suddenly: All that I have done has brought me to this, just as all that she did brought her to this same spot. We had trod a similar path, but I had not known it. I had thought I could make life go as I wanted it . . . but so perhaps had she.

Through a haze of pain and doubt I heard a voice, a well-loved voice.

"Good God!" it said. And then: "Kerensa, Kerensa!"

I was lifted in a pair of arms, tenderly, compassionately.

"My poor, poor Kerensa. . . ."

It was Kim who had come for me. Kim who had saved; Kim who was carrying me in his arms from the darkness of death into the Abbas.

I was ill for several weeks. They kept me at the Abbas and Mellyora was there to look after me.

It had been a terrible ordeal, far worse than at first I realized; each night I would wake in a sweat dreaming I was standing within the hollowed wall while devils feverishly worked to build me in.

Mellyora came over to nurse me, and was with me night and day.

One night I woke and sobbed in her arms.

"Mellyora," I said, "I deserved to die for I have sinned."

"Hush," she soothed. "You must not think such things."

"But I have . . . as deeply as she did. More so. She broke her vows. I broke mine. I broke the vows of friendship, Mellyora."

"You have had bad dreams."

"Bad dreams of a bad life."

"You have had a terrible experience. There is no need to be afraid."

"Sometimes I think Reuben is in the room, that I shout and no one hears."

"They have taken him away to Bodmin. He has been ill for a long time. Gradually getting worse. . . ."

"Since Hetty went?"

"Yes."

"How was it Kim was there to save me?"

"Because he had seen that the wall had been tampered with. He spoke to Reuben about it and Reuben said it had collapsed again. He said that he'd have it put right the next day. But Kim couldn't understand why it should have collapsed when it had been rebuilt not so long ago . . . oh you remember when . . . we were children."

"I remember well," I told her. "We were all there together. . . ."

"We all remember," Mellyora answered. "Then you didn't come home and I went to Kim . . . naturally."

"Yes," I said gently, "naturally you went to Kim."

"I knew you'd gone to the cottage, so we went there first. It was unlocked and the door was wide open. Kim was frightened then. He ran on . . . because Reuben had said something strange to him about Hetty . . . and the idea must have come to him. . . ."

"He guessed what Reuben was going to do?"

"He guessed something strange was happening and we might find out at the wall. Thank God, Kerensa."

"And Kim," I murmured.

Then I began to think of all I owed to Kim. Joe's life probably and Joe's present happiness; my life; my future happiness.

Kim, I thought, soon we shall be together and everything that has gone before will be forgotten. There will only be the future for us—for me and for you, my Kim.

I woke in the night, sobbing. I had had a bad dream. I was standing on the stairs with Mellyora and she was holding out the toy elephant to me.

I was saying: "It was this which killed her. You are free now, Mellyora . . . free."

I awoke and saw Mellyora standing beside me, her fair hair in two plaits; thick and glistening, they looked like golden ropes.

"Mellyora," I said.

"It's all right. It was nothing but a bad dream."

"These dreams . . . is there no escape from them?"

"They will pass when you remember that they are only dreams."

"But they are part of the past, Mellyora. Oh you don't know. I have been wicked, I'm afraid."

"Now, Kerensa, stop saying such things."

"Confession is good for the soul, they say. Mellyora, I want to confess."

"To me?"

"It is you whom I have wronged."

"I shall give a sedative and you must try to sleep."

"I will sleep better with a light conscience. I must tell you, Mellyora. I must tell you about the day Judith died. It was not as everyone believed. I know how she died."

"You have had bad dreams, Kerensa."

"Yes, that is why I must tell you. You will not forgive me . . . not deep in your heart although you will say you will. I kept silent when I should have spoken. I spoilt your life, Mellyora."

"What are you saying? You must not excite yourself. Come take this and try to sleep."

"Listen to me. Judith tripped. Do you remember Nelly . . . the elephant, Carlyon's toy elephant?"

She looked alarmed. Clearly she thought I was wandering.

"Do you?" I persisted.

"But of course. It's still about somewhere."

"Judith tripped over it. The scar . . ."

Her brow was furrowed.

"The tear," I went on. "You mended it. Judith's heel made that. It was lying on the stairs and she tripped over it. I hid the elephant first because I didn't want Carlyon blamed and then . . . afterwards because I thought that if it were proved to have been an accident Justin would never have gone away; he would have married you; you would have had a son who would have had everything—everything that I wanted for Carlyon."

Silence in the room. Only the sound of the clock ticking on the mantelshelf. The dead silence of the Abbas by night. Somewhere in this house Kim was sleeping. Carlyon, too.

"Do you hear me, Mellyora?" I asked.

"Yes," she said quietly.

"And do you hate me . . . for shaping your life . . . for ruining your life?"

She was silent for a while and I thought: I have lost her. I have lost Mellyora. First Granny, now Mellyora. But what do I care? I have Carlyon. I have Kim.

"It is all so long ago," said Mellyora at length.

"But you might have married Justin. You might be mistress of the Abbas. You might have children. Oh, Mellyora, how you must hate me!"

"I could never hate you, Kerensa, besides . . ."

"When you remember it all . . . when it comes back to you clearly . . . when you remind yourself of all you have lost, you will hate me."

"No, Kerensa."

"Oh you are so good . . . too good. Sometimes I hate your goodness, Mellyora. It makes you so weak. I would admire you more if you blazed at me in anger."

"But I couldn't do that now. It *was* wrong of you. It was wicked of you. But it is over. And now I want to say thank you, Kerensa. For I am glad you did what you did."

"Glad . . . glad to have lost the man you loved . . . glad for a life of loneliness?"

"Perhaps I never loved Justin, Kerensa. Oh, I am not so meek as you believe me to be. If I had loved him, I should never have let him go. If he had loved me, he would never have gone. Justin loved the life of solitude. He is happy now as he never has been before. And so am I. It would have been a bitter mistake if we had married. You saved us from that, Kerensa. For the wrong motives, yes . . . but you saved us. And I am glad to be saved. I am so happy now . . . I could never have had happiness like this but for you. That's what you have to remember."

"You are trying to comfort me, Mellyora. You always did. I am not a baby to be soothed."

"I had not meant to tell you yet. I was waiting until you were better. Then we were going to celebrate. We are all getting excited about it. Carlyon is thinking up a big surprise. It's going to be a grand party, and we're only waiting for you to be better."

"To celebrate . . . what?"

"This is the time to tell you . . . to set your mind at rest. They won't mind that I've told you . . . though we did plan to make an occasion of it."

"I don't understand."

"I knew as soon as he came back. And so did he. He knew it was the chief reason why he wanted to be back."

"Who?"

"Kim, of course. He has asked me to marry him. Oh, Kerensa, life is so wonderful. So it was you who saved me.

277

You see why I can only be grateful. We're going to be married soon."

"You . . . and Kim . . . oh *no. You* and Kim!"

She laughed. "You have been grieving all this time, thinking of Justin. But the past is done with, Kerensa. What has gone before isn't important any more. It's what lies ahead. Don't you see?"

I lay back and closed my eyes.

Yes, I did see. I saw my dreams in ruins. I saw that I had learned nothing from the past.

I looked into a future as dark as the hollows between the walls. I was walled in with my misery.

8

There are children at the Abbas now—Mellyora's and Kim's. The eldest—called Dick, after his father—is ten years old and so like Kim that when I see them together my bitterness is almost unendurable.

I live at the Dower House and every day or so I walk across the meadow, past the ring of stones to the house. All sign of the mine has now been removed. Kim says that the St. Larnstons needed to know it was there, but the Kimbers have no need of it because they will love the place and work for it so that it will always prosper while there are Kimbers at St. Larnston.

Mellyora is a wonderful chatelaine. I have never known anyone as capable of happiness. She is able to forget the hardship she endured under old Lady Larnston, the unhappiness she suffered through Justin; she once told me that she looks on the past as a steppingstone to the future.

I wish that I could.

If only Granny were with me! If only I could talk to her! If only I could draw on her wisdom!

Carlyon is growing up. He is tall, bearing scarcely any resemblance to Johnny, but he's a St. Larnston for all that. He is sixteen and spends more time with Joe than with me. He is like Joe—the same gentleness, the same absorption with animals. Sometimes I think he wishes that Joe were his father;

and as Joe has no son of his own he can't help being delighted by their relationship.

The other day I was talking to Carlyon of his future and, his eyes shining with enthusiasm, he said: "I want to go in with Uncle Joe."

I was indignant. I reminded him that he would be Sir Carlyon one day and tried to make him see the future I had in mind for him. St. Larnston couldn't be his, naturally, but I wanted him to be master of a big estate as, I pointed out, his ancestors had been for generations.

He was sad because he didn't want to hurt me, and he believed I was going to be disappointed in him, for gentle as he is, he has a will of his own. How could I expect otherwise in *my* son?

This has put a gulf between us and it grows wider every day. Joe knows of it, and feels the boy should choose for himself. Joe is fond of me, although I sometimes think he is afraid of me. Only once or twice has he referred to that night when Kim and I brought him out of the woods; but he will never forget it. It moves him deeply to think what he owes to Kim and me; and although his outlook on life is different from mine, he understands me a little; he knows about my ambition for Carlyon. After all, I was once ambitious for Joe.

He talks to the boy; he has tried to persuade him that the life of a country vet, while pleasant enough for uneducated Uncle Joe, is not the life for Sir Carlyon.

But Carlyon remains firm; and so do I. I notice that he avoids being alone with me. To know this, and to be forced to watch the family at Abbas makes me ask myself: What happiness did all my scheming bring to me?

David Killigrew writes to me frequently. He is still a curate and his mother lives on. I should write to David and tell him I will never marry again. But I avoid it. It gives me pleasure to think of David waiting and hoping. It makes me feel important to someone.

Kim and Mellyora tell me I am important to them. Mellyora calls me her sister—Kim calls me his. Kim, whom my heart and body calls out for! We were meant for each other; sometimes I almost tell him so, but he is unaware.

He told me once that he loved Mellyora first when he heard that she had taken me home from Trelinket Fair. "She seemed so gentle," he said, "and yet she was capable of such an act. Gentleness and strength, Kerensa. A perfect combination and the strength was all for someone else! That's my Mellyora! And then when she brought you to the ball! Never

280

be deceived by my Mellyora's gentleness; it's the gentleness of strength."

I have to see them together and I have to pretend. I was at the birth of the children. Two boys and two girls. There will be more. The eldest will inherit the Abbas. He is being brought up to love it and work for it.

Why should this happen to me when I planned and worked . . . and came so far?

But I still have Carlyon and constantly I remind myself that he will be Sir Carlyon one day, for Justin cannot live much longer. He is a sick man. Sir Carlyon! He must have a future worthy of himself. I still have Carlyon to work for. I shall never allow him to be the village vet.

Sometimes I sit at my window looking out on the towers of the Abbas and weep silently. No one must know how I suffered. No one must know how I failed.

Sometimes I go and stand in the ring of stones and it seems to me that my fate is more wretched than theirs. They were turned to stone while they were dancing defiance. I wish I could have been.

9

Mellyora and Kim came over from the Abbas this evening.
They were frightened.

"We want you to come back with us, Kerensa, just until
they find him."

I was cool. I have so far managed to hide my feelings; in
fact one of my triumphs—the few left to me—is the manner
in which I deceive them into thinking that I am just a good
friend to them both.

"Find whom?"

"It's Reuben Pengaster. He's escaped. They rather think
he'll come back here."

Reuben Pengaster! It was years ago that he had tried to
wall me up. There had been times when I told myself I wished
he had succeeded; if he had, I should have gone to my death
believing that Kim loved me as I loved him; and it seems that
the greatest tragedy of my life was learning otherwise.

I laughed. "I'm not afraid."

"Listen, Kerensa." This was Kim speaking, his voice stern,
his eyes clouded with concern for me. "I've heard from Bodmin. They're specially concerned. For the last days he's been
acting strangely. He said he had something to do and he was
going to do it. It was something that he should have done
before they took him, he says. They're certain he'll come
back here."

"Then they'll have guards here. They'll be watching for him."

"People like that are cunning. Remember what he almost did."

"But for you, Kim," I reminded him gently.

Kim shrugged impatiently. "Come over to the Abbas. Then our minds will be at peace."

I thought: Why should your minds be at peace? Mine has not been all these years because of you.

I said: "You're exaggerating. I shall be perfectly all right here. I'm not moving."

"It's crazy," Kim insisted; and Mellyora was almost in tears.

"We'll come over here then," went on Kim.

I was happy to see his concern. I wanted him to go on worrying about me all through the night.

"I'm not having you here and I'm staying here," I said finally. "This is exaggeration. Reuben Pengaster has forgotten my existence."

I sent them away and I waited.

Night in the Dower House. Carlyon was at school. Daisy was still with me. I had not told her because I did not want to frighten her. She was asleep in her room.

I sat at my window. There was no moon but it was a frosty night and the stars were bright.

I could just make out the ring of stones. Was that a shadow I saw there? Was that a sound I heard? A window being lowered? A door latch being lifted?

Why did I feel this elation? Apart from locking up as usual, I had taken no special precautions. Would he know where to find me? When he had been put away I was living in the Dower House. I lived there now.

Would he find some way of breaking into the house? Would I hear a stealthy step outside my door, that sudden laugh? I could still hear it. I heard it in my dreams. There were times when I saw those big strong hands about to clasp my throat.

Sometimes in the night I called out: "Why did Kim come and save me? I wish he had left me to die."

And that was why I was sitting now—half fearfully, half hopefully. I wanted to know myself, I wanted to discover whether I was glad or sorry to be alive.

I pictured him, the light in his eyes, the mad laughter.

I knew that he had broken out to come for me. He was

a sick man—fearfully, mentally sick; but Kim was right when he said such men had cunning. And when he came for me I should know.

He would kill me; perhaps he would hide me somewhere until he could build me into a wall. I knew that was what he believed he must do.

Walled up as the Seventh Virgin! I had been walled up for years, shut away from all that made life good. No sunshine to warm my bones, my life a dead thing.

Was that a footfall below? I went to my window and saw a dark figure there in the shadow by the garden hedge. My throat had gone dry, and when I tried to call out my voice made no response.

Reuben was down there. He had come for me as he had said he would. Of course he had come. Was that not his purpose in breaking out? He had something to do, and he had come to do it.

As I stood in the window, unable for those seconds to move or to plan what to do, it came back to me so vividly that I re-lived it all again—the horror of being alone with Reuben in the cottage, and later when I recovered a little of my senses and found myself in the cool night air, about to be walled up, face to face with death.

I knew then that I did not want to die. That above everything else I wanted to live.

And Reuben was down there, waiting to kill me.

The shadowy figure had disappeared behind the hedge and I knew that it had moved closer to the house.

I drew my dressing gown about me. I did not know what I was going to do. My teeth were chattering. One thought only was going round and round in my head: Oh God, let me live. I do not want to die.

How soon before he found a way into the house? Everything was locked but people like Reuben, whose minds were filled with a single purpose, often found a way.

Why had I not gone to the Abbas? They had wanted me—Kim and Mellyora. They loved me . . . in their way; but they loved each other more. Why must I always want to be the first? Why could I not take what was offered and be thankful? Why did it always have to be the best for me?

I left my bedroom and made my way through the quiet house, down the staircase to the back door. There was a glass panel in that door and my heart leaped with terror, for through the glass I could vaguely see the shape of a man.

Reuben was on the other side of that door, I told myself; and if he could find no other way he would break the glass. I could imagine his hand coming through the hole to undo the bolt. Then I should be at his mercy.

I wanted to get out of the house. I had started to run through the hall to the front door when I remembered Daisy. So I went to her room and awakened her. She had always been stupid and I did not waste time in explanations.

"Put something on quickly," I commanded. "We are going to the Abbas . . . at once."

While she fumbled with her things I was thinking: I do not want to die. I want to go on living . . . but *differently*.

Never had I realized before how precious my life was. And it seemed to me that my own thoughts mocked me. *Your* life is precious to you . . . to be lived the way you want to live it. What of others? Would they not feel the same?

I gripped Daisy's hand and ran down the stairs with her. I pulled at the bolt on the front door.

As we stepped out of the house my arm was caught in a strong grip; and in that half second of terror, I knew I was going to fight for my life with all my strength.

"Kerensa!"

Not Reuben then. Kim! His face stern and anxious.

"So . . . it is you!"

"My God," he said almost curtly, "you didn't think we were going to leave you alone!"

We? Mellyora too. It was always Mellyora and Kim.

"So it was you who were prowling round the house! You frightened me. I saw you from my bedroom. I thought you were Reuben."

"That's to the good," he retorted. "Perhaps you're ready now to come to the Abbas."

So we went. I didn't sleep all that night. I sat at my window in the house which had played such a large part in my life. I saw the sunrise in a scarlet sky that for a moment or two touched the stones with a rosy glow.

In the morning we heard that they had caught Reuben.

"Thank God!" said Kim. And I too, thanked God. For something had happened to me during that night. It was as though a chink of light had shone through the darkness which enveloped me. This was not the end of my life. I was young; I was beautiful; and Kim and Mellyora could say Thank God because I was alive.

It was a year or so after that night when Reuben Pengaster died. Mellyora brought me the news. She did not mention it but I knew how she had been shadowed by her fear for me. She was radiant on that day and I loved her. My love spread over me, warming me like the sun.

Kim joined us.

"I shall sleep peacefully again," he said. "I'll tell you now, I've lived in fear that he would get out and come for you."

I smiled at him. There was scarcely any bitterness. He was Mellyora's husband and since that night of revelation I had begun to see how right and fitting it was that he should be. I had loved him for his strength and goodness, the manliness of him; I had built him into my dream until I believed that he was as necessary to my happiness as the Abbas. But dreams could never take the place of reality; and on a night of terror when I believed that for the second time in my life I was about to face death, I began to finish with dreams.

Kim was not for me. I admired him; I loved him still, but differently. My feelings for him had gradually been changing. I had even begun to see that, had I married him, our marriage would not have been the success his and Mellyora's was. They were made for each other; outside my dream, Kim and I were not.

Granny had wished me to marry; she wanted me to know that happiness she had shared with her Pedro. Perhaps somewhere in the world there was someone who could love me, whom I could love and with whom I could prove Granny's words that happiness was as willing a guest within four cob walls as in a mansion. He would have to be strong, bold, adventurous. Perhaps more so than Kim who had settled down so happily to the quiet country life.

And Carlyon? Our relationship had changed too. I loved him as deeply as ever but I had learned how precious my life was to me, and Carlyon's to him. We had talked of the future together—Joe with us. Carlyon was going to the University and when he was of an age to decide what career he wanted, he should follow it.

"It is for you to choose, Carlyon," I told him; and as he smiled at me I knew that there was between us that trust and affection which every mother must hope to share with a beloved child.

We are together often and I have great joy in my son.

So I have come out of the darkness. I am no longer walled in by the bricks which I laid with my own hands.

There are sometimes dark days, but they pass and life becomes happier as the weeks go on. Sometimes I fancy Granny is close to me, watching and applauding. I remember the wisdom she taught me; I often repeat some of the things she said to me and I hear them with a new understanding. Perhaps I am learning to live as she wished me to, learning my lessons. I have won back my son. Kim is my friend, Mellyora my sister.

Perhaps one day I shall find a life as satisfying as that Granny enjoyed with Pedro Bee—the good life, the life that came unbidden to Mellyora and was denied to me, the life of love, for loving is giving—all giving, making no demands, living only to give.

That is what I am slowly learning and when I have mastered the lesson, who knows, the good life may come.